D1197649

4 1 0062670 6

THE
FALSE
VIRGIN

THE
FALSE
VIRGIN

A Historical Mystery
By
The Medieval Murderers

Susanna Gregory
Bernard Knight
Karen Maitland
Ian Morson
Philip Gooden
Simon Beaufort

**SIMON &
SCHUSTER**

London · New York · Sydney · Toronto · New Delhi

A CBS COMPANY

First published in Great Britain by Simon & Schuster UK Ltd, 2013
A CBS COMPANY

1 3 5 7 9 10 8 6 4 2

Simon & Schuster UK Ltd
1st Floor
222 Gray's Inn Road
London WC1X 8HB

www.simonandschuster.co.uk

Simon & Schuster Australia, Sydney
Simon & Schuster India, New Delhi

A CIP catalogue record for this book
is available from the British Library

Hardback ISBN: 978-1-47111-432-8
Trade Paperback ISBN: 978-1-47111-433-5
Ebook ISBN: 978-1-47111-435-9

Typeset by M Rules
Printed and bound by CPI Group (UK) Ltd, Croydon, CR0 4YY

The Medieval Murderers

A small group of historical mystery writers, all members of the Crime Writers' Association, who promote their work by giving informal talks and discussions at libraries, bookshops and literary festivals.

Bernard Knight is a former Home Office pathologist and professor of forensic medicine who has been publishing novels, non-fiction, radio and television drama and documentaries for more than forty years. He currently writes the highly regarded Crowner John series of historical mysteries, based on the first coroner for Devon in the twelfth century; the fourteenth of which, *A Plague of Heretics*, has recently been published by Simon & Schuster.

Ian Morson is the author of an acclaimed series of historical mysteries featuring the thirteenth-century Oxford-based detective, William Falconer, a series featuring medieval Venetian crime solver, Nick Zuliani, and many short stories set in various historical periods.

Philip Gooden is the author of the Nick Revill series, a sequence of historical mysteries set in Elizabethan and

Jacobean London, during the time of Shakespeare's Globe Theatre. The latest titles are *Sleep of Death* and *Death of Kings*. He also writes 19th century mysteries, most recently *The Durham Disappearance*, as well as non-fiction books on language. Philip was chairman of the Crime Writers' Association in 2007–8.

Susanna Gregory is the author of the Matthew Bartholomew series of mystery novels, set in fourteenth century Cambridge, the most recent of which are *Murder by the Book* and *The Lost Abbot*. In addition, she writes a series set in Restoration London, featuring Thomas Chaloner; the most recent book is *Murder in St James's Park*. She also writes historical mysteries with her husband under the name of **Simon Beaufort**.

Karen Maitland writes stand-alone, dark medieval thrillers. She is the author of *Company of Liars* and *The Owl Killers*. Her most recent medieval thrillers are *The Gallows Curse*, a tale of treachery and sin under the brutal reign of English King John, and *Falcons of Fire and Ice* set in Portugal and Iceland amid the twin terrors of the Inquisition and Reformation.

TbE PROGRAMME

Prologue; In which Karen Maitland tells how a grisly discovery in St Oswald's Church in Lythe, near Whitby, turns a Saxon princess into a venerated saint.

Act One; In which Susanna Gregory and Simon Beaufort tell how Beornwyn's hand is stolen from Lythe by two unscrupulous thieves in the year 1200, and taken to drought-stricken Carmarthen. A violent thunderstorm follows ... and so does murder.

Act Two; In which Nick Zuliani and his grand-daughter Katie travel to a Greek island on a mission for the Doge of Venice, and encounter murder and the cult of virgin saint Beornwyn.

Act Three; In which Philip Gooden describes how John of Gaunt's Thames-side place is shaken by a murder linked to a poem about Saint Beornwyn, composed by Geoffrey Chaucer, Gaunt's protégé.

Act Four; In which Bernard Knight tells how Saint Beornwyn led to a murder enquiry in 1405 in an obscure priory near the Malverns, which was resolved by Owain Glyndwr.

Act Five; In which Karen Maitland relates how a Master of the Butcher's Guild is determined to conceal the guild's valuable reliquary of Saint Beornwyn, to prevent Thomas Cromwell's most feared enforcer from destroying it. But when Cromwell's enforcer arrives in Sherwood Forest, murder follows in his shadow and threatens to destroy more than the precious relic.

Epilogue; In which Philip Gooden tells of an encounter between a dealer in saints' relics and a Russian oligarch.

PROLOGUE

Lythe, near Streanæshalch (Whitby), AD 848

On the dais at the far end of the mead hall, Badanoth, the grey-bearded ealdorman, slammed his huge fist down on the table, causing the horn beakers on it to tremble as violently as the men around him.

'Oswy is a coward and a traitor, with the heart of a bleating sheep. He will never again be received in this hall. I will not share my cup with any man who crawls on his belly to hide from the enemy. I swear on the skulls of my fathers, if Oswy or his sons set so much as a toe on my lands, I shall impale them on stakes and set them up on the beach for my men to use as targets for archery practice. That at least would put some metal into those wretches.'

One of the bondmaids, Mildryth, glanced over at Badanoth's daughter, who was staring miserably down at her clenched fists. Beornwyn's father had never been the most mild-tempered of men – not that any leader could afford to be gentle and forbearing if he had any hope of maintaining a strong rule – but since the death of his wife, Badanoth had grown increasingly irascible and violent. It was as if her passing had made him realise he was growing old and, like an ageing hound, he had to growl and snap ever more savagely to keep the young dogs from turning on him.

And turn on him they might very well do, for Badanoth

was the King's thane, sworn to uphold the law in these parts, but a king's thane is only as strong and secure as his king, and with the death of King Aethelred of Northumbria, the would-be successors were squabbling over the throne like gulls over a dead fish, with even blood brothers feuding on different sides.

The heavens, too, seemed to have joined in the argument, and the skies had sullenly refused to yield any rain for weeks, leaving the streams dry, crops withering and the livestock needing to be watered by hand from the deep wells. Mildryth sighed. More bad news at this time was the last thing Badanoth needed, but it had arrived, none the less, whether it was welcome or not.

The messenger had come not an hour since with news of another Viking raid on the east coast of the kingdom, the third since the full moon. This last attack had been against the lands of their neighbour, Oswy, a lesser thane, who'd been granted the land that lay along the coast to the north of Lythe, which he was sworn to defend. But, according to the messenger, Oswy had made no attempt to fight to defend the abbey and village where the sea-wolves had landed. His men had simply shepherded the villagers and monks to safety inland, leaving the Vikings to take whatever spoils they pleased, then torch the village and abbey before they sailed away. The flickering orange glow of the flames had been seen for miles in the darkness, making women clutch their children to them and moan.

'My own countrymen have grown soft,' Badanoth bellowed, 'too content to warm their backsides by their fires, telling stories of past glories, instead of practising for war. Ploughing fields and milking cows are all our young men are fit for now.'

He seized the arm of one of the young lads who had the misfortune to be standing close behind him. He pulled back the boy's sleeve and savagely pounded the hilt of his dagger into the muscle of his forearm.

'You think this scrawny arm could wield a sword from dawn to dusk in battle? This squab couldn't even overpower his own grandmother, much less a berserker. At his age I could fire off a dozen arrows in the time it took for the enemy to raise his bow.'

Mildryth saw the lad gritting his teeth, trying not to flinch and desperately attempting to look as if he were ready to fight the entire crew of a Viking warship single-handed. To his credit, when Badanoth finally released his arm, the boy manfully resisted the temptation to massage the bruises, though his jaw was clenched hard. But there was no mockery on any of the faces in the hall. Recounting tales of ancient wars was one thing, but Badanoth was right: it had been several generations since any in those parts had been forced to don a helmet and fight in bloody battle.

They were farmers and fishermen now. They might draw knives or even swords over slights to their honour, but who among them would have the stomach to face the fiercest of all the Viking warriors, the berserkers, men who hurtled into battle clad only in bearskins or wolfskins, who ran howling like wild beasts to hack their victims into pieces? Their onslaughts were so violent that not even hardened warriors could stand against them. Men said that the berserkers became so crazed with bloodlust that when they had slaughtered every man, woman and child in a village they would even turn upon their own comrades, disembowelling one another in their frenzied madness, and all in the name of their murderous god Odin.

Of course, Mildryth knew that all men exaggerate the strength of the enemy, especially when they've been defeated, but she had spoken to enough travellers who had seen the horribly mutilated bodies and smoking ruins of abbeys and villages to shudder whenever she heard the name.

She glanced up again at the long table where Badanoth was growling orders for the daily training of all the men, more watches to be posted along the coast, additional traps to be dug and new weapons forged. The thanes and freeborn ceorls around him looked sulky and resentful, as well they might. Trying to wrest a living from the land and sea was hard enough without squandering precious daylight hours on this.

The women shook their heads at the folly of all men. Mildryth knew many privately thought that thane Oswy had chosen the wiser path. Bury the valuables and take the families to safety. Wattle and daub houses could quickly be rebuilt, even a church could be replaced, not so people. Though Christ promised the resurrection of the dead, there were few who were so eager to reach Heaven they wanted to be sent there in pieces, hacked down by a Viking axe.

Beornwyn, with a glance over at her father, who was deep in discussion with the men around him, rose gracefully and weaved her way through the women towards the door at the far end of the hall. Mildryth followed her. She was grateful for this growing rift between Beornwyn and her father. It meant that the girl was more determined than ever to enter the religious life as Mildryth had long prayed that she would.

Outside, the evening air felt chill in contrast to the hot smoky fug of the hall. The roasting pit in the clearing in front of the cluster of long houses glowed a deep garnet red. Two sweating men, stripped to the waist, were turning a spitted sheep over the fire, while a third basted it with a long iron ladle. They barely glanced up as Mildryth hurried by.

Ahead of her, she saw Beornwyn entering the small house that her father had reluctantly granted her after the death of her mother. The bondmaid followed swiftly, closing the door behind her. Her young mistress was already kneeling before the wooden cross set upon one of the stout chests that lined the single room. Beornwyn's dwelling was plain and simple compared to the great mead hall. There was no gold leaf on the wooden carvings round the door. There were no tapestries hanging from the walls, no hunting trophies or weapons arranged above the simple bed, just plain white lime-washed walls and a fire pit in the centre of the floor. In fact, it was no grander than any of the humble ceorls' houses round about, save for the fact that, unlike their crowded homes, only she and her bondmaid occupied this one.

Mildryth sank quietly to her knees, praying, as she imagined Beornwyn was doing, for Christ and His saints to turn back the longships or hide Lythe in such a thick sea fret that the Vikings would never see the little church of St Oswald's perched high on the cliffs, and sail on by. She felt a little guilty at this last petition, as if she were sending the sea-wolves to murder others instead, but Christ would surely spare their village, if for no other reason than Beornwyn.

Mildryth opened her eyes and gazed in undisguised adoration at the beautiful face tilted up in rapture at the cross. Her mistress's long elegant hands were lifted to heaven. Her green tunic and girdle were draped in graceful folds, accentuating the rounded breasts and narrow waist. Her flaxen hair was covered by a white veil, held in place by a circlet of bronze engraved with scenes from the life of St Oswald.

If Mildryth was being completely honest, Beornwyn's hair

was more a mousy brown than flaxen, but her mistress was so seldom seen without her veil, even in private, that her bondmaid always imagined her hair to be fairer than it was. Besides, no matter what the colour, each day her mistress grew more like the Blessed Virgin Mary herself. And that holiness infused every feature with a heavenly radiance for those who had the eyes of faith to see it, which Mildryth did.

Beornwyn, with a final gracious bow of her head, finished her prayers and Mildryth scrambled to her feet to help her rise. Beornwyn had evidently been so absorbed in her devotions she had not heard Mildryth enter, for she looked surprised to find her bondmaid close to her. She smiled her thanks and sank down on the bed.

'You look troubled, my lady.' Mildryth knelt to remove her shoes, but her mistress gently pushed her hand away.

'No, fetch me your mantle. I shall need it again tonight.'

Mildryth's brow furrowed in concern. 'Please, my lady, don't go again tonight. You must rest. You've had no sleep these past three nights. You'll fall sick.'

Her mistress gave a fragile smile and patted the young girl on her cheek. 'Our Blessed Lord will sustain me. I must go to the church to spend the night in vigil. After the news the messenger brought today, it's more important than ever that I offer my prayers.'

Mildryth gnawed her lip. 'They say many churches and abbeys have been attacked and the monks and nuns slaughtered. I know that the villagers are sinful, but priests . . . nuns . . . they pray all the time. Why doesn't Christ protect them?'

'They don't pray for protection. They pray that they might be taken to be with Christ and He grants them their desire because of their faith.' Beornwyn cupped the kneeling maid's chin, raising her face so their eyes met. 'Have courage. Why should we fear death, knowing that it is but a gateway to the eternal bliss of Heaven?'

Mildryth tried hard to match her steady gaze, but even the prospect of Heaven did not take away the fear of the agony she might have to endure first. She'd heard that it took some people hours or even days to die of the terrible wounds the Vikings inflicted, and suppose she was taken as their slave – what might she have to endure then? An icy sweat crawled down her skin. 'Is that what you pray for, my lady – death?'

Beornwyn rose and crossed to the fire pit, spreading her hands over the glowing embers.

'I pray that my father will allow me to remain a virgin, dedicated to Christ.'

Her bondmaid stared aghast at her. 'But Badanoth has already agreed to that. It is settled! You are to be abbess when the old abbey is rebuilt. They've started digging out the foundations of the old ruins. You could be installed as early as next year, at least in name.'

Beornwyn grunted. 'I went to the ruins this morning. The work had already stopped, even before the messenger arrived. My father says all the wood and stone will be needed for defences and he cannot spare a single man or boy to build abbeys when we could be attacked at any time.'

'But the longboats don't come in winter. When the days grow shorter, he'll surely start to build again,' the bondmaid said anxiously.

Beornwyn shook her head. 'When the storms are too rough for the sea-wolves to come, then it's too wet and windy for any men to dig foundations or erect buildings.

Both warriors and abbesses need fine weather.' She laughed bitterly. 'Besides, it may be too late by then. If my father fears thanes such as Oswy are failing him, he'll seek to make alliances with other nobles to defend the coast. That will make him more determined than ever to use me as a peace-weaver, to marry me off to that vicious snake Aethelbald.'

She turned. The expression in her eyes was one of fear, like a deer surrounded by baying hounds. 'Pray for me, Mildryth. Pray that they will not marry me to that loath-some man.'

Mildryth understood her fear only too well, for her own fate, if Beornwyn married, would be far worse than her mis-tress's. A bondmaid would never be used as a peace-weaver, but Mildryth had been sold into bondage as soon as she was old enough to pick up kindling sticks, and knew she could be sold again or bestowed as a gift, like any cow or goat, to work or to be mated with any drooling old lecher, as her new master pleased.

'Your father would never force you into marriage. He knows you've given yourself as a bride to Christ. He wouldn't dare take you from God and give you into the bed of another.' Mildryth wanted desperately to reassure her mis-tress and, not least, to convince herself. 'I'm always telling those close to him of all the virtuous deeds you perform for the Church. They all know you for a saint. They'd speak out against it.'

Again Beornwyn gently caressed her cheek with fingers still hot from being held over the fire. 'You're a saint yourself, Mildryth, and when I am abbess, you shall be by my side, a bondmaid no longer, but a freewoman, perhaps one day even prioress to the nuns.'

Mildryth beamed with pleasure and gratitude. In truth,

she had no desire to be anything as important as a prioress. Such a role would terrify her. All she wanted was to be a simple nun, for the freedom and security that an abbey offered in this life was more to be prized than any hope of Heaven in the next.

'Now give me your cloak.' Beornwyn stretched out her arms for Mildryth's dark mantle of coarse wool, which her bondmaid wrapped tenderly about her, covering her head and tugging the edges forward so as to hide her face.

Then Mildryth crossed swiftly to the door and, opening it a crack, glanced out. Most of the villagers had vanished inside their own houses by now, or were in the great mead hall, eating or serving Badanoth and his companions. Those that remained outside were too occupied with carving hunks of meat from the roasted sheep or checking on horses to take any notice of a bondmaid leaving a house.

Mildryth turned and nodded to her mistress, who moved swiftly to the door.

'If any should come looking for me, tell them I'm stitching the altar cloth and cannot be disturbed,' Beornwyn told her.

'Let me come to the church with you, my lady. I can keep watch. It isn't safe for you to go alone. If the Vikings should come ...'

Beornwyn laughed gently. 'And what could you do if they did come? One woman alone can slip away into the night and conceal herself far more easily than two. You will do me far greater service by staying here and making sure that no one comes looking for me so that I may keep my sworn vigil undisturbed.'

So saying, she slid through the door before Mildryth could utter another word of protest, and was gone.

Mildryth turned back to the cross and offered a silent prayer for her mistress, not one a priest would ever have recognised, but a desperate plea from the heart. Christ must hear Beornwyn and keep her father from making her a peace-weaver. Mildryth was as fearful as her mistress at the idea of her marriage to Aethelbald, for what then would become of her? She'd heard of the manner in which bondswomen were treated in his hall, taken by any drunken animal that wanted to satisfy his lusts, or worked till they were near dead.

Mildryth had known from childhood that her only hope of a tolerable life was to attach herself to someone who might protect her. The old village crone who read the bones had foretold that Beornwyn's name would live on for centuries long after Badanoth's was forgotten. 'And your fate, child, is bound to hers like ivy to a tree.'

The bones had spoken and they were never wrong. So Mildryth had fought her way to Beornwyn's side, even ensuring that the former bondmaid was accused of stealing, so that she could take her place. She felt no shame about that, for God had ordained that she should serve Beornwyn, and God's will must be done. Besides, the bondmaid was a whore, one of those shameless creatures who would sleep with any man for a cheap cloak pin. She was not the kind of woman who should be allowed to soil with her filthy hands a girl as pure and virtuous as Beornwyn.

Back then Mildryth had not understood what path her mistress would follow. In her innocence she thought the bones foretold had her mistress would become a great queen. But now she knew Beornwyn's destiny was far greater than to become mere mother to a tribe. She would be a virgin of Christ, ruling over a double monastery of monks and nuns that would become even more famous than the one St Hilda had founded at Streanæshalch. There was no woman in the whole of the kingdom more saintly or more fitted than Beornwyn to become the abbess.

Mildryth added another log to the fire in the pit before scrubbing her hands in the pail of water she had set ready, using a frayed twig to lift the ingrained dirt. Then she crossed to the chest and drew out a flat package wrapped in wool cloth. Sitting on the bed, she carefully unwrapped it and withdrew the long length of fine linen and the skeins of red, green, blue, silver and gold threads. The altar cloth was three-quarters finished, embroidered with an intricate design of foliage, fruit and beasts which framed the central panel depicting the slaying of St Oswald by the pagan king of Mercia. His severed limbs and head hung on stakes. Christ on His throne looked down on the dismembered corpse with sad and wondering eyes. His hand was raised in blessing over the saint, whose face even in death was cast up to heaven, praying not for himself, but for the souls of those slain with him.

Beornwyn had begun the altar cloth some months ago, though of late, her vigils at the church had left her no time to work on it. Mildryth had carried on the work in secret while she waited for her mistress through those long evenings, so that no questions would be asked. Badanoth would never approve of his virgin daughter being alone, even while praying in a church, still less now that there was the danger of attack.

Mildryth stitched steadily, glancing now and then at the door, straining her ears for any sound of Beornwyn return-ing, and fighting the soporific effect of that warm, smoky room. But like every bondmaid she'd been up since first light

11

fetching wood and water, cooking, cleaning, milking and tending the crops, and not even such devotion as Mildryth had for her young mistress could keep her awake. Her eyes began to close.

'Who passes?' the guard bellowed over the roar of the strengthening wind.

He stepped out of the bushes, planting himself full-square in the narrow track, an arrow raised in his bow, ready to be loosed in an instant. He peered suspiciously through the darkness at the two riders on their small stocky horses.

'A friend,' Wulfred called over, holding up his free hand to show he had drawn no weapon. But he knew his brother Cynwulf's hand was grasping the hilt of his knife in his belt in readiness. Cynwulf could throw a knife as rapidly as this man could fire an arrow and just as accurately. Each man would surely end up killing the other. He prayed his brother wouldn't act in haste, as he so often did.

'Name yourselves,' the guard demanded, peering into the darkness. He hadn't lowered his bow an inch.

'Alfred and Egbert, sons of Alcuin,' Wulfred said hastily, before Cynwulf could blurt out the truth. 'Our father's lands lie to the west of the hills beyond the great river.'

The guard took a step forward, trying to catch the words, which were being blown away on the wind.

'Never heard of him, but you sound like Saxons, I suppose,' he said grudgingly. 'What are you doing here and why are you abroad so late?'

'My father sought news about the Viking raids. We must return in haste to tell him of the attacks.'

The guard finally lowered his bow. 'Aye, there's been attacks all right. My master, Badanoth, has doubled the guard, which is all very well for him, but he doesn't have to stand out here on a wild night like this, freezing his backside off. Still, I suppose better a master who is prepared to fight for his land than a coward like Oswy, who turns tail and runs away.'

Wulfred sensed the movement of his brother, and knew he'd pulled his knife from his belt, furious at the insult to their father. Fortunately the wind was tugging their mantles and causing their horses to skip sideways so the guard seemed not to notice. Wulfred kicked his beast to bring him alongside his brother and grasped his arm.

'Keep your temper, boy!' he whispered fiercely. 'Do you want to die here?'

He leaned forward to address the guard. 'Send our greetings to your master. We must press on. We've a long ride ahead.'

The guard nodded and stepped respectfully to one side. The brothers nudged their horses to walk on, but just as they drew level with the guard, a sudden flash of lightning lit up the sky. Wulfred clearly saw his face and knew he had seen theirs.

'Wait,' the guard yelled, trying to step in front of them again. 'I've seen you before. Aren't you—'

But the two brothers dug their spurs into their horses and lunged forward, forcing the guard to leap aside out of their way. They galloped off into the darkness, as the shouts of outrage behind were muffled by a distant rumble of thunder.

Mildryth woke with a start, thinking the door had opened and her mistress had returned, but the room was empty. A gust of wind again rattled the door and shutters, and she realised it was that which had woken her. The fire had burned so low it was little more than glowing embers. She hastened to put more kindling on it and blow it into life. Beornwyn should surely have been back by now, especially with a storm rising. If the wind was this strong down in the valley in the lee of the hill, it would be a hundred times worse where St Oswald's church was perched, on the highest spot above the sea.

Mildryth laid the altar cloth aside and crossed to the door. She opened it a little trying to peer out into the darkness, but the wind snatched it from her hand and flung it wide. Putting her weight against it, the bondmaid forced it shut. She stood with her back against the door, gnawing her lip. Her mistress couldn't struggle home alone in this wind. Suppose she slipped and hurt herself, or a tree came crashing down?

She hesitated. Beornwyn had given strict instructions she wasn't to be interrupted. She needed absolute peace and solitude to draw close to God. Mildryth had heard tales of men and women who'd been disturbed while they were sending their souls out among the spirits, and their souls had not been able to return to their bodies. They had woken from their meditations as the walking dead, never to return to life.

But surely the noise of the wind in the trees would have already disturbed Beornwyn's meditations. A long low rumble of thunder banished any uncertainty in Mildryth's mind. Her mistress hadn't even taken a lantern to guide her way home on such a dark night. She must go and help her.

Mildryth swiftly rewrapped the altar cloth and replaced it in the chest before lighting a horned lantern with a taper from the fire. She picked up a long sharp hunting knife and slipped it into her belt. If the Vikings came, she would feel better knowing she had something she could use to defend herself. She swaddled herself in an old patched mantle and once again wrestled with the door, having to set the lantern down and drag the door with both hands to close it against the wind.

There was no one about at this late hour. Even the hounds had taken shelter, and besides, they knew the villagers too well to bark at any with a familiar scent. The main gate in the high fence around the village would be barred now, and the watchman hunkered down behind it, trying to keep warm. But Beornwyn always came and went at night using a place in the fence behind the mead hall where several planks had been worked loose by some of the village boys who used that route to sneak in and out in defiance of their elders. It was invisible unless you knew where to find it. Mildryth found the spot and crawled through.

As she laboured up the track to St Oswald's church, the trees were bending low and the night was so dark it made her eyes ache trying to peer into it. Twigs and last year's dried leaves were dashed against her face, stinging her skin. Several times her heart thudded in her throat as she thought she saw men running towards her between the trunks, but it was only the shadows of branches whipping back and forth in the dim yellow glow of the lantern. She drew the mantle tighter about her face and struggled on up the hill, though the wind was pushing her back with every step. Every so often she stopped and cast about with the lantern in case her mistress was lying hurt somewhere. But soon she realised it was futile. First find out if Beornwyn was still in the church, then if she was not, Mildryth could make a thorough search.

The wind was gusting even more fiercely on the top of the rise. The church reared up in front of her and she struggled into the shelter of it. In the lee of its walls, the wind was considerably lighter, though as it tore through the branches of the trees on either side, the noise was so loud that an army might have been marching within feet of her and Mildryth would not have heard them.

She hesitated, then lifted the latch on the door and pushed it open, shutting it quickly behind her. The shutters of the church rattled and the flame of a single fat candle on the altar guttered wildly, then righted itself as the draught died away.

Mildryth edged forward, keeping the lantern low to the floor for fear that the light might startle her mistress from her meditation and cause her harm. As she did so, she thought she saw something long and pale lying in front of the stone altar. She stopped and slowly raised the lantern. A wolfskin was stretched out on the ground, next to a basket of meats, bread and cheese, and a flagon with two gold-rimmed horn beakers placed next to it. A woman was lying on the wolfskin. She was naked. Her long mousy-brown hair had been loosened from her plaits and fell in waves over her breast. Her face was half hidden, cradled on her bare arm and, judging by the steady rise and fall of her ribs beneath the milky skin, she was sleeping soundly.

Mildryth was so dumbfounded she could scarcely take in the scene. She stood swaying back and forth on her heels until at last a single word forced its way from her mouth.

'Beornwyn!'

The girl gave a slight wriggle and sleepily opened her eyes. For a moment she stared up at Mildryth, almost lazily as if she thought she was someone else. Then she gave a stifled cry of recognition and sat upright.

'I . . . I gave orders I was on no account to be disturbed.

How dare you follow me here?' She scrambled to her feet, her face flushed.

'The wind . . . it was strong . . . a storm's coming,' Mildryth said. 'When you hadn't returned I feared you were lying hurt somewhere.'

Slowly, slowly the meaning of what she was seeing was beginning to take form in her mind. 'I thought . . . I thought every night you'd been coming here to pray. You told me you were keeping vigil, praying that you might remain a virgin of Christ. But you're not praying . . .'

She stared at the two beakers arranged beside the flagon, at the meats, at the naked breasts of her mistress. 'You've been with someone. Who? Who have you been meeting here?'

Beornwyn came towards her, her chin lifted. 'I don't have to explain myself to you, a bondmaid. What business is it of yours who I meet?'

'But you want to be a nun, that's all you've ever wanted. You told me. You told me you didn't want to be married to Aethelbald. It's all been a lie!' Mildryth wailed.

'I can assure you, it most certainly is the truth that I don't want to marry that snake Aethelbald, because . . . because I am in love with another. There, does that satisfy you?'

'Who? Who are you in love with?' Mildryth demanded furiously. 'You are sworn to Christ!'

Beornwyn hesitated. She had the grace to look a little abashed, but the expression stayed on her face only for a moment before she lifted her chin defiantly. 'Cynwulf, son of the thane Oswy. He is the man I love. I cannot help myself.'

'But his father is the man your father branded a traitor and coward.'

Beornwyn nodded. 'Now do you see why I must meet him in secret? Do you really think my father would accept

Cynwulf as a son-in-law? What else could I do? I have to be with him. I cannot give him up.'

Mildryth took a pace back, holding her hands up in front of her as if she were trying to push the knowledge away. 'All this time I thought you were preparing to be a nun, all this time I thought you were so holy ... and you've been meeting him ... no, not just meeting him, you've been sleeping with him in this very church. I thought you were a virgin, but you're nothing but a fornicator, a sinner, wicked, wicked—'

'How dare you speak to me like that?' Beornwyn stepped swiftly forward and slapped Mildryth hard across the cheek. 'I love Cynwulf. I have always loved him and I will always be faithful to him, as if I was his true wife, which I am in all things but name.'

'No!' Mildryth sobbed. 'You promised that we would be together in the abbey. You promised to take me with you ...'

Beornwyn put both hands on her shoulders and pushed her hard. 'Get out. Go now! And if you dare breathe one word of this to anyone I will have you sold to the next slave-master who passes through the village. When you are entertaining a boatload of sailors then you'll understand the meaning of fornication!'

Beornwyn turned away and moved gracefully up the church towards the wolfskin lying before the altar. In the soft candlelight the smooth muscles of her bare back undulated beneath her skin as she walked away.

'She'll have grown tired of waiting and gone by now,' Cynwulf said angrily, as he and his brother, Wulfred, led their horses up the rise towards the church.

'It's not my fault my horse got a stone in its shoe. Besides, it's hardly likely she'd come all the way up here on such a night. Only a madman would venture out when he could be sitting by his own fire with a flagon of mead inside him. I don't know why I let you drag me out here.'

'Because I'm your little brother and you swore to look out for me,' Cynwulf said.

Although it was too dark to see the expression on his brother's face, Wulfred knew this last remark was said with a disarming smile which, ever since he'd been a little boy, had been enough to turn away the wrath of any elder, no matter what mischief Cynwulf had been up to.

When Wulfred had discovered what trouble his little brother was embroiled in this time, he'd tried in vain to talk him into giving up the girl. When Cynwulf stubbornly refused, he would gladly have left the young fool to take the consequences, or so he tried to convince himself. But with the Viking raids and the rumour that the old dragon Badanoth had redoubled the guards, someone had to watch the boy's back. And ever since the young cub had been able to haul himself to his feet, it had always been Wulfred who'd had to make sure he didn't fall down again.

Wulfred clutched his mantle tightly about him against the wind, which threatened to drag it off. He tugged impatiently on the rein of his horse, urging the beast up the last steep rise.

'Why couldn't you have fallen for some girl of our own clan? Christ knows, you only have to glance at a girl for her to throw herself at you. You're not exactly lacking in choice.'

'You may as well ask a man why he won't settle for copper when you're dangling a bag of gold in front of him. Our girls are pretty enough, but next to Beornwyn, they're as plain and charmless as mules are compared to the finest horse.'

'And have you told fair Beornwyn you think of her as a horse?' Wulfred said drily. 'I'm sure she'll be most flattered.'

By way of reply Cynwulf swung himself down from his horse and punched his brother on his arm. 'She's a jewel, an angel, the fairest swan and the purest rose dropped from Heaven itself. Satisfied? Now you wait here and keep watch. If that guard did recognise us, he might have summoned help and had us followed. So you make sure you keep awake.'

'Not much chance of sleeping in this wind,' Wulfred grumbled, as a distant rumble of thunder rolled through the darkness. 'Be quick. I don't want to be caught out in this when the storm breaks.'

Wulfred settled himself with his back to the wall of the church, drawing his mantle over his face. He watched the track intently, though unless the guard was carrying a flaming torch, on a night like this Wulfred would have been hard-pressed to spot anyone creeping up on them out of the writhing trees and bushes.

He had resigned himself to a long, cold wait, but he'd scarcely settled when he heard a shriek behind him, so loud it carried over the roar of the sea and wind. He sprang to his feet and raced up towards the church, dragging his sword from its sheath as he ran. He was about to hurl himself at the door when Cynwulf came staggering through it and collapsed into his brother's arms.

Fumbling to hold both his sword and his brother, Wulfred lowered the lad clumsily to the ground.

'Where are you injured? Who attacked you?'

Wulfred took a firmer grip on the hilt of his sword, his body tense, ready to defend them both when Cynwulf's assailant burst out of the church. But no one emerged.

Cynwulf was shaking and babbling incoherently. Wulfred could make little sense of it, but the boy didn't seem to be mortally wounded.

'Stay here,' Wulfred ordered.

The door of the church was swinging back and forth in the wind. Wulfred edged towards it, ready to strike. He slid into the church, pulling the door closed behind him as silently as he could. He had no wish to be ambushed from the back. He flattened himself against the wall, watching for any sign of movement. A candle was burning low on the altar. Nothing stirred in the shadows, but there was something pale lying on the ground. With his left hand, Wulfred pulled out his dagger and, holding both weapons ready, he edged along the wall towards the altar.

He stopped as his mind at last made sense of what his eyes were seeing in the dim light. A naked woman lay sprawled on her belly on a wolfskin. Her face was twisted sideways towards him, her arms flung wide as if she was penitent, praying. But he didn't have to touch her to know she was not praying, at least not in this life. Her eyes were wide and staring, her mouth open, frozen in a scream of pain and shock. Her back was scarlet with blood, which had run down and soaked into the wolf's pelt beneath her. She had been stabbed, not once, but half a dozen times in savage frenzy.

Wulfred hurried from the church, pausing only briefly at the door to gulp down the cold air and try to steady his thoughts. His brother was still crouching on the ground where he'd left him, moaning and rocking back and forth in misery, but there was no time to let him grieve. Wulfred dragged him roughly to his feet.

The younger lad grasped his arm frantically. 'You saw her, didn't you? You saw her ... I didn't imagine ...'

'She's dead, little brother.'

'Who did this to her, Wulfred?' Cynwulf's voice was broken by dry sobs. 'Who would want to kill such a wonderful creature?'

'I don't know who did it, but I do know who will be blamed for it. As soon as her body's discovered, all of Badanoth's guards will be questioned. The one who challenged us must have recognised us. In that lightning flash he saw our faces as clearly as if it was noon, and he saw in which direction we were headed. They'll think this is our revenge for the insults Badanoth heaped on our father.'

'Then we have to get out of here,' Cynwulf said frantically. 'We can't go home; that's the first place his men'll come searching. We have to get far away. Come on!'

But his brother pulled him back. 'If Badanoth thinks we killed his daughter he won't just seek our deaths, he'll start a blood feud between our kin that'll last for generations. We won't need the Vikings to destroy us, we'll do the job ourselves. No, we have to make them blame someone else ... The Vikings! Badanoth constantly fears a raid, and where else would they make for but a church?'

'Badanoth isn't stupid. He knows they'd never sail in a wind like this,' Cynwulf protested.

'So ... they could have been blown off course, driven to take shelter in the bay, and with the night so dark and windy they'd easily get past the guards,' Wulfred said, trying to sound more certain of this than he felt.

A spasm of grief suddenly overwhelmed Cynwulf again and he crumpled against his brother. 'But she's lying in there – dead. My Beornwyn is dead!'

'Yes,' Wulfred said grimly, 'and by dawn she must be more than a stabbed corpse.'

'What . . . what do you mean?'

Wulfred felt the trembling grip of his brother's fingers on his arm and knew that Cynwulf was not going to be able to face what must be done.

'Stay here on guard and swear to me, little brother, that whatever happens you will not set foot inside the church again tonight.'

Another flash of lightning cleaved the darkness and as the thunder answered it, the first heavy drops of rain began to fall. The storm had broken at last.

The young priest did not make his way to the church until mid-afternoon. The downpour had beaten the vegetables and fruit in his little patch into the mud, and now that the sun was shining hot and strong again, he'd spent several hours salvaging what he could and laying them out to dry before they rotted in the mud. The daily offices he'd said in haste and with a good deal of ill humour as he worked. But only when he'd saved as many of his crops as he could did he finally toil up to the church to check that the wind had not wreaked more damage than usual there.

He knew something was wrong when he saw the door half hanging from its hinges, though he tried to convince himself that the wind must have battered it open. But he smelled the stench of blood and shit before he even set foot inside.

He had taken no more than a pace into the church before his legs buckled and he sank to his knees. He didn't even have the strength to crawl outside before he vomited. It was a long time before he could steel himself to look again. A severed head with long brown hair was impaled on the top of the wooden cross on the altar. The limbs had been hacked from the corpse and hung at each corner of the church –

north, south, east and west. The feet and hands had been cut off and dangled like bizarre fruit from the windows. Blood had dripped onto the sandy-coloured stones below.

Beornwyn's flayed skin lay draped over the stone altar like an altar cloth and a buzzing cloud of flies crawled over the skinned torso, which had been dumped beneath the smashed image of St Oswald. Even as the priest stared in horror, a single blue butterfly fluttered drunkenly in through the open door and alighted on the mutilated corpse among the flies. It uncurled its long proboscis and delicately sucked the juices of the dead. The priest vomited again.

AD 864

Mildryth holds out her hand for the coin that the pimple-faced young monk proffers. She examines it carefully before sliding it away in her scrip. Satisfied, she nods and leads him up the path towards the small stone chapel that has been built a little way from the church. She gestures to him to enter and follows him in, keeping a close watch as he kneels in reverence. Thieves are always ready to steal holy relics, and monks are the worst of them all. Mildryth guards her saint as fiercely as any she-wolf protects her cubs.

A long wooden box lies upon the stone altar, surrounded by the burning candles offered by the villagers and strangers who come to pray to the saint. There have been many more strangers coming to the shrine of late. There are rumours the Vikings are preparing to come across the seas in force, not just a raiding party, but huge fleets of longboats full of warriors ready to slaughter and burn the whole kingdom. People are terrified that they will die unshriven. They come to the shrine to pray to the saint who was slain by the Vikings, for surely she has the power to save them.

The monk leans forward and presses his lips to the box containing the mortal remains of the blessed martyr. He touches his fingers to it, and then to his forehead, mouth and breast as if anointing himself with her holiness. Finally he clambers to his feet and backs out of the shrine as if leaving the presence of a great queen.

He turns and gazes earnestly at Mildryth, then seems to remember she is a woman and averts his eyes. 'They say you actually knew her. You were her closest companion, her disciple. Tell me of her death,' he begs, closing his eyes as if preparing himself for a moment of ecstasy.

Mildryth has been waiting for this. They all ask for that tale, the strangers who come to her shrine. She recites again how the virgin Beornwyn was praying alone to the blessed St Oswald when the Vikings attacked, striking her down before the very altar as she was kneeling in prayer. How, like St Oswald, she was dismembered as an offering to the god Odin, but even when the saint's head was struck from her body, her lips had continued to pray for the souls of men. The heathens had flayed her skin from her body, but the Virgin Mary had sent a cloud of butterflies, as blue as her own heavenly mantle, to cover her, so no man might look upon the saint's private parts to her shame.

It has been more than fifteen years since the night her mistress was slain and now Mildryth herself can no longer remember what is true. Sometimes in her dreams she sees her own hand stabbing the knife into that bare back, over and over again in such a murderous rage of hatred she cannot seem to stop. But when she wakes she knows it was the Vikings who slaughtered her beloved Beornwyn; everyone told her it was and how could she say otherwise?

The young monk kneels before her, takes her hand and kisses it. They think if they touch the hand of the woman who touched Beornwyn, her blessing will pass to them. She is the living link to the blessed saint, as the Bishop is the living link to St Peter and to Christ Himself. Mildryth's touch will save them.

'Ask Saint Beornwyn to pray for me,' the monk pleads.

And Mildryth will, for she is the virgin saint's guardian and protector now, just as she has always been.

Historical Note

Lythe means 'on a hill', and the church and graveyard of St Oswald are situated on a hill overlooking the sea on the Yorkshire coast. From there you can see the ruins of Whitby Abbey, several bays further along the cliffs. It is believed that the present St Oswald's church occupies the site of an ancient Anglo-Saxon church.

By AD 848, this Anglo-Saxon church was all that remained of a Celtic double monastery that was probably built around the same time as the nearby abbey of St Hilda in Whitby (Streanæshalch), housing both nuns and monks in AD 657. Unlike St Hilda's abbey, the Lythe monastery had fallen into ruins long before the time of the Prologue and only the church remained in use.

From AD 793 there were an increasing number of Viking raids on the Anglo-Saxon kingdom of Northumbria. The raiding parties often targeted churches and monasteries, because of their rich store of gold and silver treasures, but raids increased dramatically from AD 835 with a full invasion being launched in AD 865. In AD 867 the Vikings destroyed the abbey of St Hilda in Whitby. The Vikings settled and eventually converted to Christianity, burying their dead at Lythe and building a wooden church on the site. This church was replaced with a stone Norman church after 1066.

During the remodelling of St Oswald's church, Lythe in 1910, builders discovered that thirty-seven carved stones from a much earlier period had been built at random into the later Norman church walls and buttresses. Two of the stones have been dated to the eighth century. These carved stones were restored in 2007 and are now housed in a permanent display at the beautiful St Oswald's church.

ACT ONE

I

Whitby Abbey, Winter 1199

It was a pity that Reinfrid and Frossard were friends. Reinfrid was clever, and might have risen high within the Benedictine Order if Frossard had not been there to lead him astray with mischief; and Frossard might have accepted his lot as a lay brother if Reinfrid had not been constantly telling him that a son of Lord Frossard, albeit an illegitimate one, deserved better than life as a labourer.

One bleak evening, when a bitter wind turned all to ice, the two young men chanced to meet in the monastery grounds. It was Reinfrid's turn to prepare the church for compline, while Frossard had been charged to clean the stables.

'The abbot has been vexed with us ever since we let that pig into the scriptorium,' said Frossard, chuckling at the memory of scribes scurrying around in dismay while the greedy animal feasted on finest vellum. 'So I have a plan that will take his mind off it.'

Reinfrid brightened. Life had been dull since their last escapade, and his quick mind chafed at the strictures of a cloistered existence. He had never wanted to be a monk, but as the youngest child of an impoverished knight, he had been given no choice. His unhappy situation was what drew him to Frossard – the solidarity of two youngsters whose lives were blighted by circumstances of birth.

'It concerns Beornwyn,' Frossard went on, 'the virgin killed by sea-pirates up in Lythe three and a half centuries ago. She was chopped into pieces, and her flayed corpse was found covered in butterflies the following day.'

'She is not a saint,' said Reinfrid, haughty in his superior knowledge. 'The Church does not recognise her, and Abbot Peter deplores the fact that pilgrims visit her shrine.'

'Yes, and do you know why? Because it means they do not spend their money here. He would be the first to acknowledge Beornwyn if her bones were in his abbey.'

Reinfrid laughed. 'So what do you suggest? That we steal them for him?'

'Yes.'

The blunt reply made Reinfrid's jaw drop. 'But that would be impossible! They are watched day and night. We would never get near them.'

Frossard smirked. 'Oh, yes, we will. I met two of the guards yesterday, and we got talking. They are on duty tonight. They mentioned a liking for wine, so I sent them a flask – and in it is some powder from old Mother Hackness, which will make them sleep like babies. All we have to do is walk to Lythe, collect the relics and bring them back here.'

Reinfrid raised his eyebrows archly. 'And present the abbot with stolen property? I doubt that will go down very well!'

'We shall say that Beornwyn appeared to us in a dream and told us to fetch her. The fact that the guards slept through her removal will be proof that we acted with her blessing.'

Reinfrid was thoughtful. Saints were always appearing to

people in visions, asking to be toted from one place to another, so it was not beyond the realms of possibility that Beornwyn might prefer an abbey to the paltry little fishing village four miles up the coast. Frossard grinned when his friend made no further objection.

'It is a good plan, Reinfrid. What can go wrong?'

At midnight, Reinfrid slipped out of the dorter and ran to the postern gate, where Frossard was waiting. They set off together, descending the hill to the little village clustered below, where the familiar smell of fish and seaweed assailed their nostrils, along with the sweeter scent of ale from a tavern that kept notoriously late hours. Bawdy songs and womanly squeals gusted from within. The pair borrowed a boat to cross the river, then climbed past more cottages until they reached the cliff path that ran north.

It was a clear night, and bitingly cold, so they walked briskly. Both knew the shrine well. It was a pretty place near St Oswald's church, which had been built shortly after the saint's martyrdom and not changed since. It comprised a stone chapel with an altar, on which stood a plain wooden box that contained the relics. The villagers had decorated the chapel with pictures of butterflies, and candles always burned within. Relics were vulnerable to unscrupulous thieves so the shrine was never left unattended.

Frossard grinned triumphantly when they reached the building and saw the two guards slumped on the floor. The empty wine flask lay between them. Reinfrid was uneasy, though, and crept towards them to make sure they were really asleep. He touched one cautiously, then jerked his hand back in alarm at the cold skin.

'Christ in Heaven! They are dead!'

'No!' Frossard grabbed a candle to look for himself, but it took only a glance to see that Reinfrid was right. He backed away in horror. 'Mother Hackness said her powder was safe!'

'How much did she tell you to use?'

Frossard looked stricken. 'Three pinches, but I needed to be sure it would work, so I added the lot. But I did not know it would ...' He trailed off, appalled by the turn of events.

Reinfrid forced down his panic, and began to make plans to extricate them from the mess. 'You must burn the shrine with their bodies in it. Then everyone will assume they fell asleep, and failed to wake when a candle fell and set the place alight.'

'And you?' asked Frossard nervously. 'What will you do?'

'We cannot incinerate a valuable relic, so I will carry Beornwyn to the abbey and be as surprised as anyone when she is discovered on the high altar tomorrow. It will be declared a miracle – she did not want to burn, so she took herself to Whitby. Obviously, we cannot take the credit now; we must distance ourselves from the whole affair.'

'Yes!' breathed Frossard, relieved. 'The guards' families know I sent wine, but they will not want it said that their menfolk were drunk while they were minding Beornwyn, so they will keep the matter quiet. Your plan will work.'

Reinfrid shoved the casket in a sack and tossed it over his shoulder, leaving Frossard to deal with the fire. Frossard's hands shook as he set his kindling, and it was some time before he had a satisfactory blaze. He waited until the flames shot high into the night sky before turning to follow his friend. Then it occurred to him that Mother Hackness might guess the truth, so he went to her shack in the woods, shaking her awake roughly to inform her that her powder had killed two men.

'You are a witch,' he hissed, 'and the abbot will hang you. The best thing you can do is leave Whitby and never return.'

The following morning saw grief and dismay in Lythe, which had lost not only its saint, but two popular villagers.

To Reinfrid's surprise, his brethren greeted Beornwyn's arrival not with delight, but with consternation: it was not her doing, they breathed, but that of a rogue who had planned to sell her until assailed by fear of divine wrath – a thief who did not care that relations were now soured between the abbey and village.

It was too near the truth for Reinfrid's liking, so he took measures to convince the monks otherwise. He began a rumour that Beornwyn had been carried to the abbey by butterflies, the creatures that had covered her murdered corpse. He was somewhat startled when the cook and the almoner, who were impressionable and rather gullible men, claimed they had seen the casket arrive, borne on a cloud of iridescent wings. Everyone believed them, and the monks began to accept that Beornwyn's appearance was indeed miraculous.

Meanwhile, the villagers of Lythe marched in a body to the abbey and demanded their property back. They did so with such accusatory belligerence that Abbot Peter, whose first inclination had been to oblige them, could not possibly do so without acknowledging that his monastery was guilty of theft. The villagers left empty-handed and furious.

That evening, the abbot sat in his solar with his brother, William, who was visiting him from the family home at Broomhill in the Malvern Hills.

'Unfortunately, I suspect Beornwyn's bones *were* filched by members of the abbey,' he said unhappily, swirling his wine in his cup. 'There was never any miracle, and the cook and the almoner are mistaken about what they saw.'

'You do not believe in miracles, then?' asked William, surprised.

'Of course, but this affair smacks of mischief – of a prank gone wrong. And I have my suspicions as to who was behind it.'

'Then be careful how you deal with him,' warned William. 'A man who abuses sacred objects is a man with the devil on his shoulder.'

Abbot Peter worked hard for the next few days, hunting for evidence. When he had found enough, he summoned Frossard and Reinfrid to his presence. He studied them as they stood in front of him. Frossard was nervous, attempting to disguise his unease with a sullen scowl; Reinfrid, the clever one, was all innocent smiles.

Peter leaned back in his chair and picked up a beautiful silver box that William had given him. It contained a potent remedy for headaches, from which he suffered cruelly when he was under stress. And he had certainly been tense since the Beornwyn incident.

'You two have committed a terrible crime,' he began.

'Whatever do you mean, Father Abbot?' cried Reinfrid, his expression half-way between hurt and indignation.

Peter glared at him. 'Let us not play games. You both know what I am talking about.'

'Oh!' exclaimed Reinfrid, beaming suddenly. 'You refer to me slipping away from the abbey once, to pray at Beornwyn's shrine. I told her that if she ever wanted to come here, she would be welcome. I admit I should not have done it, but it is hardly a *crime.*'

'No,' agreed Frossard, taking courage from his friend's

cool composure. 'And I am sure she will be much happier here with you, sir, than in that dirty little chapel at Lythe.'

The abbot regarded them with a mixture of sadness and disgust. Reinfrid had been blessed with a keen mind, so what had possessed him to befriend the foolish Frossard? Peter blamed himself: he should have seen years ago that they were no good for each other. If he had kept them apart, they would not be standing in front of him now, with the devil on their shoulders. He set the box on the table with a snap.

'The guards' families told me about the wine you sent,' he said. 'And Mother Hackness did not go far. She told me what you threatened to do to her.'

Frossard gulped in alarm. 'Whatever she said about me is a lie. She is a witch, trying to cause friction between the abbey and Lythe.'

'Well, I believe her,' said Peter firmly. 'Meanwhile, you were both seen walking through Whitby on the night of the fire – by patrons from the tavern that stays open late.'

'Drunks,' declared Reinfrid promptly, 'whose testimony cannot be trusted.'

'You stole the relics, killed two good men and set a blaze to cover your tracks,' said Peter harshly. 'You are reckless, selfish and stupid. Unfortunately, the abbey's reputation might never recover if people find out what you have done, so I cannot make your guilt public.'

Frossard sighed his relief. 'Shall we consider the matter closed then?'

Peter eyed him in distaste. 'I want you out of my sight – permanently. Your punishment is to suffer the same fate that you tried to impose on poor Mother Harkness: you will leave Whitby and never return.'

Reinfrid frowned, confused. 'You mean you are transferring me to another abbey?'

'And letting me go with him?' added Frossard eagerly. 'Good! I shall be afforded the respect I deserve in a different monastery. *They* will not order the son of a lord to demean himself with tasks beneath his dignity. I shall never clean stables again.'

Peter smiled without humour. 'I would not inflict you two on another foundation. No, I am releasing you from your vows, Reinfrid. As from today you are no longer a Benedictine. You have always despised us, no matter how hard we tried to nurture your talents. Well, now you have your wish: you are free. Go, and take Frossard with you.'

Reinfrid regarded him with dismay. 'But go where? The abbey is all we know. And how will we live when neither of us has a trade?'

'You have your wits and your capacity for mischief,' said Peter. 'And hardship might make you reflect on the harm you have done. You will leave immediately, and if you ever come back, you will be hanged. Now get out of my abbey.'

Stunned, the two youths went to collect their belongings. Then they stared at the road that lay ahead of them, lonely, snow encrusted and unwelcoming.

'Oh God!' moaned Frossard. 'How will we survive?'

'With this.' Reinfrid reached inside his cloak and pulled out the abbot's silver box.

Frossard regarded it in alarm. 'Are you mad? His brother gave him that, and it contains medicine for his headaches. Now we shall hang for theft!'

'We did not *steal* it,' said Reinfrid haughtily. 'We took it as payment for the shabby way in which we have been treated. And it is not the only thing the abbey has provided for us: I also filched two nice warm habits from the laundry, along with this.'

He unwrapped a small bundle, and Frossard recoiled in revulsion when he saw the skeletal hand within, its delicate bones held together by blackened sinews.

'Christ God!' he blurted. 'Please do not tell me it is Beornwyn's!'

'Who else's would it be?' asked Reinfrid scornfully. 'Do not look so appalled! It is the basis for our new occupation. As soon as we are away from Whitby, we shall don these habits and present ourselves as two pious monks who have been entrusted to deliver sacred relics to another abbey.'

'Which abbey?' asked Frossard warily.

'One that lies in the direction we happen to be travelling,' replied Reinfrid with a grin. 'People will give us alms, and they will pay to petition the saint in our charge.'

Frossard regarded him doubtfully. 'Really?'

'Of course! We shall earn a fortune, and no one will harm two men of God. Beornwyn will be our protection as well as our path to a better life.'

II

Carmarthen, Summer 1200

It was the hottest August anyone could remember, with not so much as a drop of rain seen in weeks. Crops withered, cattle grew thin and the wide River Towy was reduced to a muddy trickle. Carmarthen reeked with no fresh water to wash away its filth, and its people baked under an unrelenting sun.

Sir Symon Cole dragged his heels as he rode the last few dusty miles home. His three-week foray in the forest had been unsuccessful – the ground was so hard and dry that he had been unable to track the cattle thieves who had been plaguing the town – and he was not looking forward to telling the victims of the raids that he had failed to catch the culprits yet again. As Constable of Carmarthen Castle, he had a duty to protect the town and its livestock, and its people had a right to expect more of him.

He wiped the sweat from his face, wishing he could dispense with his mail and surcoat – it would have been far more comfortable to ride without them. Unfortunately, southwest Wales had never really appreciated being ruled by Normans, and there were plenty who would love to strike a blow against the King by shooting one of his officers. As Cole had no wish to invite assassination, the armour had to stay.

His horse was panting from the heat, so he took it to the river to drink, although it was a while before he found a stretch that was not choked by the foul-smelling algae that proliferated when there was no current to wash it away. While the animal slaked its thirst, he stared downriver at the little town that had been his home for the past fifteen years.

It was dominated by four main features: the Austin priory, pretty St Peter's church, the castle and the bridge. Cole was proud of the castle. It had a motte and two baileys, and when he had first arrived, it had been a grubby collection of huts and wooden palisades. Now it boasted comfortable living quarters, a chapel and a gatehouse, while the curtain walls were of stone. He was in the process of building watchtowers along them.

'Lord!' muttered Sergeant Iefan, veteran of many campaigns

and Cole's right-hand man. 'I have never seen the valley so dry.'

Neither had Cole, and it grieved him to see the rich forest turned brown and parched, and the once-lush pastures baked to a dusty yellow. If there was no rain soon, the crops would fail completely, and they would all starve that winter.

When the horses had finished drinking, they rode on, and Cole's thoughts turned to the family that would be waiting for him. He had not wanted to marry Gwenllian ferch Rhys any more than she had wanted to marry him, but the King had been keen for a political alliance with a princess of Wales, so neither had been given a choice. After a stormy beginning, they had grown to love each other, and their marriage was now blessed with two small children. He hoped there would be more, and ached to see them again.

As he reached the Austin priory, the gate opened and Prior Kediour stepped out. Kediour's face was grim, and it became more so when Cole shook his head to indicate that he had not caught the raiders. The prior was an imposing man with thick grey hair, deep-set eyes and a dignified, sombre manner. He was respected by his brethren and the townsfolk alike. Like Cole, he had taken part in the Third Crusade, when he had been a Hospitaller – a warrior-knight. Penance for the lives he had taken in God's name had later caused him to transfer to a more peaceful Order.

'This cannot continue,' he said testily. 'We lost another cow last night, and we shall have no herd left if you do not stop these villains.'

'They are well organised,' said Cole, a little defensively. 'One group distracts us while the others strike. Yet if I divide my men, we are stretched too thin.'

'Then you will have to catch them by cunning. Ask your wife for ideas.'

Cole smiled. Gwenllian was by far the cleverest person he knew, and while other men might have bristled at the implication that their spouses were more intelligent than they, Cole was inordinately proud of his, and was always pleased when her skills were acknowledged.

'Much has happened since you left,' Kediour went on. 'You have visitors.'

'From the King?' asked Cole uneasily.

John had been crowned the previous year, following the death of Richard the Lionheart. He was a weak, vacillating, deceitful man, and Cole, plain-speaking and honest, had been unable to shower him with the flowery compliments John felt he deserved. The silence had been noted, and Cole had acquired an implacable enemy. Cole's marriage meant he had a lot of in-laws who would fight if he was dismissed without good cause, so John was busy looking for one, and a veritable flood of emissaries came to assess his accounts, watch the way he built his castle, and monitor his rule. Gwenllian was determined they should not succeed, and had managed to send each one away empty-handed. So far.

'Nicholas Avenel,' replied Kediour. 'The new Sheriff of Pembroke. He has an evil reputation, and is accused of despoiling churches and kidnapping wealthy burgesses for ransom. His henchman William Fitzmartin comes with him.'

'I do not know either.'

'John's creatures,' said Kediour disapprovingly. 'Here to find fault. They have not managed yet, but there are those in the town who aim to help them.'

'Adam de Rupe,' sighed Cole, knowing who he meant. 'The mayor.'

Kediour nodded. 'You exposed him as corrupt, which means he will not be re-elected next month. And his servants Gunbald and Ernebald hate you for gaoling them last year.'

'But they stole from the church,' protested Cole. 'They were caught red-handed.'

'Yes, but all three think they were misused regardless. And then there are Miles de Cogan and Philip de Barri. I do not trust either, despite your kindness towards them.'

'Miles is my deputy. He is not an enemy!'

'He is jealous of what you have – namely Gwenllian. He is in love with her.'

Cole gaped at him. 'He is not!'

'He is, and everyone knows it. However, Philip worries me more.'

Cole made an impatient sound. 'He is Gwen's cousin – family. Besides, if I am ousted from Carmarthen, he will lose his post as chaplain.'

'Just be careful,' warned Kediour. 'However, they and the raiders are not the only problem you need to solve. Come to the Market Square, and I shall show you another.'

Cole would rather have gone straight to Gwenllian and the children, but he dutifully followed the prior into the town centre. A crowd had gathered, and there was an atmosphere of excited anticipation, all centred on two young men in Benedictine habits.

'They claim they are taking a holy relic to Whitland Abbey,' explained Kediour with obvious disapproval. 'The hand of a saint named Beornwyn, no less. But they are Benedictines and Whitland is Cistercian. Why would one Order bestow such a favour on another?'

41

'I suppose it is odd,' said Cole. 'But hardly my business.'

'Oh, yes, it is,' said Kediour firmly. 'They announced earlier that Beornwyn grants most prayers if her palm is crossed
with silver, and several people plan to invest in a boon.
However, I have never heard of this saint, and I suspect they
are charlatans.'

'Damn!' muttered Cole. He hated problems where reli-
gion was involved.

'I shall look her up in my library this evening. However,
even if she does transpire to be genuine, I do not see why
scruffy lads like these should have been entrusted with her.'

'I will speak to them tomorrow and suggest they leave.'
Cole glanced towards the castle and wished he was in it. Not
only was he acutely uncomfortable standing in the sun in
full armour, but he objected to being kept from his family.

'They have offered to end the drought for a shilling,' said
Kediour, scowling at both the monks and the crowd they
had attracted. 'Mayor Rupe thinks we should pay.'

'Perhaps we should,' said Cole, squinting up at the cloudless sky. 'We are desperate for rain, and I am sure no
Benedictine would cheat us.'

Kediour regarded him askance. The constable had a reckless habit of taking people at their word, a facet of his
character that often stunned the prior. 'Do you really believe
that everyone who wears a habit is a good man?'

Cole considered the question carefully, although it had
been rhetorical. 'Yes, generally. I may not like them, but God
does or He would not have called them to serve Him.'

Kediour gaped his disbelief, but was spared the need to
reply by the appearance of Cole's family – Gwenllian, raven-
haired and lovely; his little son, Meurig; and the gurgling
bundle that was baby Alys. Even Kediour's stern visage

relaxed into a smile as he watched the unbridled joy of their reunion.

Gwenllian was relieved to have her husband home. Despite the recent appointment of a deputy, everyone knew it was really she who was in charge when Cole was away, and she had found the responsibility burdensome. Not only was it difficult to keep Sheriff Avenel and his unsavoury companion, Fitzmartin, entertained, but the unrelenting heat was driving even the mildest of men to ill-tempered spats. Moreover, there was a decision about the new tower that only Cole could make, and people were beginning to fear that drought and the cattle thieves would see them all starve that winter.

As soon as she could, she sent the children home with their nurse, and pulled Cole into the shop owned by Odo and his wife, Hilde, knowing the couple would leave them to talk undisturbed. Odo and Hilde sold cloth, and had been Gwenllian's friends for years, although Cole was lukewarm about Odo's gentle manners and unmanly fondness for the arts.

'There is trouble,' she began. 'Avenel and Fitzmartin arrived shortly after you left, and have been prying into every aspect of our lives ever since. They have a letter from the King, giving them leave to do whatever they like here.'

Cole sighed wearily. 'Perhaps I should resign and retire to my estates in Normandy. John will win in the end and I am tired of trying to outwit him.'

'No,' said Gwenllian firmly. 'I will not allow him to oust us from our home. You have been constable here for years, and—'

'Quite. Perhaps it is time for a change. It was never

intended to be a permanent post – not by King Henry, who put me here, or by King Richard, who confirmed the appointment.'

'If we go,' said Gwenllian, drawing herself up to her full height with all the dignity of a princess of Wales, 'it will be because *we* decide to leave. It will not be on the whim of a spiteful monarch who does not know how to rule what he has inherited.'

Cole did not have the energy to argue. Instead, he suggested they go to the castle and inspect progress on the new tower. As they aimed for the door, Hilde and Odo approached.

'What shall we do about these monks and their saint, Cole?' asked Odo. He had one hand to his back as usual; a lifetime of lifting heavy bales had taken its toll. 'Shall we pay them to pray for a miracle? Bad luck has dogged us all summer, so we could certainly do with one.'

'He will decide tomorrow,' said Gwenllian, to spare Symon the need to make a decision there and then. She smiled at her friends. 'The monks told me that they plan to stay for a few days, so there is no immediate hurry.'

She led Cole back into the blasting heat of the Market Square, where the Benedictines had finished their performance and were packing the reliquary away. Two men watched: Sheriff Avenel was a tall, bald man with the haughty bearing of the professional warrior; Fitzmartin was younger and smaller, but cast in the same mould.

'Constable Cole?' asked Avenel, coming to intercept them. 'You have been gone a long time. Can a few miserable thieves really take so long to track down?'

'He has not tracked them down,' said Fitzmartin slyly. 'They remain at large – I heard his sergeant make the announcement just now. Perhaps he would like us to help. I am sure the King will not mind us abandoning our more important duties to oblige.'

'Thank you,' said Cole amiably. He was not very good at recognising sarcasm and often wrong-footed people by taking acerbic comments at face value. 'Shall we try tomorrow?'

'No,' said Avenel, once he realised that Cole was not being impertinent. 'We have more pressing matters to concern us. And now you are home, I want to discuss them with you. Not with your wife.'

Cole bridled at his tone, and Gwenllian rested a calming hand on his arm. She had not endured the sheriff and his creature for three trying weeks just to have Cole destroy the fragile bridges she had built with an imprudent remark.

'You must excuse us, Sheriff,' she said politely. 'We have castle business to attend.'

Avenel bowed in a manner that was more insult than compliment, and stepped away, although neither he nor Fitzmartin went far.

Cole leaned down to whisper in Gwenllian's ear, 'Kediour tells me they are accused of despoiling churches. Is it true?'

'They are John's men, so it is possible.' Her attention was caught by the monks. 'Odo had a good question: what will you do about them? We do need a miracle, but I am not sure they are the ones to bring it about. Oh, no! Here comes Mayor Rupe!'

Rupe was an overweight, slovenly man who hailed from nearby Dinefwr, a fact of which he was so proud that he always wore the curious conical hat for which its residents were famous. He had been greasily obsequious before Cole had caught him misusing public monies, but was now a bitter and intractable opponent. He had insisted on holding meetings to discuss how best to catch the thieves, which he had used as opportunities to make Cole look inept and foolish in front of the town's other worthies. He was flanked by his two henchmen, an unsavoury father and son named Ernebald and Gunbald.

'It is your fault we are short of water, Cole,' he snarled without preamble. 'You should have built cisterns, not squandered our taxes on beautifying your castle. And you accuse *me* of dealing corruptly!'

'The King told him to do it,' came a voice from behind. It was Deputy Miles, a gloriously handsome man with golden hair. 'Would you have him flout a royal order?'

'The town should come first,' said Rupe stubbornly. 'And if Cole does not think so, he should resign and let a better man take the post. Such as you, perhaps, Miles.'

The deputy bowed. 'You are kind, but I should need a Lady Gwenllian at my side, and there is only one of her. Thus the post of Constable of Carmarthen is not for me. But do not despair for water, Rupe. I have a plan – if the fair lady will permit me to explain.'

Cole was not a perceptive man, but even he could not fail to notice the look of passionate longing that Miles directed at Gwenllian. He scowled, an expression that did not suit his naturally amiable face.

'What plan?' he demanded, before she could answer for herself. Avenel and Fitzmartin, aware that a possible altercation was in the offing, eased forward to listen.

'I believe I have located a hidden stream,' replied Miles, his eyes still fixed on Gwenllian. 'I did it by holding hazel twigs in a certain way and—'

'Witchery?' interrupted Avenel in rank disdain, not caring

that he was interrupting a discussion in which he had not been invited to take part.

Miles continued to address Gwenllian, much to her increasing mortification. 'No, of course not. It is a skill my mother taught me. She saved our village from drought many times. I have been surveying Carmarthen, and there is an underground stream between the town and the priory – it lies beneath the woods on Mayor Rupe's land.'

'An underground stream?' scoffed Avenel. 'What nonsense is this?'

'Not nonsense, Sheriff,' said Miles earnestly. 'It is there, I assure you.'

'You are mad,' sneered Fitzmartin. 'There is no such thing as an underground stream.'

'Bring your report to Symon tomorrow,' said Gwenllian briskly to Miles, ending the conversation before there was trouble. 'He will discuss it with you then.'

Miles was visibly crestfallen, and she was aware of Avenel and Fitzmartin chortling as they and the mayor walked away together, amused by the deputy's unseemly infatuation. Cole turned angrily to Miles, and Gwenllian was relieved when he was prevented from rebuking him by the arrival of Philip de Barri, the castle chaplain.

Philip was Gwenllian's cousin, although she could not bring herself to like him. He was an unprepossessing soul, with a wealth of irritating habits. She had not wanted him as chaplain, but there had been a vacancy when he had arrived begging for employment, and it would have been churlish to refuse. She tried not to let her antipathy show as he approached, bringing the two visiting monks with him.

She regarded them with interest. They were both young,

and had clearly not enjoyed an easy journey – their habits were threadbare and dirty, and their sandals badly in need of repair. If they were charlatans, she thought, then they were not very good at plying their trade, or they would have been better attired. The larger of the pair, who introduced himself as Frossard, had a black eye.

'A misunderstanding with a smith in Llandeilo,' he explained, raising a tentative hand to touch it. 'He thought I was going to steal a dagger.'

'Why would you want a dagger?' asked Cole, puzzled. 'You are a monk.'

'I did not *want* it,' objected Frossard stiffly. 'I was just looking. But since you ask, your domain is dangerous. Only yesterday we were obliged to watch a very desperate band of villains making off with sheep.'

'Were you close enough to see their faces?' asked Cole eagerly. The raiders tended to keep out of sight, and very few had witnessed them in action.

'Unfortunately not,' replied Frossard. 'They had hidden them with scarves.'

'There was one thing, though,' said Reinfrid quickly, seeing Cole's disappointment and hastening to curry favour. 'The fellow in charge was shrieking his orders in an oddly high-pitched voice. It made us laugh.'

'There is nothing amusing about cattle theft,' said Miles sternly.

'We would like to hear about your relic, brothers,' said Gwenllian, seeing Frossard gird himself up to argue. 'But not now – it is too hot. Come to the castle this evening.'

Gwenllian had invited a number of people to dine with her that night – Avenel and Fitzmartin, Mayor Rupe, Philip the chaplain and Deputy Miles. Then it had occurred to her that they would quarrel, so she had added Prior Kediour, Odo and Hilde, to help her keep the peace. Now Symon was home, she wished she could cancel the whole thing and spend the evening with him, but that would have been ungracious. The meal would go ahead, and she and Cole would preside together.

She had been to some trouble: the food was plentiful, the wine good, the hall had been swept and dusted, and Cole's smelly hunting dogs banished to the bailey. Musicians had been hired to entertain, and summer flowers had been set in bowls in the windows.

Cole had the pallor of exhaustion about him, so she placed Sheriff Avenel next to her, lest tiredness led to incautious remarks. Symon was not good at dissembling when he was rested, and there was no knowing what might slip out when he was tired. Miles, clad in a fine yellow tunic, had contrived to sit on Cole's left, so as to be close to Gwenllian as possible, and the feast had not been going long before she detected signs of trouble.

'. . . uncivil manner,' Cole was snapping, unusually curt. 'Do it again and I will—'

'Symon!' she hissed in alarm. 'Whatever is the matter?'

'Miles made a comment about your kirtle,' explained Cole shortly.

She smiled down at the dress in question, one that had been cut to show off her slender waist and lithe figure. 'Yes. It is a new one.'

Cole shot it a disinterested glance. 'Is it?'

'Odo and Hilde complimented it, too,' she went on. 'And even Kediour said the colour becomes me. In fact, you are alone in remaining mute on the subject. Doubtless you would pay it more attention if it was the colour of your favourite horse.'

'Yes, I would. He is piebald – large black and white patches. A kirtle in such a pattern would certainly command attention. Mine and everyone else's.'

'I had better have one made then.'

He laughed at the notion, his naturally sunny temper restored. When he turned back to Miles, she heard him begin a tale about the Crusade, which involved sufficient gore to keep the deputy's horrified attention until the meal was over. However, when the music began, she felt Miles's eyes on her again; drink had made him indiscreet in his ogling. She hastened to engage him in conversation, so he would at least have a reason for looking at her.

'Tell us more about your underground stream,' she said. The other guests pulled their attention away from the music to listen. Avenel and Fitzmartin were sneeringly sceptical, and Gwenllian hoped Miles's theory was right, just to wipe the smiles off their faces.

'As I said, it is beneath Mayor Rupe's wood,' replied Miles, unable to conceal his enthusiasm. 'I shall survey it again in the next day or so, and then we shall sink a well. Our town will never lack fresh water again.'

'That wood has always been boggy,' said Kediour. 'Yet I doubt it holds a stream, even so. The underlying rock is not the right type to support that sort of feature.'

'Did you mention using hazel twigs?' asked Gwenllian, before they could argue.

'My mother swore by them,' replied Miles, beaming lovingly at her.

'So she *was* a witch,' drawled Fitzmartin, exchanging a grin with his sheriff. 'There is a sorceress's whelp in a position of power at Carmarthen!'

'She was a good lady,' growled Cole, although he had

never met her and aimed only to defend his castle from insults. 'And I defy any man to—'

'Your destrier seemed lame today, Symon,' interrupted Kediour, earning a grateful look from Gwenllian. 'It is the drought – it has rendered the roads unusually hard for hoofs.'

'Lame?' asked Cole in alarm. He loved his warhorse. 'Are you sure?'

'A knight oblivious to the needs of his mount,' said Fitzmartin censoriously. 'King John will be interested to hear that.'

'Will he?' asked Chaplain Philip, sober and serious in his dark habit. 'I would have thought he had more urgent matters to consider as regards Carmarthen.'

'What is that supposed to mean?' demanded Miles testily.

Philip looked away. 'The cattle thieves,' he replied, although Gwenllian could tell he was lying, and it had been some other matter to which he had alluded. 'His Majesty will be more concerned about them than the constable's care of his animals.'

'He will indeed,' agreed Avenel slyly. 'Especially when he hears that they are still at large after a hunt lasting three weeks.'

Gwenllian saw a glance pass between him and Philip. Had the chaplain been telling tales, encouraging Avenel to think badly of her husband? She would not put it past him. Philip was a malcontent, only happy when he was causing trouble. Then she became aware that she was not the only one who had seen the exchange. Malicious satisfaction flashed in Rupe's eyes, and it occurred to her that he might have encouraged Philip's treachery. The mayor would, after all, lose the next election because of Cole. What better revenge than to have him dismissed?

*

The evening was one of the longest and most awkward Gwenllian could ever remember spending. Tiredness rendered Cole unusually irritable, and his temper was not improved by the attention Miles kept paying her. Avenel and Fitzmartin were critical and argumentative, and Philip's tongue wagged constantly. Gwenllian was grateful to Kediour, Odo and Hilde, who quelled many a burgeoning spat. Kediour flung priestly reproaches at anyone speaking intemperately, while Odo and Hilde kept up a flow of innocuous chatter to which no one could take exception.

'Shall we have some more music?' asked Odo, when even he had run out of bland conversation. 'I do so love a *long* Welsh ballad.'

'I would rather hear these monks tell us about their relic,' countered Avenel.

As Gwenllian doubted that he, Fitzmartin or even Miles would stay silent during a lengthy song in a language none of them could understand, the Benedictines seemed the better option. She stood to fetch them, but Miles anticipated her.

'Let me go,' he said, 'for *you*, my lady.' He smirked rather challengingly at Cole, and if Gwenllian had not been holding Symon's hand tightly under the table, she was sure he would have surged to his feet and dismissed Miles from his post on the spot. Then sides would have been taken, and who could say how such a quarrel would have ended?

The two monks were ushered in. They had smartened themselves up for their audience by washing and shaving, and their habits had been carefully brushed. They were still shabby, but at least they were clean. Reinfrid carried the little reliquary.

'We are monks from Romsey Abbey,' he began. 'And
our—'

'Romsey is a house for nuns,' interrupted Kediour, eyes
narrowing.

'Forgive me,' said Reinfrid with a bow. 'The sun has
addled my wits. I meant Ramsey. We are monks from *Ramsey*
Abbey, en route to Whitland, to deliver this sacred relic—'

'Why should Benedictines give Cistercians a gift?' Kediour
interrupted again.

'I am coming to that,' said Reinfrid, a little curtly. 'Our
abbot had a dream in which Beornwyn appeared and said
she wanted her hand taken to Whitland. Obviously, he was
no more keen to lose a relic than you would be, but she
appeared a second night, and a third, until he appointed
Frossard and me to do as she commanded.'

'I see,' said Kediour, still full of suspicion. 'And why you,
pray?'

'Because we are the youngest, strongest and best able to
travel,' replied Reinfrid, so glibly that Gwenllian suspected
the question had been put before. 'We care nothing for the
rigours of the road.' He indicated his tatty habit. 'As you
can see.'

'Who is this Beornwyn?' asked Cole. 'I have never heard
of her.'

'A virgin princess murdered by sea-pirates,' supplied
Frossard. 'She was a good lady, and she has left a trail of
miracles in her wake as we have journeyed west.'

'Sea-pirates?' asked Cole, startled. 'But Ramsey is nowhere
near the coast.'

'She was not murdered in Ramsey,' said Reinfrid, exas-
perated. 'It happened in Lythe, a small village near Whitby.
Have you heard of Whitby?'

'I have heard of its Benedictine abbey,' said Cole warily.

'A fine place, so we are told,' said Frossard blandly. 'Are you interested in petitioning Beornwyn for a miracle? Perhaps she led us here so she can help you. She has never failed us yet when we have petitioned her for mercy, and this town is clearly in need of good fortune.'

'May I see it first?' asked Cole. 'I am familiar with holy relics, having inspected many in the Holy Land – and touched them, too.'

'You *handled* sacred objects?' asked Kediour, shocked. Fitzmartin stifled a laugh at the prior's horror, although Avenel's face was stern and unsmiling.

'Do you anticipate being able to sense the sanctity of this hand, then?' asked Rupe. The question was innocent, but Gwenllian knew it was intended to cause trouble for Cole.

'No one will touch her,' said Reinfrid firmly. 'She is not for mauling by seculars. In fact, we never open her box. It would be impious to expose her to gawpers.'

'Very wise,' said Fitzmartin drolly. 'We would not want Cole struck down for irreverent behaviour, would we? It might make a mess in this beautifully clean hall.'

Rupe sniggered, then tossed a coin on the table. 'Here is a penny, and I will give you eleven more if Beornwyn brings us rain. A shilling is what you asked, is it not?'

Reinfrid grabbed it quickly. 'It is not for us, you understand. It is for Beornwyn – to continue her good works, and allow others to benefit from her munificence.'

He scowled when Fitzmartin roared with mocking laughter, then he and Frossard kneeled with as much dignity as they could muster to begin their prayers. Kediour stood abruptly.

'No,' he said coldly. 'This is sacrilege. You are imposters, and your saint is not one recognised by the Church.'

Reinfrid regarded him balefully. 'Yes, she is. She—'

'Take your so-called reliquary and leave,' ordered Kediour angrily. 'No one will pay homage to your purported saint, and we certainly do not want "miracles" that we are obliged to pay for. Real saints give them freely. There will be no more touting for business in Carmarthen. Do I make myself clear?'

His voice was so loud and authoritative that the two monks scrambled quickly to their feet, and even Fitzmartin's derisive guffaws died away. After a brief and rather tense silence, Cole announced that it was time for everyone to retire.

'Go to the kitchen,' he said kindly to the monks, seeing them look hungrily at the remains of the feast. 'The cook will feed you. You may sleep there, too, if you wish.'

'It is more than they deserve,' grumbled Kediour, watching the two lads hurry away. 'They are scoundrels, aiming to take advantage of the gullible, and their relic is a fake.'

The guests dispersed, stretching and yawning, all complaining about the sultry heat of the night. Cole escorted Kediour to his priory – he always did after dark, despite Kediour's assurance that an ex-Hospitaller was perfectly capable of looking after himself. It was some time before he returned to the castle.

'The weather must be preventing people from sleeping,' he reported, sitting wearily on the bed. 'I must have met half of Carmarthen when I was out.'

'Who?' Most of Gwenllian's attention was on little Meurig, who was shifting uncomfortably in his sleep, face flushed from the warmth of the room.

Cole listed a number of friends and acquaintances he had seen on his way to the priory, which lay on the northern outskirts of the town; he and Kediour had been obliged to stop and exchange pleasantries with them all. Then he came to those he had encountered on his way home, when he had been alone.

'Odo and Hilde were near the priory gate as I came out. They claimed they were going to walk to Merlin's Hill, to watch the stars from the top of it.'

'Then they were,' said Gwenllian sharply, not liking the scepticism in his voice. 'Odo is interested in astronomy, and he sleeps badly because of his sore back. They often rise in the night to study the heavens together.'

'Then I met Avenel and Fitzmartin, who said they were going to the Eagle tavern – the one out past the priory. Your cousin Philip was not far behind, and he told me he was following them to ensure they caused no mischief. I did not believe him.'

Nor did Gwenllian, and she wondered whether the chaplain had been going to tell the sheriff more gossip about Cole, his castle and his family. If so, the town's most remote alehouse was a good place to do it.

Cole continued, 'But the oddest thing was Rupe, with his henchmen and those two monks. They were in his wood. I saw a lamp there, you see, and went to investigate. All five were praying to Beornwyn. I suppose I should have stopped them, after what Kediour said, but I do not see what harm it can do. I left them to it.'

'Good,' said Gwenllian, not liking to imagine Rupe's reaction to being told where he could pray. His righteous indignation would have known no bounds.

'And finally there was Deputy Miles,' said Cole, disapproval thick in his voice. 'He hid behind a tree when he saw me coming, so I rousted him out like a rat.'

'You did not fight him, did you?' asked Gwenllian in alarm.

'I merely asked why he was not out on patrol, guarding our cattle as I had ordered. He said he was going to survey the coppice for that underground stream.'

'At night?' queried Gwenllian.

'I asked the same thing: he said he prefers to work without an audience. I told him to forget wild theories and concentrate on the thieves, but I doubt he will oblige. He wants to impress you with an endless supply of water. The wretched man is head over heels in love with my wife, and I was the last one to know it.'

Later that night there was a colossal clap of thunder, so loud that Cole was not the only one who thought the castle was under attack from war machines. He and Gwenllian stood at the window, watching lightning illuminate the entire countryside in almost continuous flashes.

'Is this Beornwyn's doing?' asked Cole in an awed voice, as the first drops of rain began to fall. 'Rupe paid for a miracle, and here it is?'

'Of course not,' said Gwenllian, although she was less sure than she sounded. 'It is just a coincidence.'

Then all conversation was impossible as the heavens opened, and the rain pounded down with such force that she feared the roof might cave in. The deluge stopped as quickly as it had started, and all that could be heard was water splattering from overtaxed gutters.

When it was light, she and Cole walked into the bailey which was heavily waterlogged. She smiled her relief at this sign of plenty, but he was anxious as he squinted up at the sky.

'I thought you would be pleased,' said Gwenllian. 'What is wrong?'

'The storm has not broken the weather. It will be just as hot today as it was yesterday, and that violent rain will have flattened any corn that has survived the drought. Moreover, I suspect that most of the water has run off without soaking into the soil. If this was a miracle, then it was not a very useful one.'

'Here is Kediour,' said Gwenllian, spotting the tall prior picking his way across the morass. 'I imagine he will have something to say on the subject of miracles.'

'I spent most of last night in my library,' Kediour reported without preamble, 'and I found mention of Beornwyn eventually. I was right: she is not recognised by the Church, although her cult thrives in and around Whitby. However, there is no suggestion that her hand was ever in Ramsey – or Romsey, for that matter. Those young men are lying.'

'I saw them and Rupe praying to her last night, in his wood,' said Cole. 'Do you think she made it rain?'

Kediour regarded him in dismay. 'You witnessed an act of desecration and did nothing to stop it?'

'They were praying,' said Cole uncomfortably. 'It is not for me to interrupt people's private devotions.'

'This from a man who has set eyes on the Holy Land?' Kediour was shocked. 'How *could* you ignore such an outrage? And so close to my priory, too! I must see about having the spot cleansed. You had better come with me, and point out exactly where this vile deed took place.'

'Hardly a vile deed,' mumbled Cole, disconcerted by the prior's hot words.

Kediour fixed him with a baleful eye. 'You should keep your role in this shameful affair quiet, because that rain did far more harm than good – homes flooded, crops flattened, cattle drowned. We do not want *you* blamed for the disaster. Can you imagine what Rupe and Avenel would say about it? They would use it to destroy you.'

'But it was Rupe who prayed for—' began Cole.

'He will deny it,' interrupted Kediour tartly. 'Like the liar he is.'

Cole nodded acquiescence, knowing he was right.

Gwenllian went with them as they walked to the coppice, noting a number of broken roof tiles, several people sweeping water from inside their homes and a tree fallen across the road. The sun was already hot, and the few remaining puddles were evaporating fast.

'That is odd,' said Cole, stopping to inspect a rivulet of water. 'This part of the road never usually floods.'

'It has been flowing since the storm,' explained Mayor Rupe, making them jump by speaking close behind them. 'It is running into my garden, so I hope it dries up soon. My vegetables are currently standing in a bog.'

'Perhaps you will show me the place where you and those two young vagabonds prayed last night,' said Kediour coolly. 'No, do not ask how I know. Suffice to say that I disapprove.'

Rupe began to argue, but a cold stare from the indignant prior made his words falter. Muttering resentfully under his breath, he led the way into the wood, where there was a small clearing not far from the road, reached by a narrow path. He stopped in astonishment,

'We prayed there,' he gulped, pointing with a shaking finger. 'And look! A spring now gushes from that very place. Beornwyn *has* granted us a miracle!'

'It is excess water from the storm,' said Kediour. 'There is no evidence to—'

'What is that?' asked Cole suddenly, pointing to a flash of

yellow behind a tree. Gwenllian recognised the smart new
tunic immediately, and ran forward with a cry.

It was Miles, sightless eyes gazing up at the sky above, and
a vicious red line around his neck to show where he had
been garrotted. A butterfly had settled on the wound.

Cole and Gwenllian tried to explore the wood for clues, but
Rupe's horrified wails had attracted a crowd. Kediour did his
best to keep them back, but not even his commanding figure
could control them for long, and they were soon trampling
everywhere, exclaiming in excited voices about the miracle
of the storm – the damage it had caused conveniently forgotten – and the spring that had appeared like manna from
Heaven.

'There is *another* butterfly, settling on the wound of this
murdered man,' cried Rupe. 'It is Beornwyn's spirit, weeping for the wrong that has been done next to her sacred
waters.'

'Actually, it is attracted by the moisture,' explained Cole.
'They—'

'There is nothing more to be seen here,' interrupted
Gwenllian quickly, aware of the revolted glances that were
being exchanged that the constable should own such grisly
knowledge. 'Now please go home, all of you.'

'No, stay,' countered Rupe. 'And feast your eyes on this
holy spring – a gift from the saint herself. She truly has
bestowed her favour on us – on *me*! I prayed to her, and she
has sited her stream on my land, at the exact spot where I
kneeled to petition her.'

'Actually, you were a little farther to the left,' said Cole.

Rupe's eyes narrowed. 'How do you know? Or were you
here, too, spying on us?'

'Of course not,' said Gwenllian hastily, not wanting Rupe to know that Symon had been alone in the woods where his deputy had been murdered. 'He was too tired after his three-week patrol for ferreting about in dark coppices.'

'So you say,' sneered Rupe. 'But he would have had to come past here to reach the castle after seeing Kediour home, and Miles is dead. And we all know that Miles lusted after you.'

'Symon knows he need not fear losing my affections to Miles or any other man,' said Gwenllian firmly. She was aware of Avenel and Fitzmartin on the fringes of the crowd, listening intently and doubtless eager to report Rupe's accusations to the King.

'A wife can provide no alibi,' declared Rupe scornfully. 'You would lie to save Cole, if for no other reason than that the next constable is likely to have a wife already.'

'Enough,' snapped Kediour, while Gwenllian gripped Cole's arm hard to prevent him from reacting to the insult. 'It is unseemly to quarrel over a corpse. Philip? Fetch a bier and arrange for the deputy to be carried to the castle chapel.'

'Your priory is closer,' said Cole.

Kediour's voice became gentle. 'Yes, but that is not where he belongs. And it is Philip's prerogative to stand vigil over a castle official until he is buried.'

The little chaplain looked disappointed to be dispatched on an errand when there was so much to see, and Gwenllian noted that he did not go without exchanging a quick glance with Avenel. She was thoughtful, remembering the people Cole had met on his way home the previous night: Philip, Avenel and Fitzmartin were among them. Had one of them strangled Miles? Or were the culprits Rupe and the two monks? Cole had seen Odo and Hilde, too, of course, but they were her friends and she could not believe they would throttle anyone.

'Why did you choose to pray in a wood, Rupe?' asked Cole, while they waited for Philip to return. 'Why not in the church?'

'I thought that if we were asking for rain, then we should do it outside,' explained the mayor. 'And my grove is a pleasant place to be of an evening.'

'It is not pleasant now,' remarked Kediour. 'It is a morass. My canons will fetch some stones, and we shall block the spring before it damages the road – or drowns your vegetables.'

'I do not mind, not now I know it is *sacred* water,' said Rupe. His eyes gleamed. 'I shall gather it in flasks and sell it to pilgrims.'

'It is not sacred,' said Kediour impatiently. 'Water often oozes from odd places after a violent storm, especially after weeks of drought. It will run dry in a day or two.'

'It will not,' stated Rupe loftily. 'I paid Beornwyn for a miracle and she gave me one. This wood belongs to me, and I shall build a chapel here to protect her spring, and to accommodate the pilgrims who will come. No one will block it with rocks.'

There was a determined jut to his chin, and next to him, his henchmen Gunbald and Ernebald gripped cudgels, obviously eager to use them on anyone inclined to argue. Cole's hand rested on the hilt of his sword and he drew breath to speak, but Gwenllian stopped him.

'Let them be,' she whispered. 'As Kediour says, the spring will soon run dry. It is not worth a quarrel.'

'No,' cried Kediour, overhearing. 'I will not permit it. Not so close to my priory. It would be blasphemous!'

'It is the will of God,' said Rupe gloatingly. 'You cannot

stop it and neither can Cole. The land is mine, and so is the spring. If you interfere, I shall complain to the King.'

'And the King will support you,' said Sheriff Avenel. 'He will say that a man has a right to use his own woods as he pleases. Especially when a percentage of the takings are sent to the royal coffers as an expression of fealty.'

Rupe scowled, but nodded reluctant agreement. Kediour also knew when he was beaten, although his face was black with anger as he stalked away.

'Well, *I* am pleased there will be a shrine,' said Odo, while Hilde nodded at his side. 'If any town deserves a miracle, it is Carmarthen. I am delighted with Beornwyn's favour.'

'The King's coffers will be, too,' smirked Fitzmartin.

'We need to catch Miles's killer quickly,' said Gwenllian to Cole, as they walked after the bier a little later. 'Too many people know you disliked his unseemly ogling, and Rupe will relish the opportunity to hurt you with malicious lies. We must find the real culprit.'

'Miles did annoy me last night,' admitted Cole. 'However, he was garrotted, and I am not a man to sneak up behind rivals and strangle them.'

'That will not stop Rupe and his henchmen from saying so, and Avenel and Fitzmartin will delight in carrying such a tale to the King. So might Cousin Philip, who is remarkably treacherous for a kinsman. You saw all six and those two monks on that road last night – one might be the villain, and may accuse you to draw attention away from himself.'

'So how do we catch him?' asked Cole, touchingly confident that she would know.

'You examined Miles's body.' As a warrior, used to violent

death, he was well qualified for such a task. 'Were you able to deduce anything from it?'

'Only that he was choked with something hard – not rope, which would have left fibres. And he was cold, so I imagine he died last night rather than this morning. However, it is impossible to be certain of such things. In the Holy Land, there was once a corpse—'

'What about the place where Miles died?' interrupted Gwenllian. Few of Symon's tales from the Crusade made for pleasant listening. 'Or was it too thoroughly trampled?'

'We would not have found footprints anyway – the ground is too hard.'

Gwenllian nodded. 'So all we have is what you saw last night: Miles walking alone to the coppice to look for water, ignoring your order to hunt for cattle thieves. And six suspects out here with an opportunity to kill him. Eight, if we include those two monks.'

'I saw Odo and Hilde, too,' Cole reminded her.

'Odo and Hilde are not killers.'

Cole sighed. 'Well, the culprit is obvious to me. Rupe did not want Miles telling everyone that the water was under his wood all along – and thus not holy – so he murdered him.'

'It is certainly a possibility,' agreed Gwenllian. 'Although it would mean that he did it *after* the storm, and only pretended to be surprised by the discovery of the spring today.'

'I would not put it past him,' said Cole. 'Do not forget his corrupt activities as mayor. He is more skilled at lies and deception than anyone I have ever known.'

They delivered Miles to the chapel, where Cole ordered Philip to keep vigil until the deputy was buried the following morning. The little chaplain was not amused.

'But so much is happening! The discovery of a sacred spring, talk of a holy storm. I will miss it all if I am stuck in here with a corpse. And I wanted to talk to the sheriff about . . .'

'About what?' asked Gwenllian coolly, as he trailed off guiltily.

'About Sir Symon's hunt for the cattle thieves,' said Philip with a sickly and unconvincing smile. 'How hard he has tried to lay hold of them with patrols and traps.'

'Right,' said Gwenllian flatly. 'You can do it tomorrow, when I am there to hear you. Until then, you can say Masses for poor Miles.'

'Poor Miles indeed,' muttered Philip. 'He did not deserve such a terrible death.'

'No one ever does,' said Cole grimly. 'But since we are discussing him, tell me where you went last night.'

'I was here,' said the chaplain. 'Praying for rain.'

Cole regarded him askance. 'Was it your twin I saw trailing after Avenel then?'

Philip looked away. 'Oh, yes. I forgot. The sheriff wanted me to write him a letter, so I went to the Eagle to oblige. It was afterwards that I prayed for rain.'

'What manner of letter?' asked Gwenllian, not bothering to point out that it was an odd time for clerkly activities. Most people preferred to do it in daylight, when they could see.

Philip became haughty. 'A confidential letter to the King. More than that I cannot say.'

Gwenllian nodded calmly, but she was alarmed. What had the spiteful chaplain and the sheriff written together at such a peculiar hour?

'Did you see Miles?' asked Cole.

'No, and I assumed he was out patrolling for cattle rustlers, as you had ordered. I was as surprised as anyone to hear he was discovered in the wood.'

Leaving Philip to his vigil, Gwenllian suggested that she and Cole revisit the scene of the murder to resume their hunt for clues. They walked through the town slowly, enervated by the heat, and arrived at the wood to find the little clearing thronged with people. Avenel and Fitzmartin were standing to one side, watching, while Rupe and his henchmen had filled a barrel with water from the spring, and were selling it in bowls. The two Benedictines were giving an impromptu sermon, and Gwenllian was dismayed to see Odo and Hilde among the eager listeners. Kediour was there, too, tight-lipped with disapproval.

'It is just as I feared,' he said, coming to speak to her and Cole. 'The rain did more harm than good, yet those monks – *if* they are monks – bask in their role as saviours.'

'They certainly wasted no time in buying themselves new sandals with the money intended for Beornwyn,' remarked Gwenllian. 'And they reek of ale.'

Kediour was obviously distressed. 'Desperate people are easily led, and there is something of the Devil in this cult of theirs. I fear for people's souls.'

'I fear for their purses,' said Cole. 'If the monks do not empty them, Rupe will. I thought exposing his corruption would make him mend his ways, but he is just as greedy and unscrupulous as ever.'

Gwenllian watched the mayor, who was proclaiming that last night's deluge was just the beginning of the favour Beornwyn would show him. While Kediour strode forward to inform the crowd that the Church did not recognise this particular saint, Cole drew the mayor aside.

Rupe's henchmen followed, and Gwenllian did not like the way that Gunbald pulled a dagger from his belt and looked as though he would very much like to use it. She beckoned to the two monks over, too, hoping the presence of monastic habits would forestall any violence.

'Did you see Miles here last night, Rupe?' Cole was asking.

'No,' replied Rupe shortly, while the henchmen and the monks indicated with shaken heads that they had not either. 'We were too intent on our prayers.'

'He believed he had discovered an underground stream beneath this wood,' pressed Cole. 'Which means your spring is not sacred, but was here all the time.'

'He was a fool with his hazel twigs and silly theories,' spat Rupe. 'And I would have told him so had I caught him poking around on my land. However, we did not see him.'

'Perhaps Beornwyn struck him down,' suggested Frossard. 'She disliked what he was doing, so she took a killer to him. There was a butterfly on him, after all.'

'Is she a spiteful kind of saint then?' asked Cole.

'No,' said Reinfrid, shooting his companion a cautionary glance. 'Yet it is strange that he should die next to her spring – the very thing he might have denied was miraculous.'

Gwenllian questioned all five closely for some time, but was unable to catch any of them in an inconsistency, and while she did not believe that this was indicative of innocence, it did mean that she was wasting her time. When she and Cole took their leave, Rupe was smug, the monks relieved, and the henchmen disappointed, as if they had hoped the encounter would end in the opportunity to stab someone.

*

As there were so many familiar faces in the crowd, it was a good opportunity to ask whether anyone else had seen Miles the previous night. One or two folk had spotted him near the castle, but no one admitted to seeing him near the wood. Cole, it seemed, was the last man to see him alive. Other than the killer. After a while, Rupe made an announcement.

'We should show Beornwyn our appreciation for her miraculous gift. I have bought nails for the chapel that will cover her spring, but who will provide timber for the walls and tiles for roof? Who will build an altar, and purchase candles, crosses and flowers?'

'Whoever does will be blessed,' added Ernebald, and Gwenllian could tell he had been told what to say by his master. 'Gunbald and I will give a door – you can see it over there.'

'The moment we decided to make the donation, there was a miracle,' added Gunbald, all pious gratitude. 'Our cow, which has been dry all summer, gave us milk today.'

People hastened to pledge materials and labour, and it was with astonishment that Gwenllian saw a building begin to fly up in front of her eyes. Cole muttered something about the cow benefiting from drinking her fill of rainwater, but no one listened. Avenel and Fitzmartin watched it all, their expressions disdainful.

'We should speak to them,' whispered Gwenllian to Cole. 'It will distract them from our people's foolish gullibility, if nothing else.'

She began by asking whether Cousin Philip's scribing skills had been satisfactory in the Eagle the previous night, maliciously adding that his writing was notoriously poor. Avenel exchanged a bemused glance with Fitzmartin.

'We never asked Philip to write anything,' said Fitzmartin.

'Why would we? I can write myself – an unusual skill for a knight, I admit, but one that is useful even so.'

'Did he meet you in the Eagle?' pressed Gwenllian.

'Yes.' Avenel shrugged. 'He has taken to following us around. It is a nuisance, but he wants what is best for Carmarthen. Indeed, he is rather fanatical about his hopes for the place.'

Gwenllian declined to ask what he meant, reluctant to acknowledge that she did not know her cousin as well as she had thought. 'Did you see or hear anything that might allow us to catch the killer?'

'No,' replied Avenel. 'We did not stay out long, and were back in the castle hours before the storm struck. You may confirm this with your guards. They saw us.'

They walked away, leaving Gwenllian thinking they might well have dispatched the deputy on their way home. They certainly could not prove otherwise. She glanced up as Odo approached, Hilde at his side.

'I heard what the sheriff told you, and it is the truth,' Odo said. 'We were studying the stars last night, and we saw him and his friend. They did not stay long in the Eagle, perhaps because the heat had spoiled the ale.'

'Then did *you* spot anything that might help us find Miles's killer?' asked Gwenllian.

Odo shook his head apologetically. 'My attention was on the heavens, I am afraid. I saw the storm come in, though, like a herd of horses. It was a magnificent sight, and we are indeed blessed by Beornwyn. I spent the rest of the night praying to her.'

'We both did,' asserted Hilde. 'We feel privileged to have witnessed her celestial power, and to prove our devotion to her, we shall pay for the altar in her new chapel.'

She smiled dreamily, then hurried to rejoin the builders. Odo was not long in following. Gwenllian watched, aware that there was more hammering and sawing around the shrine than there was at the new tower in the castle.

'I know they are your friends, but I think it is odd that they spend hours staring at the sky,' said Cole, also observing them thoughtfully.

'They are good people,' said Gwenllian firmly. 'They would never commit murder. They are too devout, and would fear for their immortal souls.'

'Not if they believe they were carrying out Beornwyn's wishes,' persisted Cole, then turned away to watch Rupe and his henchmen sanding the door. Gwenllian's inclination was to ignore the remark, but then it occurred to her that Odo and Hilde did seem particularly taken by the saint and her so-called miracle, and they had been out all night with no alibi but each other. Then she shook herself. How could she question such dear friends? ·

Hot and dispirited, Gwenllian stepped into the shade of the trees to think. Her attention was immediately taken by Kediour, who had approached the two monks and was addressing them in a ringing voice.

'Show us this hand you claim to have. You declined to do it last night, but now we have been "blessed" by this miracle, we must have earned the right to see the thing.'

'Yes,' agreed Rupe eagerly. 'And then we shall dip it in the spring to make doubly sure of its holiness.'

He dropped to his knees and put his hands together in an attitude of prayerful expectation. The folk labouring on the shrine did likewise, and silence descended on the clearing, broken only by a faint breeze rustling through the trees.

Reinfrid gave a strained smile as he picked up the little reliquary and handed it to Kediour.

'We are not worthy to attempt such a thing, so perhaps you will oblige, Father.'

He stepped away, head bowed, leaving Kediour grimacing his annoyance. The prior tried to open the box, but something was wrong with the lock. After several moments of futile fiddling, he thrust it at Cole.

'It is broken,' Cole said, peering carefully at it. 'Someone has tried to force it.'

'Nonsense,' declared Frossard. 'Perhaps poor Beornwyn just wants to be left in peace.'

All eyes were on Cole as he took a dagger to the lock. It clicked open after a moment, and the lid sprang up.

'There is nothing here except a piece of folded material,' he said, upending the box and shaking it with more vigour than was appropriate for a reliquary, even an empty one.

'There! What did I tell you?' said Kediour in satisfaction. 'There is no hand, and this pair are frauds.'

'No!' Horrified, Frossard snatched the box to look for himself. 'The hand is stolen! What shall we tell Whitby?'

'Surely you mean Whitland?' said Kediour, watching him closely. 'That is where you claimed you were heading yesterday.'

'He said Whitland,' said Reinfrid. 'You misheard. But how could this have happened? Beornwyn granted Carmarthen a miracle and look at how she is repaid – her relic stolen and a murder at her spring! What kind of town is this?'

'When did you last see the hand?' asked Cole, speaking quietly to calm him.

'Last night,' replied Frossard. 'We came out here to pray

with Mayor Rupe, and then we returned to the castle to sleep. It must have been stolen from us there, probably by the same person who killed the deputy.'

Cole regarded him icily. 'There are no thieves in my house. Are you sure you went there? And before you answer, be aware that my soldiers keep a record of who comes and goes after dark. Any tale you tell will be checked.'

'Well, perhaps we did pass the night in a tavern instead,' admitted Frossard reluctantly. 'And the relic was with us . . .'

Kediour's patience was at an end. 'How many more lies must we hear from this pair? They have no relic, and there is nothing to prove they ever did. It is obvious what happened: Miles guessed they were imposters and threatened to expose them. So they killed him.'

'No!' cried Reinfrid, appalled. 'We are monks, men of God.'

Kediour promptly embarked on a detailed interrogation about Ramsey Abbey, and it quickly became apparent that neither had ever been there.

'They are liars,' stated Kediour, as the pair stuttered into silence. 'They claim the saint's hand is stolen from them, but look at their reliquary – it is silver. Do they really expect us to believe that a thief took a cluster of old bones but left such a precious chest?'

'But it is what happened,' objected Rienfrid. 'It—'

'Arrest them both, Cole,' ordered Avenel. 'The prior is right: they murdered Miles when he threatened to expose their dishonesty. I shall enjoy seeing them hang.'

The townsfolk were shocked and silent as soldiers marched the two tricksters away, both howling their innocence.

Rupe quickly recovered his wits. He had not survived so

long in the turbulent world of politics without learning the skill of turning a disaster to his advantage.

'Beornwyn was petitioned and she sent us rain,' he declared. 'It does not matter that the monks are charlatans. The fact is that she graced us with a spring, and will be pleased by the shrine we are building. If we continue, she may send another storm.'

'That is true,' nodded Odo. 'The stars are favourable to such a scheme at the moment. I read them myself last night. We should persist with our chapel, and pray at Beornwyn's spring – the *real* sign that she is among us.'

Kediour tried to reason with them, but Rupe's voice was louder, and people were more inclined to listen to promises of miracles than denunciations, so he soon gave up. The people went back to their building, led by Mayor Rupe singing a psalm.

'I do not know how to convince them,' said the prior in despair. 'The spring does *not* come from Heaven – I feel it in my very bones – and it grieves me to see people led spiritually astray. I am glad Rupe will not be mayor for much longer.'

'People have short memories,' said Cole soberly. 'They will forget the money that disappeared under his steward- ship, and the dishonest arrangements he made. They will see him as the man with land blessed by a saint, which may be enough to see him re-elected.'

'Lord!' muttered Kediour, appalled. 'Yet perhaps we mis- judge him. He did buy nails for the shrine. Maybe his devotion is genuine, no matter how misguided.'

'It is the prospect of money that turns Rupe devout,' said Cole to Gwenllian, when the prior had gone. 'But we had better speak to Frossard and Reinfrid again. They are liars, certainly, but I do not see them as killers.'

Neither did Gwenllian, and the conviction was strengthened further still when she saw them huddled in a cell, pale
and frightened. She felt sorry for them, and wondered what
circumstances had led them to such a pass.

'You are in serious trouble,' said Cole gravely. 'Sheriff
Avenel wants you hanged, and I am tempted to oblige him.
Or will you earn a reprieve by telling the truth? You say you
are monks, so I would be within my rights to send you to
the bishop instead.'

The pair seized the offer eagerly, and it was not long
before the whole miserable story emerged: the prank that
had ended in disaster, their banishment, and the confession
that Reinfrid had stolen one of Beornwyn's hands and a box
in which to keep it.

'I thought it would be easy,' he finished miserably. 'That
people would pay us to pray, and we would live well. But
Beornwyn is not very good at granting requests, and last
night's rain was the only miracle she has ever performed for
us. We shall starve this winter.'

'We could not believe our luck when Mayor Rupe gave
us a penny,' added Frossard. 'After we had eaten, we hurried to his wood and prayed as hard as we could.'

'And then?' asked Cole.

'We went to the Coracle tavern, and spent the coin on ale
and new sandals,' said Frossard sheepishly. 'Whoever stole
the relic must have waited until we were drunk ...'

'If you had it at the castle last night, why did you refuse to
show it to us?' asked Gwenllian, not sure what to believe.

'Because it *is* holy,' said Frossard earnestly. 'You may not
think much of us, but we do treat it with respect. We have
never displayed it for all to gawp at. And it is fragile, anyway.
Too much pawing makes bits flake off.'

'And we can prove it was stolen *after* you saw us in the castle, sir,' said Reinfrid. 'You inspected the box very closely – you would have noticed if the lock had been broken.'

'I would,' said Cole to Gwenllian. 'There was nothing wrong with it then.'

'But we did not kill the deputy,' added Frossard tearfully. 'I saw him in the woods just after we left Rupe. He was watching us, and I had the sense that he was waiting for us to go so he could work unimpeded. Then you came along, sir, and I watched the pair of you argue.'

'You did?' asked Gwenllian uneasily. 'You did not mention this in the clearing.'

Frossard shrugged. 'Because your husband cannot be the killer, lady. We followed him back to town after the quarrel, and he was in our sight the whole time. Besides, he was kind to us – he offered us food, even after what that nasty prior said about us and Beornwyn.'

'Did Rupe and his henchmen see Miles too?' asked Gwenllian.

'It depends on how observant they are,' replied Frossard. 'He was well hidden, and Reinfrid did not spot him – just me.'

'Did you see anyone else in the vicinity?' asked Cole.

Reinfrid nodded earnestly in his attempt to be helpful. 'The same people as you, sir: Rupe and his two men, the sheriff and his friend; your chaplain; and the fat merchant with his wife.'

'Odo and Hilde,' said Gwenllian coolly. 'So who do you think killed Miles?'

Frossard and Reinfrid exchanged a glance. 'The mayor is the obvious candidate,' replied Reinfrid. 'Neither he nor his henchmen are very nice. However, any of the others might have done it, although I imagine the chaplain is too puny for strangling.'

There was no more to be learned, so Gwenllian and Cole took their leave.

'They are telling the truth,' she said, once they were in the cleaner air of the bailey. 'They did not kill Miles.'

'Do you want me to release them?'

'No, they will only run away and ply their nasty trade on others. We shall hand them to the bishop, as you suggested, and let him decide their fate.'

She glanced up to see Sergeant Iefan hurrying towards them.

'You had better come quickly,' he said to Cole. 'There is trouble brewing at the spring.'

There was trouble indeed. The crowd had grown since they had left, because Odo had fallen in the spring, and when he had been tugged upright, he claimed the pains in his back were cured. There was now a veritable army of people working on the chapel, and Rupe, Gunbald and Ernebald were selling holy water as quickly as they could put it in flasks. The heat was making people irritable, and there were scuffles and hissed arguments in the queue.

'Lord!' muttered Cole, as Odo and Hilde came to greet them. 'Their shrine has two walls built already. I have never seen anything raised so fast in my life.'

'Everyone is eager to do Beornwyn's bidding,' Odo explained, his plump face beatific. 'I feel young again now she has cured me.'

'But Prior Kediour persists in his efforts to denigrate her,' said Hilde unhappily. 'We have explained that what happened here is a good thing, but he will not listen. Perhaps you can talk some sense into him. But do it soon. People are beginning to resent his hostility.'

Gwenllian glanced towards the spring, where Kediour and his canons were imploring people to go home or, better yet, attend evening service in the church. But Rupe urged them to stay, and it was to the mayor that they listened. Moreover, there were resentful murmurings against the Austins for presuming to give orders, and it would not be long before it turned physical. Gunbald and Ernebald were armed with cudgels and knives, and it was clear they were ready to join in any trouble.

'Tell Kediour to take his canons home,' Gwenllian whispered to Cole. 'The spring will run dry soon, and when it does, people will lose interest in Beornwyn. He will not have to endure this nonsense for long.'

Cole began to weave his way through the throng, but people were packed tightly together, and he could not help but jostle a few. Inevitably, someone took exception.

'You shoved me!' screeched Rupe. He turned to the crowd. 'Did you see that? He deliberately barged into me, and almost knocked me from my feet.'

'My apologies,' said Cole. 'I was only trying to reach Kediour, so I can escort him and his canons back to their priory.'

'Then do it,' snapped Rupe. 'They are a nuisance here, and we do not want them.'

'I am not going anywhere,' declared Kediour indignantly, and Gwenllian saw with a sinking heart that he, too, was on the verge of losing his temper. 'How can I, when I see souls in peril? They will be bound for Hell if—'

'It is you who is bound for Hell,' shrieked Rupe, his voice high with indignation. He stabbed his finger at Cole. 'And

you. Beornwyn will not stand by while I am battered by a
lout who has falsely accused me of corruption. How can I be
dishonest? If I were, Beornwyn would not have put her
spring on my land.'

'Come,' said Cole, taking Kediour's arm. 'There is no rea-
soning here—'

'And now he accuses me of lying,' squealed Rupe. 'He has
already murdered Miles for ogling his wife, and now he
insults me. He—'

He did not finish, because Gunbald swung his cudgel at
Cole, who ducked away, but in so doing he stumbled into
Ernebald. With a roar of outrage, Ernebald attacked. It was
all that was needed to start a fight. Most of the canons backed
away from the mêlée, but a handful of novices remained,
trying to extricate their prior from the flailing fists.

With horror, Gwenllian saw Gunbald prepare to swipe at
Symon again. She shouted a warning, but too many others
were yelling, and Rupe's piercing screeches were especially
loud. Her voice went unheard. She saw the bludgeon begin
to descend towards her husband's head, but Avenel was there
to block it, after which his sword made short work of its
wielder.

Then Cole was on his feet, his strong voice breaking
through those of the others. She had never heard him so
angry, and the effect on the rioters was immediate. Knives
were sheathed, sticks and coshes furtively concealed, and
fists lowered. But Gunbald did not move.

Rupe rounded on Cole. 'This is *your* fault. You should not
have interfered. Gunbald is dead, and I will have vengeance.'

'Vengeance?' asked Kediour quietly. 'I cannot see your
saint approving of that.'

'Of course she will,' snarled Rupe. 'She was murdered by

villains herself, and will not sit idly while good men are slaughtered by those who are supposed to protect us. She will rise up to exact payment for what has happened. You wait and see!'

Cole's face was dark with fury and, unwilling to risk annoying a man who could put them in prison, the hotheads who had joined the brawl prudently melted away. Soon all that remained were the more sober folk, who wanted only to work quietly on the shrine. Kediour ordered his novices home in a voice that was uncharacteristically subdued, while Rupe kneeled next to Gunbald and wailed his grief. Gwenllian was sure it was insincere, that he was taking the opportunity to gain public sympathy in the hope that his past misdeeds would be forgotten, and he would be elected for another term as mayor.

'I am sorry,' said Kediour to Cole, stricken. 'I was following my conscience. I would never have pressed my point if I thought it would end in a death.'

'Go home, and keep your brethren inside,' ordered Cole shortly. 'Folk have taken this saint to their hearts, so please do not disparage her again.'

'But it is a heathen business,' objected Kediour, ashen-faced. 'I *cannot* keep silent, especially when this place is so close to my priory.'

'You must. Or Gunbald will not be the only casualty.'

Kediour shot an anguished glance at the unfinished shrine, which was already bright with votive candles. Then he gave a brief nod of acquiescence and walked after his brethren, his shoulders slumped in defeat. When Ernebald started to follow with a murderous gleam in his eye, Cole indicated that Iefan was to intercept him before more blood was spilled.

'Well?' asked Avenel, sheathing his sword. His expression was superior. 'Will you not thank me for saving your life?'

Cole grasped his hand, catching him off guard with his open sincerity. 'I will, and gladly. My wife is not ready to be a widow just yet.'

Gwenllian agreed, and was about to say so when her attention was caught by the fact that Philip had abandoned his duties at the chapel, and was whispering to Odo and Hilde. The chaplain flushed red when she approached.

'I will return to my vigil now,' he stammered, chagrined at being caught disobeying orders. 'I only left for a moment, but then the trouble started . . .'

Gwenllian pulled him to one side so they could talk without being overheard. 'Avenel claims you wrote no letter for him last night. Why did you lie?'

Philip's expression was furtive. 'I did not lie – not exactly. He *did* ask me to scribe for him, but Fitzmartin offered to do it instead. As I was there, I thought I may as well enjoy an ale before returning home. It was too hot to sleep anyway.'

'Did you see Miles?'

The chaplain shook his head. 'I would have told you earlier if I had.'

He hurried away before she could ask him anything else, leaving her staring after him thoughtfully.

'He is a fine young man,' said Odo, coming to stand next to her and smiling fondly. 'Cole is fortunate to have him as a chaplain.'

'Yes,' said Gwenllian noncommittally.

Later that evening, as the sun began to dip and the shadows lengthen, Iefan arrived at the castle to say that the cattle rustlers had been spotted a mile south. Cole prepared to ride out at once, and Gwenllian was alarmed when Avenel and Fitzmartin offered to go with him.

'Symon, no! They are suspects for garrotting Miles, and may dispatch you once they have you away from witnesses.'

Cole waved her concerns away. 'I *want* them to come, to see for themselves how difficult it is to trap these thieves. Besides, it is a good opportunity to question them about Miles. Who knows? Perhaps they will confess to his murder as we sit around a campfire.'

Gwenllian gulped her horror, before he grinned to show he was jesting. It was not funny, and she was angry with him for making light of such matters. Others also thought he was reckless to include the sheriff and his henchman in the party.

'Please,' said Odo quietly, while Hilde nodded at his side. 'I know Avenel saved your life today, but it was an instinctive reaction, and I am sure he is cursing himself now. He has changed since you came home. While you were away, he was loud and brash; now he is quiet, watchful and brooding.'

'As if he is planning something,' elaborated Hilde. 'And Fitzmartin is a beast. He punched his squire this morning for no reason. Odo and I are sure something evil is afoot.'

'I agree,' said Kediour uneasily. 'Do not forget what they are accused of – desecrating churches and holding parishioners to ransom. These are not gentle crimes.'

But Cole remained resolute, and Gwenllian could do nothing but watch as he rode away, Avenel and Fitzmartin far too close behind him for her liking. Cousin Philip stood next to her, and she happened to glance at him as he was exchanging a meaningful nod with someone. When she saw it was Odo she was bemused, but then news came that there was bloody flux in the nearby village of Abergwili, and her attention was taken in sending aid.

For the next three days, she had little time for worrying, as she struggled to run the castle, quell trouble at the shrine and be a mother to her children. Whenever she could, she continued her enquiries into Miles's murder, but despite questioning as many people as would talk to her, she came no closer to learning the identity of the killer. Rupe persisted in his claim that Cole was responsible, although few believed him, most preferring to blame the two 'monks'.

Stunned by the violence that his well-intentioned entreaties had caused, Kediour kept to his priory. Gwenllian visited him on the evening of the fourth day after the trouble, to beg more medicine for Abergwili. While she was in the priory, he voiced his continuing fear that Carmarthen was being led down a spiritually dangerous path.

'Rupe has turned Beornwyn into a very profitable business,' he said unhappily. 'He has sold countless flasks of "holy" water, and now he claims she appears to him regularly in dreams, along with "poor murdered" Gunbald.'

'I know,' said Gwenllian. 'But he is too greedy, and people resent the money he is making from them. Most have abandoned him already, and he has only a few devoted followers left. The cult will soon fizzle out completely.'

'I hope you are right,' said Kediour worriedly. 'I hate to see people misled where matters of faith are concerned. It pains me to hear him slandering Symon, too.'

It pained Gwenllian as well, but there was nothing she could do about it, especially while Cole was away. She longed for him to return, and hoped he would not be gone three weeks, like the last time. To take her mind off her worries, she reviewed what she had learned about Miles's murder.

The deputy had gone to Rupe's wood to investigate the underground stream he believed he had discovered, hoping the late hour would see the place deserted. Cole thought Miles had been dead for several hours before he was found, which meant he had been killed not long after the two of them had argued. Frossard had witnessed their quarrel, and she supposed she should be grateful that Rupe and his henchmen had not.

From ten possible culprits when she had started her enquiries, she now had six. She had never seriously considered Odo and Hilde; they were friends, and she could not believe they would garrotte anyone. Reinfrid and Frossard could also be eliminated, because they had been close on Symon's heels as he had returned to the castle, close enough that they had seen him stop to speak to the other suspects. That left Avenel, Fitzmartin, Philip, Rupe and his two henchmen, one of whom was now dead.

Her favoured suspect was Rupe, who wanted everyone to believe that Beornwyn had blessed him with a spring, and who would certainly not want Miles to claim that water had been there all along. Moreover, Rupe's alibi had been provided by his henchmen, a brutal pair who would certainly kill on his orders – and who would lie for him, too.

Avenel and Fitzmartin had no reliable alibi either. They had left the Eagle to walk back to the castle, but no one had accompanied them, and there was nothing to say they had not killed Miles en route. They were, as Kediour had reminded her, alleged to have committed other nasty crimes, so why not murder? And they certainly had a motive: the King would be delighted to hear that there was trouble in Carmarthen. Hilde and Odo were wary of them, too, and believed they were plotting something untoward.

And finally, Philip had also been near the scene of the murder with no good explanation, and he had been caught out in lies. He might be her kinsman, but she neither liked nor trusted him, and she was uncomfortable with the secret glances he kept exchanging with Avenel – and with Odo, for that matter.

She was torn from her ponderings by a rattle of hoofs in the bailey. She ran to the window, and sighed her relief when she saw Cole. Avenel and Fitzmartin were there too, and she could tell by the general air of dejection that the cattle rustlers had not been caught.

That evening, after Cole had washed away the filth of travel and had drunk more watered ale than Gwenllian had thought was possible without exploding, she told him all that she had learned during his absence. He listened without interruption.

'I think we can cross Avenel off your list,' he said when she had finished. 'He saved my life. Gunbald would certainly have killed me if he had not acted.'

'Odo says it was base instinct that drove him,' argued Gwenllian. 'I imagine he is dearly hoping that no one tells the King what he did. And do not say he went with you to catch the thieves out of goodness – he went to witness your failure for himself.'

Cole did not agree, and they debated the matter until they fell asleep, both worn out by the stresses and strains of the last four days. At dawn, the door opened and Iefan crept in.

'You can cross Rupe off your list of suspects, Gwen,' said Cole, after hearing his sergeant's whispered report. 'He is dead – garrotted, like Miles.'

Word of the murder had spread through the town long before the castle was informed, and Rupe's house was ringed by spectators when Gwenllian and Cole arrived. The more important ones were inside, where they stood in the bed-chamber, staring at the body. The only sound was Kediour's voice as he murmured prayers for the dead man's soul. Gwenllian looked around the room in distaste: it was mean and poor, suggesting that Rupe was a miser, hoarding his money and refusing to pay for clean bedclothes and decent furniture.

When Kediour had finished his petitions, Cole stepped forward to examine the body. There was not much to see: the mayor wore a thin nightshift, and had probably been asleep when his attacker had come. The bedclothes were rumpled where he had kicked with his feet, and his nails were broken, but there was nothing in the way of clues. Gwenllian's eyes were drawn to the conical hat Rupe had always worn, and she could not prevent a superstitious shudder when she saw a dead butterfly adhering to it.

'Who found him?' Cole asked.

'Me.' Ernebald's voice was hoarse with shock. 'When I brought him his morning ale.'

'When did you last see him alive?'

'Midnight. We were making plans for the chapel. His wife is away, so he slept alone.'

'She had gone to stay with her sister, because she dislikes pilgrims tramping through her vegetables,' explained Avenel. His face was impossible to read in the dim light, and his voice was flat. 'Or so Fitzmartin and I were told in the Eagle last night.'

'If he and Fitzmartin were in the Eagle, they would have had to pass this house to return to their beds in the castle,' Gwenllian whispered to Cole. 'It would have been simple to climb through an open window and dispatch him.'

'How do you know a window was open?' Cole whispered back.

'Because the hinges on the bedroom shutter are broken, and it has been tied back to stop it from rattling. I saw it from the road and so, doubtless, did the killer.'

'Rupe had lost favour since you have been away, Sir Symon,' said Philip, stepping forward to speak. 'He raised the price of his holy water, and imposed a fee for visiting the shrine. People have stopped coming, and you will find many who wished him ill. This will not be an easy crime to solve. Perhaps you should not waste your time trying.'

Gwenllian was surprised to see her cousin there. She had sent him to give last rites to someone in Abergwili, and she had imagined he would stay the night. Why was he back so soon? And why was he suggesting that they not bother to investigate a murder?

'Mayor Rupe was a businessman,' growled Ernebald, glaring at the chaplain. 'Of course he turned this opportunity to his advantage. However, it cannot be coincidence that the poor man is slaughtered the moment *he* returns.' He jabbed his finger at Cole.

'Of course it is coincidence,' said Odo impatiently, while Hilde nodded her agreement. Gwenllian was startled that they should be among the spectators: they were not usually ghoulish. 'And he is not the only one who came back yesterday, anyway.'

He did not look at Avenel and Fitzmartin, but the accusation hung heavy in the air.

'We heard the commotion when we were praying in the shrine,' said Hilde, apparently reading Gwenllian's mind and feeling the need to explain their presence. 'We had been asking for another miracle. Philip was with us.'

The chaplain gave a nervous smile. 'There is no fee at night, when Rupe and Ernebald are asleep. It was a good time for a poor chaplain to come here.'

'Never mind this,' snapped Fitzmartin. 'The question we should be considering is who killed Rupe. Personally, I agree with Ernebald: Cole is the obvious suspect. Even I, a stranger to Carmarthen, could see that he and the mayor hated each other.'

Avenel said nothing, and Gwenllian thought again of Hilde's contention that he was plotting something. Her blood ran cold. Had *he* killed Rupe, to blame Cole and give the King an excuse to be rid of him? She was devising a way to find out when a soldier arrived to report that the cattle thieves had been spotted near the bridge. Gwenllian did not know whether to be relieved or suspicious when the sheriff and his crony asked if they might be excused joining the expedition to hunt them this time.

When Cole had gone, Gwenllian made a determined effort to identify Rupe's killer by asking questions. She dismissed Ernebald as a suspect because the mayor's death had deprived him of a home, an employer and a livelihood. No other local would hire such a vicious lout, and he was now faced with a choice of leaving Carmarthen to find a new master, or a life of miserable poverty.

Assuming there was only one garrotter at large, and that a townsman had not killed Rupe for charging exorbitant prices at the shrine, she was left with three suspects from her original List: Avenel, Fitzmartin and Philip. Despite Cole's suspicions, she refused to include Odo and Hilde. She started her enquiries with the sheriff and his friend, but they were uncooperative, and professed not to recall when they had arrived at the Eagle or how long they had stayed.

'Our movements are none of your concern,' snapped Fitzmartin. He reeked of ale and his eyes were red-rimmed. Had he tried to wash the memory of murder from his mind with drink? 'And do not think that telling lies about *us* will help you. The King will take no notice.'

It was a peculiar remark, and Gwenllian had no idea what it meant, but before she could ask, Avenel had grabbed his companion's arm and pulled him away, muttering something about going to see what was happening at the shrine. Gwenllian could see what was happening from the window: two or three pilgrims were inside the chapel, but that was all. Building work had slowed since Rupe had started to charge for the honour of praying there, and although it had four walls, there was no roof. She wondered whether it would ever be finished now the mayor was dead.

'You were right,' said Kediour, following the direction of her gaze. 'The spring is half the size it was, and the town's ardour for Beornwyn is fading fast. However, a dogged minority remains, and they are fervent in their love for this so-called saint. Odo and Hilde are among them, and I fear for their souls.'

Gwenllian could see both kneeling at a makeshift altar. Then Philip approached and whispered something to them. They held a brief conversation, but all three had gone by the time she had left Rupe's house and reached the chapel.

Determined to have answers, she visited the Eagle. The landlord was reluctant to discuss his customers at first, and it took an age to persuade him, so she was tired and irritable by the time she had cajoled him into confirming that the sheriff and his friend had indeed visited the previous evening.

However, Avenel had pleaded exhaustion and had left around midnight; Fitzmartin had stayed, eventually falling asleep on the table.

'His snores kept me awake all night,' the landlord grumbled. 'I would have poked him, but he has a nasty temper so I did not dare. He slept until dawn, when word came about Rupe.'

So, thought Gwenllian, Fitzmartin was not the killer, but the landlord's testimony put Avenel out alone at the salient time. She walked slowly back to the castle, deep in thought.

As she passed the shrine she saw Avenel slouching towards it from the direction of the town. Hilde was right, she thought, watching him covertly: the sheriff had changed from the arrogant, superior man he had been when he had first arrived. He was quieter, sombre and definitely troubled. Was it his conscience, uneasy with murdering civilians?

After a moment, Fitzmartin appeared, and stalked towards the priory gate, where Kediour was chatting to a lay-brother. The henchman snarled something in a low voice, and ended his words with a hard poke in the chest that made Kediour stagger. Gwenllian ran towards them, ready to berate Fitzmartin for laying hands on a priest. He sneered at her before going on his way.

'He is vexed with me for asking questions about the churches he is said to have despoiled,' explained Kediour, rubbing the spot where he had been jabbed. 'He threatens to kill me if I persist, which hardly leads me to think him innocent.'

'Then stop,' said Gwenllian, alarmed. 'Symon will lose his post for certain if *you* are murdered. A mayor and a deputy may be overlooked, but not an important churchman.'

Kediour smiled fondly at her. 'Do not worry about me. I have not forgotten all the skills I learned as a Hospitaller, and besides, I suspect Fitzmartin is all wind.'

Gwenllian was not so sure. Then she frowned. 'Is Odo rubbing his back?'

'Unfortunately, his "cure" was only temporary. It is a pity. I would have liked to have seen something good come out of this miserable business.'

They glanced up at the sound of hoofs, and Gwenllian felt a surge of joy when she saw Cole. Behind him, his soldiers grinned as they escorted a score of bound men. The prisoners were sullenly defiant, and nearly all wore the conical hats popular in Dinefwr – the kind that Rupe had favoured.

'There is a good reason why we caught them so quickly this time,' said Cole as he dismounted. 'Their leader – and fellow Dinefwr man – was not available to give them details of our patrols and plans.'

Gwenllian gaped as she struggled to understand the import of his remark. 'What are you saying? That *Rupe* controlled them?'

Cole nodded. 'I should have guessed when Reinfrid described what he had observed about the thieves – that their leader shouted orders in an unusually high voice.'

Gwenllian recalled Rupe's falsetto screeches during the scuffle in which Gunbald had been killed. 'A local leader would explain a great deal.'

'Especially one who attended meetings in which our strategy for tracking the thieves was discussed. Moreover, several prisoners have already told me that the raids were all his idea.'

'But why?' asked Gwenllian, shocked by the betrayal. 'He is . . . *was* our mayor.'

'Dinefwr is also suffering under the drought, and Rupe has family there. He knew he was finished here, so he decided to avenge himself by stealing our livestock – and helping his kin at the same time. Of course, that was before the "miracle" he claimed to have funded. After it, he must have begun to hope that he might be re-elected.'

They both turned as someone approached. It was Fitzmartin, Avenel at his side.

'We have just been informed that Rupe was behind these raids,' the henchman growled. 'When the King hears, he will confiscate every last penny that villain owned. He will crush his treacherous relations, too.'

'No,' said Cole sharply. 'The dry summer has brought death and famine to Dinefwr, and there is nothing to be gained from persecuting them.'

'Besides, I suspect Rupe has already given them most of what he owned,' added Gwenllian. 'You must have noticed the shabby furnishings in his home. And there is the fact that he was obliged to ask for donations to help him build Beornwyn's chapel.'

'But he publicly accused you of murdering your deputy,' said Avenel softly to Cole. 'Why not let his thieving kin pay the price for his flapping tongue?'

'Because it is better for the region that we do not,' replied Cole. 'It would lead to all manner of feuds. Please do not mention it to the King. Simply say the culprits have been caught.'

Avenel stared at him with an expression that was impossible to fathom. It made Gwenllian acutely uneasy, but there was no time to ponder, because Iefan had arrived. The sergeant's face was pale with shock as he blurted his news to Cole.

'Those two monks are dead, sir,' he gasped. 'Strangled, like the others.'

'Well,' drawled Fitzmartin slyly. 'I suppose that proves *their* innocence.'

It did not need a close look to see that Reinfrid and Frossard had died by the same hand as Miles and Rupe. The only difference was that Frossard had a bruise on his temple.

'He must have been stunned by a blow to the head,' surmised Cole, 'allowing the killer to dispatch them one at a time. Frossard is larger, and would have put up more of a fight, so he was disabled first.'

'When did you last see them alive?' asked Gwenllian of the gaoler.

'Noon,' said the gaoler wretchedly. 'Two hours ago.'

'I assume you were at your post all that time,' said Cole. 'Who came down here?'

The gaoler was as white as snow. 'It is so hot today, sir, so I went to the kitchen for a cool ale . . . But no one ever comes down here! I did not think it would matter if I left them alone for a short while.'

He stopped when he saw Cole's disgust, and scurried away with relief when he was ordered to remove the bodies so that the cell could be used for the cattle thieves. Their arrival and the interviews that followed kept Cole busy for the rest of the day. Gwenllian spent her time with the children, but they were asleep by the time Cole had finished with his prisoners. He trudged wearily into their bedchamber just as the last of the daylight was fading.

'If your gaoler is telling the truth about the time,' Gwenllian began, having thought about the most recent murders all afternoon, 'we can eliminate Odo and Hilde as suspects, not that they were ever serious contenders in my eyes. They were at the shrine when the monks were killed. I saw them there myself.'

'Who is left then? Fitzmartin? He seemed unmoved by the news of their demise.'

'He has an alibi for Rupe, which means he did not kill the monks either – I am sure we only have one garrotter at large. Our sole remaining suspects are Philip and Avenel. I cannot see my little cousin as a killer; he does not have the strength.'

'It takes no great power to strangle a man from behind,' said Cole soberly.

'I was alluding to a different kind of strength. I do not believe he has the *fortitude* to dispatch four victims.'

Cole was about to argue when there was a commotion at the bottom of the stairs. Within moments Avenel burst in, an indignant Iefan at his heels. The sheriff was agitated, and made no apology for invading their privacy.

'I cannot find Fitzmartin. He was meant to meet me in the Coracle, but he is not there.'

'Are you his keeper then?' asked Cole archly. 'He cannot look after himself?'

'Of course he can,' snapped Avenel. 'But he told me that he knew the killer's identity, and would reveal it when I arrived at the tavern. I have a bad feeling that he has put himself in danger in his eagerness to make amends.'

'Make amends?' queried Gwenllian. 'With whom? You?'

'Yes. Your chaplain has uncovered evidence that proves Fitzmartin has desecrated churches and ransomed their parishioners. Needless to say I am unimpressed, and Fitzmartin has been at pains ever since to win back my approbation.'

'It is a trap, Symon,' whispered Gwenllian as Cole stood. 'Do not go.'

'I never thought you were the killer, Cole,' said Avenel, stepping closer as he tried to hear what she was saying. 'I would not have saved your life if I thought you were. Fitzmartin disagrees, but he is a fool – he thinks you weak for declining to expose Rupe's perfidy, but I see wisdom in the decision. You and your lady are good rulers, and I shall say so to the King.'

'Thank you,' said Gwenllian coldly. 'However, Symon is still not going with you. We shall lend you some soldiers, and they will help you search for your friend.'

Avenel smiled slyly. 'I outrank him – he cannot refuse me. However, I would rather he came willingly. It would be so much more pleasant for us all.'

'Then I shall come, too,' determined Gwenllian.

'No!' exclaimed Cole in alarm.

'Of course you may,' said Avenel smoothly. He held out his hand. 'I shall escort you myself.'

With the sense that matters were moving far too fast for her to understand, Gwenllian allowed the sheriff to lead her down the stairs and into the bailey.

The dark streets were oddly empty as they hurried through them, because people had sought cooler places to be – taverns, the church and even the parched river, where some still bathed in its fetid shallows or slumped on its banks in the vain hope of catching a breeze.

Gwenllian's heart pounded with anxiety. She knew, with every fibre of her being, that something bad was about to happen, and wished she had had the presence of mind to grab one of Symon's daggers before she had left.

'Look,' said Avenel suddenly, ducking into a doorway and indicating that Gwenllian and Cole should do the same. 'Odo and your cousin. They have been together a lot of late, but when I ask them why, they tell me they are praying.'

'Perhaps they are,' said Gwenllian, trying to control the tremor in her voice.

'Yes,' said Avenel, with one of his unfathomable looks. 'But it is an odd alliance, do you not agree? And where can they be going at such an hour?'

Gwenllian had no answer, but was indignant when Avenel began to follow them. She opened her mouth to shout a warning, but the furious look he shot her made her close it again. Cole held her hand as they walked, and together they saw Odo and Philip stop briefly in the church, then aim for the road that led north. The moon was almost full, and was shockingly bright in the clear sky, so trailing them was ridiculously easy.

'They must be going to the shrine,' whispered Avenel.

But Odo and Philip continued past it and the priory, so that Gwenllian could only suppose they intended to visit Merlin's Hill, from which Odo liked to study the stars. She wondered why Philip should have chosen to go with him: the chaplain had shown no interest in astronomy before. Avenel stooped suddenly and picked something up from the road. It was a buckle, distinctive for being elaborately engraved.

'Fitzmartin's,' he said, peering at it in the moonlight. 'From his tunic. There must have been a struggle and it fell off.'

'Here is blood,' said Cole, bending to inspect dark spots in the dust. He soon found more on the well-worn path that led to the shrine. 'It is damp, so it has not been here long.'

'The killer has abducted Fitzmartin,' declared Avenel. 'The fool! He should have confided his suspicions to me, and we would have tackled the villain together.'

'I do not trust any of this,' hissed Gwenllian, plucking at Cole's sleeve to whisper in his ear. 'It has a contrived feel. Avenel intends to win the King's approval by luring you to the chapel – it will be deserted at this time of night – and killing you.'

'Hurry,' ordered Avenel sharply, and Cole had no choice but to obey.

Gwenllian could not move fast enough to keep up with them. She lagged behind, hampered by her skirts, and feeling sick when she saw more splashes of blood. Absently, she noticed that the stream flowing from the spring was now no more than mud; it would not be long before it dried up altogether.

The shrine looked forlorn in the dark, with no roof and no pilgrims, although there was a rosy glow inside where candles had been left burning. Then she heard a familiar voice. It was Kediour.

'Gwenllian?' he called. 'It is safe now. A sharp blow to Avenel's head has put an end to his mischief. Symon is tying him up for me.'

Gwenllian hurried forward, but stopped in alarm when she saw not Cole securing the sheriff, but both men sprawled senseless on the floor. Then the door slammed behind her, and she turned very slowly to see Kediour holding a crossbow.

'I am sorry,' said the prior softly. 'I had hoped to resolve this business without further loss of life. Now I am afraid you must die, too.'

Gwenllian gaped at Kediour in disbelief. There was a knife in his belt and the crossbow was unwavering. With lurching terror, she recalled that he had been a Hospitaller, a warrior-knight who had earned his spurs in the bloody slaughter of the Crusade. Then she glanced at Cole and Avenel. The sheriff was beginning to stir, hand to his head, but Cole lay still.

'I was obliged to stab poor Symon,' said Kediour, in the same apologetic voice. 'I wish it could have been avoided. I liked him, even if he did admit to manhandling sacred relics in the Holy Land. I only stunned Avenel, though, as I shall need his help to arrange the bodies.'

'Bodies?' whispered Gwenllian.

'Fitzmartin,' replied Kediour, and she saw a third man on the floor. He had been garrotted, and drips from the wound had left the trail that Cole had followed. She noticed the fine metal chain that held Kediour's pectoral cross, and recalled what Symon had said about the murder weapon: that it was something hard, not rope that would have left tell-tale fibres. 'He made accusations, so I had no choice. I brought him here, knowing it would be empty. You were right: people are already forgetting Beornwyn and her so-called miracle spring.'

'Fitzmartin is the King's man,' said Gwenllian shakily. 'So are Symon and Avenel. His Majesty will send emissaries to discover what has happened to them, and—'

'His Majesty will have heard the rumours about churches despoiled and parishioners ransomed,' said Kediour in the same soft, sad voice. 'He will not look too carefully at the disappearance of Fitzmartin and Avenel, while you and Symon have long been thorns in his side.'

Gwenllian looked at Cole, and felt anger replace shock. 'I suppose you think you acted righteously,' she said contemptuously. 'To prevent a shrine being founded for a saint not recognised by the Church.'

'I did act righteously,' averred Kediour. 'God will not want a blasphemous cult on the doorstep of a holy priory, and it was my duty to crush it. I sincerely doubt those monks had Beornwyn's real hand, given the inconsistencies in their tale, and the whole thing was based on deceit. The souls of hundreds were in peril, and I did the right thing.'

'I see it all now,' said Gwenllian, not concealing her distaste. 'Indeed, I should have known you were the killer when you refused to have Miles's body in your priory. You could not bear to let a victim into your domain.'

Kediour grimaced. 'A foolish superstition for which I am sorry. I was doing God's will, and I have no cause to feel guilt or remorse.'

'You were never a suspect because Symon did not know that you had sneaked out of the priory after he had taken you home. But sneak out you did, and you saw Rupe, his men and the two lads praying to Beornwyn. You could not fight five of them, so you decided to secure Symon's help in cleansing the spot the following day. But Miles was there, too—'

'Performing heathen tricks with his hazel twigs,' said Kediour in rank disapproval.

'And you feared that if he did discover water near where Rupe and his companions prayed, it might be interpreted as the saint's doing.'

'Well, I was right,' said Kediour acidly. 'That is exactly what happened. I thought the affair would be over with Miles dead and the wood defiled by murder, but then the storm came, and what I had hoped to avoid came to pass anyway. The Devil was busy that night.'

'He still is busy,' said Gwenllian coldly.

'I cannot tell you how shocked I was when I saw the spring

the following day,' Kediour went on, his eyes distant. 'Of course, the really irritating thing was that it did *not* flow from the place where they prayed – as Symon noted, it was further to the left. Rupe lied.'

'And so you killed him, too.'

Kediour regarded her bleakly. 'He was not only deceiving people with his false miracle, he was profiting from it – taking money from the desperate and the poor. I cannot imagine a greater crime. And now it transpires that he was a cattle thief, too.'

'Reinfrid and Frossard were next,' said Gwenllian. 'It was easy for you, a regular visitor to the castle, to wait for the gaoler to slink away for ale. But why bother with them?'

'Because Cole was going to hand them to the bishop, rather than hanging them as they deserved, and they might have escaped to ply their evil trade again.'

'It was you who stole their relic, of course,' said Gwenllian. 'You knew they would celebrate their good fortune in a tavern, so you waited until they were too drunk to notice and took it from Reinfrid's pack. Then you insisted on seeing it the next day, hoping that an empty reliquary would expose them as charlatans.'

'It should have done,' said Kediour bitterly. 'But Rupe salvaged the situation. He would have found some excuse for the spring drying up, too, and gullible folk would have accepted his lies. It had to be stopped, Gwenllian. You must see that.'

Gwenllian saw that Avenel had regained his senses and was listening. Then with a surge of relief she saw that Symon's eyes were open, too. She stepped towards the spring, ostensibly to dip her hand in the mud, but really so to shield him from Kediour's sight. She was aware of him and Avenel exchanging a silent signal. They had a plan, although she could not see how they would prevail against a skilled warrior who held a loaded crossbow.

'Stand up, Sheriff,' said Kediour abruptly. 'And drag Fitzmartin and Symon to the altar. There is wood enough for a fire, I think.'

'A fire?' asked Gwenllian in alarm. She straightened quickly, her hand dripping with thick brown muck.

'I shall follow the example set by those false monks, whose wickedness began this miserable affair. They started a blaze to conceal what they had done, and so shall I.'

'Why should I?' asked Avenel, although he scrambled upright. 'You will kill me anyway.'

'Because there are many ways to die,' said Kediour softly. 'Quickly with a crossbow bolt, or slowly in an inferno. The choice is yours.'

Avenel moved towards Fitzmartin, regarded him sadly for a moment, and then grabbed his legs. 'None of your victims were good men,' he said quietly. 'Miles lusted after the constable's wife, Rupe was a thief, Reinfrid and Frossard lived by deceit, and Fitzmartin did some terrible things. But Gwenllian is innocent. Let her go.'

'I wish I could,' said Kediour sadly. 'But no one can know what I have done. They will not understand, and might turn against my priory. Now pull Symon to the altar and let us end this miserable business. I have no wish to prolong the agony.'

Avenel bent, and in one smooth move had snatched the knife Cole passed him and lobbed it at the prior. Unfortunately, his aim was poor and it passed harmlessly over Kediour's head. The prior's eyes blazed with fury, and the crossbow started to come up. Gwenllian knew it would not miss. More out of desperation than rational thought, she flung the grainy sludge that clung to her fingers at him.

Her aim could not have been better, and the crossbow discharged harmlessly into a wall as mud flew into Kediour's eyes. Avenel lunged towards him, and there followed a furious tussle. Gwenllian tried to pull Symon to his feet, but he was heavy, and she could not do it. Then Avenel knocked Kediour into a row of candles, all of which went flying. They caught the tinder-dry wood of the walls, and she saw the prior was going to have his fire after all.

The flames took hold quickly, and a shower of sparks sprayed across Kediour's habit. The wool began to smoulder, then it ignited. Kediour tried to bat out the blaze with his hands.

'Help him,' gasped Cole, when Avenel came to haul him to his feet. 'Do not let him die in here.'

Avenel ignored him, but once they were outside there was no question of anyone going back. The entire chapel was ablaze, sending orange flames leaping high into the night sky.

'You asked me to keep the truth about Rupe's evil deeds from the King,' said Avenel softly. 'Well, let us do the same for this misguided prior. We shall invent a passing outlaw to take the blame for these murders, and we shall say Kediour died trying to save the chapel.'

III

The fire burned itself out quickly, and by the time the townsfolk came hurrying to see what was happening, there was nothing left but smouldering planks. Kediour's body was retrieved and carried back to a priory that would genuinely miss him, and Avenel took the opportunity afforded by the canons' stunned distress to reclaim Beornwyn's hand with none of them any the wiser. He offered to return it to Whitby, and left the next morning. By the evening of the same day it had started to rain.

The land recovered quickly once the weather reverted to the cool, wet, grey days its people knew and loved. The river ran full and fat, trees and hedgerows regained their colour, farmers reported that some of the harvest might be saved, and livestock began to fatten.

'Miles was mistaken,' said Gwenllian one evening. Cole's wound was taking too long to heal, and she was concerned by his continued pallor. 'There is no underground stream in Rupe's wood, and the water that bubbled from the ground was just a result of that unusual storm. There is a lot of water around now, yet there is no sign of it.'

'Good,' said Cole. 'I am sure shrines are good things, generally speaking, but they do bring out the worst in people. In the Holy Land . . .' He trailed off when she shot him a warning glance. 'Well, suffice to say they are not always sites of peace and serenity.'

'We were wrong about Avenel,' said Gwenllian. 'He had nothing to do with despoiling churches or holding people to ransom – that was all Fitzmartin.'

'And Cousin Philip found the truth,' added Cole. 'Odo said we were lucky to have him as a chaplain, and he was right. I do not know why we had to send him to Brecon.'

'He deserved a promotion after all he did,' said Gwenllian. Then she grimaced. 'He might have been on the right side in the end, but he is still a very *slippery* character, and I was glad to see him go. Much of what he discovered was with the help of Odo and Hilde, yet he never acknowledged the role they played. He kept the credit for himself.'

Cole smiled his understanding. 'So that is what they were doing with their muttered discussions and secret glances! But why did they go to Merlin's Hill on the night of the fire?'

'To talk without being overheard. It was a sensible pre-caution. Fitzmartin had intimidated a number of people into spying for him. He would have killed them if he had found out what they had discovered and were passing to Avenel.'

'Avenel was horrified by their revelations. He is a decent man. Incidentally, I advised him to hide his goodness when he visits the King. John does not want honourable, intelligent men in his service.'

'No,' agreed Gwenllian, 'although it was unwise of you to say so. However, I trust Avenel to be diplomatic. He might even persuade the King to leave us alone.'

'It was good of him to take Beornwyn's hand to Whitby,' said Cole, more gloomily than was his wont. 'It might be some time before I would have been able to do it.'

'It would indeed,' she said with mock indignation. 'You have been gone far too much of late, and I intend to keep you here with me for several months at least.' Then she became serious. 'Yet I am glad Beornwyn has gone. She did no good here.'

'Perhaps she objected to her limbs being toted around the country and exploited by unscrupulous men. When I am well, I shall light a candle for her in the church. She was a real person, whether a saint or not, and does not deserve to be treated so.'

Gwenllian made no reply, and they sat in companionable

silence, listening to rain patter in the bailey below and the other familiar sounds of castle life – the clatter of pans from the kitchens, the rumble of soldiers' voices from the barracks and the contented cluck of hens scratching in the mud. Then a butterfly flitted through the window, dancing haphazardly until it landed on Cole. He let it stay, studying its pretty blue markings and the way it flexed its wings. Then it took to the air again and was gone.

'I hope that was not the same one that danced over the wound in Miles's neck,' said Gwenllian in distaste. 'Or kin to the dead one I saw on Rupe's conical hat.'

Cole laughed, the first time he had done so since the fire. 'I would not think so. But do you know, Gwen, I am feeling much better. Perhaps we can light Beornwyn's candle tomorrow.'

Whitby, Winter 1200

Abbot Peter was appalled when Sheriff Avenel brought him the sorry tale of Reinfrid and Frossard. The hand's theft had been noticed, of course, and had caused even further friction between Lythe and the abbey. Now, a year after the original affair, Peter had had more than enough of Beornwyn and everything connected to her.

'She has been a bane to me ever since I came here,' he said irritably to his brother, William. He rubbed his temples. His headaches had grown worse since the trouble, although the medicine William had brought would ease them. He had somehow mislaid the last box, and had had to manage twelve months without it. William had been too busy to bring a replacement batch sooner, because he had been busy founding his own priory. It was to be near their family home at Broomhill in the Malvern Hills.

'Has she?' asked William sympathetically.

'She was a nuisance when she was in Lythe, because pilgrims would insist on going there instead of here,' the abbot continued waspishly. 'And now she is here, the villagers accuse us of theft on a weekly basis. I have a good mind to send her packing.'

'Really?' asked William, regarding him intently. 'Because if you are serious, I have a new monastery that is sadly bereft of relics. Beornwyn would make a big difference to us – perhaps even the difference between survival and ignominious dissolution.'

'I wish you could take her,' said Peter fervently. 'But relations with Lythe would never recover if I were to dispatch their beloved saint to a place that none of them have heard of. I fear I am stuck with the wretched woman – and will be until the end of my days.'

'Not necessarily,' said William, settling more comfortably in front of the fire. 'You are right in that you cannot *give* her away, but what if she were stolen? Lythe cannot blame you for that – it is how they lost her themselves.'

Peter laughed without humour. 'I think they would guess what happened if Beornwyn suddenly appeared in the priory founded by my own brother!'

'Would they?' asked William seriously. 'How? Broomhill and Lythe are many miles apart, and both are remote. How would your villagers find out?'

Peter stared at him. 'Do you think it would work?'

'Why not? Relics are always being filched by unscrupulous thieves, and this will be just one more instance of it.'

Peter considered the matter, but then shook his head. 'No,'

he said with real regret. 'It would make me no better than the young men I banished.'

'It is not the same at all,' argued William. 'They took her for mischief, whereas you are trying to heal a rift that is damaging both the abbey and Lythe. Your monks gloat and the villagers hate them for it – such sentiments will see them all in Hell. Removing her will eliminate a source of discord and thus save their immortal souls.'

'Well, if you put it like that . . .'

'Good,' said William briskly. 'However, it will have to be done properly, so there can be no question of skulduggery on your part. Leave it to me, brother.'

He was as good as his word, and the following day, the monks reported with dismay that burglars had smashed a window in the chancel and made off with a number of relics, Beornwyn's among them. A week later, most were found abandoned in a church in Scarborough, but Beornwyn was believed to have been tossed into the sea.

When William presented the relics to Broomhill, he told the new prior that he had bought them in France. No one ever questioned him, and the shrine thrived, especially after a wealthy Venetian merchant named Marco Giuliani was cured of deafness. Giuliani promptly made the abbey a handsome donation, then offered to double it if they would sell him one of Beornwyn's fingers. The prior demurred, but William opened the reliquary one night and saw the hand lying on top, almost as if it were begging to be removed. Thus Giuliani had his relic, and the priory received funds for a beautiful new Lady Chapel.

But Lythe's distress tore at Peter's heart, and nothing he did relieved the ache of guilt every time he saw a villager kneeling at the altar where Beornwyn had rested. He lay awake at night wondering how he could make reparation, and then an idea came. He would write her story. He would set his best scribes to illuminate it, and he would present the finished manuscript to Lythe as an acknowledgement of the part Beornwyn had played in all their lives.

Filled with vigour, he snatched up his pen and began at once, transferring all he knew of her to parchment, and even inventing a few details, intended to make her sound more saintly. He wrote in the vernacular, thinking the villagers would prefer it to Latin. He laboured for days, watched wryly by his good friend Prior Richard, head of the Cluniacs in Bermondsey, who happened to be visiting.

Eventually, the manuscript was finished, and Abbot Peter summoned the villagers to receive his gift. They stared at it in bemusement, before informing him that it was very pretty, but not something that was much use in a place where no one could read.

'Never mind,' said Richard kindly, when they had gone. 'God will appreciate what you have done, and that is the most important thing.'

'Will He?' asked Peter bitterly. 'Then why do I feel as though Heaven is frowning on me? My headaches are worse than ever and I am very tired.'

Richard regarded him in concern, then became practical. 'Beornwyn has caused you far too much trouble, and it is time for it to stop. We shall expunge all trace of her from your abbey, and the monks will be forbidden to speak her name. We shall use her shrine for other relics, and the people of Lythe will have to go elsewhere to petition her.'

Peter nodded wearily. 'Very well. And I shall burn the manuscript.'

'No, I shall take it to the library in Bermondsey,' said

Richard, loath to see such a beautiful thing reduced to ashes. 'Then she will be truly gone, and you must forget her.'

'Yes,' said Peter, nodding. 'I shall. It is for the best.'

He leaned back in his chair and rubbed his eyes. Then he started in alarm when something spiralled past his face to land on the table in front of him. It was a dead butterfly.

Historical Note

Nicholas Avenel was Sheriff of Pembroke in 1202, and he, along with William Fitzmartin, was accused of despoiling churches belonging to Gerald de Barri, Archdeacon of Brecon (more famously known as Gerald of Wales). They were also said to have harried parishioners by kidnapping them and holding them to ransom.

Symon Cole was Constable of Carmarthen in the 1190s, and Lord Rhys of Deheubarth had several daughters named Gwenllian.

In the last quarter of the twelfth century, one Adam de Rupe left provision for masses for his soul. He had a tenant named Gunbald, son of Ernebald. Witnesses to the deed included Philip de Barri and Odo of Carrau. A similar grant was made for the soul of Miles de Coggan.

There was an Augustinian priory in Carmarthen in 1200, but the name of its then prior is unknown, although Kediour is mentioned in deeds dating to the 1180s.

Finally, the first head of the Benedictine abbey at Whitby was Reinfrid, and Frossard was lord of the manor at Lythe. The abbot in 1200 was probably Peter, and Richard was Prior of Bermondsey from 1189 until about 1201.

ACT TWO

It wasn't my idea of paradise – a godforsaken lump of rock thrust up in a sea full of similar outcrops, where the population was outnumbered by the goats – but Katie loved it. As we got off the galley at Kamares, she looked up at the mountains that surrounded the harbour, and cried out with joy.

'Oh, Grandpa, it's beautiful . . . magical!'

I cringed at her calling me her grandfather, even though it was true. It made me feel old, though that was also true. You see, I gave up counting my years when I passed seventy. And I didn't want to be reminded of the fact every time Katie opened her mouth. I pulled a face.

'I told you to call me Nick.'

Katie frowned and tugged at the golden hair that cascaded down over her shoulders. It was a mixture of her grandmother's ash-blond hair and my red locks. Though my hair was more salt and pepper now.

'I'm sorry, Grand— Nick. But I haven't known you all that long, and I love having a real grandfather.'

Maybe I should explain why she hasn't known me all her life. My name is Niccolo Zuliani of Venice, though my friends call me Nick, a name my English mother gave me. And I have spent most of my life on the furthest edge of the world. The Mongol Empire of Kublai Khan had drawn me like a magnet from the earliest time I heard stories of its fabled wealth. I had travelled there and made some good friends, even becoming a high official at the Khan's court. But I had always yearned for home, as all Venetians do. And finally I had returned to discover that my long-lost love, Caterina Dolfin – the lithe and sexy Cat of my younger days – was still alive and kicking, with a granddaughter called Katie Valier. It had turned out that the pretty girl, who now stood before me on the quay at Kamares, was my grandchild by the son I had never known. That son had been a seed that I had left spawning in Cat's belly when I went to seek my fortune on the other side of the world. Now, having discovered my granddaughter, I was striving to make up for lost time. I sighed, knowing that I was already giving in to her every whim.

'Then you may call me that, but only in private. Every other time it must be Nick, or Messer Zuliani. Now, where is Querini? I was told he would be here to meet us.'

We had been standing on the quay for some time by now. Our baggage was already piled there too, and the oarsmen of our speedy Venetian galley were beginning to file off the boat. But there was no one to greet us. Each oarsman – who was a free Venetian, not a slave, as in other galleys – saluted us as he passed. The men were chosen by lot from each parish, and their families were supported by the remainder of the parish while the rowers were away carrying out their duties. We had been on our travels so long that I had got to know them individually, at least enough to recognise their faces. I saw the cocky one called Stefano, who was working off his debts. Debtors often paid off their obligations by rowing in the galleys along with oarsmen chosen by lot. He grinned at me as he passed.

We were still left waiting after the oarsmen had all gone to find their lodgings. At last the Doge's private secretary, Bertuccio Galuppi, who had travelled with us on this long journey to the Greek island of Sifnos, came hurrying back down the quay. He had gone to see why no one was waiting for us on our arrival. As he got closer, I could see his face looked like thunder.

'Messer Galuppi, what is wrong? Is there some delay? I do hope not, as I am quite parched, and standing in this sun is not a good idea for an old man with a thirst.'

Galuppi shook his head. 'I fear we have a problem, Messer Zuliani.'

'None greater than my thirst, I can assure you.'

Galuppi, who acted as though he had a rod up his arse at the best of times, bristled at my levity.

'It is far worse than that. Niccolo Querini is . . . indisposed.'

'Indisposed? That is an insufficient excuse when the Doge's representative lands on this little excuse for an island.'

That's me, by the way – the Doge's representative. I'll tell you later how Nick Zuliani, of dubious origins and shady repute, came to be occupying such an elevated post. But right then I needed to throw my weight around a little. I scowled at Galuppi.

'Tell him that I don't care if he's dying of the French pox, I want him here now.'

Galuppi's face turned puce, and he anxiously inclined his head to remind me of the presence of my granddaughter. I suppose he imagined such language should not be spoken in the presence of a lady of such tender years. Especially not one from the noble houses of Dolfin and Valier. I had no such compunction. Before I had known of her existence, Katie, dressed as a boy, had spied on me. It had been only when I turned the tables on her and grabbed her that I had felt her burgeoning tits. She had cursed me then in a language that was as robust as any Venetian sailor cursing drunkenly in a tavern in the Arsenal. Which is probably where she had learned it as the wild child she had been before I met her. I had tried my best to be a good grandfather and to put her on the straight and narrow, but to no avail. Besides, I was secretly proud of her vocabulary, and had learned a few choice expressions from her myself. I was tempted to use one or two now, but saw that it would be counter-productive with the sober-sided Galuppi. Instead, I laid an arm over his shoulder, and drew him aside.

'Bertuccio, tell me, what has indisposed Querini?'

His stiff demeanour bent somewhat, and he leaned towards my ear to whisper into it.

'He is dead—'

'Dead?' I cried. 'Why didn't you tell me?'

He shook his head vigorously. 'No, no, not dead. Merely dead drunk. He is incoherent and sleeping it off in the tavern along the street.'

I glowered. 'We shall see about that.' I turned to Katie. 'Wait here, the shipmaster will ensure no harm comes to you. I have some business to attend to.'

I saw that she was about to protest at being treated like a child. But she knew the nature of my temper, and decided to save up her complaint about her treatment for when we were in private. I had no doubt I would be called 'grandfather' in the frostiest of terms, but I could bear it. Rather that than she get involved in a scene with Querini that could become nasty. She sat down on one of our trunks, and rested her chin in her hand in a way that suggested she was not happy with me. I ignored her gesture and indicated that Galuppi should lead me to our drunken host.

In actual fact, Niccolo Querini was not who I was sent to meet by the Doge. The focus of my long and arduous journey from Venice around the southern coast of Greece and out into the Aegean Sea was Querini's wife, Speranza Soranzo. Her father, Giovanni Soranzo, had earned a reputation as the hero of Aegean naval operations. He had taken twenty-five galleys up to the Black Sea and the Crimea, restoring Caffa to Venice and taking it away from the hands of the Genoese. He became Head of the Navy, and Governor of the Gulf and Islands of Venice. In 1309 he was appointed Attorney General jointly with Marco Querini, whose son, Niccolo, had married Giovanni's daughter. All had then seemed well in Soranzo's world.

But a year later, the Querinis became embroiled in a conspiracy to overthrow Doge Pietro Gradenigo. The plot failed – not without some conniving on my part – and Niccolo Querini and his wife were banished to Sifnos, an island belonging to the Soranzos. Now, two years on, Giovanni Soranzo had been named Doge himself, and his daughter's life was about to change. I was on Sifnos, that aforementioned chunk of rock in the Aegean, to talk to Speranza about her return to Venice, and the terms on which it would be possible. But first I had to deal with her drunken husband.

Galuppi led me past a noisy boat-builders' yard and down a narrow cobbled lane to a small doorway pretentiously carved in stone with a coat of arms on the lintel. I didn't recognise the armorial bearing, but I certainly did the body inside. I had met Niccolo Querini when I had toyed with joining the plotters in the 1310 conspiracy. Then, he had been a hothead with a powerful chest and strong arms. The man slumped over the low table in the anonymous tavern had gone to seed. He had put on a lot of fat round his waist, and his once well-groomed hair was greasy and long. Clearly, Niccolo had not survived his exile well. I grabbed his unwashed locks and lifted his head off the table. He didn't protest at the mistreatment, merely dragging one bleary eye open to see who it was who was molesting him. The solitary eye was bloodshot, but gave signs of recognition. He propped his heavy head on his palm, which allowed me to let go of his hair. Thankfully, I wiped my greasy palm on the shoulder of his tunic. When he spoke, his speech was slurred and jumbled.

'Zulz ... Zuliani. Good to see you, man. How's things?'

I peered angrily into his one functioning eye.

'They could be better, Querini. I have just come through a big storm that threatened to wreck my galley off the Peloponnese. Then we were attacked by pirates who could have been under the command of the Duke of Milan, for all I know. And when I arrive at Kamares, desirous of a soft bed and a roof over my head, I find my host has drunk himself silly in a cheap tavern.'

My last words were shouted right in Querini's face. He flinched and held his head in both hands, no doubt to try to control the headache that raged within.

'It's not my fault, Zuliani. It's hers.'

'By 'hers' I suppose you mean your wife, the daughter of the Doge. Why is it her fault?'

Prising both eyes open, he gazed at me miserably.

'She's forsaken me for a monk. And now she's gone and shut herself in a nunnery.'

His head fell to the table with a loud clunk, and I could see

I would get no more sense out of him. I left Querini to bemoan his fate and asked Galuppi to make arrangements to transfer our baggage across the island to the Querini mansion in the south. He asked about a courtesy visit to the capital, Kastro, but I waved his suggestion aside. The people I needed to see were ensconced in the south and the capital of this little island was in the east. I use the word 'capital' advisedly. It doesn't take much to be the biggest place on an island in the back of beyond. No, the Tou Kontou peninsula was where the Querinis were settled, and that is where I would move my household during my stay on Sifnos. Galuppi hurried off to arrange the required transport.

As I walked back to the quay to meet up with Katie, I pondered on Querini's words. I was not surprised to find the Doge's daughter lodged in a religious house. She was supposed to have been living in the monastery of St John the Theologian at Mongou as the terms of her exile. That she would actually be living with her husband, however, was taken as read, and the Querini mansion was close by the monastery. So I assumed she had taken herself off to Mongou in anticipation of my arrival, just for form's sake. But what had Querini meant about her leaving him for a monk? I would have to do some digging to discover what had been going on here on Sifnos.

My task had all started with a letter. As soon as Giovanni Soranzo had become Doge, the letter had arrived from his daughter, begging to be allowed back to Venice. Soranzo was a canny enough bird to know that as Doge he had to act cautiously, and not show preference to family. Especially family who had plotted against the previous Doge. What he had done had been a surprise to me as much as to others around him.

I had been dining with Cat in Ca' Dolfin, her family home, where I had been living since my own house had burned down. Both of us had finished the meal, and we were talking finance. It was my favourite subject.

'I have put what money I have in the Florentine Bank of Peruzzi. They are financing the Venetian bullion trade, which is huge. Twice a year a bullion fleet of twenty to thirty ships, under heavy naval convoy, sail from Venice to the eastern Mediterranean coast or to Egypt, bearing primarily silver. And they sail back to Venice bearing mainly gold.'

'What profit is there in that?'

I sighed. Cat had the old aristocracy's lack of understanding of how trading worked.

'Because it is a trade between regions that value gold and silver differently. Some merchants are making annual rates of profit of up to forty per cent on very large, short-term investments.'

Cat yawned and I knew to stop my monologue. Then I saw by the growing look in her eyes that she was thinking pretty much the same as me. It was still only a month or two since we had found each other again, and the forces of nature worked strongly in both of us. As soon as we could slip Katie's attention, we would be dashing off to bed together. Old man I may be, but my lust was aroused by the still lithe and sensuous body of Caterina Dolfin. But we were destined never to get there. A scratching at the water door of Ca' Dolfin had heralded the arrival of a mysterious emissary clad in a hooded cloak. It had turned out to be Bertuccio Galuppi with a strange commission. The Doge wanted to find out discreetly about his daughter's situation, and have his man recommend what to do about fetching her back to Venice. It seemed I was the man for the job, due, according to Galuppi, to my legendary negotiating skills and discretion. I think he meant I was a slippery and underhand customer, who could be relied on to sneak in and out of Sifnos without anyone knowing. After Galuppi had delivered his message, Cat and I spoke about whether I should take the job. She was adamant I should.

'You can't refuse. It's the Doge who is asking. That means it is a command.'

I snorted. 'That's what you members of the *case vecchie* think. We mere merchant classes need a good deal to be on offer.'

I often teased Cat about her family being of the old aristocracy, which excluded such as the Zulianis from power. It was one of the reasons I had left Venice. Her father had deemed me too common for his snooty daughter. Now I had my feet under her table, but it had taken me forty years, the death of her father, and a trip round the world to get there. Our argument would have raged on, but for the intervention of the one thing that united us both. It was Katie, who had been listening to our row, who finally resolved it.

'Of course you must go, Grandpa. Then you will have the Doge in your pocket, and eternally grateful to you.'

I pointed at my granddaughter in triumph.

'See. She is more of a Zuliani than a Valier or a Dolfin. She gets straight to the nub of the matter in the most businesslike way.' I hit the table with my fist, causing my wine goblet to spill over. 'I will go.'

Katie smiled, righting my goblet and wiping the spilled wine with her hand. She licked her fingers.

'Good. And in return for my sound advice, you will take me with you.'

*

Eventually, after a bone-shaking ride over the hills of Sifnos, Katie, Galuppi and I managed to settle ourselves in Querini's estate in Moussia. I had to admit the views were spectacular. Venice hunkers down low at sea level, whereas this mansion was perched high on a hill overlooking the bright blue sea. From the balcony of the main room, I could see a curious white chapel stuck out on the peninsula, and beyond it nothing but water. It was a good place to keep a lookout for marauding pirates and had escape routes by the beaches to the west and the east. I reckoned I had appropriated Querini's own room, but I was not concerned about that. The fool could stay in the stables, for all I cared. If he ever got back from the other end of the island after sleeping off his binge. As for me, it was time to tie one on before embarking on my official business, and I had plenty of Querini's best wine over dinner.

I awoke the next morning with a hangover, but knew it was nothing that a brisk walk in the fresh air wouldn't cure. Time to acquaint myself with Speranza Soranzo's hideaway. Standing on the balcony, I could feel that the morning was warm but the onshore wind was cool. So I pulled a sleeveless velvet robe over my tunic and leggings, and went to see to it that Katie would be entertained while I met the Doge's daughter. Walking through the archway into the inner courtyard of the Querini mansion, I saw the back of a slim pageboy I had not noticed amongst the servants during last evening's meal. I called out to him, intending to get him to fetch Katie. When the boy turned round, I saw it was Katie herself dressed in the way I had first seen her when she was stalking me in Venice.

'What the hell are you doing in that garb?' I exploded.

She grinned and spun around, showing me the full effect of the white tunic, red tabard, and grey leggings she wore.

'Don't you think I would pass as a pageboy? I fooled you at first, didn't I?'

She had tucked her radiant hair under a red sugar-loaf hat, and I had to admit she was a passable youth. Albeit one that someone with a taste for downy-faced boys might prefer.

'But why do you want to pass as a boy?'

She pouted in a way that was all female. 'I knew Galuppi wouldn't let me come with you on your investigations dressed as myself. He is so stuffy and old-fashioned, and thinks a woman should sit at home and spin and embroider.' She grabbed my arm and pulled me to her. 'But you will arouse no alarm being accompanied by your page, will you?'

I knew that pleading tone, and was aware I could not stop her once her mind was made up. I sighed deeply.

'Very well. But don't let Galuppi see you. And keep your mouth shut when I am with Querini or his wife. Pages are seldom seen and never ever heard.'

Katie grinned and put a finger to her lips, sealing her vow of silence. I wondered how long it would last.

'Besides, I am not investigating anything, but merely ascertaining if the Doge's daughter is suitably chastened by her banishment, and will not stir up feeling on her return.'

Katie shook her head vigorously, almost releasing her long locks. 'Fat chance of that happening. Speranza was always too full of her own importance. Now she is the Doge's daughter, she will lord it over everyone.'

She started to walk ahead of me, but I grabbed her arm and held her back.

'You mean that you knew her before her exile? Then she will recognise you, and your little subterfuge will be in vain.'

Katie blew out her cheeks in exasperation. 'Of course she

won't, Grandpa. I was only twelve when she last saw me. I've grown since then.'

I shrugged in defeat, not wishing to note that she had also grown tits, which were now well concealed, thank God, or the disguise would have been useless. I did have one command for her, though.

'You will have to walk behind me and not at my side or ahead of me. From now on, you are not my granddaughter, but my servant.'

Katie bowed deeply, put on a solemn face and hung back as I crossed the courtyard. Which was just as well as it meant she didn't see the big grin on my face caused by her feisty impudence. She was without a doubt a Zuliani.

The land was scrubby and sere between the mansion and the monastery, our feet raising dust that clung to our clothes. It was a far cry from Venice, where dampness and the sea were on every hand. Soon we could see the thick walls of the monastery, which was set on a small rise in the land. Over the doorway hung a bell set in an arch with a thick rope hanging from it, which stirred lazily in the hot wind that blew across the dried-out land. The door to the monastery lay open, its timbers bleached and cracked in the sun. I stepped through the archway and into an open yard. There was no one around, though I got the impression that a black-clad figure had just disappeared through one of several doors to my right. Straight ahead of me, though, stood the church and another open door. On reaching it, and looking into the gloomy interior, I felt rather than saw its enticing coolness. Katie came up close behind me and whispered in my ear.

'Did you see that priest run off when we arrived? Don't you think it's odd that no one has come to ask who we are? Let's just grab the church silver and run.'

I glared at her, and stepped into the cool interior, which was only sustained by the narrowness of the windows. The interior of the church was dark and sombre. Beyond the sanctuary screen, a solitary candle burned close to the altar, and I could just make out a kneeling figure in the circle of yellowish light it cast. From the slightness of the figure I guessed it was a woman. No doubt this was the Doge's daughter. I held up my hand to indicate to Katie that she should stay put, and started to make my way down the central aisle. I had got only half-way when someone I had not noticed loomed out of the darkness. He stood in my way. It was a man in a drab brown robe with its hood pulled up, half masking his face. He held his hand palm outwards to stop my progress.

'You may go no closer. Who are you?'

His words were spoken in a hoarse whisper, as though he were trying not to disturb the prayers of the woman he protected. I had no such compunction, and made my voice boom out echoing around the church.

'I am Messer Niccolo Zuliani, come to speak privately with the Doge's daughter, Speranza Soranzo. Who might you be? Take off your hood and show yourself.'

I could see beyond the monk's shoulder that the kneeling figure, hearing my voice, had turned to look at me. Apprehension was written on the pale face that glowed in the light of the candle. My adversary raised his hand and deftly flicked back the hood of his monkish robe, revealing a tonsured head and a grave, angular face. Though the rest of his features seemed chiselled and lined, and his nose slightly bent, his lips were as full and red as a woman's. He licked them with the tip of his tongue, betraying a new nervousness.

'I am Brother Hugh, Mistress Soranzo's spiritual guide.'

So this was the monk who had stolen Speranza from her

husband. He was not the most manly of rivals for Querini, so I could see why Niccolo had turned to his cups in despair. Perhaps it was his religious message that was irresistible. I was to find out the truth of that soon enough. The woman in white had risen from her knees by now, and approached my little confrontation with the charismatic monk. She was more composed now, and calmed him down with a few gentle words.

'It's no problem, Brother Hugh, I have been expecting Messer Zuliani.'

She stepped past the monk and gave me a bow that was no more than a curt nod of the head. I suppose I shouldn't have expected any more. I was a common trader, and she the daughter of the Doge of La Serenissima and a member of the same élite ruling gang in which my own Cat Dolfin had her origins. I gave her my best cold stare that had many a business opponent quivering in his boots, but she merely ignored it and ploughed on.

'I am sorry that I was not at my husband's house to greet you. We thought the storms at sea would have delayed you.'

I saw from her tone that she wasn't sorry, and that the 'we' she referred to was not herself and her husband, but herself and her monkish mentor. She had slightly inclined her head to indicate him as she spoke. I tipped my own head to acknowledge her comments, and assured her that our stout Venetian galley had weathered the storms easily.

'We even outran the pirates that seem to infest this region. Now, Domina Soranzo, I need to arrange a time when you and I can speak. In private.'

I made it clear what that meant for the monk, and blushing, he retreated from our presence and walked through the sanctuary arch to where Speranza Soranzo had been praying. I noticed that he picked up a small gilded box from the altar before he snuffed out the candle and plunged the sanctuary into darkness. When he turned the box had disappeared somewhere in his robes. Querini's wife drew my attention away from his activity by taking my arm and walking me away.

'I regret I cannot see you in the monastery as I have a private cell not suitable for visitors.'

By her tone of voice I assumed she meant not for male visitors. She was clearly either taking her pretence of following the terms of her exile to an extreme, or she truly had shut herself off from her husband. I guessed the monk was the key to what she was up to, and mentally noted I would have to find out more about him.

'Then we should talk at your husband's house. I take it that propriety will not be offended if you met me there. After all, my granddaughter will be there too.'

I looked over my shoulder at Katie who, in her pageboy disguise, had been skulking in the shadows all this time. 'Won't she . . . Sebastiano?'

Katie glared at me in giving her such a stupid name, and with as gruff a voice as she could muster replied, 'Indeed, master.'

Katie need not have been concerned at me drawing her to Soranzo's attention. The Doge's daughter hardly deigned to look at the page who attended me. But I did notice that the monk gave 'him' a sharp look. Perhaps he was a more dangerous adversary than I had at first suspected. From his mangling of Italian I guessed he was an Englishman, so maybe I could speak to him in his own language. I had learned some of the rough tongue from my own mother, and could speak it passably. It would pay to know where he stood in the Soranzo household before I questioned Speranza more closely.

After she had agreed to meet me at her husband's mansion

the next morning, I left the monastery with 'Sebastiano' trailing sulkily after me. It didn't take long for Katie to emerge
from her mood, though. She grabbed a long, dry twig and
started slashing at the trailing brown grass on our return path.
Gradually she speeded up and came up to my shoulder. She
was bursting to tell me something, but was going to make me
repent for treating her badly first.

'Sebastiano? Where did that stupid name come from?'

I smiled evilly. 'The way you were behaving, I just thought
you resembled a martyr.'

'Oh, very amusing, *Grandfather.*'

To be deliberately reminded of my advanced years hurt,
and I winced at the jibe.

'Very well. You are obviously bursting to tell me something you know. So I apologise for the slur on your
manhood . . .' She swished at my legs playfully with the twig.
'. . . and am ready to listen with ears wide open.'

Katie pouted in that endearing way of hers, making a play
of deciding whether or not to tell me what she knew. But it
was obvious that she would without any further encouragement, and she managed a pause of a few moments.

'I have seen the monk before.'

'Brother Hugh? Where?'

'Why, in Venice, of course. Before you came back from
your travels. He was a sought-after guest in the houses of
Granny Cat's friends. The more vacuous ones.'

Katie had some choice words at her disposal, revealing
her fine education at the expense of the Valier family, whose
name she bore. 'Vacuous' was one I would remember when
it came to the *case vecchie* of La Serenissima. I laughed.

'And what was he peddling? Indulgences to save them
from Purgatory?

Katie grinned in a way that suggested she had a salacious secret to reveal. 'No. Something far more valuable than that.'

'Oh, what?'

'Virginity.'

Once we had returned to the Querini mansion, and I had persuaded Katie to dress like a proper girl once again, she told me the story. We first ate a quiet meal with Galuppi, and I sank a few goblets of Querini's good red wine. Eventually, the fussy secretary saw that his presence was not wanted, and he bowed and left. Relieved by his disappearance, Katie threw her legs over the arm of the chair she had been sitting demurely in, and clasped her hands behind her head.

'Lord! I thought he'd never go, Grandpa Nick.'

'Is that why you were sighing heavily all the time? Bertuccio Galuppi is a good man, you know, and doesn't deserve to be on the end of your bad manners.'

She waved one hand in the air. 'I'll apologise to him tomorrow. Now, let me tell you the story of Brother Hugh.'

It seems that the monk had turned up in Venice three years ago in search of a relic. He had come all the way from a place called Carmarthen somewhere in the badlands beyond the edge of England. He was peddling a story about a finger bone belonging to a saint that a Venetian merchant had long ago purchased.

'My great-uncle Marco!' I exclaimed. 'It must have been him. He went all over the place collecting relics to resell at a profit.'

Katie hushed me, and kicked her legs in anger.

'Let me finish. This Brother Hugh was nothing much of an attraction at first, according to Granny Cat.' She looked across the table at me. 'You can see he's not much to look at, and his message was all about a saint no one had heard of. But then he somehow laid his hands on the relic, and it all changed.'

At a gathering of bored matrons of noble lineage to which Hugh had been invited, more out of habit than expectation of something exciting, a stir had been created. The monk had produced a small gilded box, and announced he had the relic of St Beornwyn.

'Who?'

Katie sat up and stamped her foot. 'You're always interrupting, Grandpa.'

'Well, what sort of outlandish name is that? Be-orn-wyn.'

'It's English ... or Welsh ... or something. Anyway, I don't suppose she's a proper saint like Mark or Agnes, just one of those false Celtic ones.'

I was getting impatient, and tried to hurry Katie along. Like all Zulianis, she did like to tell a tale. I had been accused of telling a million lies when I came back from Xanadu.

'So where does virginity come into it? On the way back from the monastery, you said he was peddling virginity.'

She grinned broadly. 'Yes. That was what turned Brother Hugh into a sensation. Imagine what little a gathering of bored Venetian wives, weighed down with the riches of generations, didn't have and couldn't buy. Brother Hugh told them that, if they venerated St Beornwyn, and lived as she did, they would somehow regain their virginity.'

I fairly bellowed with laughter, so much so that one of the servants came running to see what was wrong. After I had shooed him away, and wiped the tears from my eyes with the end of my expensively fur-trimmed robe, I asked Katie to run that by me again. She looked at me as if I was some monkey that a crusader had just brought back from Afric lands. And not a very bright or well-trained one at that.

'Let me explain, Grandfather.'

That name again. I kept my face straight and nodded.

'This St Beornwyn was apparently a noble Englishwoman who was betrothed to a local lord. But she was renowned for her nightly vigils at the local church, where she prayed for the salvation of her father's land from invading pagans. And for her own perpetual virginity.'

Katie glanced at me to see if I was going to break out into laughter again. But I managed to look serious. She went on.

'While she was living she was called a saint, offering up her virginity and her regular vigils for the good of others. Then one night the invaders came and struck her head from her body. They flayed the skin from her body and draped it on the altar, but the Virgin Mary sent blue butterflies to cover her nakedness. So you see she was an exemplar of the virtue of virginity.'

I grunted. 'It didn't save her life, though, did it?'

'Oh, Grandpa Nick, you have no soul.'

I summed up. 'So St Beornwyn is a saintly virgin, and Brother Hugh was holding her up to the *case vecchie* as a figure to emulate. What did the husbands of all these newly created virgins think of this?'

'Granny Cat said they were probably mostly glad to concentrate on their mistresses, and not to have the attentions of their wives to cope with. It was lucrative for Hugh for a while, as the women would offer gifts to St Beornwyn.'

My ears perked up when I heard that. I loved a good scam.

'Ah, so he got rich with his little cult.'

'For a while, until the women got bored. Then Hugh

decided to concentrate on one of his followers who had been most devoted to the saint.'

'Let me guess. Speranza Soranzo.'

'Exactly.'

'He could see by then that her father was a hero of the Republic, and well on his way to becoming Doge. If he snared Speranza, then he would revive his fortunes. Unfortunately, her husband went and got himself involved in a little conspiracy, and Hugh's acolyte was banished to a Greek island.'

I waved my arms to encompass the isle of Sifnos, where we were lodged. 'This very enchanted isle.'

Katie nodded.

'To give him his due, Hugh followed her into exile. And maybe his gamble will now pay off. If you can persuade the Doge to allow her and her husband back to Venice, Hugh's fortune will be made again.'

I scowled at my granddaughter. 'It's my job to decide if his daughter won't be an embarrassment to Giovanni Soranzo, not to act as Speranza's agent and persuade him to allow her back.' I knew what I had to do. 'I need to know more about Brother Hugh and his virgin saint. Especially if he is to come back with Speranza and her husband. And where is Querini, anyway?'

It was getting dark outside, and Querini still had not put in an appearance. Maybe he was still sleeping off his binge at the harbour. But I thought he was less of a man for getting in such a state, and for avoiding me into the bargain. Was he afraid of coming back to Venice, where he had attempted to oust the former Doge? Or was he embarrassed by his wife tossing him out of the marriage bed for a monk and a cult of virginity? I suddenly realised that Katie had said something and I had missed it.

'What was that, girl? Your grandpa is getting deaf in his old age.'

She laughed. 'I don't think so. You're as sharp as that knife you carry at your waist.'

I touched my favourite dagger instinctively, and Katie carried on.

'I said let me approach Brother Hugh as a possible convert to St Beornwyn. I can then find out more about him, and about Speranza.'

I scrubbed at my beard, worried about what my granddaughter might get herself into. However, it was a sound proposition.

'I suppose it's not a bad idea. After all, you are young and virginal.'

I thought I saw a blush emerge on her throat, just for a moment. She coughed delicately.

'It's certainly true I'm young enough to remember what virginity is like.'

I guessed she could see the storm brewing in my look, because she quickly held up her hand.

'Don't even ask, Grandpa. That's a girl's secret, and not even her future husband has a right to know the truth.'

I was about to say it surely was his right to know if his bride was a virgin or not, but I stopped myself. How times must have changed since I left Venice for the distant lands of Kublai Khan. And I had to remind myself that I had left behind in Cathay a black-haired, dark-skinned beauty, who had been part of a virgin tribute to Kublai before I relieved her of her qualification to belong the group. I sighed at my recollection of dear Gurbesu, but then put her to the back of my mind.

'It's a good idea, and you should act on it – the sooner

the better, in fact. So make a start tomorrow. By then perhaps Niccolo Querini will be available for me to question
also.'

It turned out that that was wishful thinking on my part.

Katie arose bright and early, eager to carry out her task of
insinuating herself into Brother Hugh's exclusive circle. So
she wasn't present when the furore began. I was eating a
slow and luxurious breakfast, mulling over what I might ask
Speranza Soranzo, when Galuppi burst into my room. He
was so agitated he stumbled over his words, finally manag-
ing to get one sentence out.

'He really is dead this time.'

I calmed him down a little and asked him to repeat what
he had said, though I already suspected what he meant.

'Who is really dead?'

'Niccolo Querini. His manservant was giving his hunting
dogs some exercise this morning close to the shore below
here. When they ran off, he followed them and found
Querini lying on the strand just above the tideline. He came
back for assistance, and alerted me to the situation. They've
all gone off to bring the body back.'

I cursed. 'Damn them. I would have liked to have seen
the body in situ.'

Galuppi looked puzzled. 'Whatever for? His man said he
must have fallen from the cliff. He was drunk and paid the
penalty for incaution.'

I wished life – or more precisely, death – was that simple.
Not for the first time since returning to the West, I longed
for the assistance of Masudi al-Din. I had met him in the
heart of Kublai's great Mongol empire at a crucial moment
in my investigation of a murder. He was an Arab from Yazd,

with a cornucopia of knowledge about the human body. He could examine a body, and tell you all sorts of marvels about it. How the man had died – either by accident or design. What weapon had been used – poison or blade. He could even say how quickly the victim had died, and whether in pain or not. And when he opened a body with his sharp knife, it was like he was opening a book. He had always taught me never to jump to conclusions, so I needed to hurry if I was to see Querini's body where it had fallen. I threw a tunic over my shirt, and dashed from the room as fast as my old legs could carry me. Galuppi roused himself enough to chase after. I ran down the path he indicated that led to the beach below the mansion. It was one of the sea escape routes in case the mansion was ever attacked from the landward side. I heard the loud barking of the hunting dogs before I even saw the gaggle of servants around Querini. They were bent over the body, in the process of lifting it. Despite my ragged breathing from the unusual exertion, I mustered a loud cry.

'Leave him where he is.'

Fearfully, the servants looked up at the vision of a red-haired demon descending on them down the cliff path. In China I had earned the nickname of Zhong-Kui, a demon who sets wrongs right. That is how I must have seemed at that moment, even though my hair was no longer quite as flame red as once it had been. I strode over the sand, and the group of men around the body stopped what they were doing, and parted for me. Niccolo Querini lay face up, his arms spread wide and his dull, lifeless eyes staring into the heavens. There was no point in looking at the ground around him for any signs because the sand had been churned up by the restless feet of the servants and the dogs. Even now, the two large hounds were snuffling round their dead master, licking his face.

'Get these dogs out of here.'

I snarled the command at the man who I knew was Querini's servant, Antonio. It was he who must have been the one who discovered the body. He hung his head, and muttered an apology, grabbing the dogs by the scruff of their necks, and dragging them away. I looked up at the cliff above where the body lay and at the back slope at its foot where it was supposed to have landed. Mentally noting what I saw, I indicated to the servants that they could now carry out their mournful task. I would examine Querini's body in detail in the comfort of the mansion, not here on the strand, where the sun was already beating down on the back of my neck. Besides, I needed a good goblet of wine to steel myself for the task ahead. I hated the sight of blood.

I hurried up the slope, anxious to precede the body back to the mansion. Speranza Soranzo would be waiting for me, and I didn't want her to see her husband before I had spoken to her. Bertuccio Galuppi bustled along breathlessly at my side.

'There is no question, is there, that it was a terrible accident? I am sure that is how Doge Soranzo would wish it to be.'

I stopped in my tracks, and stared at Galuppi.

'Is that why you are here? To ensure I do the Doge's bidding as you see it?'

For a moment the secretary's façade slipped, and a sneering look transformed his face.

'You don't think the Doge sent you here because of your diplomacy skills, do you, Zuliani? You're here to provide the common touch, and be your usual slippery self when it comes to winkling out secrets. But now that the main impediment to the Lady Soranzo's return is conveniently dead, I see no further need for your services.'

I smiled politely, and carried on back to the mansion. He ran to catch me up, and grabbed my arm.

'Did you hear me, Zuliani? You are no longer needed.'

I shook his hand off my arm disdainfully.

'Oh, really? And you will tell that to the Doge, will you, when you return with the lady and her monkish lover in tow?'

I loved the way Galuppi's face went puce on such occasions. Feed him something he didn't know and put him in a sticky position, and he fairly exploded. Of course I had no proof that anything irregular was going on between Speranza and Brother Hugh – especially as he was apparently extolling the virtues of virginity. But it did no harm to overstate the case with Galuppi – he was bound to back off. And so he did, but with ill grace.

'I am sure you are maligning the lady most foully, but have your way. I will only be the happier when you fall over your own clumsy feet. Then I shall tell the Doge what you said about his daughter with the greatest of pleasure.'

He stormed off in the opposite direction, which was quite amusing because it meant he was walking away from the mansion, and would get tangled up with the impromptu funeral cortège. Let him think what he did about me in his snooty supercilious way. I was the one who had the confidential talk with Doge Soranzo, Hero of the Aegean, Head of the Navy, and Governor of the Gulf, Ambassador to Sicily and Egypt. He told me he had worries about the behaviour of his daughter, not about that of Niccolo Querini. He didn't tell me exactly what concerned him, only that I had to find out for myself.

'I don't want to prejudice your opinion of her, Zuliani. But there is a serpent in her bosom, and I want you to tell me if she is too dangerous to bring back to Venice.'

His voice still rang in my ears. I had thought he meant his son-in-law, but now I had some inkling of what form the serpent had truly taken. I would let Galuppi do his job as he saw it, but I wouldn't allow him to impede me in doing mine. As I approached the mansion, I could see a figure in a white dress standing on one of the balconies. Katie never wore white, and besides, she would still be with Brother Hugh. So I guessed it was Speranza Soranzo spying out the return of her husband, like a sailor's wife who had been told some bad news. Then I suppose she saw me because she slipped back through the window.

When I entered the great chamber of the Querini mansion, she was once again on her knees in the little chapel alcove at the far end. It was as if she were deliberately reminding me of our first encounter at the monastery. And of her piety, though I wondered if she should be wearing black. Maybe she imagined herself royalty, now her father was Doge. Many queens wore white mourning garb, just as she was. Whatever her plan was, the sombre effect was spoiled by the sight of a large red boil on the back of her neck. I could see it because of her bowed head.

'Domina Soranzo, I imagine someone has already given you the bad news. You have my condolences.'

She sighed dramatically, and held out her arm, asking for my assistance in raising her to her feet. It was all a little ponderous and imperious, and an attempt to put me in my place, but it would have been churlish to refuse the assistance. I took her weight and she rose up. Our proximity allowed me to get a closer look at her face than she might have wished.

For a woman of only thirty or so, she looked quite careworn, and she clearly had plucked her eyebrows out of existence. Her face was pale without evidence of those foul lead-based whiteners some women used. Though I have heard that some women swallow arsenic to make themselves pale. Masudi al-Din told me this could result in headaches, confusion and hair loss, if not death. So perhaps Speranza Soranzo followed this cosmetic regime. She certainly sounded a little confused when she replied to my half-question about receiving news of Querini's death.

'Yes. Antonio told me, when he came back with the dogs. They will be so upset, you know. They loved Niccolo.'

It took me a moment to realise she was talking about the dogs. And it was probably true they loved Querini more than she did, I thought. She gave no sign of sadness at her husband's passing, or even made an enquiry as to the cause of his death. Instead she rambled on about the dogs and Querini's manservant.

'He told me that when he approached the body, a cloud of blue butterflies rose up around Niccolo. It was a sign, of course.'

Of what, she clearly wasn't going to tell me, though it rang a bell with me. Something Katie had said, but I wasn't able to recall it. And before I could try, she cast a nervous glance towards the door of the great chamber. There had been the sound of shuffling feet, and subdued voices. It was as if she were afraid her husband might not be dead after all, and would come striding in from the strand. Instead, his lifeless body was unceremoniously borne in like someone who had passed out after a night of heavy drinking. One servant clasped him by the armpits, and another by his ankles. His head was turned at an acute angle on the leading servant's arm. They paused upon seeing the mistress, but she waved a hand, and they carried on with their task of laying the body in the chapel. Once he had been arranged on the stone altar, she drifted over to the body, and peered closely at it as if reminding herself of what her husband looked like. Her hand went nervously to the back of her neck, where I knew the suppurating boil would be giving her pain. Then her hands closed in prayer, and I knew it was no use questioning her today. Nor would I get to examine the body more closely for a while. I gritted my teeth, and walked out of the great chamber, leaving her to her own thoughts.

'Niccolo Querini is dead?'

Katie shook her head as she asked her question of me. I had been waiting for her in the shade of the ancient olive tree, which was set in the centre of the courtyard of the Querini mansion. I sat for a long time before her smiling face appeared in the archway. She had skipped over to me, no doubt full of what she had learned from Brother Hugh. But I had to tell her my news first, before she learned of it from somewhere else. I thought it would have upset her, but I didn't really know my granddaughter that well yet. Her eyes opened wide, and a look of excitement pervaded her beautiful face.

'Was he murdered?'

Trust my Katie to get straight to the point. I shrugged and waggled my head in a noncommittal way.

'I can't say yet. The grieving widow is with the body.' I indicated the doorway to the great chamber and chapel. 'Perhaps when she has completed her obsequies, she will allow me to examine him. But from what I saw on the beach, there is no way that he fell from the cliff.'

Katie squeezed my hand. 'Tell me what you saw that made you come to that conclusion, Grandpa Nick.'

We had both already worked on the case of one murder together, and I knew how she loved the mental exercise involved. And her enthusiasm stoked the fires of my own.

'The body was at the foot of the cliff, from where it was presumed he had fallen.'

Katie quickly interrupted me. 'Who presumed this?'

'Why, Galuppi, of course. He pretty much told me that was the conclusion that the Doge would want me to come to.'

'Ohhh, Galuppi.' My granddaughter waved her hand, dismissing Galuppi's opinion.

I went on with the explanation for my suspicions.

'The cliff edge is crumbly at that point where the loose soil overrides the rock. So it's true, a fall was possible. But there was no sign of disturbance above, and no evidence of loose soil on the sandy beach. No, Querini didn't fall from the cliff, or even get pushed. Of course, he could have died naturally of a failure of his organs. He was a heavy drinker. But I don't believe that was the case either. I will know more when I can examine the body.'

'Yes, we can examine it together.'

I knew that was as close Katie would get to a request to be present when I looked at Querini's body. And to be honest, I didn't mind the thought of having her as a companion. As I said, blood always turns my stomach. I had already allowed her to see a much more gruesome body when we explored my burned-out house in Venice for any remains. We had come across the body of a man that was no more than a blackened cinder. Katie had a strong stomach and a good eye for detail too. I nodded my agreement.

'Now tell me what you learned from Brother Hugh.'

She laughed. 'He showed me his most precious possession.'

I looked suitably concerned for her modesty, just as she
had intended with her ambiguous comment. But it turned
out that what she referred to was the relic of St Beornwyn.
The finger that Great-uncle Marco had originally brought to
Venice. Katie was convinced that the monk truly did revere
the saint and what she stood for. He came from a small community based in a place called Carmarthen on the edge of
the English king's territories. He had been offended when
Katie had called him English, and insisted he was Welsh. I
had heard of these hill-dwelling people on the fringes of
King Edward's lands. Troublesome and independent-
minded, they had taxed the patience of the older King
Edward, now his son was not doing any better apparently.
Perhaps that was why he was borrowing so much money
from the Bardi and Peruzzi banks, where I had my own
funds invested. If Hugh was Welsh he would be an opin-
ionated fellow, no doubt.

'I told him I had heard of St Beornwyn and the tale of her
saintly devotion to keeping her virginity. He blushed a little,
but explained more of the saint's history to me.'

It appeared that Beornwyn had been betrothed to a local
lord in the north called Aethelbald, or some such barbaric
name. Beornwyn, however, though being the daughter of
another lord and therefore always likely to be married off
for dynastic purposes, wished to dedicate her life to Christ.
There was a belief that as long as she remained a virgin, the
pagan invaders would not devastate her father's lands.
Refusing Aethelbald, she maintained a nightly vigil at a
remote chapel. Hearing this, I snorted in derision.

'It sounds like she had a younger lover and her vigils covered some sort of assignation with him. She didn't want to give him up for some old baron.'

Katie pouted. 'Grandpa, you are so coarse. The story is beautiful. Anyway, finally the invaders did come, and they murdered Beornwyn when she refused to give up her vigil. They even flayed the skin from her body and hung it on the chapel altar. And that is why she is the saint of virgins, and people with skin diseases.'

'Hmm. And the relic?'

'When he had finished his story, Brother Hugh produced this small gilded box from his sleeve. He opened it and inside, laid on red velvet, were the bones of St Beornwyn's finger held together with gold wire.'

I pulled a face.

'I have always thought there was something gruesome about holy bones. I mean, how is a saint to be clothed in flesh again at the Resurrection, if his body is scattered all over the Christian world?'

Katie's laughter was like a tinkling silver bell. Unfortunately, at that very moment, Speranza Soranzo emerged from the great hall into the sunlight. Maybe it was our levity that caused her to screw up her face, or maybe it was the brightness of the sun. Whatever it was, she stormed past us and out the archway. And there went my chance of questioning her about Querini and the cult of virginity. I wearily pushed myself to my feet, my knees protesting at the effort. Katie almost put out a hand to assist me, but seeing my glare, stopped herself. I would be fooling myself if I thought that I still had the physique to give her a run for her money. She would soon outstrip me. However, my mind had not dulled yet, and it occurred to me that she could be my eyes and ears with Domina Speranza Soranzo. But I would leave that until later.

'Come. Let's take a look at Niccolo Querini before anyone prepares him for his funeral. They could wash away a lot of evidence.'

The interior of the great chamber was suitably sombre with no candles lit. The small slit windows let in little light as well as keeping the hall cool in high summer. Someone, presumably Speranza herself, had lighted a solitary candle inside the chapel, which was located at Querini's head. I was glad of it, for it would give me some light for the next task. As we got closer to the body, I saw that she had also placed her husband's hands in a prayerful pose on his chest. I moved them apart, examining the hands closely.

'What are you looking for?'

Katie's question was a good one. I wanted to see if there had been a struggle.

'A man may have traces of blood on his hands, if he was in the act of defending himself when he died. I see nothing here, though.'

I placed his hands at his side, and proceeded to pull up his eyelids, peering into his eyes. Katie was full of curiosity.

'I thought it was nonsense to imagine that the image of the murderer was left fixed on the victim's eyes. Is it then true?'

I smiled at her misunderstanding of my actions.

'You are right to think it ridiculous. And in response to your enquiry, I was looking to see if the eyeballs were spotted with blood in any way. Masudi al-Din told me that if a person were strangled or smothered, blood vessels in the eyes would be burst. Again nothing.'

I gazed at the torso of Querini, stroking my hands over his chest.

'Ah, here is something odd.'

'What?'

Katie leaned forward eagerly. I smoothed out the outer jacket, which was laced up the front over his undershirt, and pulled the opening a little wider. There was a patch of blood on the dark red shirt that had not been noticeable before. And I could see a small hole in the shirt, which I could just poke my finger in. Not caring about the evidence I was now destroying – for who but I cared about it? – I ripped open the hole and revealed a similar hole in Querini's chest. Swallowing the bitter taste of vomit rising in my throat, I poked my finger in the hole. It ran deep, probably as far as his heart. The wound made a sucking noise as I withdrew my finger. Katie was fascinated, quite unmoved by the presence of blood and violent death.

'Is this how he was killed? Stabbed to death? Such a small wound and so little blood.'

'I have seen this before, though. A thrust to the heart with a slim bassillard can kill as effectively as chopping a man to pieces with a sword. And the blood can stay inside the body because the puncture in the skin is so small. You heard how it sucked closed after I pulled my finger out.'

Katie stared at me, her eyes big with an excitement that I suddenly regretted exposing her to. She whispered the word that was in my head.

'Murder for certain, then.'

I nodded, and added the inevitable question.

'But who did it?'

The following morning I had my first intimation of what might have happened. Katie had already left for Mongou monastery in the hope of speaking again to both Brother

Hugh and Domina Speranza. We had spoken briefly about what information she should gather. Ostensibly, her task was to discover more about the cult of St Beornwyn, and Speranza's adherence to it. But if in the process she learned more about Querini and his life on Sifnos, then that too would be very useful.

All I knew about him was that he had no obvious income other than his wife's money, but was living the life of a lord with a heavy drinking habit. It was Antonio, the manservant, who began to explain that conundrum. I requested his presence soon after I had finished my breakfast. I found the heat of midday intolerable, causing my brain to boil and prevent concise thought. Mornings and evenings had become the time on Sifnos for me to apply myself, leaving the middle of the day to eat and rest. A timid tapping on the door alerted me to the arrival of Antonio. I called him in, and observed him closely for the first time. He was a dark-complexioned man with thick black hair, more like a Saracen than a Venetian, and it confirmed that he must be a local man. The Greeks were closely intertwined in physique to the Turks who ruled them, though they were loath to admit it.

'Is your name really Antonio?'

The man blushed, and shook his head. 'That is what my master called me. He liked to imagine he was still in Venice, I think. My real name is Antonis.'

'Antonis, I want to ask you about your master, and why he should have been on the strand in the first place. It is pretty much out of his way if he was coming back here from Kamares harbour. Even drunk, he would know his way home.'

Antonis dropped his gaze to the floor, examining his sandals quite extensively. I had obviously hit a nerve, and needed him to explain. I waited only a moment, then bellowed in the most intimidating way I could muster.

'Come, man. Tell me what you know, or by the will of the Doge, it shall go ill for you.'

The cowed servant looked over his shoulder, as if fearing that Querini would rise from the altar and stop his words with a ghostly hand.

'Master, please tell no one or they will surely kill me too.'

This was getting interesting.

'Who will kill you? Do you then know who killed Querini?'

He licked his lips nervously, and I sought to reassure him.

'Speak up, and I promise no one will know from me what you said.'

'The master needed money because the domina had stopped giving him any.'

So Speranza, who no doubt had funds provided by her family, gave nothing to her husband to sustain him in his miserable exile. That of itself was interesting in terms of her immersion in the Beornwyn virgin cult and of her devotion to Hugh. Perhaps the monk was receiving what Querini had lost. I returned my gaze to the man before me, and encouraged him to go on.

'So how did your master sustain his style of life here?'

Antonis shrugged and remained tight-lipped. But I would not give up, though it took some time before I got the facts from him. It seemed that to supplement his income, Niccolo Querini had resorted to clandestine piracy, along with some of the inhabitants of Sifnos, who were long used to making a living from the pickings of the sea. For many years small trading vessels were boarded and robbed of their goods. Not enough was taken to cause a major problem, which would have resulted in someone like Giovanni Soranzo, in his days

143

as Head of the Navy, cracking down on pirates. They took just enough to feed and sustain a few men and their families. Querini's role was mostly to discover news of the passage of vessels, but he also relieved his boredom with some active participation too. Antonis was clearly hinting that there might have been a falling out of thieves on the beach.

'Chlakopo beach is where the pirates bring their loot ashore, you see.'

That was the fearful servant's last offering. It was going too far for him to offer names. After all, he had to live on this island after we had all gone. But there was one question I had to ask.

'When you found the body, Domina Speranza said there was a . . . cloud, I think she said . . . yes, a cloud of butterflies that rose up from it. Is that true?'

I had remembered in the meantime why her description had chimed with something in my mind. Katie had related to me Speranza Soranzo's own account of the discovery of St Beornwyn's flayed body. It had apparently been modestly enveloped with blue butterflies. I was wondering if the miracle had been repeated. Antonis snorted in disbelief.

'I told her the dogs disturbed some purple butterflies, and that to Greeks they represent the souls of the dead. But there were only two or three. Hardly a cloud.'

Not a miraculous cloud then, more like a figment of Speranza's fond imagination. I dismissed Antonis, and he practically flew from the room, relief written on his swarthy face. My throat felt dry, and I poured myself a quite palatable Cretan wine of Querini's. I believe it came from Candia. I decided I would have to follow up Antonis' information, and find out the names of these petty pirates. The reason why I hadn't pressed him for the names – besides not having him fear for his life – was that I was unconvinced that Querini's death had been due to a brawl between thieves. Querini's hands bore no signs of bruises or scrapes such as he would have got in a fight. However, it was important not to dismiss the idea out of hand. Someone could have crept up on him, and done him in. Besides, what other possibilities did I have at the moment? Katie might come up with something, but until she did, I decided my investigations warranted a journey back to the harbour at Kamares. Querini must have had drinking companions there who could have loose tongues. And the only other avenue I had was Galuppi. If he really did have any orders from the Doge that I was not party to, they may relate to clearing the husband from the scene in order to allow the daughter to return unencumbered. But that was going to be a hard one to tackle. A sojourn in an unnamed tavern close to the harbour had greater appeal as a line of investigation. I would get Querini's servants to saddle a horse for me.

In the end the horse turned out to be more of a mule, and that was being kind to its ancestry. Perhaps donkey was a more accurate description. Its broad back and recalcitrant ways made the journey over the high back of the island long and sweltering. So I was glad to flop in the shade in one corner of the tavern where I had first seen Querini. In response to my demand for a good red wine, the tavern-keeper brought a jug of something he called Xinomavro. When I poured it into the cracked goblet he provided, it looked as black as old blood. I drank the first draught deeply and incautiously, and my mouth was sucked free of all moisture, leaving me thinking dried blood was an accurate description. I learned later that the name he gave it meant 'sour black', which was quite to the point. At first, I didn't know if I was being played a trick on like some innocent traveller. But everyone else in the tavern seemed to be drinking the same wine, and there were no furtive glances to see if I had been taken in. I poured a second goblet, and took it more slowly. Soon the taste began to grow on me. It was either that, or I was getting drunk enough not to care. I smiled gently and looked around. Several of the faces were familiar from the time I had stormed in to confront Querini, and I wondered if they now knew of his death. And if they did, was it because one of them had been involved in his demise? They all looked like brigands to me.

When I had consumed most of the blood wine, I waved the jug at the tavern-keeper, whose lack of a name made him as anonymous as his hostelry. He brought another jug over, and plonked it on the table by my elbow, splashing some of the wine on my shirtsleeve. I half expected it to burn through the material, but it didn't. Before he could leave, I grabbed his arm and asked him to sit a while. Reluctantly he did so, casting a defiant glance around the low-ceilinged room in case any of his cronies was of the impression he was consorting with the enemy. I broached the subject on my mind.

'Querini. Was he a regular here?'

The stubble-chinned man scowled. 'Why do you want to know? Going to pin his death on one of my customers?'

His Italian was good, which was fortunate. My Greek was execrable. But at least I had learned one thing quickly from his response. They knew Niccolo Querini was dead. I suppose I should not have been surprised – on such a small island bad news would travel fast. It was either that or someone in the tavern had murdered him and boasted of it.

'Not unless someone here is guilty of his murder. I did hear that he had some ... dealings ... with local sailors that might have resulted in a falling out.' I looked around the tavern. 'Does anyone here fit the bill?'

The tavern-keeper let out a guttural laugh and spat on the rush-strewn floor.

'Has Antonis been blabbing?'

I kept my mouth shut and my face impassive so as not to give the manservant away. So the tavern-keeper carried on.

'You don't need to say anything. He would spread any tale to divert attention from himself.' He saw the surprise on my face. 'Oh, yes, he's dabbled in some offshore *fishing*, too, if you take my meaning. Him and that little pig-sticker dagger of his. But in answer to your question, there's some here bold enough to steal, but no one with enough balls to kill a nobleman.'

I nodded sagely. 'That's as I thought. But tell me, did Querini talk about his wife much when he drank here?'

Another gob of spit splattered on the floor.

'That witch? God rot her and her little familiar that follows her around.'

I guessed by the witch's familiar he meant Brother Hugh. It was not very complimentary for a man of God, but quite apposite. I thought I would stir the pot a little and see what brewed.

'They say the monk convinced her to deny Querini his rights as her husband, and to play the virgin.'

That amused the Greek, and he chortled deeply in his phlegmy throat.

'She's a fake virgin, if you ask me. But it's true, what you say. Querini always used to boast how wild she was in bed, but recently she had denied him. He used to come here and drink the jug dry and bemoan his fate. He said he wasn't getting anything from her purse either, though he always paid his bills here.'

We were back to Querini's illegal business again, and I felt there was nothing more the man could offer. So as I had learned all I was going to from the tavern-keeper, I gave him a coin in way of payment for his information. He got up and shambled back to the corner of the room and his wine barrel, from where he presided over his domain. I too started to get up, but I had been sitting so long, my knees were stiff. They almost gave way under me, and I had to grip the edge of the table for support. It was a toss-up between whether it was infirmity or the effects of the Xinomavro. Whatever, I stayed where I was for a moment, and that slice of pure good luck meant I was not crossing the tavern floor when Galuppi entered. He had a black cloak on with the hood thrown over his head, but I recognised him all the same. No one else in Kamares had the gait of a man with a rod up his arse. I sat back down sharply, and leaned over my jug like some drunken Greek, hoping Galuppi wouldn't spot me. I watched out the corner of my eye as he spoke briefly to the tavern-keeper. Then he was ushered through a door that presumably led to the owner's private quarters. I waited to see what would happen next and was rewarded by the swift arrival of another familiar face. It wasn't a local, but the debtor who was working off what he owed by being an oarsman in the galley that had brought us here. I racked my brain to recall his name, cursing age and poor memory, until it came. What was a common labourer like Stefano doing meeting up with the patrician Galuppi in an anonymous Greek tavern?

I didn't want to be in the tavern when Galuppi or Stefano came out of the back room, so I got up, paid my bill, and went out into the coolness of the early evening. Walking past the boatyard, I watched idly as a gnarled old man worked on the beginnings of a boat. He drove long nails into the over-lapped planks, then bent the nails' end back into the plank on the inside. I ambled past and, further along the quayside, I noticed a burly figure that I recognised. It was a ship's cap-tain I had used on a few *colleganze* – business enterprises overseas to you. I called out his name.

'Captain Doria! What are you doing here?'

The grey-bearded, old sea dog looked up furtively from making a written record of the goods being loaded on his boat. He looked very concerned that someone had recog-nised him. Then he realised it was me.

'Niccolo Zuliani, by the Devil. I might ask the same of you. I noticed that sleek vessel in the harbour, but I would hardly have associated it with you.'

His own vessel was patched and the wood grey and worn. But I knew it to be seaworthy, having trusted my money in it more than once. I gave him a vague explanation of my apparent improvement in fortune.

'I wish it were mine. It's borrowed, as I'm on some busi-ness for a big man in La Serenissima. But why all the muscle on your ship?'

I had noted the two finely honed men staring disdainfully at me, as if I were a dog turd on the sole of their boots.

Doria cocked a thumb at them, and whispered in my ear, 'Oh. I've got quite a lot of gold on board. The deal has been to buy cheap gold from the Saracens with silver coins. The Doge is behind most of it.' He tapped the side of his nose, and laughed. 'Soon, there won't be any coins to buy goods with anywhere in Europe. It will all be in the hands of the infidels. Not that it will matter to the English. They say the

149

English king is so far into debt with the Peruzzi and Bardi banks, he won't be able to pay them in the end anyway.'

Doria's chatter sent a shiver down my spine. What money I had was in those banks, and he had just told me a good recipe for their crashing soon. I asked him to do me a favour when he returned to Venice, and took the quill from his hand. On his bill of lading, I quickly scrawled him an authorisation to arrange the removal of my money from both banks. I cursed the Doge for engineering the crisis, and for keeping me in Sifnos when I most needed to be home.

'Take this and hold my money for me until I return. There will be a percentage for you.'

Puzzled but compliant, Doria took my note and strode back to his ship. I hoped to God he realised the urgency of the document I had given him. So, what with all that distraction, I think I must have missed Galuppi and Stefano's emergence from the tavern. I hovered by the end of the cobbled street where the tavern lurked, but it got later and later with no sign of either man. Finally, even the boat-builder gave up his work for the day. The sun was sinking, and I had to get back on my donkey and make for the other side of the island before it got completely dark. I didn't want to fall over a cliff like I had been told Querini had. My late arrival at the Querini mansion meant that I didn't know that Katie had not returned until the following morning.

I got anxious when she didn't appear for breakfast. I thought she would be up promptly in order to tell me what she had found out the previous day from the domina and Brother Hugh. So when she wasn't, I became concerned. So concerned that I didn't even talk to Galuppi about being in Kamares the previous day. That would have to wait until I discovered where my precious granddaughter was. And the obvious place to start was the monastery at Mongou.

I hurried across the open fields surrounding the monastery, sweating in the morning sun that was already getting hot. The sound of a doleful bell carried across the valley, and despondency clenched my heart tight. I had a bad feeling about what I might find at the monastery of St John the Theologian. The bell had stopped ringing when I reached the main gateway to Mongou, but it still swung backwards and forwards, and the rope that worked the bell was swinging too. Someone had just left it and disappeared. The doors to the church inside the walls of the monastery were open and I could hear monotonous chanting coming from inside. I peered into the gloom, and saw for the first time the black-clad monks that occupied the monastery. For once they weren't avoiding me. The heavy aroma of incense hung in the air, and clouds of it drifted on the breeze through the open doors. As a Venetian, I was familiar with the Orthodox heresy. I was old enough to remember tales of Venice's role in the shambles that was later called the Fourth Crusade, when the Latin Church invaded Constantinople and ousted the Roman Empire and its faith. Venice profited mightily from its fall. That state of affairs didn't last long, though, and in my youth the Greek Emperor and the Orthodox Church took it all back. Being Venetians, we made deals with the Emperor in the same way we had with the Latin crusaders sixty years earlier. So the bearded black monks were a familiar sight to me, but I had not seen such fervent prayer as was presented to me that morning. I felt awkward about disturbing them, even though I feared that they might be praying for Katie's soul. I turned away to try and find either Brother Hugh or Domina Speranza, but was blessed

instead by the happy sight of Katie Valier rushing across the
open courtyard towards me. She almost bowled me over,
and hugged me hard.

'Grandpa, you must have been worried when I didn't get
back to the mansion yesterday.' To my surprise she then
scowled at me. 'I thought you might have come searching for
me last night.'

I smiled broadly, and tried, albeit half-heartedly, to extract
myself from her embrace.

'You can let go of me now. And I am sorry I didn't come last
night. I didn't get back until late myself, and assumed you were
already abed. It was only this morning that I knew otherwise.'

She finally pulled away, much to my regret. I was glad of
her warmth, as I had feared deep down that I might have
next seen her cold and dead. If this was what it was to have
family and blood relatives, it was not entirely pleasant. I
shook the bad thoughts from my brain, and asked her what
all the fuss was about.

'I have not seen the black crows so agitated.'

'Nor I. They are usually hidden away in their cells.
Women are not something they like to feast their eyes on in
such holy surroundings, I am told. But I can tell you why
the monks are so excited.'

Her eyes gleamed with a burning desire to tell me what
she had discovered yesterday, and the reason why she had
been unable to return last night. But she restrained her natural exuberance in the desire to lay out her facts cogently.

'I must tell you the story in sequence, so that you understand how it came about.'

She dragged me over to a stone bench that was in the shade
created by the walls of the church. As she spoke, her tale was
embellished by the hypnotic chanting of the monks inside.

'When I arrived yesterday morning, I couldn't get in to see Speranza because the door to her cell was locked. From the inside. Brother Hugh was already at the door trying to talk to her, but she wasn't answering.'

Katie explained to me that Hugh expressed a worry that something might have happened to Speranza. But on putting her ear to the door, Katie heard sounds from within. It was a low mumbling and the rustle of a linen dress. She reckoned that Speranza was alive and talking to herself. Assuming she was in no immediate danger, she convinced Hugh to leave his benefactor alone for a while. She brought him to the very bench we were now sitting on, and asked him why he thought Speranza had done this.

She looked at me. 'He said that since her husband's death, she had been distant and uncommunicative. He had been concerned for her sanity.'

I snorted. 'More concerned that his meal ticket was slipping away from him.'

'Perhaps. He did seem to be showing real concern, but I can't fathom his true feelings. What Grandma told me about him left me with an impression he was a fraud and a charlatan. And it's true, he did seem more worried about the disappearance of the relic than for Speranza.'

'The relic has gone?'

'Yes.'

Apparently, Hugh had placed the saint's finger on the altar, where Speranza liked to pray, that morning. And when he returned, both the domina and the relic were nowhere to be found. He at first suspected the monks because they had expressed admiration of the relic when he had first shown it to them. And he didn't think Speranza would have taken it, as she had always left it for Hugh to collect after her prayers.

But now that she had locked herself in her cell, he was beginning to suspect otherwise. Katie had asked him if it truly was the finger of St Beornwyn.

'Oh, yes. Her hands were once brought to Carmarthen by clerics from Whitby. She had lived her mortal life nearby in Lythe. What we know of her comes from the very lips of her constant companion, Mildryth. She was St Beornwyn's maid in life, and cared for her. After her mistress's death, Mildryth became the virgin saint's guardian and protector. Many pilgrims went to her to kiss her hand, for if you touch the hand of the person who touched the saint, then her blessings will flow to you. Mildryth herself told the story of her virgin mistress many times. As for the relic, I wasn't born when the saint's hands were in Carmarthen, but I traced them to Broomhill Priory. It was there I learned that a Venetian merchant had obtained one of the fingers. I have to admit to my shame that I coveted a relic of St Beornwyn, so I followed the trail to Venice . . .'

Katie then told me that Hugh failed to get any further because at that moment a piercing scream came from the direction of Speranza's cell. He and Katie leaped up and ran across the courtyard. Her door was now ajar, and Katie, arriving ahead of the monk, pulled it open.

Katie stopped her story for a moment and stared at me wide-eyed.

'Oh, Grandpa Nick, you should have seen the blood.'

'Blood?'

I was chilled by Katie's revelation. Was Speranza dead too, and the monks' chanting a Mass for her? Katie grasped my hands tightly with hers.

'She stood in the centre of the room with her arms outstretched, making the shape of Christ on the cross. And her hands – her palms were oozing blood.'

Katie's eyes were wide open, as if she had witnessed some miracle.

'You mean that she was marked with ...?'

'Stigmata, yes.'

No wonder the monks were singing. They had a genuine miracle taking place in their own obscure monastery, which could be very lucrative for them. Of course, you would have to put me in the category of sceptic when it came to miracles. Like Doubting Thomas, I needed to see this for myself.

'Come, show me.' I could not keep the irony out of my voice. 'Is the domina approachable by the mere mundane?'

'Oh, yes. She has calmed down now, and even let me bind her wounds yesterday. She slept last night, but I have not checked on her this morning yet. We can go and see how she is, if you like.'

I followed Katie to the range of buildings where the monks' cells stood. I refrained from suggesting we should be relieved it was merely the Lord's wounds that marked Speranza. If she had copied the virgin saint's affliction, she would have been flayed alive. Katie poked out her tongue in response to my scepticism. She knocked on the cell door, announcing herself to the woman within. A muffled voice gave us permission to enter.

Speranza Soranzo was kneeling beside a simple pallet bed, which was the only furniture in the room. In fact, it was the only item in the room other than the woman herself and a wooden cross on the wall. It was truly a bare, ascetic cell. Believe me. I scanned it carefully, expecting to see something with which the supposed stigmatist could have wounded herself. But there was nothing.

She turned to look at me, a nauseatingly beatific look on

her bland face. I could see a growing crop of boils on her neck, though. The saint had not seen fit to cure her of those. Perhaps I was being too cynical, and decided to ask if I could see her wounds. As if more than willing to display the evidence of her special status, Speranza held out her bound hands, and I noticed the bandage on her left hand was partly unwound. I kneeled before her and took the hand in mine, unwinding the loose bandage fully. There was indeed a puncture wound the size of a finger in the centre of her palm, and it was still oozing blood slightly. I sniffed the wound because it is said that holy wounds, like the bodies of dead saints, exude the odour of sanctity. I could smell nothing. I wrapped the bandage back around her hand, and thanked her for her courtesy. It was a puzzle that I could not explain, and I didn't like the fact.

Having retreated back to our bench in the courtyard, I asked Katie where Brother Hugh was.

'I don't know. I have not seen him this morning. You would think, wouldn't you, that he would be fussing around his great prize? I mean, he not only has a well-connected convert to St Beornwyn's cause, he now can parade her as a stigmatist.'

A voice spoke up from the porch of the church.

'Is that what you think of me? That I am doing all this for fame and fortune?'

It was the missing Brother Hugh, still worked up about his missing relic. Apparently he had been hunting in the church for it again, when the Greek monks had filed in. He had been trapped in a side chapel, and had to endure the whole service, which was a lengthy one as Orthodox services are. He had only just been able to escape.

I grunted noncommittally, neither confirming nor excusing my opinion of him.

'Did you find what you were looking for?'

'No, but I have not searched the domina's cell yet.'

With a determination that I had not seen in him before, he crossed the blisteringly hot courtyard, making for Speranza's cell. Katie made as if to get up and follow him, but I stayed her with my hand.

'Leave them to it. I have no doubt that Speranza has the relic. It's just a matter of whether she will give it back to him.'

Katie nodded, then tilted her head to one side as she watched Hugh disappear round the corner of the dormitory range.

'Did you notice something about Hugh's robe?'

'No, but I'm sure you have.' Katie's young eyes were far better than mine, and I had to rely on my wits and longer time on this earth to stay ahead of her.

'Yes. The hem of his robe, where it brushes the ground, has a faint white mark around it just above the edge of the robe.'

I frowned, not sure what she was suggesting. 'Well, I would guess that Hugh has only one robe, and it's probably been dragging in the dust.'

Katie clapped her hands together in triumph. 'No, it's not dust. It's more deeply stained in the brown wool than that. It's like when a man sweats in the heat and then the sweat under his armpits or across his back dries, leaving a white mark. Only that wouldn't happen to the edge of his robe. It looks to me like sea salt has dried around the bottom where he has got his robe wet in the sea.'

I suddenly saw what she was suggesting.

'Or on the shoreline at Chlakopo beach, where Querini's body was found.'

I clapped my hands on my knees and rose, rather too

abruptly for my creaking knees. But I was determined on action at last.

'Katie, tell Brother Hugh and the domina to make ready. I intend to sail for Venice tomorrow, and they will both come with me.'

'You will take her back home along with the killer of her husband?'

I lifted an admonitory finger in the air. 'If he is the murderer, then he will face justice in Venice. If not, well . . .'

I strode across the courtyard grinning, knowing that I would have frustrated my granddaughter with my unfinished sentence. The truth was I didn't know what the alternative was. There were so many possible suspects for Querini's murder, and I still needed to talk to a few of them. When I got back to the crusader mansion, I told all who were to travel back with me to pack for a long journey.

The first man I summoned was Antonio-Antonis. I was troubled by what the tavern-keeper had said about him. He had referred to the manservant's involvement with Querini's piracy, and mentioned his 'pig-sticker dagger'. I had not given Antonis enough consideration, thinking him just a bystander to the death of his master. As I began to pull my spare clothes out of the chest, he arrived in answer to my summons.

'You wanted to talk to me, sir?'

I looked carefully at his belt. No dagger. Did that mean he had hidden it after sticking his master through the heart? He certainly looked wary at my examination. I had no time for finesse, even if I had been capable of it in the first place.

'Yes. Give me your dagger.'

I held my hand out with a lot more authority than I felt. If he decided to oppose me, he could easily kill me where I stood. Instead he wavered, and looked around as if for a way of escape.

'My . . . dagger? Sir, I don't wear one when I am about my duties.'

That enough was true. I could not recall having seen one at his waist, not even when I had seen him out with the dogs at the scene of Querini's murder. But I needed to be sure he didn't have the sort of dagger that could have made the small but deadly wound to Querini. And if he was the killer, I could not leave him free on the island after our departure.

'Except when your duties are standing side by side with your master robbing honest traders of their goods.'

His face went deathly pale at my accusation.

'Who told you that?'

'Never mind who did. I can see from your face that it is true. Where is the bassillard you used to stick in the heart of those you robbed?'

My reference to the sort of narrow, slender-bladed dagger that could have done for Querini seemed to puzzle Antonis. He fell to his knees, clutching at my fur-trimmed robe.

'I don't now what you mean, sir. Yes, it's true my master persuaded me to help him once or twice. But I never killed anyone. None of us did. It was enough to wave a good heavy sword in the air, and they usually let us take what we wanted. A little bassillard would have had no effect on them, sir.'

I believed the grovelling servant, and extricated my robe from his grasp. I told him to go, and he would hear nothing more of this. He gasped out his thanks and ran from the room. I felt confident I could eliminate him from my list of suspects, as I had thought all along. Had I not seen there were no signs of a struggle on Querini's body, and no cuts or bruises on his knuckles? If Antonis had turned on him, he surely would have put up a fight, even drunk as he had been. Querini's dogs had been another indication of his innocence. Domina Speranza had told me how much they had loved her husband. If Antonis had already been out walking them when he encountered his master and then had slain him, the dogs would have been more agitated around Antonis. And if he had killed Querini without the presence of the dogs, it would have taken a stout heart and great cunning to leave the scene of the murder, walk back to the mansion, collect the dogs and 'accidentally' discover the dead body. No, Antonis was off my list of suspects.

As I was completing my preparations for the return to Venice, Bertuccio Galuppi strode into my room.

'What's this I hear? We are to return to Venice all of a sudden? Does this mean you have satisfied yourself of the domina's suitability to present herself before the Doge, her father?'

I grinned in a way I hoped was enigmatical. 'Indeed. I am assured of her almost virginal status, in fact.'

Galuppi didn't know what I was talking about, having not been a party to the details of Katie and my examination of Speranza Soranzo's relationship with Brother Hugh. But of course he knew of the monk's existence after I had made reference to him as the domina's possible lover. So, unsure whether he was being mocked, he narrowed his eyes in suspicion.

'You mean the monk will be coming back with us, too?'

'Oh, yes. He is an essential part of my plans for Domina Soranzo's return to Venice.'

Galuppi shrugged in resignation. 'Then I shall ready myself for the journey.'

He turned to leave, and I was tempted to confront him

with my knowledge of his trip to Kamares, and his meeting with Stefano the oarsman. But I wanted to face them with that fact together. On board ship and before we reached La Serenissima would be time enough. In fact, I was confident that, with all my suspects on board, all would be revealed before our return. If it wasn't, I would have failed in my mission for the Doge.

It was the following day before we got to sea. It took longer than I thought to move all the baggage across the island to the harbour, and then to load it. I noticed that Captain Doria's ship had left, and hoped that he would carry out my request to pull my money out of the two banks. I would be only a few days behind him, but those days might be all it took for the banks to crash. We were also delayed by a row over the allocation of cabin space. The domina wanted her own quarters, and the best ones too. Galuppi, Katie and myself had to take second best. In the end the captain of the ship reluctantly gave up his cabin, and everything was settled. But by then it was too late to set sail, so we spent an uncomfortable night on board waiting for the morning. The oarsmen, including the debtor Stefano, had gone back ashore and spent the night in various taverns around the quayside. Their pulling on the oars in the morning had therefore been sluggish at best. But at last Sifnos had disappeared over the horizon, and we were on our way towards the southern coast of Greece. Here we would rest and reprovision before heading north for La Serenissima.

Two days into our homeward journey, I decided it was time to pull at a few threads and see what unravelled. The first person I came across on deck happened to be Bertuccio Galuppi. He was staring out beyond the prow of the ship as if seeking the first sighting of Venice lagoon and its protective shingle bank. We had hardly spoken since getting on board, each of us avoiding the other for whatever reason. Now, I would confront him with his suspicious meeting with Stefano. He was concentrating so much on the vista ahead that he didn't hear me until I was right behind him. Suddenly realising I was there, he turned to go, much as he had done for the past two days. I grasped his arm abruptly.

'Don't go, Messer Galuppi. There is something we must discuss.'

He looked down at my fist crushing the cloth of the arm of his fine jerkin, and tried to release himself from my grip. I was unmoved, and pulled him closer to my face.

'You may think you are something special here, Galuppi, seeing as you are old family and all that rubbish. But I am the person the Doge confided in, and I will be reporting to him when we return. And I may have to tell him about your rendezvous with a common oarsman in some low tavern, and the conspiracy that it no doubt points to. So you'd better listen to me.'

Galuppi did that sneer that is a part of the armoury of the upper classes. In fact, I was afraid he saw through my feeble reference to a conspiracy, and could tell I had no idea why the two men had met.

'Oh, so I must listen to you, must I, Zuliani? Well, let me tell you something. Your little task for the Doge was only a pretty charade to cover up the real reason we were on Sifnos. I was charged with the task of getting rid of Niccolo Querini by any means available. So while you were stumbling around talking to the domina and that monk, I sought out a likely member of the crew to assist me. The debtor Stefano was ideal. A man who would do anything for money. If you saw us together the other day, it was when I paid him off. He told me he had carried out his orders to the letter. Now, let go of my arm.'

Stunned by his admission, I did so, and he pushed past me. He was making for the cabins at the stern, but stopped for a parting shot.

'And don't think of running to the authorities with this. It was all done at the Doge's behest, so no one will care to listen to you.'

With that final warning, he went through the door to the cabins, and I was left clutching thin air just as a wave broke over the bow. I would have been swept off my feet and perhaps over the side, had not a firm hand taken hold of me as I tumbled. Down on one knee and staring over the rail at the worsening grey sea, I blurted out my thanks.

'I thank you, sir, for your life-saving timeliness.'

I heard Katie's bell-like laugh, and realised the steely grip had been that of my own granddaughter.

'Your eyesight is fading, Grandpa, if you think I am a man. I think I am more offended even than when you grabbed my tits at our first meeting.'

A passing sailor, sent to trim the sails, gave me a strange look on hearing Katie's comment. Embarrassed, I hustled her back towards our cabin. I think I have mentioned our first encounter, when Katie had dressed as a boy and was stalking me. I had lurked in wait, and grabbed her roughly round the chest, not expecting a womanly figure to appear under my hands. But the sailor was not to know that.

'You should not say things like that in front of others. That man will think I am some sort of incestuous pervert.'

Katie laughed. 'He is probably jealous of your intimate knowledge of my luscious body.'

'There you go again, Katie. Please stop it.'

She could see I was really embarrassed, and put her solemn face on.

'Sorry, Grandpa.'

The truth of the matter was that I just didn't get this parent business. I wanted to be a good example to my grand-daughter. But whatever I did, it soon degenerated into the usual fun and games, it seemed. However, Katie did have something serious to tell me.

'I have just been talking to Speranza, as you requested.'

'Did you see the crucifix around her neck?'

A few days ago, I had noticed the leather thong around Speranza's neck that disappeared under the front of her dress, and was curious what it held.

Katie frowned. 'No. I went to touch the thong as I asked her, and she quickly put her hand over her chest to protect it. She said it was a family heirloom and personal to her.' Her eyes lit up. 'You don't think it is the saint's missing finger, do you?'

I shrugged noncommittally. 'Maybe. Now, tell me. Is she all right? Her wounds, are they healing?'

'No, the wounds are open and they are bleeding again. I can't figure it out, unless they are truly stigmata.' She said this in such a way that I knew she didn't believe in the phe-nomenon any more than I did. 'But that isn't what I want to talk to you about. You see, while I was looking at her hands, she said something to me.'

'What was it?'

'She looked at me, all innocently in that virginal way she has now, and said she thought that Brother Hugh had killed Niccolo in order to ensure her husband did not lead her away from St Beornwyn. She sounded quite sure of it.'

I pulled a face. 'That gives us two murderers in the space of a few moments.'

I explained to the puzzled girl the result of my confrontation with Galuppi. She was as surprised as I was at what he had said.

'Galuppi involved in a murder plot? With direct orders from the Doge? I don't believe it.'

'What's so unbelievable? That stiff, strait-laced Bertuccio Galuppi could arrange the murder of a man, if it suited the Republic? Or that the Doge – our noble hero of the Aegean – could order it done in the first place, if it fitted in with his own personal situation?'

Katie stamped her foot in frustration. 'Damn it, Grandpa, why are you always so good at seeing through all the sham?'

'Because I have lived a long life surrounded by hypocrites.' I gave her a rueful smile. 'I fear it is something you will learn too, if you stick around your grandfather. In the meantime, I need you to tutor me about aspects I find much more difficult to comprehend.'

'What's that?'

'Families and marriage. Now there are two things that completely fox me.'

As well as Katie teaching me what went on between men and women inside families – a story with which I was completely unfamiliar – I had another task to perform. This occasioned delving deep into the bowels of the ship where the pitching and yawing was more stomach-churning than on deck, and the odours were of men's sweat and bodily excretions. But it was worth it. Once I had found out what I had all along believed, I was ready to confront the killer of Niccolo Querini. I was glad to get back on deck and breathing in the clean, fresh air coming off the Adriatic, even if it was whipping up to gale force and throwing a stinging spray into my face. Being thrown from side to side, I reeled back to my cabin, and planned my next step. I hoped it would finally serve to unpick all those threads I had been teasing away at for the last few days.

The seas eventually eased, and I sent a message to the people concerned to meet me on the rear deck. I did it through Katie, because none of them would refuse a pretty girl. I didn't tell her that, though – she would have slugged me. I stood on the deck with my back to the setting sun, so that when the others looked at me they would have to squint. Bertuccio Galuppi was the first to arrive.

'What's all this about, Zuliani? Hasn't everything been settled to your satisfaction already?'

'We shall see, Messer Galuppi. I just thought we should get our story straight before we reach Venice.'

'What is there to get wrong? I told you . . .'

He paused because the next person to come onto the rear deck was the oarsman Stefano. Galuppi stared at me angrily, and then waved a dismissive hand at the man.

'What are you doing here? Get below where you should be. You stink.'

In fact, Stefano had taken some care to wash the sweat of below-decks off his body. His hair was wet and droplets of water glistened on his face and arms. I guessed he had scooped up a bucket of sea water and poured it over himself before climbing to the upper reaches of the ship. Still, he hung his head and was about to turn away, when I stopped him.

'I requested his presence, Messer Galuppi, by the same fair messenger who gave you your summons. I got permission from the ship's captain first, naturally. We don't want the ship going round in circles because one of the oarsmen is not pulling his weight. But seeing as his evidence is somewhat compromising, perhaps we can have him speak now, and then I can dispense with his services before the domina comes on deck.'

Galuppi tried to give me an intimidating stare, but the sun behind me simply made him squint like some poor idiot. He mustered as much authority in his voice as he could.

'If we are talking about Querini's death, you know we have talked over this man's evidence. And it does not need to go beyond the three of us.'

I put on as cynical a voice as I was able. 'Oh, you are referring to Stefano's assertion that *he* killed Niccolo Querini?'

Stefano winced, and looked over his shoulder to see if anyone else had heard me. Galuppi too was disconcerted by my clear statement.

'Keep your voice down, man.'

I pressed on regardless. 'He told you this in the tavern over a few goblets of Xinomavro, no doubt. And you believed him.'

A look of uncertainty came over Galuppi's face.

'What do you mean – believed him?' He turned to the red-faced Stefano. 'What does he mean?'

Before Stefano could speak, I intervened, looking Galuppi straight in the eye.

'You told me that you plotted with this man to murder Niccolo Querini.'

Galuppi foamed at the mouth at my accusation.

'You know at whose instruction it was.'

'I know who you *said* it was, and you might have even believed it. Though I think you read more into the words of ... this person of note ... than were there in the first place. But that is neither here nor there. What is clear is that what Stefano told you was untrue.'

Galuppi rounded on the embarrassed oarsman, who flinched and shook his head.

'I only told you what you wanted to hear, messer. And I figured that, if Querini was dead, I might as well claim it was me did it, so you would pay me.'

I smiled beatifically. 'So you see, Galuppi, you have nothing to tell the Doge after all.'

Galuppi wasn't giving up, however.

'The man is lying now. You have persuaded him to lie to thwart me. Of course he did away with Querini.'

I shook my head as though chiding a troublesome youth. 'Not so. You see, I went down to the oar deck to talk to Stefano earlier. I asked to see his knife. It was a wide-bladed dagger, and quite short in length. It is a slashing knife, not an assassin's blade. Nothing like the murder weapon at all. And when I professed to admire his killing skills, and asked him to tell me how he did it, he told me a pack of lies about stabbing Querini in the gut three times and twisting his knife so.' I made a twisting motion with my hand held in a fist as if thrusting with a dagger.

'Needless to say, there were no such marks on Querini's body.'

Galuppi growled and demanded his money back of Stefano. He would have struck the man if I hadn't stopped him.

'No. You have been taken for a fool, and the loss of money will serve to teach you a lesson. Stefano, you can go.'

Mumbling his thanks, the oarsman returned to his nether world, and left us gentlemen to ours. There were a few moments of awkward silence between Galuppi and myself, but then the others arrived. Katie was leading, and Domina Speranza was relying on the sturdy arm of Brother Hugh to prevent her from falling as the ship rolled in the rough seas.

'I hope you will make this brief, Zuliani. I would rather lie on my bed than try to stand upright in such weather.'

Speranza Soranzo's words were peremptory, and to my ears bore no sign of the forbearance due from the follower of a Christian martyr. But then I had my doubts about Beornwyn anyway. The daughter of a nobleman – which the saint had been – was not someone used to self-sacrifice, as the domina herself clearly exemplified. I thought Beornwyn was as false a virgin as Speranza was, despite the stories spread by her faithful maidservant. She herself, whose name I had forgotten, would have had a vested interest in creating the myth of her mistress. She probably made a lot of money from pilgrims and the like. It was such a good scam I wondered why I had never tried it myself. Maybe because I was never in the company of virgins. This thought made me look guiltily at my granddaughter. A man who had spent his life enjoying the company of a certain type of woman, and coming late to family obligations, had little to judge a good woman by. But I knew that, virgin or not, Katie was, like her grandmother, the best of women. And far and away above Speranza Soranzo in nobility, even though she had a ne'er-do-well for a grandfather. Oh well, time to pull the final threads of the unravelling tapestry that was Niccolo Querini's death. I took a deep breath, and began.

'Before we arrive in Venice, I must conclude the matter of the murder of Domina Speranza's husband.'

The woman in question opened her mouth to speak, but I raised my hand and surprisingly she remained silent, contenting herself with a deep sigh. I went on.

'Firstly, there is no truth in the story that he fell to his death accidentally.' Galuppi glared at me, but I pressed on. 'It has also been suggested that he was killed in a ... brawl – shall we say – between colleagues embarked on a private venture.' I almost said the word 'pirate' but held back to spare the domina's embarrassment. 'This I have dismissed because of lack of evidence of a struggle on the body. His hands and knuckles were not—'

This time it was the monk who tried to intervene.

'Messer Zuliani, does the domina need to be subjected to these intimate and disturbing references? It is her husband's body to which you are referring, after all.'

I tilted my head to acknowledge his concern. 'As you wish. I will not go into detail. Suffice it to say that none of the inhabitants on Sifnos, or the servants in the Querini mansion, were guilty of murder. Similarly, none of the crew on this ship were involved.'

I stared hard at Galuppi and defied him to object to my raising this point. He merely stared off to the horizon, which was beginning to tilt alarmingly as the ship rolled on the growing sea. Of course, I had not excluded Galuppi specifically from my list of suspects when I mentioned the crew. But it was to Hugh that I next turned.

'Brother Hugh, I know you profess to be a man of God, and I have no reason to doubt your sincerity.'

The monk's eyes narrowed in suspicion as to where my speech was leading.

'I am glad you acknowledge the nature of my vows, messer. But I detect a note of caution in them. Where is this going?'

Hugh took a step or two away from me as he spoke, leaving Speranza reaching out for support to a rope that angled up to the ship's mast. Hugh stood with his back to the handrail around the edge of the deck, and he clutched at it as he staggered a little on the lurching deck. I stood with legs apart and my knees flexed as my father had taught me when a boy. Father had been a cruel and harsh man, but he had passed on all I needed to know about ships. I carried on with my investigation of Hugh's recent behaviour.

'You have worked hard to bring Domina Speranza to an appreciation of the value of St Beornwyn's virtues. Her virginity. In the process, you have managed to cut her husband out of her consideration.'

Hugh cast a look around the deck as if seeking an exit.

'It was the domina's own choice to reject her husband, and return to the values of virginity. I had no hatred of Querini.'

'Hatred was not the motive I was looking for, merely expedience. How much more suitable that Niccolo Querini was out of the way permanently, than as an encumbrance that could keep popping up at awkward moments. So when you found him on the strand, drunk and argumentative, you decided to take action, did you not?'

'I was not there.'

The monk looked hunted now, and kept casting a pleading look at the domina. I thought my plan was progressing well, and pointed dramatically at the hem of his robe. The same robe he had been wearing since I had first met him.

'Then tell me where you got the stain of sea salt on the hem of your robe, if not on Chlakopo beach.'

'It wasn't me. It . . .'

Brother Hugh's cries were drowned out by a demonic wail, taking us all by surprise. Before I could do anything to prevent her, Speranza threw herself at Hugh, spitting and clawing.

'Devil in disguise, you killed my husband. You killed him.'

He looked at her aghast. 'You know why I was on that beach.'

Before he could finish, she struck him a blow on the head that sent him reeling. The ship lurched, and he didn't stand a chance. Losing his footing completely, Hugh pitched over the handrail and into the boiling sea.

We rowed in circles as best we could in the gale, searching for him, but it was hopeless. Finally I agreed with the captain that we should give up, and he plotted a course for Venice. I sat disconsolately in my cabin, with Katie perched on a stool close by me. The space was so small that we filled it, our knees touching. There was nowhere for me to brood in solitude.

'Well, that wasn't as I had planned it.'

'Why not, Grandpa? You uncovered the murderer, didn't you? It is a shame that he drowned rather than face justice in Venice. But in the end it all worked out.'

I sighed, and patted Katie's knee, which was pressed against my thigh.

'Did it? Brother Hugh may have been guilty of many sins, but he didn't deserve to die in that way. And it is time I did something about it.'

I slapped my hands on my knees, and prised myself up, taking care not to bang my head on the low ceiling.

'Come, Katie. I must set matters right and do it now.'

'Where are we going, Grandpa?'

'To speak with Domina Speranza.'

I was in no mood for courtesy any more, and burst into the lady's cabin without knocking. I groaned at the sight facing me. Katie peered over my shoulder, and gasped.

'Lady Speranza, your hands.'

Speranza Soranzo sat at the small table in the captain's cabin with her hands laid out the surface, palms upwards. The stigmata were once again leaking blood onto the table's surface. She looked up at us slowly, a serene expression on her face, and held out the evidence of her saintliness. I growled in anger, and sprang across the room.

'Enough of this mountebank tomfoolery.'

I knew what I had to do, and stared the fake virgin in the eyes.

'I know all, you see, domina. I had planned to scare Hugh in order for him to tell me what he knew about Querini's death, but you stopped him.'

Her voice, when she spoke was languid and distant.

'I shall carry the sin of his death on my conscience for ever, but I don't regret what I did. He killed my husband.'

'Oh, no, he didn't. I think he was on the beach when Querini was murdered, but was unable to do anything about it. And he was just about to tell us who did kill Querini, but you prevented him. And you know why? Because it was you who killed your own husband.'

Katie gasped, but Speranza merely smiled beatifically.

'How could I have done that? A poor, unarmed woman.'

'But you are not unarmed, are you? You killed him with the same implement you use to fake your stigmata. I couldn't figure it out at first, but it's obvious just looking at you.'

Katie peered at the domina.

'Where, grandfather? Where is it?'

I pointed at the leather cord round her neck.

'We all thought that was a crucifix. But if it were, why is it hidden, when the domina is so religious? Why is it not on display?'

Speranza's hand went to her breast, trying to cover what was on the end of the cord, but I was too fast for her. I grasped the leather cord, and yanked on it hard. The knot snapped, and I pulled it away from her breast. On the end dangled a long and viciously sharp ship's nail with a rounded head. There was blood on it from her efforts to open her own wounds, but I had no doubt that at some point it had also borne Querini's blood. In cross section the nail was square, and tapered to a point. If it was held by the flat head in a fist with the point protruding from the knuckles, anyone of moderate strength – even a woman – could punch it deep enough into a body to reach and rupture the heart. It fitted the small but deep wound I had found on Querini's body perfectly.

Speranza Soranzo turned her head away from me as if not caring one jot what I knew. She wrapped her bloodied hands around her and began to rock slowly backwards and forwards. Katie and I retreated from the cabin. There was a key in the door lock on the inside. I transferred it to the outside and turned it. The murderer of Niccolo Querini would be safe until we reached Venice.

Once on deck, and breathing fresh air again, Katie and I stood in silence for a while, each contemplating the recent events as darkness fell around us. It was my granddaughter who spoke first.

'What are you going to do, Grandpa Nick?'

I shrugged. 'What can I do? She may be a murderer, but her victim was *persona non grata* in Venice, involved in plotting against the previous Doge. And she is still the present Doge's daughter. I can only tell Soranzo what I know, and leave it to him to deal with it. It's family matters, and as I said to you, I'm not good with those.'

Katie rubbed my arm gently. 'I think you underestimate yourself. You make a fine grandfather.'

She poked around in the little purse hanging at her waist.

'I was going to give this to Speranza. I found it on the deck after Hugh fell overboard.'

She showed me what she had. It was a series of finger-bones bound with gold wire. The relic of St Beornwyn. I laughed.

'Well, you can keep it now. It is quite valuable.'

She gave me a strange look, and shuddered.

'What? Keep some relic that ensures virginity? I can't think of anything worse.'

She raised her arm, and without a second thought, tossed the saint's finger into the sparkling sea.

Footnote

You will no doubt have in your mind the question of the truth of all this. After I returned from my adventures in the far distant land of the Great Khan Kublai and told the people of Venice of the wonders I had seen, many chose to disbelieve me. I was branded a liar at worst, and a story-teller at the very least. Another Venetian to return from a similar place, Polo by name, was dubbed *Il Milione* – the Teller of a Million Lies. In the future I may be said to be worse than a liar, and be seen as no more than the figment of a deranged imagination myself. But history will tell you who to believe. Certainly there is some dispute about Niccolo Querini's end, due no doubt to the fact that Speranza murdered her own husband. To obscure the fact, a story went round that he didn't die until close to 1326. But one thing is certain. After the events of 1310, once his property was forcibly liquidated in Venice and a price was put on his head, clandestine piracy must have been his only means of survival in exile. And the plain truth is that Speranza Soranzo, sometimes called Soranza Soranzo, did return to La Serenissima hoping to be received as the daughter of the Doge. Instead, Giovanni Soranzo ordered her excluded from the Doge's palace for life. She was to spend the rest of her days in the monastery of Santa Maria delle Vergini in a secluded cell, apart from other nuns, in the occasional company of a servant. She was forced to apply to the Council of Ten for permission to visit her family on very special holidays, or for medical reasons, when she had broken out with boils and stigmata. Upon those occasions, the lady Soranza, by order of Venice, was directed to arrive inconspicuously at a side door of the palace, at night, and in a covered boat – in order to remain undetected.

And by the way, the Italian banks did not crash in my lifetime, after all. But I guarantee that, if you are reading this twenty years or more after I am gone, they will have, creating havoc in the world. History will confirm my good sense in taking out my money before they did.

Niccolo Zuliani, 1314

ACT THREE

I

June 1376

It was Hugh who saw him. At first they thought he had
drowned. The body lay face up on the foreshore of the river
as if deposited by the tide, waiting to be revealed by the
growing light of a summer's dawn. But when Hugh and
Alfred clambered down from the landing stage and
squelched across the mud to the corpse they saw that the
visible areas of clothing and hair were not waterlogged but
dry. The face was composed.

From a distance the two men also assumed this must be a
member of the household. The tunic the corpse wore was of
blue and white, the livery of the house of Lancaster. But
when they drew closer they saw the cloth was of much finer
quality than anything they wore, and the colours more subtle
in their dye. They soon forget these distinctions anyway, for
blotting out the centre of the chest was a circle of dried
blood. Hugh and Alfred did not recognise the dead man
even though his features were not disfigured.

'He did not die natural,' said Alfred, shielding his eyes
against the early morning sun as he gazed at the red spill
on the dead man's tunic.

Hugh crouched down to examine the man's face closely.

Alfred, older and more stiff in the joints than his fellow, stayed upright.

'This is one of *hers*, not ours,' said Hugh, standing up and jerking his thumb towards the great white palace that stretched along the river front. Eager to show how he came by this conclusion, he went on: 'His face is darker and his beard is not after our fashion and, besides, he does not look English.'

'Who did this?' said Alfred.

'That is not our business,' said Hugh. 'Go and fetch help to carry him inside. Don't waste time, the tide is coming in.'

Alfred was not as quick-witted as Hugh and usually deferred to the younger man. He did as he was told and, while Hugh waited on the foreshore, he made his way up through the terraces that lay between the river and the palace. Hugh looked at the body once more. He was certain that this gentleman was exactly that, a gentleman, and part of the Queen's company and therefore a stranger, a foreigner. What or who was the cause of his death? Not our business, he'd said to Alfred, but it was peculiar all the same. He'd surely mention it to his brother John who, though claiming to despise the palace and its occupants, was always eager to hear titbits of gossip from within its white, fortified walls.

The incoming tide was only a few feet away from the body by the time Alfred returned with half a dozen members of the household – not that so many were required but they were drawn to the spot by curiosity – and a makeshift litter. One of the household stewards, Thomas Banks, was with them. Hugh, who'd been enjoying his place in the sun as the finder of the body, had to give way to the steward. Hurrying to remove the dead man from the mud, they were lifting him up as water was starting to lap at their feet. The body was easy to handle, quite pliant. They carried the litter up through the green, flowering terraces. Because it was still early in the day, no one, or at least no one of any importance, was wandering in the gardens. Directed by Thomas, they toted the body through some cloisters and so into his office. The room was chill and gloomy, with sunbeams penetrating a narrow window.

Once there, Thomas Banks swept the cushions from a ledge of stone, which functioned as a bench, and indicated that the body should be laid down there. He had said very little so far. Hugh sensed he was troubled. A sure sign was the way the steward frequently clasped his chain of office.

'Which of you found the body?'

Glancing at Alfred, Hugh nodded.

'Your name is Hugh . . . Hall, isn't it?'

'Yes, sir,' said Hugh, surprised and slightly alarmed that he was known to the steward.

'You are to stay, Hugh. The rest of you may leave.'

'Should we get a priest?' said one of the other servants, reluctant to quit this interesting scene. Thomas Banks gestured impatiently. 'Time enough for priests later. Go now, I say. And make no mention of what has happened. I know you all, and if this discovery becomes the common talk, I'll hold you responsible for it, every single one of you.'

The group filed out wordlessly, until there were only three left, two living, one dead. Hugh was more uneasy than pleased at being instructed to stay. He watched as Banks stooped over the body, clutching at his golden chain with its motif of S-shaped links. The sunlight coming through the window fell directly on the red stain on the dead man's tunic.

'You found him lying on his back, as he is now?'

'Yes, sir. He was quite dry on the front so he did not drown,' said Hugh. 'You can tell by the marks there ... by the blood ... that he did not drown. I think he must have been ...'

Still bending over the body, Thomas Banks fixed Hugh with a look that caused the servant to falter.

'I did not ask you to think, Hugh. It may be that this individual *did* drown, whatever you believe. It may be, eh?'

The steward stepped away from the corpse. He smiled tightly. He held his hand palm outwards towards Hugh Hall, as if to demonstrate he had nothing to hide.

'I can see that you are a sharp man, Hugh. It must be plain to you that this individual here is not one of us, not English. He is not one of the Duke's men, as we are. Discretion is required. You understand me?'

Hugh nodded. He didn't trust himself to say anything further.

'In the meantime,' continued Thomas Banks, 'you may assist me by examining this unfortunate person's wound. Yes, that's right. Approach the body. Unbutton the tunic. Let us see now.'

Wondering whether this was the reason he'd been told to stay behind – so that the steward could avoid dirtying his hands – Hugh drew near to the body on the stone ledge. For a moment he paused, out of respect or apprehension or both. Then he began the awkward process of unbuttoning the blood-stained upper garment. It was a snug fit and the reason became apparent after a moment. There was another item of clothing wadded inside, some kind of undergarment, or a part of one, but so saturated in blood that it was impossible to tell the original colour. It must have been

placed there in the attempt to stanch the flow from the body.
Hugh pulled the bloody material a little to one side. It came
away with a little tearing sound, far enough to expose a sticky
gash below the region of the heart. By now, Thomas Banks
was standing at his side. Together steward and servant stared
at the wound. The sunlight coming through the window had
shifted onto the bearded face of the corpse. The expression
was oddly peaceful, considering that death must have come
suddenly and violently.

'You are right, he did not drown,' said Thomas. 'But the
river is generous and offers deaths by other means than
water. For example, there are stakes protruding from the
mud, there are outcrops of rock.'

To Hugh's eyes, this fatal injury was caused by the
hand of a man. Still he said nothing. His eye was caught
by something white tucked into the dead man's armpit
and he reached over to tug it out. It was a scrolled parchment. One end was reddened as if it had been dipped in
a pool of blood but the rest was untouched. Perhaps the
position of the body, the way the parchment was tight
against the man's right side, had protected it from the
worst effusions of the wound. As Hugh pulled out the
papers, he also detached a thin golden chain from which
was suspended a precious stone. One of the links had
snapped. Perhaps it had been damaged in the attack on
the man.

Thomas Banks was more interested in the papers than
the stone. He almost snatched the item out of Hugh's hands.
The servant watched him unfurl the cylinder of parchment,
which contained lines of script. Of no use to Hugh Hall,
who was not able to read. He rubbed his fingers together.
They were sticky with little flakes of dried blood and threads

of material adhering to them. He felt he had earned the right to ask a question.

'Do you know who this is, sir?'

'What? Oh, yes, I know who it is. He is one of the Queen's company.'

The steward spoke distractedly. His attention was on the parchment, which he angled so that the words captured the light. He nodded a couple of times as though what he read was familiar to him. He sighed. He glanced at Hugh.

'These are verses,' said Thomas. 'A strange thing to find on the body of a dead man, eh?'

Hugh was not really surprised at anything done by the higher-ups in the palace. They had their own whys and wherefores. A corpse carrying a poem did not seem so very odd to him. The steward continued: 'I have heard these verses before. I heard them recited only last night by the very man who composed them. It is the story of a saint. A virgin saint.'

Now Hugh held up the chain and the steward took it. The dark red stone echoed the blood that had spilled from the body.

'That's a ruby, isn't it?' said Hugh.

'He wore it as a protection against poison and other evils,' said Thomas Banks. 'Much good it did him.'

II

Two Months Earlier

'The last time you were here, a murder took place,' said Richard Dunton.

'More than one of them,' said Geoffrey Chaucer, surprised that his friend was raising the subject at all. 'I remember there was a mason and another workman, and then there was—'

'A member of our order who also died,' said the Prior of Bermondsey.

Geoffrey noted the tactful way in which Prior Richard was referring to the death of the monk, as if it had been a natural death or an accident.* And he still wondered why these unhappy events were being mentioned at all until the prior explained.

'I know that the subject must be at the front of your mind. How can it be otherwise on your return to Bermondsey Priory? So I thought I would raise the matter first to get it out of the way. We are still grateful here for your discretion in that unfortunate business and we are glad to see you back, Geoffrey. I am glad.'

'Let us talk no more of murder then,' said Geoffrey. 'I am here for some peace and quiet to write.'

'And you have travelled from one mighty house on the Thames to another,' said the prior. 'The Palace of Savoy must be like a hive of bees, always busy, always buzzing.'

There was more than simple curiosity in Dunton's tone. A note of envy was detectable too. From his previous visit to Bermondsey, Geoffrey Chaucer remembered how knowledgeable Richard Dunton was about the outside world, or at least the royal part of it.

'Savoy is not so productive as a beehive. It's more like a nest of wasps or hornets. I do not visit there much anyway.'

'I remember you have a house in Aldgate as well.'

* See *House of Shadows*

'My books are there but the lodging is above the city gate itself, good for seeing life, not so good for writing about it.'

'Where your books are, there your heart surely is, Geoffrey?' The prior leaned forward in his chair and said, 'But your wife, Philippa, spends most of her time at the Savoy Palace, doesn't she?'

'She is one of several ladies in the service of Queen Constance of Castile,' said Geoffrey. 'Or in the service of the Duchess of Lancaster, if you prefer her English title.'

'And Philippa's sister is also in royal service?'

'Not exactly. Katherine helps to care for the children of John of Gaunt by his late wife.'

'So she is the *magistra* to the Duke of Lancaster's children, she is their director and guide.'

The prior spoke slowly as if instructing a class of children himself. Chaucer nodded but said nothing, hoping to cut off this line of talk. He did not want to talk about his sister-in-law. He was fairly sure that Richard Dunton wasn't so ignorant about Katherine Swynford's position in John of Gaunt's household as he pretended. Was he probing Geoffrey for extra information, or was he testing how much Geoffrey himself knew?

As if sensing his guest would give away nothing more, Richard Dunton sat back in his chair and took another sip of wine. They were sitting on either side of the fire in the prior's lodgings. It was a bright, cold evening in the spring. The abbey was poised between the canonical hours of vespers and compline. The day was drawing to a close. Soon supper would be brought in. Chaucer had little doubt that, because they were dining privately in the prior's quarters, they would be eating better than the monks in the refectory. It was almost three years since he'd last seen Richard Dunton and in the interim the prior had grown a little plumper in the face. The old adage about self-denial, that 'the sacrament makes a good breakfast', did not apply to him. But then, Geoffrey reflected, the same might be said of himself. Those early years during which he did service as a squire and a soldier had been followed by a more sedate, indulgent existence.

'Do you have a subject, Geoffrey?' said the prior, his eyes darting to an item that lay on a nearby desk. 'I mean, a theme to write about?'

Geoffrey shrugged. He did have a couple of possibilities – for example, the tale of a pair of star-crossed lovers in the ancient city of Troy – but he was curious to see what Richard Dunton was about to suggest. The prior rose from his seat and fetched a roll of parchment from the table. Still holding it, he returned to his chair by the fire.

'Have you heard of a saint called Beornwyn?'

'The virgin martyr? Yes, but she is little more than a name to me.'

'So many saints, so many stories,' said the prior. 'But this one is unusual.'

'They're all unusual,' was Geoffrey's response, then, seeing the look on the prior's face, somewhere between disappointment and disapproval, he drew up a fragment from the well of memory: 'Wasn't her modesty preserved by a veil of butterflies after her death?'

Prior Dunton looked pleased at that and then, deftly, he outlined the tale of St Beornwyn. The setting on the North Sea coast among local kings and warring tribes, the refusal of the noble-born Beornwyn to marry according to her father's wishes, her growing reputation as a virgin dedicated to Christ, her charity to the poor, the way an angel materialised to assist

185

her with copying out a psalm, and other marvels. Then came the darkness and violence as well as the real miracles that must appear in all saints' stories.

There was the slaughter of Beornwyn at the hands of coastal raiders, a slaughter that involved violation and sacrilege when the young woman was taken by surprise, at prayer, inside a cliff-top church. Yet the dire details of Beornwyn's death were transfigured by the butterfly veil, just as the story of her life transformed the lives of others. Her memory would draw warring peoples together. Her example would give heart to those embarking on the lonely path of virtue and self-denial. As he told this tale, Prior Richard's tone and expression fitted the moment: doleful, earnest, joyous. He barely glanced at the manuscript but made jabbing motions with it to emphasise particular points.

Almost despite himself, Geoffrey's imagination was stirred by what he heard. Perhaps it was the desolate scene of Beornwyn's martyrdom in St Oswald's church perched above the waves of the sea. Perhaps it was that blue winding-sheet composed of hundreds of butterflies.

'How did the manuscript come into your hands, Richard?'

'It has been lying here all this time, in the Bermondsey library. It is the belief of Brother Peter that the manuscript was deposited in our library more than a hundred years ago by another prior, also called Richard.'

Geoffrey remembered Brother Peter from his earlier visit, an elderly, stringy man who peered through his spectacles at one's face as if he were reading a book. He was glad to hear the librarian was still alive.

They were interrupted by the arrival of supper, brought in by two lay brothers. With reluctance Geoffrey and Richard shifted from their places by the fire. The prior replaced the manuscript on his desk and the two men moved to a table near a window, from which there was a view of the conventual church, a great shadow looming over the cloisters in the dusk. Candles were lit, food was served, fresh wine poured, and the lay brothers withdrew as wordlessly as they had come.

At first they ate in silence. Geoffrey was right. Fish of this quality – turbot and sole – would not be served up in the refectory. Nor would the open pie of cheese and the custard dishes that followed. Enjoying the food and wine, Chaucer was happy to wait and see where the Prior of Bermondsey would lead the conversation. He didn't think it was a coincidence that Richard Dunton happened to have on his desk the manuscript with the Beornwyn story while he was welcoming a new guest. And the prior had not recited that same story with real feeling just to show off his oratorical skill.

The prior complimented Chaucer on the lucrative post to which he had recently been appointed: controller of the taxes paid on both the wool and the wine passing through the port of London. Since it was John of Gaunt who was responsible for the double appointment, Chaucer played down his own merits and said something about the Duke of Lancaster's generosity. The prior's reply was that John of Gaunt had good reason to be grateful to Geoffrey. Chaucer thought they were getting close to dangerous territory again but it turned out that Richard Dunton was referring not to any secret understanding between Chaucer's sister-in-law and Gaunt, but to a poem that he had composed a few years earlier in memory of Gaunt's first wife, Blanche. The poem was called *The Book of the Duchess*. Copies of it were circulated in court, where it was also recited, and Geoffrey knew that the grieving John was consoled by the praise that he bestowed on 'my

Lady White'. Now, the Prior of Bermondsey claimed that he too had been moved by this elegy to a noble woman. As he mentioned this, his glance shifted towards the Beornwyn manuscript lying on his desk.

'So you think I might do the same for the virgin saint?' said Geoffrey, understanding the direction of the talk. 'Do you believe that Beornwyn deserves a memorial in verse, Richard?'

'Far be it from me to dictate what you should write,' said Dunton, leaning back in his chair, replete with food and drink, dabbing with a napkin at a spot of grease on his upper lip. 'I am merely offering it to you . . . so you might read the story at your leisure.'

'Then I'll look at it,' said Geoffrey. 'Thank you.'

Although Chaucer took the thing out of courtesy, he had no intention of reading it through. The more the prior pushed the subject at him, the more he resisted. He'd glance at the manuscript before handing it back together with some appropriate comment. He suspected that Richard was press-ing the Beornwyn story on him because, if Chaucer were to turn it into verse and circulate copies among the noble ladies and gentlemen of the Savoy Palace, then the whole business would reflect well on Bermondsey Priory and on Dunton himself. Cynical to think so, perhaps, but Geoffrey couldn't blame him for trying.

While the prior went off to compline, Chaucer returned to the guest-chamber that had been prepared for him. He was conducted there by a lay brother. The chamber was fur-nished with a bed, a large chest, a stool and a small table set under a window, which was shuttered. Geoffrey was half amused, half irritated to see that on the table top was an array of quill pens, pots of ink and sheets of paper. Not only was the prior determined he should compose a story (about St Beornwyn) but he was even providing the tools for the job, even if he had not gone to the expense of providing proper parchment to write on.

Apart from the writing gear, the simple furnishings of the room were very different from the comforts of the Savoy Palace or Chaucer's own accommodation at Aldgate. But he liked it in this place. Being on the far side of the river turned London almost into a foreign country. His life in the city itself was his public life. Yet, while Geoffrey's official positions at the port of London were lucrative, as the prior stated, they were not very onerous. In the meantime his wife was attached to the Duke of Lancaster's court and therefore better provided for than anything he could arrange for her. Philippa kept the children, Elizabeth and Thomas, with her too. He was happy to see them – and their mother – now and then. Geoffrey found himself with time on his hands. Time to write. The priory was a place where he was able to write. No doubt it was as riven with jealousy and pettiness as any place on God's earth must be, but nevertheless the atmosphere of labour and outward piety at Bermondsey was for Geoffrey Chaucer a spur to composition.

The bed in his room was well enough equipped to have a candle fixed to a bracket, which extended from the frame. Visitors were evidently expected to read and study. Once the lay brother departed, Geoffrey stretched out on the bed, intending merely to cast his eye over the tale of St Beornwyn before settling himself to sleep. But half an hour later he was still reading, although now with much greater alertness. He couldn't have said exactly why. The story of Beornwyn was related in a dialect with which he wasn't completely familiar, and therefore not always to be

understood straightaway. And, as he'd said half humor-
ously to the prior, the unusual features of this life were
actually quite normal, for a saint. So what gripped him?
Was it the setting on the rocky coast in the north country?
The butterfly veil? The image of a woman, alone and
assailed by attackers rising up from the sea? Some combi-
nation of these perhaps. Almost against his wishes, he
found himself becoming interested in this Beornwyn.

Eventually he put down the manuscript and lay back with
his hands cradling his head. He no longer felt tired but fresh
and lively, in mind at least. What could he do with St
Beornwyn now? Was she really as she had been written up
in this story? The virgin who rejects an arranged marriage,
the pure woman who keeps company with the angels.
Geoffrey thought of his sister-in-law, Katherine Swynford,
another woman with a name for piety. Katherine was a
young widow. She was also the lover of John of Gaunt, the
third son of King Edward but in point of importance the
second man in the kingdom. Given the King's decrepit state,
some would say he was first in the land. When a respectable
interval had elapsed after the death of his wife, Blanche,
whom he had sincerely loved, John married Constance, the
daughter of an ousted (and now dead) king of Castile. By so
doing, John had been anointed King of Castile, even if a
rival claimant was inconveniently in possession of the throne.
Though Constance was a beautiful and highly eligible bride,
this was a marriage of power and expediency. Geoffrey
Chaucer didn't think that John of Gaunt's heart was in the
union, whatever his head and his father – Edward III – dictated. No, John's heart and his other parts rested with
Katherine.

Chaucer wasn't certain when Katherine and John had

become lovers but it must have been at least four years previously because there was a child of their union, a boy now
rising three. He could ask Philippa, of course, but his wife
might not tell him, even assuming she was intimate with all
of her sister's secrets. But whenever it was that John and
Katherine began their liaison, both were widowed at the
time. Now Gaunt had a queen and a mistress, the two often
living under the same roof. Fortunately, the roof of the Savoy
Palace was very extensive. To the outside world, Katherine
had a reputation as a pious lady (the true parentage of the
child was known to very few). Yet while Katherine was genuinely devout, as Geoffrey was aware, she also had a hidden
passion for John of Gaunt.

He wondered if St Beornwyn had been, in truth, as pure
and pious as *she* was painted. An unholy thought occurred to
him, like a little imp darting through his head. Suppose
Beornwyn were no different from most other girls and
women. Suppose she had rejected her father's choice of husband not out of any desire to lead a virginal life but because
she already had a lover. A lover, whose identity or even existence had to be concealed for some reason – say, because
he was low-born or came from a rival family. All speculation,
of course, and probably a slander on the dead lady. But no
more unlikely than the story in the manuscript that the
Bermondsey prior was urging on him. In fact, if Richard
hadn't stressed Beornwyn's virginity so much, then Geoffrey
thought he might not be responding like this, with scepticism and a mischievous wish to undermine the legend.
Chaucer did not disbelieve in the legends of saints. But he
didn't quite believe in them either.

Almost before he knew it, he was lighting the candles that
stood on the little table, sitting on the stool, picking up one

of the quill pens, dipping it in the ink-pot and scrawling a few lines on a sheet of paper. The outline of the piece was clear in his head. He would cast it in the form of a dream. The first few lines turned into a page and then several pages. The thing flowed, via his hand, from his head onto the white sheets on the desk. He must have been writing for some time for he was dimly aware of the ringing of the matins bell, a time when it was closer to dawn than to dusk. The candles burned down, and still he scrawled away. Eventually, as light was creeping back into the sky and the birds were beginning to sing, Geoffrey rubbed his eyes. Now he was tired, but he was also satisfied. He left the scrawled sheets, returned to bed and settled down to sleep.

He woke at around the hour of terce, well into the day, so far as the monks were concerned. It was a sharp morning, the wind rattling at the shutters in the window of the guest-chamber. Geoffrey returned to the desk, sat down and read through what he had written in one continuous rush during last night. Strangely, it seemed to have been written by a different person from the one who was scanning it now. The piece began quietly enough, with the writer's inability to get to sleep after hearing the tale of the terrible martyrdom of a pure and virtuous woman. Then, when at last he begins to slumber, he starts to dream. In his dream the martyred woman is a very different being, a devotee not of Christ but of her passion for a man. She dies at the hands of the man's rival although the rumour is put about that she perished for her faith. When the dreamer awakes he is unable to decide which version to believe.

> Alas, I know not how to deem,
> To trust the story or the dream?

Geoffrey yawned. The piece needed plenty of work but the basic idea was there. It would surely go down well with a worldly audience such as the one at the Palace of Savoy. He wondered what his wife, Philippa, would make of it.

Meanwhile Chaucer's wife, Philippa, was not thinking at all of her husband, tucked away in Bermondsey Priory. If she had been thinking of him, then it would most likely have been in a baffled sort of way. For she could not understand his attraction to Bermondsey. It was a hushed, bookish spot, full of men, away from the colour and flurry of court life at the Savoy.

Like her husband, Philippa Chaucer owed her present position to John of Gaunt, and to the court service she had done for John's mother, the late Queen, also called Philippa. Now she was nominally in service of another queen, John's new wife from Spain. But like her husband, she found herself with time on her hands. Her duties at court were so light that they scarcely existed. She made a point of seeing her children often, but their immediate care and instruction was in the hands of others.

Philippa had just been talking with Elizabeth, her ten-year-old. Every morning she ran through what the girl had learned the previous day and gave her encouragement for the one to come. Because she was not from England, Philippa was concerned that her daughter in particular should be familiar with at least the French and Dutch languages. Her son, Thomas, showed less inclination for learning and, anyway, she felt boys were better able to fend for themselves.

After Elizabeth left, Philippa remained sitting by the fire. The morning was cold, with gusts of wind rattling

the windows. There was a knock at the door. She recognised this knock and called out for the visitor to enter.
Carlos de Flores came in, bowing his head a little. She
indicated he should sit opposite her, in the place recently
vacated by Elizabeth. He smiled and sat down, all the time
regarding her with his steady brown eyes.

When John of Gaunt brought his new bride home to the
Savoy Palace, the Castilian princess did not come alone.
Constance arrived with a retinue of counsellors, priests and
servants. And there were others whose precise functions were
not so well defined but who had to be found well-appointed
lodgings somewhere in the rambling spaces of the palace.
Carlos de Flores was one such individual. His English was
near-perfect and he had the manners of a courtier.

'I trust I find you well, madam.'

Before Philippa could reply another gust shook the panes
and cold air swirled round her feet.

'Well enough ... considering this weather.'

'Ah, yes,' said the Castilian. 'The weather. Before I came
to your country I was told that, of all things, the English like
to talk about their weather.'

'That must be because there's so much of it to talk about.'

Smiling to show that he had understood Philippa's joke,
Carlos de Flores said, 'You show yourself a true Englishwoman by saying so, madam, yet you are from Hainault
originally, are you not? You and your sister?'

Philippa wondered why de Flores was bothering to
mention this. It was no secret that she and Katherine were
the daughters of a knight who came from a small country
snuggled into a corner of Europe. Either the Castilian was
just passing the time or he was showing that he had dug a
little way into their histories.

'We come from Hainault, yes,' she said. 'This England was hardly more than a place across the seas where our father went to serve the Queen. Yet the weather in Hainault was very similar to here, Señor de Flores. In fact, I'd say it was worse.'

In her mind's eye Philippa saw the great flat spaces of her childhood scoured by wind and rain. She remembered the high summers, when the ditches dried up and she and Katherine, having nothing else to do, would watch the men at work in the fields. All this time she was conscious of the Castilian's gaze. He was stroking his hands on the arms of his chair as if they were made of fur rather than wood. His long fingers were adorned with rings.

'You are thinking of your country?' he said.

'That was many years ago, in my childhood.'

'Surely not *so* many, madam, to see you now.'

Despite herself she coloured slightly and said, 'I am past my youth.'

Seeing his success, de Flores persisted. 'We have a saying in my country. Only the owner closes the door on his youth – and its pleasures.'

I'm almost thirty, she wanted to say. I have two children and my husband has absented himself again. I know I am no beauty. If you want to compliment someone then go and talk to my sister. Her husband is dead and she is linked to one of the very highest in the land. I think you'll find she is more apt for this kind of talk than I am.

But she said none of this.

Then she saw his brown eyes looking at her in the eager way of a dog when it wants something, a kind word, a scrap of food. Perhaps he was in earnest after all. He was about the same age as she was. Darker complexioned, of course. You couldn't deny he was handsome, although his nose was too small for her liking. She smiled slightly at his gallantry.

'In this country you cannot tell what season it is, but in Castile we would have put the winter and spring behind us by now,' said de Flores, as if returning the conversation to a more innocent level. 'Everything would be set fair for many months.'

'You miss your homeland, Señor de Flores?'

'I go where my duty calls me, madam. And I am surrounded by my countrymen here. Countrymen and countrywomen. There is little chance to be – how do you say it? – to be sad for the home. Besides, one may be sad anywhere. Even at home one may be sad, wouldn't you agree?'

'Your duty, Señor de Flores? You mentioned your duty. What exactly is your duty here? I am confused, there are so many visitors to this household and they have so many functions.'

'Mine is simple. I am here to serve the Queen of Castile.'

'The Duchess of Lancaster, you mean.'

'They are one and the same.'

'But we are in England now, and so she has become a member of the house of Lancaster.'

'Madam, it would gratify me to believe that we are on sufficiently good terms for you to call me Carlos. After all, we both serve the *Duchess* – however she is styled.'

'So it is good that we at least know our functions, Carlos,' she said.

'Yes. And now I must take my leave . . . madam.'

De Flores half levered himself from the chair and paused as if giving her the opportunity to say that he too might call her by her given name of Philippa rather than the formal 'madam'. But she said nothing. As he was leaving the chamber, he turned round by the door.

'Where is your husband?'

'About his own business.'

'He is away for long?'

'He too has his duties,' she said, evading the question. 'He'll return when they are done.'

Carlos de Flores smiled and closed the door. Philippa went to stand by the window. No boats were visible on the river apart from a barge that was wallowing in midstream. She didn't altogether trust Carlos the Castilian yet she couldn't, at this stage, see what he might be after. To get to her sister, Katherine Swynford? Perhaps. It was even possible that de Flores was hoping to gain access to John of Gaunt through her. But why? And if that was his intention, the shorter route would surely have been through Constance herself since the Castilian was already a member of the Duchess's extended entourage, much closer to her than Philippa would ever be.

There was another, more remote possibility. It was that de Flores was interested in Philippa Chaucer for herself. The notion was so far-fetched that she almost laughed aloud. Yet she remembered his attentive brown-eyed gaze, almost wistful. There'd been his remark about youth and pleasure. His query about Geoffrey's absence. Did he somehow want to take advantage of it? Because the idea was attractive (though far-fetched of course) she did her best to crush it.

The next day they met twice. The encounters looked accidental. But on both occasions Philippa Chaucer had the sense that Carlos de Flores had been waiting to catch her.

The first time was in a public passageway. De Flores seemed on the verge of going beyond the normal pleasantries but, with his eyes flickering over the frequent passers-by, he evidently thought better of it. The second occasion was in the gardens of the Savoy Palace. It was calm and bright now. Philippa was walking by herself in one of the orchard alleys. Apple blossom strewed the grass. Carlos de Flores suddenly appeared at her side. He made some remarks about their second encounter of the day and about the change in the weather and then jokingly suggested that such a comment showed he was turning into a true Englishman. Philippa smiled. She knew the Castilian wasn't going to be put off.

'A beautiful day, as you say.'

'A day for poets.'

'I suppose so. My husband would know. He is the one who writes verses.'

'I've heard great things of your husband – and of his verses. The Duke of Lancaster values him highly.'

Philippa was always slightly surprised by the esteem in which Geoffrey was held. She was not, however, surprised that de Flores should know of her husband's verse-writing since the Castilian seemed to have set himself the task of finding out about her and her family. They turned from one orchard alley to another. The river glinted through the trees. The gardeners, at work, scarcely looked up as the finely dressed couple walked by.

'John of Gaunt, now, he also values your sister highly,' said de Flores after a pause.

'The Duke of Lancaster knows how to esteem those who do him service. He is a generous man.'

'Service takes many forms, Philippa ...' said de Flores, hesitating for an instant in case she objected to the familiarity. 'You are close to the lady Katherine?'

Philippa Chaucer stopped in the middle of the walkway, compelling de Flores to stop also. She looked him straight in the eye. She'd never had much time for evasion.

'You ask if we are close, Katherine and I? Well, we fought as children and did not like each other very much for long periods. Afterwards our paths went in different directions. She married a knight who was like my father. I married a man who is most comfortable among his books. Even though Hugh Swynford is dead now, Katherine is ... you might say that she is well provided for. Better than I, perhaps. Yet we remain sisters, tied by blood and memories.'

'Thank you,' said de Flores. 'Your husband has written poems for her, has he not?'

Philippa laughed. 'There you are wrong. Geoffrey wrote about John of Gaunt's first wife, not Katherine.'

'I apologise for my error.'

He seemed about to say more but broke off and glanced down the alley. Between the line of trees three men were advancing towards them, sombre against the blossom. Philippa recognised the person in the middle as a Castilian by the name of Luis, one of several priests in the service of Constance. This individual stood out, mostly on account of a large pectoral cross, which gleamed with precious stones. The other two, by their dress and the way they inclined their heads respectfully towards Luis, were his countrymen.

'Let us speak of some other subject, madam,' de Flores said, pointing at the nearest apple trees. 'Grafting, for example.'

And, as the three men passed them, de Flores talked loudly of 'slips' and 'scions'. While he was speaking, he gave the merest tilt of his head to Luis, who nodded in return. The priest was touching his cross, dabbing his hand to it. He wore yet more emeralds and sapphires on his fingers. The other men looked curiously at Philippa and de Flores.

When they were out of earshot, Philippa tried to make light of things and said, 'I did not know that you were a gardener, Señor de Flores. Slips and scions indeed!'

'I am no gardener. But I have talked to some of those who work here. I have listened to their words. It is surprising what you learn.'

Philippa knew that he was referring to more than the gardeners' terms about grafting. They reached another crossing-point in the garden walks.

'I shall go this way,' said de Flores. 'It would be best if we parted for now. But I hope we shall meet again. These gardens are a pleasant place for walking and talking, especially in such delightful company.'

He bowed slightly and strode off. Philippa returned to the palace. She was more confused. What was he after? Why the questions about Geoffrey's verses? She wondered why de Flores suddenly started talking about an innocent subject as they passed the priest. She thought the glances and nods that passed between the two Castilians were not just a greeting. There was something complicit in those glances and nods.

III

Geoffrey Chaucer remained at Bermondsey Priory for another ten days, enjoying the hospitality of the prior and the ordered shape of the life there. He wrote and he read and he talked with the prior and with the aged librarian. Brother Peter. When he left, it was with his work about St Beornwyn revised, rewritten and completed. He handed the original manuscript back to Richard Dunton, thanking him for telling him the story of the saint's life in the first place. Dunton was pleased. Chaucer didn't spoil his mood by telling him he might not be quite so glad when he eventually read the piece for it cast a not altogether complimentary light on Beornwyn.

Geoffrey returned to his lodgings in Aldgate, and greeted Joan, the woman who cooked and kept the place for him in the absence of his wife (and his wife was almost always absent). She was a good housekeeper who tended to treat his presence as an intrusion. She looked more like a grand-mother than a mother but had a young son, called Thomas, whom Geoffrey was teaching to read, in a fitful way. The boy was about eight, younger than Chaucer's own son, also called Thomas, and he was useful round the Aldgate lodg-ings. Once Geoffrey had attended to some customs business, he visited a copier near St Paul's and arranged for three copies to be made of the Beornwyn poem. Two of these he would give to the more discriminating members of the Savoy Palace household. At a later date, if invited, he would recite the poem to an audience, a select one.

As it happened he'd been reminded of the Savoy Palace even before crossing the bridge back into the city. Leaving Bermondsey Priory on foot, Chaucer stopped off at the Tabard Inn. This was one of his bolt holes in Southwark, not so respectable as the priory, of course, but more reputable than some of the commercial establishments further west along the river, among which were many brothels. In fact, the host of the Tabard, Harry Bailey, was making efforts to attract a better class of customer, for example by purchasing higher quality wines. This particular location in Southwark, on the main road leading towards the southeast, was a natural gathering-place for those intending to start on the pilgrimage to the shrine of Thomas Becket in Canterbury. Chaucer thought he could identify a few pilgrims assembling here now, quite early on this spring morning. It was not only their travelling clothes but their expressions, somewhere between excited and smug, which gave them away.

Harry Bailey was pleased to see Geoffrey. The host was an ample, cheerful figure, naturally interested in his customers and not only for the sake of business they bought. He recommended his Rhenish – 'New in yesterday, sir. Go down to the cellar and see the markings on the barrel for yourself' – but Geoffrey apologetically explained that he'd had enough of good wine while at Bermondsey and ordered honest ale instead. He went to sit in a corner and watch the world go by. He was amusing himself by guessing at the professions and trades of the pilgrims gathering in a group at one end of the room when his attention was caught by a penetrating voice from closer by. He turned to look. Not all of Harry Bailey's guests were of the pious pilgrim type, and the cluster of men crowding round a neighbouring table were what you might call old Southwark.

'He is a changeling, I tell you! His filthy riches stink to high heaven. His white house is finer than the King's! And his new duchess is a foreign bitch who cannot even wrap her tongue round God's good English.'

The speaker was a man with a stubbly scalp, which showed beneath an undersized red cap. His drink sat neglected on the table in front of him as he used his right forefinger to tick off his accusations on the fingers of his left hand. The other four individuals round the table said nothing but nodded or remained still. They were sitting back slightly as if wary of these fierce words, and so giving Geoffrey a clear view.

'How much longer must we bear this tyrant? How many more insults must we endure from the very existence of the traitor? How often will we be forced to bow the knee before this whoreson prince?'

Now the speaker was using his fist to thump on the table, emphasising each angry question. Geoffrey sighed. He glanced across at Harry Bailey but the Tabard host was busy chatting to a couple of the pilgrims. Chaucer did not think Bailey would appreciate the kind of talk coming from the next table. He didn't appreciate it himself. Had it been overheard by someone with real authority and the desire to exercise it, then the speaker could have found himself in serious trouble. For the subject of the man's rant was John of Gaunt, the Duke of Lancaster. The references to his great wealth, to the white house that was finer than the King's, to his foreign wife, made it clear enough. In addition, there was the mention of John being a changeling. This was a rumour, lately creeping about London, to the effect that thirty-five years previously, Queen Philippa, the wife of Edward III, had given birth to an unfortunate girl which, like a sow, she had overlain and suffocated. Terrified of telling the truth to her royal husband, she substituted a baby boy for the girl child. To compound the insult, it was said that the boy was the son of a labourer from Ghent.

Wearily, Geoffrey Chaucer got to his feet. He moved the short distance to the table where red-cap sat among his companions. It looked as though he was about to launch on another string of insults and rhetorical demands.

Chaucer, clutching his drink, said mildly: 'Excuse me, but I couldn't help hearing what you were saying.'

The man with the little red cap looked up in surprise. The others round the table instinctively shifted further away on their stools, trying to dissociate themselves from their friend.

'So what if you did hear?'

'I have news for you,' said Chaucer. 'That story you were telling about John of Gaunt being a changeling . . .' He noticed the expressions on the faces of the men. Now they were really worried.

'Well, that is what he is,' said the speaker, although his tone was a little less certain. 'What is your news?'

'Gaunt is no changeling but he is something stranger, much stranger.'

All the time Geoffrey was speaking low, as though imparting a secret. Then he leaned forward and placed his wooden mug on the table, allowing the curiosity of the men to build up, making himself part of the group. When he judged the moment was right, he said: 'Much stranger, I say again. I have it on good authority that the Duke of Lancaster is the offspring of a dragon and a mermaid. Furthermore, he was conceived during a thunderstorm.'

'Authority? Whose authority?' said the one who'd claimed Gaunt was a changeling.

'I have sources inside the Savoy Palace at the very highest level,' said Geoffrey. 'I will take an oath on that.'

'Is it true? Is Lancaster really the child of a dragon and a mermaid?'

The speaker was another young man at the table. His voice was naturally high, not only with surprise at what he was hearing. His words caught the attention of a tall, lanky fellow who was passing and who stopped for a moment to listen.

'Yes, it is as true as I'm standing here,' said Geoffrey, thinking that there was a kind of truth to what he was saying, the same sort of truth as in the story of Beornwyn. He could see that his quiet confidence was having an effect, not so much on the original speaker as on the others, including the tall man who was still hesitating nearby. Their glances flickered towards the red-capped man, who said: 'It's absurd! How would a dragon and a mermaid have congress?'

Chaucer raised his eyebrows slightly as if the question itself were absurd. 'By asking that, you betray the limits of your understanding, my friend. The laws that apply to mere mortals do not apply to the gods – or to dragons and mermaids. No more than they apply to basilisks, griffins or unicorns. Only an ignorant individual would think otherwise.'

There were signs of agreement from the listeners round the table. The high-voiced young man was nodding his head in a sage sort of way. The tall fellow was perhaps not so convinced, since he merely raised his eyebrows before moving off. Satisfied, Geoffrey picked up his pint pot and returned to his seat. He knew not to press home his advantage. Leave the group to mull over the idea he'd planted in their heads. He had succeeded in his principal aim, which was to quieten the fiery man in the red cap. Geoffrey shifted his attention back to the pilgrims at the far end of the room. Two or three individuals more had joined since he last looked, including the tall man. Out of the corner of his eye he observed the group at the neighbouring table as it broke up until the only one left was the speaker. When he'd finished his drink he too got up to leave. On the way out he paused by Chaucer's seat.

'It is I who am right, my *friend*. John of Gaunt is a changeling, and not what he seems. Just as the house where he lives is a front for all manner of corruption and iniquity, and full of foreign filth. You say you have sources inside the Savoy Palace. Well, so do I, I tell you.'

Chaucer kept his face impassive at these last words, the only unexpected thing the man had uttered. This lack of response provoked him further. He leaned in slightly and said: 'The day will come when all the fine folk within Savoy walls will tremble at the wrath of the common people. The day will come when that white house is reduced to a pile of grey ash.'

This was very dangerous and foolish talk. Geoffrey was losing patience but he still did not respond, simply staring calmly at the man. Finally, realising he wasn't getting anywhere, the red-cap stalked out of the Tabard with a curious, stiff gait. Chaucer finished his own drink, giving the other time to go a distance, and then, after promising Harry Bailey that he'd try the Rhenish on his next visit, he made for the door. Standing in his way was the tall individual who had listened in on the earlier conversation.

'A dragon and a mermaid! Ha! I would rather have said that John of Lancaster was the offspring of Mars and Venus.'

Geoffrey had to look up at the speaker, who was more than a head taller. His face was battered and scarred but he wore an amused look.

'The child of Mars and Venus? That would turn Lancaster into Cupid, wouldn't it?' said Geoffrey, struggling to envisage Gaunt as a plump, mischievous child with a quiverful of arrows slung over his shoulder. Well, yes, he might

have been like that once. The other man must have come to
the same conclusion for he too smiled.

'You were having trouble over there?' said the man, nodding his head towards the place that Geoffrey had just left.
'I saw that insolent person trying to bait you. I almost came
across to give him a piece of . . . my mind.'

Geoffrey shrugged. A brawl was exactly what he had
been trying to avoid. He recognised the man in front of
him, recognised not who he was but rather what he was.
While they were talking he'd been running his eyes over
the other's clothing. Like his face it was battered but of
sound quality. His tunic, of thick fustian, was patterned
with a network that looked like rust. It was the imprint of
the chain mail he had been wearing. That, together with
his assured voice and manner, was enough to tell Geoffrey
that here was—

'Sir Edward Jupe, at your service,' said the man, thrusting
his hand forward.

They shook hands. Geoffrey introduced himself. Sir
Edward scratched his head as if he might have heard the
name. Geoffrey asked if he was going to join the pilgrimage
since the knight seemed to be part of the group assembling
in the Tabard. Also he was aware that fighting men of Jupe's
rank often went on a pilgrimage after campaigning, either as
a way of giving thanks for their survival or perhaps because
they simply couldn't settle down.

'No, Master Chaucer, there is no pilgrimage for me. I am
acquainted with a couple of the gentlemen who are on their
way to Canterbury, that's all,' said the knight, glancing
towards the company. 'I have delayed here a moment to
greet my friends. My destination is much closer. I have not
seen my lady for these many months.'

And so, thought Chaucer, you show your eagerness by visiting her with your tunic unchanged and rust-spotted. It occurred to him that the marks might equally well be blood. Still, that was what some ladies liked in their men, newly returned from the wars. He didn't ask where Sir Edward had been campaigning. There was always a war going on somewhere.

'I hope you find her well . . . but not too well.'

'What do you mean?' said Sir Edward, an angry look replacing the previous good humour. 'What do you mean, sir?'

'Only that your lady must surely be feeling the absence of her knight, and that your return will restore her to perfect health. Nothing more than that.'

'Ah, just so. If you'll forgive me,' said the knight, bowing before making to withdraw towards the group of pilgrims. Chaucer at last was permitted to quit the Tabard, and to reflect on his two meetings. The encounter with the red-capped man had not been pleasant but he knew that what the agitator said was not so different from what many Londoners believed, even if few would dare to say it out loud. John of Gaunt was unpopular not merely on account of his fabulous wealth and because he had been unsuccessful in various recent military adventures, but because he had married a foreign queen, Constance of Castile. He was thought to be over-mighty, arrogant and devious. There was some truth in all of these accusations.

Geoffrey Chaucer was pleased with his quick invention in the Tabard Inn. The claim that Gaunt was the product of a dragon and a mermaid had a kind of poetic truth to it. After all, what was Edward III in his younger campaigning days but a dragon heaping fire and destruction on his enemies?

And Queen Philippa, dead these last seven years, had been in her young days a notable beauty: like a siren, like a mermaid. Thinking these things, Geoffrey felt the sheaf of papers inside his coat. The story of Beornwyn.

Once he had called at his Aldgate lodgings and visited the scribe by St Paul's church and handed him the sheets with instructions to make three copies, Geoffrey Chaucer proceeded westwards towards the Savoy. He intended to visit his wife and children. The morning was warm and bright, and the streets crowded. He thought of the pilgrims about to set off from Southwark, and half envied them their ride away from the smoke and smell of the city. It took him about half an hour to reach the area of the palace. The Strand was paved until this point and then the paving gave up, as if the thoroughfare was not interested in anyone who wanted to travel beyond the Savoy.

The section facing the street gave little idea of the beauty and splendour that lay within. A long, fortified wall prevented passers-by from seeing or even guessing at anything of the interior. In the middle of the wall was an enormous gateway, secured by a portcullis. Since this was only raised for ceremonial entrances and exits, the usual way in was via a pedestrian gate – itself by no means small – a few yards away from the principal one. This gate was not kept closed, because there was so much traffic in and out, but a couple of liveried members of the household kept a discreet watch on everyone.

As he was approaching this entrance, Geoffrey was surprised to see someone who looked like the irate man from the Tabard Inn walking ahead of him. And even more surprised when red-cap turned into the Savoy gate. Any doubt about his identity was dispelled when he cast a quick look behind him as he entered. Chaucer ducked his head just in time. He noticed that the man was not intercepted by the gate-keepers, which suggested that they knew him. He recalled what the man had said about having his own sources inside the Savoy. Perhaps he was speaking the truth.

Geoffrey waited a few moments. When he passed through the gate, he nodded at the gatemen, who dipped their heads slightly as a mark of deference. Geoffrey was known to them – as the husband of a demoiselle serving Queen Constance and as the brother-in-law to Katherine Swynford – but he was not important enough to merit a proper bow. He stopped and spoke to the sharper-looking of the doormen.

'Someone came through here a few moments ago, a man wearing a red cap. You know who it was?'

'I believe his name is John.'

'It is John Hall, sir,' said the other doorman. 'I know him because I know Hugh, his brother, who is in the household. John is often here.'

That explained red-cap's familiarity with the Savoy. Chaucer thanked them. He said nothing more to the door-men but decided to report John Hall to one of the stewards. Violent and seditious talk against the Duke of Lancaster by one who regularly visited the Savoy could not be tolerated.

Immediately inside the entrance and to the right was a chapel and a library, and beyond lay some of the extensive accommodation for the servants, as well as the stables. The bigger apartments and the state rooms were on the river side of the palace. Geoffrey made his way along passages and up and down stairs and through cloistered spaces towards his wife's lodgings. As he drew nearer to them, the very fabric of the building seemed to grow lighter and more airy. He arrived at the ornate lobby outside Philippa's door and was taken aback to encounter a group of men waiting there in sober silence. He recognised one of them, a steward called Thomas Banks. The others were regular members of Gaunt's retinue.

Geoffrey's first response was one of alarm. He asked what was wrong and then, when Banks put a finger to his lips as a sign for quiet, asked again more loudly. The steward was prevented from replying by the opening of the door behind him. A long face looked out. A long body followed. At once the gaggle of men drew right back as if they were trying to sink into the rich hangings on the walls while Banks himself bowed deeply. As did Geoffrey Chaucer, for the man who had emerged from Philippa's chamber was none other than John of Gaunt, the Earl of Richmond and Derby, of Leicester and Lincoln, as well as the Duke of Lancaster and the King of Castile.

'Geoffrey! How very pleasant it is to see you again. May I entreat you to enter your own wife's quarters.'

Chaucer was conscious of Gaunt's retainers looking at him with respect – that warm, almost eager welcome from their master! – perhaps tinged with amusement. Was anything mischievous intended by that remark about his wife's quarters? Gaunt himself held the door open for Geoffrey to go in. He did it with a touch of mock servility. He was in a good mood. The reason became apparent the moment Geoffrey got inside his wife's chamber. On the far side of the room, close by the windows overlooking the Thames, stood Gaunt's mistress, Katherine Swynford. She smiled to see him. Her smile warmed his heart in a way that his wife's did not, even though the women were sisters.

'Philippa claims that the view from here is even better

than the one from my apartment,' said Katherine. 'The
Duke of Lancaster decided to see for himself.'

'You may not believe it, Geoffrey, but there are rooms in
the Savoy that I have never entered,' said John of Gaunt.

Since there were hundreds of rooms in the palace, most of
which Gaunt would never dream of visiting, this was hardly
news, but Chaucer put on a face suggesting mild surprise. He
understood that it might be useful for Katherine and Gaunt
occasionally to meet out of the public eye – if you disregarded
all those retainers waiting outside. What place more conven-
ient than Philippa's chamber, at the other end of the palace
from the area reserved for Constance of Castile and her party?
Gaunt was lately returned with his duchess from Bruges,
where he had concluded a peace treaty with the French. He
had been parted from Katherine for some time. Not that anything improper had been occurring just now. The two lovers
had evidently been chatting and laughing together, like any
couple at ease in each other's company. Gaunt was dressed in
a dark blue jupon, sparsely tagged with gold buckles and hangings, quite informal. Katherine was likewise clad in blue, a
tight-fitting gown that emphasised her full figure.

'Where have you come from, Geoffrey? You look as
though you've walked a distance.'

'I've come from Aldgate, my lord, and before that I was at
Bermondsey Priory.'

Gaunt picked up on the priory reference, as Geoffrey perhaps intended he should. He started asking questions, staring
hard at Chaucer. An aquiline nose – his father's legacy –
separated penetrating eyes. As always when he was talking to
Gaunt, or rather being talked to, he was conscious of the
Duke's height. The questioning continued. What had
Chaucer been doing at Bermondsey? Writing. Ah, yes, of

course he had been writing. His subject? A poem about a saint. Who? Beornwyn? No, I have not heard of her.

'That's because she is known for her virginity,' said Katherine to John, and gave a small laugh. Her laugh was one of her most attractive features. She added: 'And St Beornwyn is chiefly known for the fact that her violated body was shrouded by butterflies.'

Gaunt and his mistress were curious now. Geoffrey was encouraged to produce this latest offering, encouraged to distribute the poem, to read it aloud to his friends and admirers at court. Geoffrey put up the tiniest show of reluctance and, secretly delighted, agreed to produce the copies as soon as possible. Then they seemed to remember why he was here in Philippa's chamber. Katherine said: 'If you are looking for your wife, Geoffrey, she is walking outside on the terraces. The day is a pleasant one for exercise.'

It was a polite dismissal. Bowing to Gaunt and Katherine, who were now standing side by side, Geoffrey withdrew. The retinue outside the door relaxed when they saw it was only he who was emerging from the room. Geoffrey nodded at the steward, Thomas Banks. As he was threading his way through yet more corridors and cloisters, he remembered that he'd intended to tell someone about John Hall, the man in the Tabard. Yet, inside the Savoy and its vast precincts, the firebrand's words seemed rather puny. To attempt anything against the palace and its inhabitants would be like kicking against the side of a mountain.

Once outside, he paused to admire the view. Geoffrey knew that Gaunt took a well-informed interest in the Savoy gardens, an interest that accounted for their colour and their order. Rose gardens and borders of flowers were interspersed with orchards, while each end of the terraces was given over to herb and vegetable plantations, together with a couple of well-stocked fish ponds. In between were paths and gently graded steps leading down to the low wall fronting the sweep of the river

There were quite a few people outside, apart from the gardeners, strolling singly or in pairs and small groups. Shading his eyes against the sun, Chaucer glanced about for Philippa, without expecting to see her so soon. Indeed, he nearly missed her because she was in company and not female company either. She walked past almost directly below where he was standing on the topmost terrace, about three levels down. He did not recognise the gentleman deep in conversation with his wife. The man was elegantly dressed but not in the English style. Their heads, when they could be glimpsed through new foliage and branches, were close together. The couple reached a clear space at the end of a walk, turned round and paused before retracing their steps. Chaucer heard Philippa's laugh, distinct, louder than her sister, Katherine's. Her companion grasped her by the upper arm. Or perhaps he simply touched her there. Geoffrey couldn't be sure at this distance. He stood in thought, undecided what to do, before a bell sounding twelve, from one of the newly installed clocks in the palace, brought him back to himself.

He went down the nearest flight of steps until he reached the terrace where Philippa and her friend were strolling. Except that they were no longer together. Coming towards him along the walk between trees and shrubs was the well-dressed individual. He was handsome with a neatly cut beard. Definitely not English, and so probably part of the Castilian company. He was moving rapidly and scarcely looked at Chaucer as he passed. At the far end of the walk Philippa was standing motionless.

Geoffrey went towards her. When he was close enough, he called her name and raised his hand slightly in greeting. She did not smile as her sister had done. She looked neither pleased nor displeased to see him. Instead she looked pre-occupied. Perhaps it was something the Castilian had said to her. Chaucer didn't ask. He gave no indication that he had been watching her, let alone asking who it was she had been walking with.

Philippa and Geoffrey Chaucer talked cordially enough. He asked about the children. She asked what he had been doing at Bermondsey Priory. He explained that he had encountered the Duke of Lancaster and Katherine in Philippa's chamber. And so on ...

If Geoffrey had turned and followed the Castilian instead of going on to speak to his wife, he might have discovered something more interesting, even worrying. Carlos de Flores was walking fast because he had suddenly remembered that he was due to meet someone. It was the same sound of the noon-day clock bell that Geoffrey heard that prompted him to leave Philippa in a hurry. He walked up the gardens on a diagonal slant and then through the palace. Much of the Savoy was still a maze to him although he was familiar with parts of it, such as the route to the stables. Waiting for him in a shaded corner of the large, high-walled yard was the red-capped individual whom Chaucer had encountered in the Tabard Inn. No courtesies were exchanged between the two men, they fell to talking straight away. Anyone observing the two – the Castilian and the Londoner – would have realised that they had business together, and that something about their postures suggested that it was confidential.

The red-cap did most of the talking, while de Flores nodded from time to time. Then they must surely have had some sort of disagreement for red-cap started to raise his voice, as he had in the tavern. There was no one about, only some liveried grooms keeping to the sunny side of the great yard, but the foreigner put his hand on the other's shoulder, to soothe him or control him. The hand was angrily shrugged off and red-cap stalked away with that stiff gait that Chaucer had already observed. He went off in the direction of the gate on the Strand. De Flores stared after him for a while before retracing his steps to the more refined area of the palace.

Yet this meeting had not gone unobserved. A woman had been keeping a distant eye on de Flores for the last half-hour or more. She had already witnessed his deliberate encounter in the gardens with Philippa Chaucer and his abrupt departure from her. The expression on her face as she saw the Castilian and the Englishwoman was not difficult to read. It was one of anger. She scurried to keep up with Carlos de Flores as he strode through the palace and then, keeping in the shadows, she watched the Castilian meet the man with the red cap. She had distinctive features, this woman in the shadows: a hawk-like nose, black eyes, a smile that could quickly be replaced with an angry baring of the teeth. But it would have been difficult to interpret her reaction to what she had been watching for the last few minutes, Carlos de Flores in conversation with a red-capped man. Neither pleasure or displeasure, but curiosity perhaps.

IV

So things went on quietly enough for a couple of months. Spring turned into summer. Philippa Chaucer continued her sojourn at the Savoy Palace. Geoffrey spent most of his time at Aldgate and at Wool Wharf, down by the river, attending to his duties as Controller of Customs. But things were not so quiet for Geoffrey's patron, John of Gaunt. With the King's oldest son, Edward, close to death and the King himself in a decline that was scarcely less steep, John was forced to attend Parliament to hear charges that the King was burdening his people with too much tax, and – although these accusations weren't made so explicitly – that the money raised was being wasted or used for corrupt purposes. Geoffrey Chaucer heard from Philippa and other insiders reports of Gaunt's fury at the insolence of the Commons. Yet however much Gaunt might storm and vow to crush the upstarts, for the moment the tide of events was against him and his family, and so he was compelled to make concessions.

It was perhaps for the sake of diversion from all these troubles that Geoffrey was encouraged to recite his latest work, the story of St Beornwyn, to the cream of the Savoy court.

Thomas Banks himself passed on the word. 'My master – our master – would be glad to hear your tale of the saint and the butterflies,' he said. The steward was obviously in the confidence of the Duke of Lancaster. Perhaps there was more to him than there appeared.

Chaucer visited the St Paul's copier to whom he had entrusted his original script and, after paying the two marks agreed on, he received three copies in return. Back in Aldgate, he checked through the manuscripts for accuracy. They were neat and clean, though in no way decorated or ornate. Geoffrey remained pleased with his invention in the story of St Beornwyn, the way he had subtly cast doubt on the truth of the legend. Now he intended to send two of the copies to the palace in advance of his public reading. It helped if a handful of his audience was familiar with what he was about to say. It was like seeding the ground in the hope of a good crop of applause and praise.

Late one sunny morning a couple of days afterwards, Chaucer was returning from his office at Wool Wharf. His head was full not only of wool but of wine, or rather the columns of figures, weights, bales, tuns, shipping rosters and commissions that made up most of his reading at work. It was only as he got to the front door of his Aldgate lodgings that he noticed, to his surprise, that the door was ajar. This was unusual because the flow of traffic through the nearby gate, which was the principal route in and out of this eastern part of the city, made it unwise to leave the place open or unguarded. Geoffrey pushed at the door. Inside was a sparsely furnished lobby, with one spiral flight of steps leading up to Geoffrey's set of rooms, which straddled the gate itself, and another, smaller flight going straight down to a cellar. The only illumination came through a narrow, barred slit in the stone wall beside the front door. But now, by the sunlight streaming in from the street, Chaucer saw Joan bending over a diminutive figure who was slouched on a bench against the wall.

To his alarm, he realised that it was young Thomas. His mother was using a cloth to try to stanch blood dripping from the lad's head. Alerted by the sound of the door and the increase of light, Joan looked round. The fear on her lined face was replaced by relief.

'Thank God it is you, sir.'

'What's happened? Is he all right?'

The boy himself raised one hand slightly in response but said nothing.

'I need to get water and a poultice.'

'Go on, Joan. I'll stay and look after him.'

Geoffrey took the sodden cloth and kept it pressed against the boy's forehead. With his other hand he cradled the back of Thomas's head. It did not appear that much damage had been done, only a nasty though superficial gash producing blood that was already flowing less freely. Joan disappeared up the spiral stairs. Chaucer made reassuring sounds to Thomas. He was fond of the lad. He allowed him to call him Geoffrey. He thought that he probably saw more of this Thomas than of his own son. He glanced round. The door was still half open. From the street came the rumble of carts and carriages and the constant shuffle of pedestrians converging on the gate. Chaucer wondered what had happened.

Joan returned with a container of water, more cloths and other gear. Geoffrey was glad to hand back responsibility to her. He waited until she had cleaned up the boy's wound and applied a poultice to his head before fastening the front door. Then together with Joan he assisted the lad up the steep steps to the first floor. The boy was shaky on his legs but otherwise seemed all right. He kept apologising to Chaucer for something he'd done – or hadn't done – and muttering some words about a king, but Geoffrey waved it aside and was relieved when Joan dispatched him to lie down in the little chamber that mother and son shared.

It took him some time to piece together everything that had happened. He had an account from Joan and, later, when the boy was almost fully recovered, from little Thomas. It seemed that a well-dressed individual had come knocking at the Aldgate door, which was opened by Thomas, his mother being occupied on the upper floor. The man explained that he was calling on the King's business and that it was most urgent he should see Master Chaucer. Was the gentleman in? Thomas said not (and Geoffrey reflected that anyone knowing his routine would also know he was unlikely to be in at that hour of the morning). The stranger asked if he could wait for the master of the house in his office. The matter was very urgent, very important. The King's business, the King's business. He repeated this many times over. He waved some scroll with a big red seal attached. By this time Joan had appeared. She didn't say so but Geoffrey guessed she was a little overawed by the visitor's manner, by his talk, by the sealed scroll. He was shown up to Geoffrey's domestic office, which occupied a central space over the gate itself. She did not think to ask the guest's name. Besides, what harm could he do in a musty old room full of books? Joan didn't say this either, but Chaucer was familiar with the housekeeper's opinion of his room and his books.

It was Thomas who did not trust the stranger or who became curious. After a few minutes, the boy crept to the door of Geoffrey's room, which was not shut tight, and heard the sound of papers being rustled and the soft thud of items being shifted about. Thomas knew that something wasn't right. He pushed his head round the door and saw the stranger bending over Chaucer's desk, hurriedly pushing volumes and manuscripts to one side as if he wanted to be rid of them. Then he gasped and took a manuscript over to the window to look at it in a better light. He nodded to himself, went back to the desk and scooped up several more loose sheets of paper. Then he glanced round and saw the boy standing in the doorway.

All of this Thomas related in a clear, almost descriptive

manner. He turned it into an exciting story. He even imitated the stranger's sigh as the man realised he had found what he was looking for. Chaucer was proud of Thomas. He reassured the boy, who seemed more anxious that Geoffrey might not want to continue teaching him to read than he was concerned about anything else. Unlike his mother, he had a respect for the twenty-five or so handwritten volumes that had pride of place in the office and that Geoffrey regarded as his real treasure. Thomas had respect not only for vellum and paper but for the words written on them, even if he was not able to understand many of them yet.

Maybe it was this respect that caused him to start forward in an attempt to intercept the thief as he sprang from the room, carrying the bundled manuscript and papers. The man lashed out with his free arm and knocked the boy aside, but Thomas succeeded in regaining his balance and pursued the man along the passageway and down the spiral staircase. At the bottom of the steps he tripped and landed on the rush-strewn flagstones of the lobby. His mother, alerted by the noise, was not far behind. By now, the stranger had unlatched the front door and vanished into the street. Joan helped Thomas to the bench and started to mop at his wound. Shortly afterwards Geoffrey arrived home.

Thomas was not sure where he had received his wound. Geoffrey had noticed some drops of blood on the floor of the upper passage so he thought it might have been as a result of the blow from the man. Was he wearing any rings? he asked.

Joan could not remember but Thomas said, 'Yes, Geoffrey, here and here and here.' He indicated most of the fingers on his own hands. 'And all different coloured stones too.'

Thomas was quite recovered by now and enjoying the attention.

Geoffrey thought that it was probably one of the visitor's rings that caught the lad across the forehead. But if the individual was wearing rings set with different coloured stones, then he was no impoverished thief. He was no ordinary thief either, to be going and taking manuscripts.

Geoffrey went outside and questioned William, the porter who had a little wooden lodge on the inner side of the Aldgate arch. His job was to keep an eye on the comings and goings through the gate, which as well as being a busy entrance was a spot where various ne'er-do-wells were inclined to gather if not shoo-ed away. William's work did not stop there. Every cart arriving with goods from the country had to pay a small fee, which went towards paving the streets. Early in the morning William removed the drawbars and swung back the great oak doors that kept the city safe during the hours of darkness, and last thing in the evening he did the same in reverse. William knew Geoffrey Chaucer, of course, the person with royal connections who lodged over his head. Geoffrey enjoyed his company and a chat every now and then. But the porter could be no help on this occasion. No, he had not witnessed a man making a hasty exit from Chaucer's front door, let alone seen in which direction he might have gone.

Geoffrey had not held out much hope from William and he returned to his upstairs office and started to tidy the room. The thief had been searching for something specific and only disordered the owner's documents and books, as Thomas witnessed. Even so, it took Chaucer some time to return everything to its place, checking to see that nothing was damaged. What was missing was, as he half expected, one of the copies of his poem about St Beornwyn, one out of the three manuscripts for which he had paid the St Paul's copier two whole marks. In addition, a clutch of his official documents had vanished, material to do with the wine and wool imports. Geoffrey kept an orderly desk and had a fairly good idea of what had been taken: lists of quantities and commissions, mostly. None of it was a proper secret and none of it would be of much use to anyone outside the office of Controller of Customs. He suspected that the thief had snatched these pieces either in a panic or as a cover for his real objective, which was the Beornwyn story.

Well, if he was hoping to deprive the world of the fruits of Chaucer's poetic skill then he was too late, for there were already two copies of the poem in circulation among John of Gaunt's retinue at the Savoy. And Geoffrey still had possession of the original, which he'd penned at Bermondsey Priory.

Geoffrey couldn't imagine who would take the trouble to make off with a poem. The only people aware of its existence were John of Gaunt and a handful of others in the Savoy, such as Thomas Banks. Yet if anyone in the Savoy was eager to see it then he merely had to lay hands on one of the copies that Chaucer had dispatched to the Palace. The description provided by Joan and young Thomas left no doubt that the thieving caller was a gentleman, one with many-ringed fingers, someone on the King's business – though that part must be a lie surely. But nevertheless he was a person who was well-to-do, if not noble. It made no sense.

Then he spotted an overlooked manuscript lying in a dark corner. He picked it up. It was a scroll, fastened with an unbroken disc of red wax. The gentleman thief had arrived at Aldgate brandishing a scroll with a red seal. He must have dropped it in the rush to get away. Chaucer went over to the window and examined the seal. He thought he recognised the device imprinted in the wax, a rudimentary castle with three towers. He broke the seal without any qualms and unfurled the document.

He stood there for some time, squinting at the unfamiliar script and scratching his head. He did not know much of the language but he knew enough to obtain a general sense of what the document contained. It appeared to be about the purchase of some plot of land, not land in England but in Castile. The thing was in Spanish.

Despite its size the audience chamber was full, or so it seemed to Geoffrey Chaucer. He glanced round, dazzled by the wealth of candles on display, candles whose beams were intensified by their reflection in so many mirrored and plated surfaces. The candles were a sign of splendour and abundance, and scarcely needed since the evening was fine with sufficient light still coming through the ample windows to read by.

Geoffrey was standing at a lectern, ready to recite the story of St Beornwyn. Directly in front of him, seated on a great chair, which was almost a throne, and under a canopied dais, was John of Gaunt. At a discreet distance from the Duke of Lancaster were seated Katherine Swynford and other ladies of the household, including Philippa Chaucer. Further back in the room were yet more ladies, with a scattering of gentlemen as well. Chaucer had been surprised to recognise a couple of them. One was Sir Edward Jupe, the lanky knight from the Tabard Inn. He greeted Geoffrey warmly, saying that he thought he recognised his name on their first encounter but had not realised he was addressing the illustrious poet or 'maker', as he put it. Standing to one side was a demure-looking lady who glanced repeatedly at Sir Edward, as he did at her. Chaucer assumed she was the one he had been racing to see, wearing his rust-patterned tunic and all. He was better dressed now, though in a style befitting a knight who has neither the time nor the resources to waste on the latest fashion.

Thomas Banks was also in attendance, an unusual honour for a mere steward, but it confirmed that his place in the Lancaster household was more important than it appeared. A greater surprise was to see the handsome Spanish man, the Castilian, whom Chaucer had glimpsed in company with his wife. He asked Philippa who he was, pretending that it was an idle query and claiming that he had glimpsed the gentleman round the Palace. Was it his imagination or did Philippa look uneasy? She told her husband that this individual was called – and here she paused as if struggling to recall his name – Carlos de Flores and that he was part of the retinue of Queen Constance. Something in Philippa's hesitation wasn't convincing. As for Queen Constance of Castile, she was not in the audience chamber, of course. Indeed, she only kept company with her husband on public occasions, and not always then. There were other Castilians in the room, including a round-faced priest with a prominent pectoral cross.

Geoffrey regarded these individuals with some suspicion. He'd come to the conclusion that the thieving visitor to his lodgings must have been someone connected to Constance. It was obvious, really. Knowledge of the Beornwyn poem was restricted to the Savoy, where almost anyone on the English side might have been able to have a sight of it since he had already dispatched two copies there. But the nest of Castilians in the palace might not have been aware of this. If they wanted to read about Beornwyn, for reasons Geoffrey couldn't yet fathom, then the only way would have been to go to the source himself, or rather to Aldgate. More conclusive evidence of a Castilian visitor was that the legal document was in Spanish (it was indeed about the transfer of a parcel of land). Geoffrey's belief was that the caller had simply snatched up the scroll at random to impress whoever he found in Aldgate. The red seal with the device of the three-turreted castle signified the house of Castile. When Geoffrey talked more about the robbery to Joan and Thomas he discovered that mother and son had not detected any foreign accent but, to them, he was a gentleman and all gentlemen talked differently – or oddly.

John of Gaunt cleared his throat as a sign that Geoffrey might begin. The gentle conversations in the chamber died away. Geoffrey glanced down at the sheets before him, the version of the saint's life written out in his own hand. He started to recite, working half from memory, half from the words before him.

> 'God grant that all our dreams are fair,
> For certain in this life is care
> Enough without there be more strife
> From sleep than in our waking life.'

After a while he realised that he was not receiving the response he expected. Quiet attentiveness, yes, but with an undertone of coldness, even disapproval. Some of the court ladies glanced at each other. When Chaucer came to the part of the story, the dream sequence, speculating that

Beornwyn might not have been a pure maid after all but a woman like any other, the glances became more frequent and there was even the odd bout of muttering. All at once he understood what he should have understood before: that a saint's life, however remote and unlikely in its details, was nevertheless a kind of sacred object, not to be tampered with. He realised too that although he had sent copies to the Savoy it seemed as though no one had looked very carefully at the poem.

It was fortunate he concluded the poem by stressing Beornwyn's purity, and dwelling on her butterfly cloak and other miracles. Even so, the applause at the end, led by John of Gaunt, was muted. The only individual to compliment him was – and this was most odd – the round-faced priest with the cross, whose name was Luis. He had a large, fleshy hand, which he offered like a lump of meat, the fingers weighted with rings, Geoffrey noticed.

'Master Chaucer,' he said, although he had difficulty getting his tongue round the name, 'your fame is spread far and wide. Now with this romance of your saint from the north, her fame is spreading too. But you do not think she was such a saint, eh?'

Geoffrey gave some bland answer to the effect that it was a story, and so something half true, half invented. He was starting to regret ever having heard of Beornwyn, although he did not say this.

But Geoffrey's regrets on this evening in the audience chamber of the Savoy were as nothing to his regrets a day later when the news reached him that a man had been found dead on the Thames foreshore and that, tucked away inside the corpse's tunic, was a copy of his very own work.

V

It was the morning after the discovery of the body on the foreshore. Once again, Geoffrey was at the Savoy, although not in the light and luxury of the audience chamber or in the comfort of his wife's quarters. Instead he was sitting in a chilly, cramped office that had been put at his disposal. He couldn't help feeling that the meagre quality of the room was an implicit rebuke or even a warning. Geoffrey was out of favour with John of Gaunt, and this was a bad position to be in.

It was not only that Chaucer had written and recited a poem that was coldly received by its listeners on account of its disrespectful, even irreverent treatment of a saint who – for God's sake! – Gaunt had not even heard of until a couple of months ago. It was more than the fact that a member of the retinue of Queen Constance had been discovered dead by the river. Worse still, from Geoffrey's point of view, was the copy of the Beornwyn poem that had been found on the body of Carlos de Flores. It seemed as though he was somehow being held responsible for de Flores's death, at least in part. As far as the riverside corpse was concerned, the story was being put about that he had drowned. But the truth, that he'd sustained a vicious attack, was also starting to circulate, despite the best efforts of Thomas Banks to prevent it getting out. Furthermore, the fatal injuries had probably been made with a knife. It was not known whether these rumours had yet reached the ears of Constance but they surely would.

'Our master has asked me to ask you to look into the matter, to ... resolve it somehow,' said Thomas Banks.

The steward was sitting across from Chaucer in the little room. He tugged absently at his chain of office. This request from Gaunt, coming via Banks, was more of an order. And Chaucer couldn't help feeling some involvement in the whole business anyway. He had never spoken to the dead man but he had spied on him. Geoffrey couldn't help wondering how well his wife had known de Flores. He guessed that the copy of the poem on the body was the one that had been stolen from Aldgate. In which case, de Flores was almost certainly the thief.

'You will do this, resolve the matter or clear it away,' said Thomas Banks. Again, it was more instruction than request. 'Our master is preoccupied, he has other things on his mind. You may have whatever you need, speak to whoever you want. Our master has put me at your disposal.'

Geoffrey was irritated by these references to 'our master', as if Banks were determined to show himself the perfect, diligent servant. Yet the steward was right to say that Gaunt was preoccupied. His older brother, Edward, was very near to death, it could be only a matter of days. When that happened, and because of the infirmity of his father, John's position in the country would be all powerful. The last thing Lancaster needed was some scandal to do with a courtier from his wife's company of foreigners.

Nevertheless Geoffrey tried to take things in a different direction.

'Isn't it possible that this de Flores was attacked by a stranger, by someone who has nothing to do with the Savoy Palace? Perhaps he was the victim of a robbery?'

'No,' said the steward. 'For one thing, the only way down to the river shore where he was found is through the palace gardens. For another, not a thing was taken from his body. His rings, his jewellery, everything was there. Including this.'

From a pocket Banks fished a thin golden chain. It was broken. There was a small ruby set in the chain. Banks laughed, a dry, humourless sound.

'This ruby did not protect him from harm.'

'May I have it?' said Geoffrey. 'I'd like to show it to someone.'

The steward shrugged, as if to say: do what you please. Now Chaucer picked up the copy of the Beornwyn story, which Banks had earlier presented to him as if it were evidence of some crime. And it was evidence in a way. After all, there was blood on one end.

'I suppose it is a coincidence de Flores had this with him when he was found?'

'I do not think so, Master Chaucer.'

'That's what I was afraid of. I cannot see any reason why he should have it, though.'

'Oh, I can help you there. I have a . . . witness . . . one who has a story.'

Banks left the room. Geoffrey thought about his predicament. He would have to talk to Philippa, at some point, about the man de Flores.

The steward returned with someone else. To Geoffrey's amazement it was the red-capped person from the Tabard, the firebrand, the one he'd seen entering the Savoy several weeks before. He remembered now that he'd intended to report on the man's fiery words to Thomas Banks. Not necessary now since the two were obviously acquainted. The man was just as surprised to see Chaucer. But Geoffrey seized the advantage in greeting him by name: 'John Hall.'

'Why, it is the man who says John of Gaunt is the issue of a dragon and a mermaid.'

Now it was Banks's turn to look confused.

Chaucer said, 'We have met, we two, and not under auspicious circumstances. The last time I saw you, John Hall, you were spouting seditious words against the Savoy.'

Hall did not reply. He looked at the steward.

'The words you heard should not be taken at face value, Master Chaucer. This one is in my pay. By coincidence – yes, this is a genuine coincidence – it was his brother and another man who discovered de Flores's body yesterday. Hugh Hall is a member of this household. It gives brother John a pretext for visiting from time to time.'

'I see,' said Geoffrey, though he didn't.

'Explain yourself,' said Thomas Banks to Hall. He returned to his seat. Chaucer had not left his. Hall remained standing. In his posture and tone was a mixture of defiance and deference.

'I am in the *secret* employment of this gentleman here,' he said to Geoffrey, who noticed that he used the word 'employment' instead of 'pay'. 'My work makes for strange bedfellows, whether in the Tabard Inn or elsewhere. If you want an explanation for my "seditious words", sir, it is because sometimes the discontented and the treasonous have to be smoked out of their lairs. Pretending to be one of them is a way of doing it.'

Geoffrey observed how, as he was saying this, Hall's eyes darted repeatedly towards Banks. Hall was definitely a spy of some kind but Geoffrey wondered whether the steward knew the real force of Hall's rants against John of Gaunt and the house of Lancaster. He wondered what the red-cap actually believed, whose side he was on. The uncertainty was not cleared up when Hall continued: 'Also, sir, I have been reporting to a gentleman in the Spanish party here in the Savoy.'

'The dead man, de Flores?'

Hall ducked his head slightly in acknowledgement. 'Yes. His death had nothing to do with me.'

'No one said it did,' said Geoffrey.

'The Spaniard believed I was telling him things even while he was telling *me* things, all unawares. Things that I passed on to my employer here.'

'Did you get paid by the dead man for your things?'

'No ...' Then seeing the expression on Geoffrey's face, he said: 'Not much anyway ... not enough ...'

'You had a disagreement over payment. You had a fight.'

'We had a falling out,' said the man, choosing his words with care. 'But I did not kill him, I say.'

'No one said you did, John Hall. What did you learn from this de Flores?'

'The Castilian was interested in causing a division here in the Duke's court. He talked of a poem.'

'A poem?' said Geoffrey, feeling a chill that was not caused by the dank chamber.

'A poem about a lady who was not what she seemed. I didn't understand what he was talking about.'

'You were not dispatched on any errands by de Flores?' said Geoffrey. 'For example, you did not visit a house in Aldgate to – obtain an item – through deception?'

Either the look of bafflement on the other's face was genuine or John Hall was a fine player. But Chaucer did not believe that he was the one who'd stolen the Beornwyn piece anyway. Nor did he seem to have any notion of why the Castilians might wish to get their hands on the poem. Geoffrey nodded at Thomas Banks as a sign that his man could go. The steward waved the spy away and Hall moved out of the room in his stiff-gaited way.

When the door had closed, Banks stood up, arms akimbo.

'Well, Master Chaucer, I must confess that I am not much the wiser.'

Geoffrey shrugged as if he too were in the dark. But an idea was beginning to take shape in his head. He rose.

'You will excuse me, steward. I have to visit my wife.'

'I did not care for that poem about the saint, Geoffrey,' said Philippa.

She spoke regretfully as if she would like to have liked it. Husband and wife were sitting in Philippa's apartment, the one where Chaucer had encountered John of Gaunt and Katherine Swynford together a few weeks earlier. The most uncomfortable part of the conversation was over. Geoffrey had asked Philippa directly about her friendship with Carlos de Flores. She didn't seem put out by his words. Perhaps the man's death made such questions seem necessary, instead of painful or impertinent. Philippa replied that the Castilian was a friend to all ladies, and that she was not such a fool as not to see what kind of a man he was. Besides, she added, he was interested in her more on account of her sister, and that not because *he* was such a fool to believe he could have Gaunt's woman for himself but for some other reason. And de Flores also asked several questions about him, Geoffrey, her husband.

It was now that Geoffrey started to talk about the Beornwyn poem, the one Philippa didn't like.

'I wrote down the account of a saint, which I heard first at Bermondsey Priory. As I was writing it I found that the picture of the woman, Beornwyn, began to change in here –' Geoffrey tapped his temple, '– and I wondered if she was as pure and holy as she'd been reputed. I meant no harm in

233

what I did. The woman was long gone, and her life and her death were rich but faded like an old tapestry. Why not add another thread to the picture? I did not reckon on the audience at the Savoy Palace being so . . . so . . .'

'So pure, so holy?' said Philippa, with amusement. 'You must remember, Geoffrey, that though all of us might be educated and sophisticated people we also have regard to the proprieties. My sister is a devout woman.'

Geoffrey nodded. That was true. He continued: 'I believe that the Castilians, or some of them, want to create a division between your sister and the Duke of Lancaster. They do not like the fact that she lives in the same house as their queen. I think they plan to use my poem to help open up the division by suggesting that Katherine is like Beornwyn, devout and pure in the eyes of the world, but . . .'

'Like all women,' said Philippa. 'Someone with her own wishes and desires.'

'Just so,' said Geoffrey, grateful that she had put the matter in her own way and, in his gratitude, thinking that he ought to keep company with her more often.

'But none of that explains why de Flores was killed,' said Philippa. 'If he *was* killed, that is.'

'What happened on the night when I read the poem?' said Chaucer. 'Later on, I mean. Did you catch sight of Carlos de Flores?'

Geoffrey himself had not remained long in the audience chamber. He could see the recital had not gone down well. He had no wish to stay and receive tepid compliments. By the late light of the summer evening he returned to Aldgate by himself, just as William the porter was about to close the city gates.

After a pause, Philippa answered him: 'I saw de Flores

talking to someone, a man. They were standing close together in a corner by a window. The chamber was not so full by then, John of Gaunt had already left and my sister followed shortly afterwards. I recall thinking it was unusual. If de Flores was going to be discovered talking quietly in a corner, I'd expect a woman to be involved. He and the man did not know that they were being observed. It was growing dark outside. There was some dispute, I think. De Flores suddenly strode out and the man seemed to go off in pursuit of him.'

'You know who the man was?'

'No, and I have not seen him here in the Savoy before. But he had a battered countenance – and, Geoffrey, now I remember that you were talking to him before you read out your poem!'

'Then it must be Edward Jupe, the knight. The knight of the battered countenance describes him well. He was in company with a lady, a demure-looking lady.'

'Oh, it is Alice Osterley. She is one of the Queen's demoiselles, like me, though I scarcely know her.'

'Where was she when this dispute was taking place?'

'I don't know. She was not in the corner with the men.'

'Was it possible the argument was over her?'

'Geoffrey, I cannot say for certain. But, yes . . . Carlos de Flores had been . . . paying attention to Alice, I believe . . . as he paid attention to several of Constance's women.'

Now Chaucer stood up. It was obvious who should be questioned next.

He thanked Philippa, and noted the slight disappointment on her face as he left. He turned back and they kissed. Yes, he really must keep company with her more often.

He returned to the cell-like office, wondering where and

how he would lay hands on Sir Edward Jupe. The answer
proved easier than he'd expected once he talked to Thomas
Banks. He began by asking what Banks observed on the
evening of the Beornwyn reading before leading the conversation round to Sir Edward. The steward explained that
he quit the audience chamber shortly after his master, John
of Gaunt. But Banks was able to tell Geoffrey Chaucer a
little about the knight's history.

Although Jupe came from a family that could hardly count
itself as noble, a family that possessed nothing more than
some desolate acres in Lincolnshire, the knight had done a
great service to John of Gaunt on the borders of Aquitaine
several years ago. He protected the Prince during a fierce
skirmish with an advance guard of the French, protected
him almost at the cost of his own life. Of course, any knight
would have done the same, willingly laid down his life for his
liege lord. But, said the steward, something about the way Sir
Edward bore himself after the attack, together with his modesty and meekness in response to Gaunt's gratitude, caused
the Duke to take Jupe to his heart. He seemed to the Prince
the very model of what a knight should be: courteous, coura-
geous and chivalrous. He might not be as well-born as some
but he had an innate nobility. He became a friend of
Gaunt's, as far as a king's son may have friends. Chaucer
nodded. He knew that the Duke of Lancaster was loyal to his
friends.

Then, after the French war, Sir Edward dedicated himself
to other causes, even campaigning in the cold northern
countries near the edge of Russia. Always he wore his lady's
favour. This was the opening Geoffrey was looking for.
Almost casually, he asked Thomas Banks about Sir
Edward's lady. Was she in the court of Savoy? Indeed, said

the steward, he believed that the knight was favoured by Alice Osterley. In fact, she too had been present on the evening of the Beornwyn reading. Yes, said Chaucer, pretending to remember, I saw them together!

Not a single word that Thomas Banks said indicated he was aware of any unhappiness between the knight and his lady. Any unhappiness, any dispute or jealousy. Chaucer had that knowledge only from Philippa. But then his wife was likely to be better informed than the men in the household.

'Tell me, Geoffrey, you surely don't suspect Sir Edward of having a hand in this matter?'

'Not in the slightest,' said Chaucer, reflecting, not for the first time, how easy he found it to tell a lie. 'It is only that he may have some information about Carlos de Flores. I would like to speak to him. Do you know where I might find him?'

'I believe he and his page lodge somewhere south of the river. He is often to be found in a tavern on that side, though its name escapes me.'

The Tabard in Southwark?'

'It may be.'

This was enough for Geoffrey. Within the hour he found himself once more back inside the Tabard. He was greeted cheerfully by the host, Harry Bailey. He even took a drinking cup of the Rhenish wine that Bailey had been pressing on him. (It was as good as the inn-keeper claimed.) There was no thin-lipped, red-capped firebrand to disturb his drinking with talk of reducing the Savoy to a pile of ash. There were no pilgrims assembling to begin their journey to the shrine in Canterbury.

But there was a lanky knight sitting in a corner. Sir Edward Jupe was by himself. He was staring at a wooden pint pot on the table in front of him. He did not look up as

Geoffrey approached. The knight of the battered countenance had turned into the knight of the woeful countenance.

'I hope I find you well, sir,' said Chaucer, feigning surprise.

'Who …? Oh, it is the maker. The poet, Geoffrey
Chaucer.' The slightest smile of recognition passed across Sir
Edward's gloomy features.

'I last saw you at the Savoy Palace,' said Geoffrey, as if that
encounter had taken place months before rather than a couple
of days earlier. He sat down on the bench by the knight.

'Do not talk to me of that evening, Master Chaucer. I
prefer to forget it, and to forget the night that followed. It was
a bad business.'

Chaucer nodded, not expecting to get to the quick of the
matter so soon.

'I wish I had stayed my hand,' Sir Edward continued.

Chaucer wondered whether he was about to hear a confession of murder but what the knight said next left him
more baffled.

'What were those lines in your piece?' Jupe took a swig
from his pint pot before, furrowing his battered brow, he
recited from memory:

> 'For woman may seem holy, pure and true,
> Yet, all within, be frail as I or you.'

It took Geoffrey a moment to recognise his own handiwork.
This was a rhyming couplet – and not a very good one
either – from his poem about St Beornwyn. It occurred
when the narrator was speculating that the good woman
might not have been quite so good, after all. Sir Edward
Jupe had seized on these unremarkable words after hearing
them just once, he had stored them in his head, and was

repeating them back to their creator. In other circumstances, Geoffrey might have been flattered. Now what he felt was a creeping dismay.

'I don't understand you, Sir Edward.'

'What you said about women is all too true, Master Chaucer. Nevertheless, I regret what I have done.'

'But I do not know what you have done.'

'Why, I put pen to paper, as you do.'

If Chaucer had been baffled before, he was now utterly confused.

'Sir Edward, let us speak plainly so as to avoid all misunderstanding. We are talking here of a Castilian gentleman by the name of Carlos de Flores?'

'Oh, him.'

The expression on Jupe's face was unreadable. Was it a grimace? A sneer? A trace of guilt?

'You were observed talking with him at the Savoy Palace. You were angry.'

'We exchanged words, it is true.'

'Words before blows?'

'No blows. I did not offer him violence,' said the knight, in a mild, almost surprised fashion.

'But you were seen following de Flores out of the room.'

'I did not *follow* him, Master Chaucer. I merely left shortly after him.'

'You did not see where he went?'

'No, and I do not care where he went either. As far as I'm concerned he may go to . . . to the lowest pit.'

'Sir Edward, you are aware that Carlos de Flores is dead? He was found on the foreshore of the river next morning.'

This time the knight did respond. His lined face became suffused with a dull red. He fumbled with his hands on the table and knocked over his pot of ale. Liquid dribbled, unregarded, onto the floor. This was no act, Geoffrey reckoned. Sir Edward was genuinely shaken by the news. It was some time before he said anything more, and then it was only to ask for confirmation. Briefly, Geoffrey Chaucer described the outward circumstances of the Castilian's death.

'So then, the fellow is no more. You cannot think I had anything to do with it, Master Chaucer. If I had fought with that foreign gentleman, it would have been done in the open and in an honourable manner, not using a knife in the dark down by the water.'

'Yet you were in dispute with him over a lady?'

'I discovered that my lady Alice had been . . . I found out that he had been pressing his attentions on her . . . and though she struggled to resist his blandishments . . .' Sir Edward sighed.

Chaucer waited, but when no more came, he said: 'What did you mean about regrets then? About putting pen to paper?'

'When I left the Savoy Palace I returned to my lodgings on this side of the river. I fear that I was not altogether in my right mind. That very night I sat down and wrote to my lady Alice in a manner that was impetuous and foolish. I did not address her dishonourably but I believe I did not use those terms of respect and esteem that are her due. When I . . . when I came to myself again, it was too late to recall the letter. It had already been dispatched to the Palace. I sent my squire with the thing and he put it into my lady's hands himself. And now she has opened it and, without a doubt, she has read my unkind words and read them again . . . and again . . .'

Sir Edward Jupe seemed to notice for the first time that he

had spilled his drink on the floor. He watched the ale settling into the grooves between the flagstones.

'Your squire can confirm all this? That he took the letter to the palace and so on.'

'Why, yes. Simon would no more utter a falsehood than—'

The knight faltered. Geoffrey realised that he'd been about to say that he would never lie. Perhaps he thought it was too boastful a claim to make about himself. Chaucer clicked his fingers for the pot-boy and ordered another pint for the disconsolate lover. He might as well drown his sorrows. And Geoffrey too felt a certain sorrow for Sir Edward. He did not think that the lanky individual next to him had killed the Castilian. He was capable of killing, of course, but he would not do it on the sly.

When the fresh ale arrived, Chaucer took his leave of Sir Edward Jupe. On the way out he settled his score with Harry Bailey.

'A good man, that,' said the landlord, slipping the coins into his apron, and indicating the knight in the corner.

'Yes,' said Chaucer.

'One of my most devoted customers too.'

Instead of returning to the Savoy, Geoffrey went back to Aldgate. There he was able to clear up at least one part of the mystery. To Joan and young Thomas he showed the ruby on the golden chain, which the steward had taken from de Flores's body. The housekeeper did not recognise the item but Thomas, who had had enough presence of mind after the attack to enumerate the rings that the thief wore on his hands, said he was almost sure it was the one around the man's neck. Geoffrey complimented him once more on his sharp eyes. Then he went into his office to think.

It was plain enough that Carlos de Flores was the one

who'd stolen the Beornwyn copy from this very room. And the reason for the theft was that the Castilians in the Savoy wanted to get their hands on the poem to see whether they could use it as a weapon in their campaign against Katherine Swynford. They must have heard something of its contents but not been able to lay hold of one of the two copies that Geoffrey had already sent to the palace. The more he thought about the matter, the more obvious it seemed. Quite against Geoffrey's intentions – indeed, the notion had never occurred to him – the poem about St Beornwyn worked subtly in their interest. That is to say, it could be interpreted as being against Katherine and so in favour of Constance.

Why else had the priest, Luis, been the only person to single Chaucer out for congratulations on the night of the reading, and why had he done so in a very public manner? The fact that Geoffrey was Katherine's brother-in-law might be very useful to them. See, the Spaniards could say, even the family of John of Gaunt's mistress disapprove of her and of her behaviour. Why, the poet Geoffrey Chaucer has penned a story about a woman who pretends to be pure but who is, in reality, driven by her passions, by her appetite for men. In itself, these whisperings would hardly be enough to drive a wedge between Gaunt and Katherine but it all helped to spread unease and distrust in the household. Once again, Chaucer wished that he'd never heard the tale of Beornwyn from the Prior of Bermondsey. It had brought him nothing but trouble.

But was the killing of de Flores connected to the wretched poem or not? Geoffrey had already spoken to two men, John Hall and Sir Edward Jupe, with reasons to dislike, even to hate, the Castilian. He still did not think that Jupe had killed de Flores. He believed the knight was genuinely a man of honour. But was it not conceivable that he had pursued his rival all the way down to the foreshore of the river and there, in a fit of drunken madness, stabbed him to death? Jupe would know where to strike quick and deep. It was the sort of violent action he could perform in his sleep. And, by his own account, he'd been the worse for wear. 'Not altogether in my right mind' was his roundabout way of describing his condition while writing the fatal letter to Alice Osterley. Geoffrey had just seen for himself that the knight was as ready to wield a pint-pot as he was a sword. And hadn't the landlord of the Tabard called him one of his most devoted customers?

Yet, of the two suspects, it was John Hall who seemed much the more likely to have done the deed. As a secret agent in the pay of Thomas Banks, he had easy access to the Savoy. He was also working for Carlos de Flores, or pretending to work for him. At any rate he was being paid by the Castilian. Not paid enough, though. Suppose there had been a prearranged meeting down by the river that night and then a row over money during which Hall stabbed de Flores? The red-capped man was capable of anger. Chaucer remembered his outburst in the Tabard.

De Flores must have had other enemies. Given his womanising reputation at court, there must be any number of husbands and lovers and suitors bearing a grudge against him. With a mixture of amusement and discomfort, Geoffrey considered that he might even be counted among them. After all, he'd seen for himself his wife and the Castilian strolling easily in the Savoy gardens. Had heard her laughter, seen his casual touch on her arm. Bearing a grudge wasn't the same as sticking the knife in, but one might easily lead to the other.

It was with relief that Geoffrey turned back to some paperwork that had to do with his wine and wool responsibilities. There was something simple and clean about the lists of quantities, about the additions and subtractions and the rates of duties and tax that was far removed from the messy, bloody world of human affairs.

The next morning Chaucer returned to the Savoy Palace, intending to see Thomas Banks and to report on his progress, or lack of it. He had it in mind to question John Hall again. But Geoffrey had no sooner entered the cell-like chamber set aside for him, than there came a tap at the door.

He was surprised when the round-faced priest, Luis, entered and asked to speak to him. Chaucer noticed that he avoided using his name. Otherwise his English was good. Geoffrey motioned Luis towards the only other chair in the room. But the priest shook his head.

'Not in here, if you please, Master ... Here there are too many sharp ears. Please come to our side.'

Curious, Geoffrey followed the black-clad figure along passages and up and down flights of stairs until they arrived at a part of the Savoy that was quite strange to him. It was probably no coincidence that they were at the opposite end of the palace to the area where Katherine Swynford and Philippa Chaucer were lodged. For these were the apartments belonging to Queen Constance and her retinue. Luis led Chaucer into a chamber that was as finely furnished as any he'd seen. There was an abundance of gold and silver plate, and of silk hangings. It was a room that openly proclaimed the pious nature of its occupant. Geoffrey observed the images of the Virgin in recesses and a sculpted relief of the crucifixion set on an altar-like table. Scattered across other surfaces, with casual deliberation, were devotional

books bound in gem-encrusted leather. There was an orna-
mental folding screen in one corner, the wooden handiwork
of which, to Geoffrey's eyes, looked Spanish. In the air hung
a faint incense-like smell.

Luis, more at ease now that he was back in his own surroundings, indicated that Chaucer should seat himself in a
chair to one side of the fireplace. He sat down opposite. For
a moment he dabbed at the gem-studded pectoral cross,
uncertain how to begin.

'You told a story in this house quite lately, a story about a
saint whose name I find it difficult to get my teeth around.'

'Beornwyn,' said Chaucer, before adding half under his
breath, 'Beornwyn, yet again.'

'Yes, just so. I too have a story to tell you. It is a short story,
Geoffrey – can I call you that? I can get my teeth more easily
round Geoffrey. Yes, good. It is a short story about a lady. She
is from my homeland of Castile. She marries a man of rank
and wealth but, of the two of them, it is she who brings
more to the union because her title raises him up higher.
They live together under one roof, away from her homeland.'

Chaucer sighed inwardly. Had he been brought to the
priest's chamber to listen to a tedious allegory about
Constance and John of Gaunt? Some impatience must have
shown on his face because Luis waved a soft, placatory hand.

'No, no, this is not what you think, Geoffrey. I am not
speaking here of the Queen in whose service I toil. I am not
speaking at all of your master, Lancaster. I am talking of
someone else. This lady, as I say, lives under the same roof as
her husband. But her husband has an eye that will not stay
still. Is that how you say it in English? An eye that moves all
the time?'

'A wandering eye, you mean? He can't keep his gaze away from other women.'

'It is not a question of eyes only. Ever since they have arrived in this foreign land, husband and wife, he has wandered with his eyes and with more besides.'

'Let me be clear,' said Geoffrey. 'We are talking here about Carlos—'

'Hush,' said Luis. 'No names, no names. In the end, the lady can bear it no longer. Perhaps her position is made worse because she is dwelling in a foreign land. Her husband will not moderate his behaviour but he becomes more shameless, more lacking in honour. One night not long ago, she finds him emerging from a chamber where he should not be. In her anger she pursues him until they meet and they are – how do you say it? – face to face. They are by the river. Fearing he is about to do her violence, she seizes a knife, which he carries, and she turns it upon him, like this.'

The priest leaned forward and, with surprising nimbleness, mimed a thrust with a dagger. The jewelled cross swung like a little pendulum.

'He falls to the earth. At first she tries to stem the flow of blood by tearing a strip from her chemise and applying it to the wound. But it is too late. She runs away. The next day the body is discovered by the river. The lady, she comes to me. She confesses her crime.'

'She comes to you because you are a priest? Because you are from the same country as her?'

'Not for either of those reasons. Wait, and you will understand. I know how much the lady has been provoked, but it is still a crime. Geoffrey, believe that I break no secret of the confession. I say again she did not tell this to me as a priest . . .'

Chaucer felt the ground slipping from beneath his feet.

What was the purpose of telling him this confession, relaying it at second-hand? Who was the woman? The wife of Carlos de Flores? He didn't know de Flores had a wife. But then why should he know? What response was the priest expecting from him?

'I ask you, Geoffrey, what would happen to the lady under English justice?'

Chaucer hesitated. He did not know. A nobleman had the right to be tried before his peers. But a noble lady? And, anyway, this was a killing of a stranger by a stranger, not by an Englishwoman of an Englishman. Whose business was it to adjudicate?

'I don't know,' he said.

'Probably better not to bring it to the test?'

'Probably not.'

'I am glad you agree, Geoffrey.'

There was a pause. Chaucer detected that incense-like scent in the air again.

The priest continued: 'I offer a contract, not one that is written down or signed, but a contract all the same. Lately there has been some agitation on this side of the Palace of Savoy about a certain lady who dwells on your side. Indeed, I believe she is a kinswoman of yours by marriage, Geoffrey. Various people on my side have been stirring themselves to cause doubt and confusion on your side – including the gentleman who met his fate down by the river. My idea is this. All doubt and confusion will cease. There will be no more whispers about your lady. In return, the story will be put about that the gentleman died by drowning. We can all agree on that, the English and the Castilians. An unfortunate accident. The dangers of the river. Our troubles will be over. The whispers will stop. We shall live happy and be together.'

'And the lady?' said Chaucer. 'What of her?'

'Oh, she has agreed to all of this. She is ashamed of what she has done, deeply ashamed. She wishes to retire from life in this great house. Indeed, she wishes to retire from the life of the flesh altogether, as far as one can do so and still remain on this earth. The lady will join the Benedictines near here at . . . I cannot recall the name of the place but it begins with the letter B—'

'Barking, the abbey at Barking,' said Geoffrey. That made sense. It was a place that enjoyed royal patronage. Only the daughters of the wealthy and the well connected were admitted there.

'If you doubt my words, you can ask her yourself,' said Luis, rising to his feet. Indicating that Geoffrey should follow him, he moved towards the Spanish screen in the corner. He folded back one of the panels. Sitting behind it, on a stool, was a young woman. She was handsome, with a hawk-like nose and bold dark eyes. Geoffrey was shaken to realise that, all this time, there had been a third person in the room. He realised too that the pleasant incense-like smell was the scent that she was wearing. She said nothing but nodded her head, once, with abrupt decision.

'Behold,' said Luis. 'My niece, Isabella, widow of the late Carlos de Flores.'

Still she said not a word. Simply nodded, as if assenting to everything her uncle had said.

She rose to her feet. She was tall, taller than Geoffrey and her uncle. After a moment she leaned forward and took hold of the cross that the priest wore about his neck. She touched her lips to the ruby set on the crosspiece. Then she strode out of the room.

*

So it was solved. Or at least it was resolved. The lady Isabella, whose uncle was the priest Luis, took herself away from the world and retreated into Barking Abbey. The story got around the Savoy Palace that the unfortunate Carlos de Flores had, after all, and despite those earlier rumours, been a victim of the river. At the same time, the whispers and the stories against Katherine Swynford and her connection with John of Gaunt also died away, at least for a time.

Thinking about the whole matter later, Geoffrey reflected on the strange parallels in what had occurred. Carlos de Flores had gone in quest of a poem that he could use against Katherine Swynford, a woman whose devout exterior masked her real and passionate self. The Beornwyn poem had dealt with the same subject, a woman with a hidden life, buried feelings. And de Flores had met his fate at the hands of a woman whose fires of rage and jealousy, banked down for so long, had finally burst forth. For all that, the woman, Isabella, said not a word in Chaucer's hearing. She had been a mute witness to the discussion of her crime and its consequences. Was this silence a self-imposed penance? He could not forget the way she had stooped and kissed her uncle's cross. In that gesture was surely acceptance, though he could not tell whether it was angry or resigned.

Quiet returned to the Savoy Palace, although not to the life of John of Gaunt, for his older brother died very shortly after the events related here and the Duke of Lancaster became the most powerful man in the kingdom, in reality if not in title. His liaison with Katherine Swynford continued in the precincts of the Savoy and elsewhere.

Sir Edward Jupe was reconciled with his lady, Alice Osterley. It seemed that the impetuous, drunken letter that he wrote to her was not couched in such disparaging terms after all. It may have been mildly reproachful but it was also truly loving. Elsewhere, the death of Carlos de Flores might have caused a few female hearts in the Savoy to skip a beat but, if so, there was no one ready to own up to it, and certainly not the unknown lady from whose chamber de Flores had been spied creeping on the night of his murder. Geoffrey returned to Luis the ruby on the gold chain, which had been worn by de Flores. He had no wish to retain something worn by a murdered man.

And it happened, some weeks after all this, that Geoffrey Chaucer and John of Gaunt were talking together. Good humour was restored. The poem of St Beornwyn was all but forgotten. As far as Geoffrey was aware, every copy had been destroyed.

John of Gaunt said: 'I heard a most absurd story the other day, a story about myself.'

'You did, my lord?' said Geoffrey.

'A rumour appears to be circulating in London that I am the issue of a dragon and a mermaid.' Gaunt's tone suggested mockery at the credulity of ordinary folk, but there was also just a note of pleasure in the rumour. 'Where do you suppose that started?'

'A dragon and a mermaid, eh?' said Geoffrey Chaucer. 'I really have no idea.'

ACT FOUR

Herefordshire, August 1405

Prior Paul wore his usual benign smile, which was pasted on as he woke every morning in the affluent little priory of St Oswald and lasted until he went to bed. However, secretly he was very worried. A gnawing concern was eating away at his placid nature and every few minutes, he wandered restlessly over to one of the windows of his parlour in the prior's house to stare across at the woods to the west. The morning was perfect, the warm sun dappling the bright green of summer and the swelling fruit in the orchards, but he was looking beyond these, fearfully seeking the approach of what might be their nemesis.

Soon he moved over to another window in his corner room, where he had relief from the westerly view, as he could look up at the blunt end of the Malvern Hills, where the earthworks of the so-called 'British Camp' crowned the Herefordshire Beacon. It was an ancient place, where some said the hero Caractacus had fought against the Roman invaders, but the prior pushed aside any thoughts of armies and battle, as they reminded him too clearly of his present concerns.

The door opened and a mellow voice caused him to turn from his sombre meditations. It was his secretary, Brother Mark – a good-looking and ambitious young man who quite openly admitted his intention of one day becoming an abbot in their Benedictine order. He came across with a couple of sheets of parchment, which he laid on the prior's table.

'Brother Patrice's order of services for the coming week, Prior,' he said. 'And Brother Arnulf's accounts for the visitors' donations last month, as he described in chapter this morning.'

Paul laid a hand on the documents and thanked his secretary, but his mind was not on chanting or money, important though they were.

'Is there any news from Wales?' he asked, his smile still in place, but his tone anxious.

'The porter was told by one of the carters who takes our wool that he saw thousands of men camped in the fields beyond Monmouth,' replied Brother Mark. 'But that is a good many miles away from here.'

The prior nodded and sank into the chair behind his table.

'We can only pray to God that they will pass by this place,' he said fervently. 'Tell Brother Patrice that we will include extra prayers in every service until this danger is past.'

After discussing a few more routine matters, the younger monk left the prior to his worries and went down the stairs and out into the inner courtyard of the monastery. Although he had been there for almost a year, Mark was still beguiled by the attractive appearance of the place. Surrounded by a high wall of warm Cotswold stone, the priory was a stout oblong nestling under the shelter of the Malvern Hills, a high ridge that stretched northward for some twelve miles. It was virtually the boundary of Wales, and it was said that eastwards there were no other hills worthy of the name until one reached Muscovy.

At the end of the priory nearest the hill lay the church, a

neat cruciform building with a squat tower surmounted by a pointed roof. The church was built almost against the wall, this situation being dictated by the spring that came up under the floor of the chancel, directly in front of the altar. Brother Mark knew that the priory had been founded here before Norman times because of this spring, which had a wide reputation for healing, especially of ailments of the skin.

When he looked away to the right, he saw that a score of yards in front of the main door of the church, a transverse wall ran across the oblong compound, cutting it in half. It was pierced by a central gate and beyond this, the more secular part of the establishment lay separated from the monastic area around the church. It contained the guest-house, kitchen, stables, laundry, brewhouse and accommodation for the lay brothers, who did all the manual work in the priory and in the fields outside.

As he stood on the steps of the prior's house, built at the inner angle of the cross wall, Mark looked again at the creamy stone of the frater and dorter on his left, where the monks ate and slept. The dorter was connected to the south transept of the church by a passageway that led to the night stairs. This allowed the monks to enter the church for the nighttime services directly from their dormitory over the refectory, without being exposed to the elements. The young monk was well aware that the Benedictine Order was often accused of soft living, which had given rise to several splinter groups, who practised a more ascetic way of life.

His contemplation of the architecture complete, Mark crossed the inner courtyard to the opposite side of the church, where the chapter house and infirmary occupied that corner of the enclosure.

As he approached the infirmary, he saw the infirmarian coming towards him.

'Have you much trade today, Brother?' he asked Brother Louis in a mildly jocular way. The French infirmarian, who had studied medicine at the prestigious school of Montpellier, looked sternly at the younger man, critical of his light-hearted manner.

'If you mean that we have a number of souls needing treatment for their ailments, then yes, trade is good,' he said haughtily. In fact almost everything about Brother Louis was haughty. He was a thin, erect and stiff-necked man of about fifty, very conscious of his good education and medical skills.

Not at all chastened by this, Mark delivered a message from Brother Paul.

'The prior wishes to know how Brother John is faring,' he said. 'We were all worried about him last evening when he had another of his seizures.'

The infirmarian shook his head, more in exasperation than concern.

'Our Brother John is getting on in years. In fact, that is his main problem, as there is little physically wrong with him. He is frail and all we can do is humour him and keep him comfortable for the remaining years of his life, which I fear may not be all that many.'

Having put the younger man in his place, Louis stalked on towards the long building in the lower corner of the inner compound, opposite the prior's house. This was the domain of Brother Jude, the cellarer, who was responsible for all the stores, including those that made life comfortable for the residents. A couple of lay brothers were unloading casks of wine from an ox-cart and carrying them through the large doors into the capacious storerooms, but the Frenchman entered through a smaller door into the cellarer's office.

Brother Jude was a large, somewhat obese, monk with a full pink face and a red nose, which suggested that he was conscientious in sampling much of the liquor that entered his vaults. Indeed, the first thing he did was to offer the infirmarian a cup of best Burgundy wine and keep him company with a similar libation while they discussed the list of medical supplies that Louis had placed before him.

When this was done, Jude also enquired after the health of the older brother, John, who had collapsed on his way to matins the previous midnight, after having one of his shaking fits.

'He has been getting worse for months,' commented Jude as he finished the last of his wine. 'I often see him from here, walking about the precinct talking to himself, staring up at the sky with his hands clasped as if he is speaking directly to God himself!'

Louis shrugged indifferently. 'Perhaps he is, for all we know. There is little I can do about it, as he has no physical infirmity that I can treat. He has been having these fits these many years, but at least they are not getting worse.'

After a little more conversation about the state of the world, and especially the concerns about the political unrest in the country, the infirmarian walked in his stately fashion back to his hospital. Though its primary function was to treat the occupants of the priory, the small population of only eighteen brothers and a score of lay brothers provided relatively little work for the doctor. However, much of his labour went on the treatment of visitors, who came with a variety of ailments, seeking relief both from his medicines and through the miraculous water from St Beornwyn's spring. Though some of these supplicants were common folk, the reputation of the priory for its medical care was such that a considerable income was obtained from rich merchants and manor-lords who came from all over the Midlands, the Marches and the West Country.

Once inside his infirmary, which was a long, low building, roofed in slate like the rest of the priory, Brother Louis went to the room at one end, which acted as his office and dispensary. A table and two chairs represented his consulting room, the rest of the chamber being given over to cabinets and shelves filled with various herbs and drugs, together with his paraphernalia for rolling pills and mixing tinctures. He poured a small quantity of a reddish liquid from a flask into a small earthenware cup and went into the main ward, which had half a dozen low beds, each consisting of a straw mattress resting on a low wooden plinth. Beyond was a short corridor leading to four cubicles, used either for patients wealthy enough to pay for a private room or those who were very sick. Only two were in use at the moment, one for a fat burgess from Hereford with a disfiguring skin disease of his neck, and the other for a wealthy fish merchant of Bristol suffering from weeping ulcers of his legs. The main ward contained only one patient and it was to that bed which Louis now went, holding up his cup of medicine as if it were a Communion chalice.

'Drink this down, John,' he commanded imperiously. 'It will settle your mind after your disturbance of last night.'

'It was no disturbance, Louis, it was a message from Heaven telling me to expect grave news!' quavered the old man indignantly.

'Just take this sedative, John, then get some sleep,' urged the infirmarian impatiently. 'You should be fit enough to attend compline later today.'

With this admonition, he walked away towards the private cubicles, where his bedside manner improved markedly as he enquired solicitously after the health of the two rich patients.

At St Oswald's they subscribed to the tenets of the Benedictine Order, founded by the great man many centuries earlier, but they did not adhere as strictly to the rules as did the Cistercians or the Cluniacs, who had diverged from them because of their perception that the Benedictines had gone soft. Though, as in all monastic establishments, there were nine offices each day devoted to praising God, this small priory had compromised by joining several services together, so that they were actually only held on five occasions. That morning, terce, sext, nones and High Mass had been combined into a forty-minute observance that ended in plenty of time for midday dinner.

The black-robed monks trooped into their refectory and sat at the three oak tables set in a U-shape. At the centre of the top table sat Prior Paul, with his sub-prior, Matthew, on his right, and Pierre, the sacristan, on his left. The prior often ate alone in his house, but today he ate with his flock, anxious to hear if any of them had picked up any gossip from the lay brothers about the army that lay over the horizon.

'The dray-man who brought that special ale up from Ross said he saw no signs at all on his journey,' offered the cellarer, Jude, as one of the servants placed a trencher of roast pork with beans and cabbage on the table before him.

'Yet there are reports of some peasants fleeing with their belongings on the road from the west towards Hereford,' contributed Arnulf, the hospitaller, who tended to get most news of the outside world because of his dealings with the visitors who stayed in his guest-house.

The conversation lapsed as the serving men hurried in with more food, placing thick slabs of yesterday's bread before each member, loaded with meat and vegetables. These trenchers used to be laid directly on the scrubbed boards of the tables, but recently the brothers had become sophisticated enough to lay them on pewter platters. Another servant came around with a jug of wine and yet another with a large pitcher of ale, and soon the community was tucking in to an abundance of food and drink, far removed from the Spartan origins of the monastic movement.

As Prior Paul slowly ate his meal, he looked around at his brethren and wondered what some of them were thinking. In spite of his bland, amiable appearance, he was an astute judge of men, as well as being an able administrator. He was well aware that his deputy, Brother Matthew, hungered after his own position as prior and was no doubt patiently – or perhaps, impatiently – waiting for his death or retirement to a hermitage. However, Paul was only sixty years of age and had no intention of handing over the reins for some time yet.

He looked across at the sub-prior now, studying his cadaveric face and his unbending and humourless manner. A large Roman nose with deep furrows on each side of his mouth suggested that life at St Oswald's would not be so comfortable under his authoritarian direction.

On his other side, Brother Pierre, the sacristan, sat fastidiously picking at his food with his eating knife and delicately washing his fingers in a bowl of rosewater set before him. Dedicated to his task of administering all the physical aspects of the priory church, his nature was tarnished by his permanent disdain for all things English, his French origins oozing from every pore. He had come two years earlier from a large monastery on the Loire and made no secret of the fact that he hoped to be recalled there before his life amongst the barbarians became intolerable.

The other Frenchman, the infirmarian, Louis, sat at the top of one of the side tables. Thankfully, Paul knew that his Gallic tendencies were not as blatantly obvious as those of Pierre, but his rather aloof and sarcastic manner was born of his pride in his professional background, as he never let an opportunity pass to remind his fellows that he had trained at the most eminent centre of medical learning in Europe.

As the prior's eye roved over the other monks, almost a score in number, he mused on the fact that he knew many of their secrets. At least two of them regularly visited women in the nearby village. and he suspected another of attending cockfights. Though the monks were supposed to be confined to the priory, many of them had reason to leave during the day, to supervise work in the fields or travel about the nearby countryside collecting alms from other villages. Twice a year a retinue of brothers carried the feretory around the district, the ornate reliquary that usually rested on the altar of the church. This heavy embellished and gilded box contained the skull-cap and some bones of the blessed St Beornwyn and was hawked around the hamlets and churches of the area to collect donations for the priory, accompanied by the monks chanting and ringing handbells.

In the relaxed atmosphere of St Oswald's, there was no code of silence at meals, as was usually enforced by the Cistercians and other stricter orders. There was hardly noisy chatter, but certainly plenty of subdued conversation as the brothers worked their way through their ample meal. The main topic of conversation was the threat from the advancing army, now not many miles away, and this continuing anxiety led Prior Paul to ask Louis, Matthew, Jude and Pierre to come to his parlour after the meal.

An hour later, they sat on stools before his desk, the prior's secretary standing discreetly in the background.

'We need to decide what preparations we should make should this rebellion overtake us,' began Paul. The seriousness of the situation had by now caused even his habitual smile to fade somewhat. 'Though it seems that these brigands have halted their advance, we cannot expect it to be other than a temporary reprieve.'

The thin lips of the sub-prior pursed in disagreement. He never missed a chance to contradict his superior.

'One can hardly call their leader a "brigand",' he complained. 'This Glendower is a landed gentleman of mature years, a qualified lawyer and one who, in the past, has given loyal service to King Henry.'

The physician, Louis, nodded his agreement. 'I have heard from France that he is well looked upon there – and that he has been offered military assistance by the royal court in Paris.'

Pierre snorted in disgust. 'Some gentleman! He has rebelled against his king and for five years he has rampaged throughout Wales, sacking and burning towns. He has killed thousands and God alone knows what damage he has done to religious houses!'

The prior held up a placating hand. 'The politics of the matter are none of our concern, but our survival and the protection of our community and property most certainly are. We need to plan how we might best limit the damage should Glendower's army overrun us.'

'Damage has already been done, just because of the threat of this rebellion to the countryside,' snapped the sub-prior. 'We heard from Brother Arnulf at the chapter meeting this morning that the value of donations from pilgrims and supplicants has decreased appreciably in the past few weeks. People are becoming afraid to travel here, as we are in the path of this Welsh army advancing into England itself.'

The infirmarian nodded his agreement. 'Several of our wealthy patrons who were due to come for my treatment have sent messages to say that they are remaining at home until all trouble has passed.'

The prior shrugged. 'There is little we can do about an advancing army, save pray earnestly to God in the hope that He will divert it. However, we have treasure and valuables here which would be the first target of a despoiling horde.'

Brother Jude, whose mind worked more slowly than the sharper Frenchmen, frowned as he mulled over his superior's comment. 'You mean we should bury our money and hide our silver chalices and patens?'

Prior Paul nodded. 'Perhaps not actually in a hole in the earth, but certainly in a good hiding place. We must think about this now, so that if Glendower's rabble come close, we can rapidly hide our treasure away somewhere.'

They discussed this for several minutes and eventually came up with a provisional plan to use an old stone coffin in the crypt beneath the chancel. This crypt had not been used for a century, as the infrequent burials of deceased monks were now made in a plot alongside the church, near the chapter house.

'We will keep this to ourselves for the time being,' ordered Paul. 'The lay brothers need not be made aware of it, as they might be forced by these rebels to disclose the hiding place.'

'May God give me strength to keep this secret myself, if I am subjected to violence and torture!' said Pierre fervently.

'What about our saint's reliquary?' asked the cellarer. 'The outside is finely chased with gold and silver, and there's a heavy gold band around the relic itself.'

The prior nodded again as he agreed with Jude. 'The reliquary is too large to conceal, but we must preserve the skull-cap. Indeed, that is our most prized possession and must be kept safe at all costs.'

The object in question was kept on the high altar, but an hour after the prior's meeting it was being used in the chancel of the church. A dozen pilgrims and supplicants were gathered in the empty nave, having come to the priory either indifferent to, or ignorant of, the presence of a hostile army just over the horizon. Most of them had some ailment, ranging from weeping skin ulcers to severe arthritis, but a few were ordinary pilgrims, curious about the well-known cult of St Beornwyn.

Today it was the turn of Brother Louis, the infirmarian, to administer the cures. Half a dozen of the monks occupied the quire stalls on each side of the chancel, providing harmonious chanting while Louis went to the altar. With repeated genuflection, he opened the gilded doors of the reliquary and removed the most precious fragment of their beloved Beornwyn, which lay amongst other parts of her skeleton.

It was a bowl-shaped calvarium, the top of the skull of the beautiful saint, which had been embellished with a wide band of heavy gold around the circumference, into which a repetitive motif of butterflies had been engraved.

Turning, Brother Louis held the relic high above his head and, as the chanting changed, began intoning a litany of Latin prayers. The small congregation in the nave dropped to their knees on the cold flagstones and crossed themselves, murmuring their own prayers as the infirmarian advanced towards the holy well, placed beneath the chancel arch, at the foot of the steps leading up to the presbytery.

It was an ornate structure of pink marble standing head high, the base carved with cherubim and seraphim. The upper part was a large alabaster statue of St Beornwyn herself, gazing down benignly into a large marble bowl shaped like a seashell, lying at the foot of the edifice. Just above the bowl, a kneeling angel held a pitcher under his arm, from which a small cascade of water fell into the bowl, almost filling it until the excess ran off through an overflow. The water passed into a conduit under the church and reappeared at a much more mundane spring in the outer courtyard, where it was used for everyday purposes in the priory and also for bathing the feet or other afflicted parts of supplicants who desired external treatment of their diseases.

Louis stood before the fountain and, with a stately bow, bent and held the ornate skull under the jet of water until it was half full.

The first supplicant who had come for a cure moved forward and kneeled before the priest, who with a sonorous stream of Latin, blessed the limpid fluid in the skull. Then bending, Brother Louis held it to the lips of the pilgrim who took a sip, or rather a gulp, as he was determined to get his money's worth. This was repeated for each of the supplicants who were waiting patiently in the nave, and after much genuflection and mumbling of prayers, they lined up again before the infirmarian, who gave them a general blessing and then directed them to seek further diagnosis and treatment at the infirmary, if they so wished. Though he did not say it directly, there was a tacit understanding that such additional medical care would come at a price, though, to be fair, this was graded according to their apparent means and for those who were sick but obviously near-destitute, the treatment was free.

Later, one of the supplicants took advantage of this invitation and sought out Louis in his consulting room. A rotund cloth merchant from Evesham, he was suffering from severe flatulence and pains in his belly after eating. After examining him, which included prodding his corpulent belly, Louis suspected that much of his problem was due to overweight, but produced an earthenware pot, sealed with a wooden stopper.

'At the end of each meal, swallow as much of this as would fill half an eggshell,' he commanded. 'And cut down drastically on your victuals, especially fatty pork and other greasy food.'

Handing the jar to the merchant, he told him to return when it was all used, or go to an apothecary in Evesham and buy more. He handed the man a slip of parchment on which were written some cabalistic marks, as a prescription for the apothecary.

Gratefully, the clothier departed, placing a liberal pile of silver pennies on Louis's table. Before he left, he enquired about the saint who, he hoped, would work miracles upon his belly, aided by the infirmarian's mixture of chalk, valerian and peppermint.

'How did this priory come to be established in such a lonely place?' he asked.

The infirmarian was quite willing to engage in conversation with this intelligent and liberal fellow.

'It is said that a healing well has been here since time immemorial,' he said, sitting back in his chair. 'Even in the time of those Ancient Britons that we read about in Geoffrey of Monmouth's famous book, people came from far and wide to drink and wash in its waters. There are several such wells along the Malvern hills, but this one has the best reputation.'

'But why did this one have a Benedictine house placed over it?' persisted the inquisitive merchant.

'Before the Normans came, a daughter of the Earl of Hereford suffered from the falling sickness, which was cured by the waters of this spring,' replied Louis. 'The Earl was so impressed that he granted not only twenty hides of land here, but also gave a generous endowment for the priory.'

'But why dedicated to St Oswald and St Beornwyn?' asked the merchant.

'The earl was influenced by his confessor, a Benedictine monk, who came from the Shire of York and was devoted to the memory of St Oswald, so the priory is named after him. Oswald was King of Northumbria in ancient times and, although a ferocious soldier, became a saint after his death in battle at Oswestry, because he had converted the pagan Northumbrians to the way of Christ.'

The clothier's forehead wrinkled in puzzlement. 'So why is the church dedicated to this St Beornwyn? Who was she?'

Brother Louis, ever an impatient man, was beginning to get a irritated by the merchant's persistence, thinking that he was demanding a lot for his silver pennies. However, he decided to humour him one last time.

'Several hundred years after Oswald's death, which was a violent dismemberment, the same thing happened to a devout virgin in a church dedicated to St Oswald near

Whitby. She was horribly mutilated by Viking berserkers on one of their raids upon the Northumbrian coast, and for her virtue and martyrdom she was herself elevated to sainthood. Some two hundred years ago, some of her bones were given to this church as holy relics.'

Satisfied at last, the clothier ambled away clutching his pot of stomach medicine and with a sigh of relief, the infirmarian rose and went into the ward where Brother John was sitting up on his pallet. After a perfunctory examination, Louis stood back and told the old monk that there was no reason why he should not rejoin his fellow monks.

'You can eat in the frater and sleep in the dorter as usual,' he declared. 'Tomorrow you can go back to your duties in the scriptorium. Doing your usual tasks will keep your mind off your strange delusions.'

Brother John had become too feeble and unreliable to continue his old duties about the farm or dealing with the pilgrims, so the prior had relegated him to the scriptorium, a small chamber above the chapter house. This housed the priory's small library and was where any work on manuscripts was carried out, directed by the sacristan. John had been given the task of making copies of psalms and chants for the choir and any other calligraphic work that was needed.

After supper, in the mild light of the summer evening, most of the monks congregated for a social hour in the 'warming room' situated at the end of the refectory. The fireplace was now empty, but in the cold weather it contained the only fire in the monks' accommodation, apart from that in the prior's parlour.

They sat around the stone benches built into the walls to discuss their activities and any local news and gossip. Of course, the rumours about the advancing Welsh army were a major topic.

'I am told on good authority that Glendower has a sizeable contingent of French troops with him now,' declared Jude, the cellarer, without disclosing who his good authority might be.

'I still fail to understand how this Welsh barbarian is able to command the support of the French,' grumbled Brother Pierre. 'Nor why he is able to defeat a much mightier nation like England.'

'In the hills and valleys of his rugged country of Wales, he is able to run rings around the English forces,' replied Mark. 'In a pitched battle on the open field, the King's troops would defeat him, but as they have done since Roman times, the Welsh wage a guerrilla war, darting down from their rocks and crags upon tired soldiers, wet and dispirited after their long march from the Midlands into the forbidding mountains.'

Louis, ever contentious, pointed out that the Welsh leader had virtually annihilated a much stronger English army at the battle of Brynglas.

'Their archers are the most skilful in Europe, which is why they are hired as mercenaries by many countries, even including England itself!'

The conversation and argument about warfare and tactics went on for some time, a somewhat incongruous subject for a group of monks, but eventually one of them changed the subject to Brother John, who like some of the other monks, had taken himself to his bed, to get as much sleep as possible before they were awakened at midnight for matins.

'Old John is becoming a serious liability to the welfare of this priory,' grumbled the cellarer. 'I sometimes see him stumbling about the courtyard, mumbling to the sky and waving his arms about. It is an embarrassment to the supplicants who come here. They must wonder what sort of place this is to have a madman wandering about.'

Brother Arnulf, the hospitaller, agreed with him.

'Several of the guests who stayed with me have been concerned about him and it cannot do the reputation of this place any good. The prior should think about settling him in one of our sister abbeys, which have places for such aged brothers in their declining years.'

The younger secretary, Mark, was not so ready to condemn the old man.

'He seems quite harmless, surely little damage can be done by him. His fantasies can be quite interesting, for only a few days ago he told me that he had spoken with an angel during the previous night, who informed him that we need have no fear of the advancing army for at least another two weeks.'

Some of the monks chuckled, others clucked their tongues at this further evidence of Brother John's dementia.

'Perhaps our Lord God has set one of his Angels with the keenest eyesight on top of the Malverns, to spy out the movement of Glendower's troops for us!' suggested Pierre sarcastically.

For the next two days, little was seen of Brother John, as he spent most of his time in the quiet of the scriptorium, seated at his high desk with a quill and ink. He was copying out a dozen duplicates of a new chant, which Patrice, the precentor, intended to add to the choir's repertoire. In spite of his age and other problems, John still had a sharp eye and produced excellent black-letter copies on sheets of parchment. He attended the frater at mealtimes and his appetite seemed undiminished. He was very quiet, but otherwise did nothing to give the other monks any cause for concern or irritation.

However, on the third morning all this changed.

At dawn, the brothers went down the night stairs into the church for prime, the first service of the day. The fact that Brother John was not amongst them failed to register, due to their sleepiness, until the office was over, when they trooped out into the early morning light of the inner courtyard. Here they found the old monk pacing up and down, shaking his fists at the heavens and muttering angrily at some unseen person apparently hovering above him.

'This is becoming insufferable!' snapped Matthew, the sub-prior. 'Someone call Brother Paul. He must do something about this man.'

As Arnulf hurried across the precinct to the prior's house, Mark went to the old man and gently placed a hand on his shoulder.

'What is troubling you, John?' he asked. 'Have you been hearing voices again?'

The aged Benedictine lowered his arms and turned an angry face towards the younger man. 'A message directly from St Oswald, no less! We are undone, this house is a sham and must be abandoned!'

Some of the other monks had begun to drift towards the refectory for their breakfast, but the vehemence of John's voice caused them to turn back and stare at him. The infirmarian, in his role as a doctor, joined Mark at the old man's side in an attempt to pacify him, for he seemed to be in a towering rage.

'John, John! Why are you so troubled?' Louis asked soothingly.

John glared at him scathingly. 'I tell you, all is lost with this place! We have been tricked for centuries.'

'Have you had more strange dreams?' asked Mark gently, but this seemed to annoy the elderly brother even more.

'Dreams? Not dreams, boy!' he ranted. 'St Oswald came to me in the night – or rather, I went to him.'

Louis decided to humour him once more. 'You went to him? Just where was this meeting – in the dormer?'

The elder monk's lined face looked at him pityingly. He raised an arm and pointed a quivering forefinger at the hill visible above the priory wall.

'Up there, at the British Camp.'

Brother Louis's eyebrows rose. 'On the top of the Herefordshire Beacon? Really, Brother, you test my patience. Those old legs of yours would hardly take you to the foot of that hill.'

John scowled at him. 'I was taken up there by a pair of angels. They held my arms and we drifted up there as gently as a butterfly.'

'And St Oswald was there waiting for you, I suppose?' said Pierre sarcastically.

'He was indeed, standing in the centre of that great earthen circle built by the ancients.'

By this time Arnulf had returned with the prior hurrying behind him. Paul went straight to John and held both his hands in his.

'Brother, you must try to restrain yourself with these wild tales. They do no good for the reputation of our house.'

'Our house no longer has a reputation!' bellowed the old man defiantly. 'We have been living a lie these past two centuries.'

The prior turned to the infirmarian. 'Brother Louis, will

you take our old friend to your sickroom and give him something to calm his spirits? Perhaps a good sleep will settle his mind.'

He laid a calming hand on the sleeve of John' s habit, but the old monk irritably shrugged it off.

'I'll not go to bed. It's not long since I rose!' he declared loudly. 'I must proclaim this message of deceit to the world.'

He began shuffling towards the gate between the inner and outer precincts, repelling all attempts to restrain him. However, at a sign from the prior, his secretary ran forward and closed the large wooden gate that sealed the archway.

'Brother, where do you think you are going?' coaxed Paul. 'Come back with me to my parlour and take a cup of wine to settle your spirit.'

Frustrated at having his exit cut off, John began mumbling again and waving his hands to heaven, but after few moments, he seemed to sag into submission, allowing Mark and the prior to lead him slowly back towards the house in the corner of the inner court. The dozen monks, who had congregated around them, watched as they reached the entrance porch.

'The poor man has lost his mind altogether now,' observed the sub-prior, not without a tinge of satisfaction unbecoming in a servant of God. 'If I was the prior, I would get him to a place of refuge without delay. He does this house no good with his bizarre behaviour.'

Pierre, the sacristan, privately had his own ungodly thoughts, thanking Heaven that the austere Brother Matthew was not yet prior, but aloud he joined in the general agreement that something must be done about old John.

'I wonder what our patron saint told him up there?' mused

Arnulf, the hospitaller, pointing up towards the Beacon, which hovered over the priory.

Jude grunted. 'As always, no doubt our prior will listen politely to John's ramblings. He has the patience of a saint himself.'

A few minutes later, the agitated old monk was seated on a stool before the prior's table, behind which Paul was beaming at him with his inevitable fixed smile. Mark was hovering to one side, after providing the other two with cups of wine from the prior's cupboard.

'Now, Brother John, tell us why you were so set on leaving the priory just now,' asked Paul gently, 'and where did you think you were going?'

The seemingly innocent question set off the old man's temper once again. His hand shook and some of the red wine spilled onto the polished floorboards.

'Where? Anywhere, out of this accursed place!' he quavered. 'But I will soon direct my feet towards the bishop in Hereford or Worcester – and then to Canterbury, or even Rome, if needs be!'

Paul shot a look at his secretary, his eyebrows raised in surprise. Mark shrugged, then spoke to the aged brother.

'John, that is an ambitious enterprise! I doubt you have been further than Worcester in your life?'

'I will find a way. The Lord and St Oswald will guide my steps.'

Prior Paul felt it was time that they got down to essentials.

'John, dear brother, what exactly is it that so disturbs your mind?' he asked gently. 'You speak of betrayal and shame, but what is in your turbulent mind that so distresses you, at a time of life when peace and tranquillity should be your lot?'

John's lined face looked from one to the other of the men who were trying to soothe him, but the wildness did not leave his eyes.

'St Oswald has chosen me as the channel to deliver the truth to the world!' he declared. 'I am in honour bound to carry out his sacred mission, no doubt ordered by the Almighty Himself!' He rocked on his stool as he crossed himself at these words, spilling more wine in the process.

Mark rolled his eyes at his superior and Paul sighed; even his fixed smile was weakening a little at the old man's intransigence, and he responded more firmly.

'Brother John, you must tell me what exactly *was* this vital message that you feel so fervently bound to convey it to the highest levels of our Mother Church!'

A life-time of vows of obedience surfaced in the monk and he bowed his head in submission. The secretary retrieved the cup from his fingers before what was left of the wine was spilled, as John began to speak.

'I have been troubled for some weeks by feelings of impending doom, Prior,' he said in a low voice. 'It was as if a malignant thunder-cloud was hovering over the Malverns and over our house. I knew something bad was going to happen and at first I thought it was the destruction that might be wrought by these advancing Welshmen.'

Paul nodded sagely. 'A natural enough fear, Brother. I doubt there is one of us who has not been touched by such apprehension.'

John shook his head, still looking down at the floor. 'No, it was not that, for the blessed Oswald assured me that we would suffer little harm from Glendower, who he said was a devout man and a protector of God's houses in Wales.'

The prior privately thought that this might not apply to

England, but he kept his doubts to himself. 'So what was it?' he persisted.

Brother John took a deep breath, then let it out in a long sigh as he committed himself to exposing his secret.

'He told me that all those centuries ago, the woman Beornwyn, who has become our patron saint and whom we praise and revere every day, was a brazen hussy, a whore who even fornicated in God's house, in the church of St Oswald himself! She was not killed by berserk Norsemen, but rightly executed for her profligate lewdness.'

The prior's face paled and his famous smile dropped from it like breeches falling when a belt breaks.

'That is a terrible thing to say, Brother!' he gasped. 'I am your confessor and I will have to give you a severe penance for such evil thoughts.'

'His mind is deranged, Prior,' murmured Mark. 'He is not responsible for his fantasies.'

But aghast at this sudden blasphemy, Prior Paul's habitually placid nature crumbled and he rose to point a shaking finger at the old monk.

'I will listen to no more licentious slander against our beloved Beornwyn!' he howled. 'Go to your bed and stay there until I have decided what to do about you!'

As John stumbled to his feet, the furious prior turned to his secretary.

'On second thoughts, escort him to the penitentiary cell and make sure that he stays there. Say nothing to the others. We cannot have the rest of our brotherhood tainted with his vile accusations!'

Mark took the culprit by the arm and gently led him away. John went unprotestingly, his eyes lowered to the floor as they left the prior to simmer down in his parlour.

As they walked across the inner courtyard, some of the other monks were still standing there, looking expectantly at the couple as they made their way to the chapter house, where a tiny cell was attached to the side of the building.

Brother Matthew, the sub-prior, came across to intercept them. 'What has happened?' he demanded imperiously. 'Why are you shutting him away?'

Mark raised a hand warningly at Matthew. 'Our brother here is unwell. The prior wishes him to be kept alone for a time.'

Matthew glowered at the young secretary. 'I am the sub-prior. I demand to know what's going on!'

Stubbornly, Mark shook his head. 'You must speak to the prior yourself, Brother. Those are his orders.'

Matthew angrily marched off towards the prior's house, leaving Mark to shepherd the old man into the small room that was kept for those who had offended in some way. It was rarely used, save for occasionally housing a brother who came home drunk from the village or was repeatedly late for holy offices.

Reluctantly, Mark ushered John to the hard chair, which, along with a lumpy mattress and blanket on the floor, was the only furniture, apart from an empty bucket and a large wooden cross on the wall.

'Sit there and rest, Brother,' he said compassionately. 'Lie down, if you wish, though it's early in the day for sleep.' As he went to the door, he turned to look at the old monk sitting with downcast eyes. 'I'll get one of the kitchen boys to bring you some broth, bread and water.'

Getting no response, he went out and pulled the door shut behind him. There was a key on the outside, but the prior had not told him to lock the old man in, so he left it there and went back across the precinct. Inside, John stirred himself and went to the small window, an unglazed square with bars across it. The only view was of the bare stone of the outside wall of the church, but as he held on to the bars, a blue butterfly fluttered in and alighted on the back of his right hand. With a strangled cry, he jerked away and as the creature flew off, he collapsed onto the hard bed and cried piteously, his chest heaving with sobs.

At about the ninth hour, after the office of prime, the monks all trooped into the chapter house for their daily session, which was part service, part business. As the priory had no novitiates at the moment, all the brothers had taken their vows and could remain for the whole meeting. One began by reading a chapter from the Rule of St Benedict, then the date, calendar and phase of the moon was announced, together with the names of the saints that were commemorated on that day. Prayers were said for the King and for the dead, then the daily schedule of services and duties were read out.

At chapter, any brothers who had offended in any way were brought before their fellows and penances ordered where necessary by the prior or his sub-prior. Today, the usual dull routine had been broken by John's weird behaviour, and the monks were eager to hear it discussed. From his chair facing the half-circle of benches where the brothers were sitting, Prior Paul began the proceedings, his face looking uncharacteristically drawn and sombre.

'We need to consider what must be done about the affliction of our Brother John, who, I must remind you all, has been a faithful member of this community for more than thirty years. His mind is now obviously deranged, but the

distasteful nature of his recent fantasies is such that we must
seriously consider how we should deal with him.'

At this, Brother Luke, one of the older monks, stood up to
ask a question.

'Prior, we have only heard rumours of what John alleged
this morning. Can you please tell us what he said?'

Paul looked very uncomfortable at this, but he had little
option in the fraternal nature of their closed community.
He cleared his throat.

'It is a hideous blasphemy, which I am loath to repeat,
but you will have to acknowledge that it comes from a dis-
eased mind. Brother John, in his demented state, alleges
that St Oswald of blessed memory had told him that our
dear patron, Beornwyn, was not a pure virgin, but a fornicator who actually committed her sins in a house of
God!'

There was a hiss of disbelief and a wave of muttering
amongst the brothers, but it was cut short by the harsh voice
of Matthew, sitting on a chair at Paul's right hand.

'Forgive me for interrupting, Prior,' he snapped. 'But I
find to my horror that this is the most foul and terrible accusation that it has ever been my lot to hear! To malign and
slander our beloved patron, who cannot answer for herself,
is an injustice that has no equal in my memory.'

He was almost quivering with anger at this slur on his
heavenly heroine, the virtues of whom he had always
extolled to an extent that bordered upon an obsession. He
was not finished yet and, red-faced with temper, addressed
the prior directly.

'I would advise that we should not proceed any further
without John being brought before us to answer for his sin.
It is always customary for brothers who have offended to be

faced directly with their misdeeds before this chapter and I feel it even more necessary now!'

Everyone knew that the sub-prior was flexing the muscles of his ambition, laying further claim to succeeding Paul when the time came. He rarely lost a chance to qualify or even contradict the prior over any lapse of custom or procedure, to emphasise his dislike of the more lenient regime favoured by Paul.

This time, however, the prior dug his heels in.

'All in good time, Brother! But first I wish to hear what others have to say about this unfortunate matter. We all have a right for our opinions to be heard.'

'John claims that angels took him up to the Beacon where he met St Oswald?' said Brother Arnulf, who was in charge of the guest-house.

'I suppose that is not impossible, though it would indeed be a miracle! Are we to believe that part of his story, even if not the more scurrilous aspects?'

The sub-prior again jumped in to reply before Paul could answer. 'Being taken up a mountain is not uncommon in religious history,' he grated. 'Was not the Muslim prophet Mohammed taken on his night journey by angels from Araby to the Mount of Jerusalem? And did not our own Lord Jesus Christ Himself go up to a mountain with Peter, James and John to meet Moses and Elijah?'

The prior's smile came back fleetingly as he responded. 'Indeed, Brother Matthew. And did not your namesake also record in his gospel that after forty days in the wilderness, Christ Jesus was taken to a mountain to be tempted and that angels then came to minister to him?'

The sub-prior nodded his agreement, but used the opening to come back at his superior.

'As always, you are right, Prior. But on that occasion it was Satan who transported him to that high place! Can we be sure that the same has not happened to Brother John and that this was not possession by the Devil?'

There was a fresh bout of murmuring amongst the assembled monks, which the prior brought to end by raising his hand.

'Then we will question our sick brother as he stands before us, as Matthew has suggested.'

He directed his secretary to fetch John from the penitent's cell and there was an uneasy silence in the chapter house as the younger man went on his mission. The monks shuffled their feet and looked uncomfortable, sensing the antagonism between their prior and Brother Matthew, as well as their concern over John, who until the last few days, they had looked on as a harmless, if eccentric, old colleague.

Then the door jerked open and the prior's secretary stood there, looking flustered. "He's gone! The cell is empty!'

Paul jumped to his feet. 'Gone? Where can he have gone? He must be somewhere in the priory!'

The irate Matthew strode towards the secretary and pushed him aside at the door. 'Why was he not locked in?' he snapped. 'Do I have to check everything myself?'

He marched out, followed by Mark, then the prior himself at the head of a ragged procession of brothers.

'When was he last seen, Mark?' demanded the prior. 'He can't have gone far on those old legs of his.'

His secretary, feeling guilty for not turning the key, said that the last person to have seen him must have been the lay brother who took him some food, now several hours ago. The sub-prior was barking out orders, and within minutes all the monks and a number of lay brothers and servants were

combing the various buildings in the inner and outer courtyards. It was only when a door-ward, disturbed by the
commotion, stumbled out of a privy near the outer gate,
that a sighting of the old monk was obtained.

'He passed out onto the lane to the village about an hour
ago,' the porter announced in an aggrieved voice. 'I didn't
know anyone was looking for him.'

The prior sighed. 'John would try the patience of Job,' he
complained. 'Mark, send a couple of servants after him –
and go with them yourself, as you seem most able to calm his
madness.'

Two of the ostlers quickly saddled up a trio of ponies and
minutes later, they were jogging briskly along the track that
joined St Oswald's priory to the outer world. It passed
through the handful of cottages that made up the village of
Broomhill, almost all of whose inhabitants were dependent
on the priory for their livelihood. As they passed, one of the
ostlers called out to a woman who was tying her goat to the
stakes of her garden fence.

'Good-wife, have you seen an old monk passing this way?'

She waved a hand onwards. 'Brother John went by less
than an hour ago. Never so much as returned my greeting,
neither. He'll surely be past the crossroads by now.'

They kicked their ponies into a trot and soon reached the
junction of the track with the wider road that came up from
the Forest of Dean and led towards Worcester.

'Which way now, Brother?' demanded one of the servants.

Mark rapidly considered this and felt that, given John's
threat to report his fantasies to a bishop, it was more likely
that he was aiming for Worcester. They turned left and
within half a mile, they saw the old man limping ahead of
them. When they caught up with him, Mark saw that John

was exhausted, only his fanatical willpower keeping him on his feet.

'John, John, what are we going to do with you?' sighed the younger monk, as he gently helped to lift John on to his own pony.

'I'll be locked up this time, boy,' croaked the old monk. 'But St Oswald will find a way to get my news proclaimed abroad.'

Mark led the pony towards home, sending one of the grooms ahead to tell the prior that the fugitive had been found unharmed. When they reached the priory, they were met by a silent group in the inner courtyard, a grim-faced sub-prior pointing at the infirmary building.

'In there with you, John,' he ordered in a voice of stone. 'You are not to leave, on pain of excommunication.'

As Mark and Brother Louis led him to the sick ward, the infirmarian decided that they would use one of the single rooms to hold John.

'They are unlikely to become full after the rumours that must already be spreading, thanks to the carters,' said Louis, somewhat bitterly. 'This will badly affect both our reputation and our treasure chest. We have had several more messages from patrons to say that they have called off their visits.'

'Maybe the threat of the Welsh advance is the reason for that,' countered Mark.

They settled John in one of the small chambers at the end of the main ward, the old man being silent now, but Mark noticed a sly glint in his eye as he watched them leave.

'Behave yourself now, Brother,' admonished the secretary, but John made no response. Outside the room, Mark was concerned that there was no lock on this door, but Louis seemed unconcerned.

'I spend much of my time in here and will keep an eye on him. Anyway, the prior has set a permanent guard on the gate between the courtyards. There is no other way out, except over the wall, and I doubt that even our intrepid old escaper will attempt that, especially as I will give him a good dose of laudanum to dull his warped senses.'

As the small community tried to get back to its normal routine, a quite different concern gripped them later that day, making them all but forget the peculiar behaviour of their oldest brother.

Lay-brothers and villagers who were working in the more distant fields and pastures began to notice an increase in the number of travellers using the lanes and tracks coming from the west. All were moving in the same direction, away from the Welsh border, and instead of the usual traffic of pedlars, carters and merchants, whole families seemed to be on the move, some with wagons or handcarts piled with possessions. The village reeve of Broomhill went to question some of the refugees and felt obliged to come up to the priory to report what he had heard.

'It seems this Glendower's army is on the move,' he told Arnulf, who was the most approachable of the monks, as he spent much of his time in the outer courtyard attending to the guests and visitors. 'The Welsh and these new Frenchies have been camped up for a couple of weeks, licking their wounds after being badly beaten near Usk. But it seems the English forces have pulled away and these barbarians are starting to advance again into the Marches.'

The hospitaller hurried with the news to his friend Jude, the cellarer, and in turn they went to the prior's house to give him even more to worry about. They found him in the parlour with the sub-prior.

'We had better set about hiding our treasures, as I suggested earlier,' was Paul's immediate response. 'Brother Matthew, will you ensure that the old crypt is cleared out? It may be that we will need to wall up the entrance to conceal its existence.'

As usual, the sub-prior was reluctant to hasten to carry out Paul's suggestions.

'I doubt there is much need for urgency, Prior. Monmouth is a long way off for a rabble travelling on foot – and no doubt stopping every few yards to loot and ravish.'

'Nevertheless, see that it is done,' retorted Paul irritably. 'We had better make sure that Beornwyn's skull is safest of all – apart from our devotion to it, it has an appreciable amount of gold around it.'

After vespers later that day, the usual relaxation and gossip hour in the warming room was dominated by talk of the approaching invaders. More reports had come in as the priory workers returned from the fields where early harvesting was in progress.

'It is said that the Welshmen are destroying every castle and manor house,' said Brother Jude, with an almost salacious delight.

'But they are respecting churches and holy houses,' countered Louis. 'No doubt the influence of their French allies is moderating their behaviour.'

Mark, always mild and conciliatory in his speech, reminded the French monk of his previous opinion. 'I recall you saying that the Welsh leader was an educated and cultured man – is that really true?'

The infirmarian nodded gravely, pleased to be a

Frenchman who could teach an Englishman some British history.

'This Glendower is a relatively wealthy man with several estates of his own. As well as being a soldier, he studied at the Inns of Court in London to be a lawyer. Not only that, but he married the daughter of one of the King's judges. He is descended from the princes of North and South Wales, but has been in the service of several prominent English nobles, fighting for them, and indeed, for King Henry himself.'

The prior's secretary admired Louis's erudition. 'You seem unusually well informed about these matters, Brother.'

The infirmarian smiled smugly. 'I like to keep abreast of what is happening in this country. One never knows when it might come in useful.'

Big, amiable Brother Luke joined in the discussion. He was a large, slow-moving man, content to supervise some of the lay brothers in the fields – and often chose to labour alongside them.

'If this Glendower served the English aristocracy and even the Crown so well, why is he now campaigning against them?'

'I can answer that, as I came here from the priory of Bangor in North Wales,' volunteered David, one of the younger monks. 'He has become disaffected since the death of one of his major patrons and then being overlooked for advancement by other nobles. Also he had a serious dispute over land with a powerful English neighbour in Ruthin, which triggered the present conflict.'

Louis nodded his agreement. 'That dispute has escalated into a nationalist rebellion and flocks of Welshmen – even students from Oxford – have been streaming back to join his army.'

'What about the involvement of the French?' asked Mark, always keen for enlightenment.

The sacristan, Pierre, answered this one. 'Paris has no love for the English king,' he said cynically. 'This was a chance to foment rebellion against the unpopular Henry by joining with the Welsh and several powerful lords in the North of England.'

'I heard tell of something called the "Tripartite Indenture",' observed Mark.

Louis nodded again. 'You are well informed yourself, Brother. Yes, recently Glendower agreed with those northern lords that, with the help of the French, they would defeat the King and divide up England and Wales into three separate provinces, each under their own control.'

Jude, the cellarer, sneered at the notion. 'That's a fantasy worthy of Brother John!' he scoffed. 'Our King, God bless him, will never let his kingdom be stolen from him like that! He will fight like a lion – and no doubt the French will then see reason and run home as usual!'

This started a squabble between the French and English factions amongst the brothers, which the sub-prior had to suppress with threats of penances for this unchristian behaviour. By the time they had settled down, the hour was late enough for them to seek their beds until the call for matins at midnight.

For the rest of the evening, the priory slumbered peacefully under the silvery light of the full moon. High above, the Herefordshire Beacon was silhouetted against the sky and, beyond it, the rest of the Malverns marched away to the north. The guard posted on the gate of the inner courtyard snored his way through the hours, but had the foresight to tie a cord from the latch to his wrist as he lay slumped against the gatepost.

Just before midnight, the night-porter in the dormitory began ringing the bell for matins and almost a score of sleepy monks clambered from their palliasses. After a perfunctory wash in the basins at the end of the dorter, they donned their habits as the prior arrived from his quarters, then began filing through the door at the opposite end. This led them down the night stairs into the south transept of the church on the way to their places in the quire.

They all carried lighted candles, which were to be placed in sockets in the choir stalls, and this dim illumination was sufficient to cause the leading monk to stop dead as he reached the crossing of the nave.

It was Brother Pierre, the sacristan, and he let loose a sound partway between a scream and a sob. Close behind, still only half awake, Brother Luke bumped into him with a muttered expletive, which was rapidly converted into a gasp of surprise.

'Holy Mother of God, what's happened? Who's that?'

Within seconds, the rest of the monks had formed a half-circle around the spring of St Beornwyn. Her alabaster statue had fallen forward from its pedestal and lay face down in the wide basin below, but even more alarmingly, it was obscuring the upper half of a body, also face down in the healing pool. Water had splashed out and lay on the slabs below the steps leading up into the quire and presbytery.

The sub-prior pushed forward and was first to reach the inert figure lying bizarrely in the sacred spring. Both Mark and the sacristan were close behind him and all three crouched alongside the victim of what appeared to be an extraordinary accident. By now, Prior Paul, who brought up the rear of the procession, had hastened to the fore and taken charge.

'Get that statue off the poor fellow!' he shouted, for once uncaring about the sanctity of the surroundings. He grabbed one shoulder of the stone saint and with Matthew and Mark grasping the head and opposite shoulder, levered up the full-size effigy and swung it sideways to rest across the top of the basin. It was extremely heavy and there was an ominous 'crack' as part of the retaining edge of the pool broke away, allowing more water to stream across the floor.

'Lift him out, for Christ's sake!' howled the prior, but it was an unnecessary command, as Matthew and Mark were already pulling the victim up from the basin. Then with Brother David and the precentor carrying the legs, they staggered across the flooded floor to a dry patch of flagstones and gently turned the figure face up as they laid him down.

'It's old John!' said Pierre flatly, though this surprised no one, as he was the only one missing.

'And he's dead!' added the infirmarian, after bending for a few seconds over the inert figure. There was a murmur of concern and a flurry of making the sign of the cross.

'I have heard of some supposedly drowned men who recovered after having the water squeezed from their chests,' suggested the prior tremulously, thinking that this looked like being the worst week of his life.

Louis shrugged, but, to appease Paul, bent again and pressed hard on John's chest a few times with both hands. There were wheezing sounds from the dead man's mouth, but no water emerged and the infirmarian stood up again.

'I doubt that he drowned, as there's no froth at his lips or nostrils,' he pronounced grimly. 'I was once physician to an abbey in the marshes of the Carmargue, where I saw many drowned people, so I am familiar with the signs.'

The prior stared at him. 'But nothing else could have killed him? His face was under the water!'

Brother Matthew jumped to contradict Paul. 'At his age, surely many things could have caused him to collapse. An apoplexy or a stroke? After all his strange behaviour lately, it should be no surprise that his brain has become severely disordered.'

Louis had been crouching to examine the corpse more closely during this exchange, running his hands over the soaking white hair and feeling the scalp. He now stood up and looked gravely around the ring of anxious faces in the flickering candlelight.

'Our brother's brain has certainly become severely disordered – but not by an apoplexy. His skull has been fractured!'

Again a ripple of consternation passed around the onlookers.

'Hardly surprising, after that statue fell upon him,' observed Matthew caustically. 'It must weigh several hundredweight.'

'It was not the statue,' declared the infirmarian. 'Old John has been deliberately struck upon the head!'

'It must have been the statue!' wailed the prior. 'It is unthinkable that anyone would have offered that poor man violence.'

Louis shook his head vehemently. 'There can be no doubt – he was struck upon the head. He must have been dead before his face went under the water.'

It was obvious that the audience of monks were unwilling to accept the physician's pronouncement.

'It must have been the statue!' cried Arnulf. 'St Beornwyn

was surely bringing down retribution upon John for his slanderous sacrilege against her.'

There was a chorus of agreement from the circle of his colleagues standing around the corpse.

'What clearer sign do we need?' cried Jude. 'There has been no earthquake, so why should our beloved Beornwyn's image fall at the very moment that her denigrator was beneath it?'

Louis, the physician, was unmoved by the arguments. 'But did it fall? Or did someone help it on its way?' he asked.

'I respect your expert knowledge, Brother, but in my long experience, the most obvious explanation is usually the correct one, 'said the prior, his placidity beginning to return in spite of the stressful circumstances. 'Even if he did not drown – and I have to accept your opinion on that – the fall of such a heavy weight upon his head can surely be the only explanation for his grievous injury.'

Louis, his face devoid of expression, shook his head. 'Normally, I would submit to your wise opinion, Prior. But unless Beornwyn's retribution was even more miraculous than it appears, that explanation cannot be accepted.'

'On what grounds do you so stubbornly contradict our prior?' snapped Matthew indignantly.

'There are two reasons,' replied the infirmarian evenly. 'Firstly, the fractures are on each side of the head rather than on the top or back, which one would expect from a statue falling on him. But far more telling is the fact that there are two separate injuries, one on each side of the head. It is too much to accept that the statue had fallen twice!'

There was a silence, then the circle of monks moved nearer so that the physician could point out the areas of blue-red discoloration above each ear.

'He has suffered bruises, but the skin is not broken,' explained Louis. 'However, I can feel fractured bone beneath each injury. The poor man was twice struck violently with a blunt object and probably died rapidly.'

During this altercation, the deceased monk lay in his sodden habit, staring up at the darkness of the roof high above. His pallid face was wet, his mouth partly open as if protesting against the discomfort that he was suffering.

'What shall we do with him?' asked the practical Mark. He had already plunged his arm into the basin to remove the wooden plug from a drain at the bottom, to stop the leakage over the cracked rim, which was threatening to turn the crossing of the nave into a duck pond.

After some discussion, the prior, sub-prior and sacristan decided to place the body on a bier behind screens in a corner of the south transept, well away from the flooded floor – and from the curious gaze of the depleted number of visiting pilgrims. Two of the monks went for the bier, which was hanging on a bracket at the back of the church. It was a stout stretcher with handles each end and four sturdy legs, used to carry bodies and coffins at the infrequent funerals. John was reverently lifted onto it and his soaking habit removed, to be replaced by a shroud fetched from the vestry.

'Matins shall be devoted to prayers for our departed brother,' announced the prior. 'Naturally we shall be holding a full Requiem Mass for him when the time comes.'

As they filed into the quire stalls above the shattered function, Brother Matthew murmured into the prior's ear. 'We must discuss this in chapter as well as between we senior members. It may not be appropriate to offer the full rites of the Church to someone who may have been possessed by the Devil!'

*

Next morning, before the chapter meeting, the prior, his secretary, the sub-prior, the sacristan and the infirmarian went back into the empty church to examine the damage to the shrine of St Beornwyn. A couple of burly lay brothers lifted the heavy statue from across the wide bowl and laid it on the flagstones. A stonemason from the village, who did any building work that was required in the priory, was called to examine it. He declared it undamaged apart from some chips from the base, which fitted into a socket on the back of the bowl.

'Someone has jammed a crowbar or such-like under there and levered her off the supporting peg,' he declared confidently, causing Louis to smile smugly at this confirmation of his theory. The mason promised to return with cement to set Beornwyn more firmly back on her pedestal and to repair the broken rim of the basin. When he had departed with the lay brothers, the senior monks were left alone to consider the situation.

'Much as it pains me to accept it,' began the prior, 'it seems that you were right about this being a deliberate act, Louis. But I feel it flies in the face of reason to believe that anyone would so cruelly murder this poor old man. What earthly motive could anyone have?'

The sub-prior was ready with an answer. 'None of us was happy about Brother John's lewd fantasies, especially as they were likely to drastically reduce our income from pilgrims, which finances the comfortable way of life enjoyed by this house!'

Brother Paul sighed. Matthew never missed a chance to snipe at what he considered a lack of asceticism at Broomhill.

'That could never be a motive for murder, especially in an institution devoted to God and good works,' he protested.

'You are too unworldly to be fully aware of the working of men's minds, Prior,' retorted Matthew cynically. 'Men will kill for a couple of pennies, let alone the many pounds that pilgrims and supplicants bring in to St Oswald's.'

'But we're not just *men* here, we are a special breed who have given our lives to the Almighty,' said Mark, vehemently.

Again the sub-prior gave one of his supercilious smiles. 'You are young and innocent, Mark. When you have lived in the world for another twenty years, as I have, you will know that there are good monks and bad monks, just as in any other walk of life.'

The physician Louis decided to put an end to this pointless argument. 'The fact remains that our Brother John was foully murdered. There is no avoiding that conclusion, so whatever the motive, there is a killer amongst us.'

Prior Paul became agitated, his hands fluttering in front of his ample stomach. 'Amongst us? Surely we must look for some evidence that an outsider committed this foul crime?'

The infirmarian shrugged. 'I am merely a physician, who can tell you that John was deliberately slain. I cannot venture any opinion as to *why* or by whom.'

'What about *when*?' asked the prior's secretary.

Louis nodded sagely. 'I wondered when someone was going to ask me that. We found the body shortly before matins, at around midnight. He was still warm and his limbs were still pliable. I last saw John in his room when I gave him a sleeping draught earlier that evening.'

'At what time would that be?' asked the prior.

'I took myself to my bed in the dorter at about the seventh hour, though it is difficult to be precise.'

Though some large abbeys and cathedrals had installed large clocks many years previously, they were still not

common. At St Oswald's, the bellringer who alerted everyone to the times of all holy offices, used a large graduated
candle to inform him of the time.

'So the despicable deed must have been perpetrated
during the five hours between those times?' persisted Mark.

'It would appear so,' agreed Louis. 'But no one has asked
me *where* it was committed. That is just as well, as I have no
answer. Poor John could have been struck on the head in his
room in the infirmarium – or in the church, or anywhere
between. There is no way of telling.'

After this there was a strained silence as no one could
think of any further questions – or, indeed, answers.

'We must leave this now,' ordered the prior. 'When we all
meet in the chapter house, I will solemnly enjoin every
member to examine his conscience and to confess any sins
that may have a bearing upon the tragedy.'

'Not only any sins, but any information that might be
useful,' added the sub-prior, determined to get in the last
word.

Twenty miles away, in a barn set on a piece of common land
outside a village in the land of Gwent, another conference of
a very different sort was in progress. Around a rough table
taken from the reeve's house, half a dozen men sat on a
couple of benches looted from the same place. From a chair
at the head of the table, Owain Glyndwr was listening to
reports from his lieutenants and making plans for the morrow.

'The further we go into England, the more difficult it will
be to feed them and our horses,' growled Evan ap Collwyn,
one of the prince's quartermasters.

'Soldiers will always find a way of getting food from somewhere,' retorted another giant of a man, Iestyn Goch.

'Six thousand mouths need a lot of victuals,' retorted Evan. 'They have been on a very short commons since Brecon, and the way ahead looks unpromising.'

Owain, the true Prince of Wales, listened carefully to all the opinions, absently pricking the reeve's table with the point of a small dagger. He was a large man, though not on the scale of Iestyn Goch. Handsome at fifty, with light brown hair and beard to match, he had an avuncular calmness that belied his prowess as a fighter and a politician. This rebellion – better termed a war of independence – had been running for five years and until Usk a couple of weeks ago, had been increasingly successful with every passing month. However, that battle at Pwll Melyn had seen the death of his brother, who was his chief supporter, as well as Bishop Thomas, a fighting cleric who had won over the priesthood of Wales to his side. Equally tragic was the loss of Crach Ffinant, his bard, soothsayer and prophet. In addition, his son had been captured and dragged to the Tower of London. However, this severe setback had not weakened his determination to advance into England, threatening the very heartland of the unpopular tyrant King Henry IV. Thankfully the French had now kept their promise and landed almost two thousand men at Milford Haven, who were now joining his forces. However, as Evan had pointed out, an army marches on its stomach, and at the moment those particular organs were pretty empty.

'Until now, we have been campaigning in Wales and have seized our sustenance wherever possible from towns, manors, castles and courts belonging to Englishmen or Welshmen who have sold out to them,' observed Glyndwr. 'As I have always insisted, we have never stolen from our own peasantry, the very people for whom we are fighting. However, now that we are on the very edge of England, we need not be so sensitive. We have suffered oppression and humiliation, with untold cruelty from them for over a century, since they murdered Prince Llewelyn at Cilmeri. So now we will take what we need, to show them that the tables have turned.'

He transferred his gaze to another man, a sallow, black-browed fellow with a shock of dark hair and a turn in his eye.

'Mostyn Gam, what have your scouts reported about our route towards Worcester? What prospects are there for feeding our men and beasts on the way?'

Mostyn looked pessimistic. 'Not very good ones, *arglwydd*. There are few great houses and estates, most of the farms are small and half of them only grow bloody apples!'

'What castles will we have to contend with? They are usually well stocked with food and fodder.'

Mostyn Gam pulled out a small roll of parchment from his pouch and flattened it on the table. Entering England was a new experience for the Welsh army and their knowledge of its geography was sparse. Though the coastline was well known, the inland areas were familiar only to those who lived there, as there were no reliable maps and only the main roads between towns were recorded, their distances often being speculative.

'Our priest from Talgarth went disguised with one of the scouts. He drew this chart when he came back, marking the places where he felt meat, grain, hay and even money might be taken.'

They pored over the crude map for a time, noting where castles, manors and villages were sited near the route they proposed for reaching Worcester.

'What's this one, marked with a cross near this line of

hills?' asked Evan ap Collwyn, jabbing a large finger onto the parchment.

Mostyn squinted at it with his lazy eye. 'He said it was a small priory, dedicated to some English saint or other. It's isolated and, with a bit of persuasion, may well yield up something useful. They're bound to have livestock for us to slaughter, as well as a mill stocked with flour and grain.'

'And some gold and silver cups on their altar, as well as a fat money chest in their chancel,' suggested another man, a cousin of Owain's from Builth.

The prince held up a cautionary hand. 'We are fighting the King of England, remember, not the Holy Catholic Church! I respect those religious houses in Wales who support our cause and if English priests and monks do not oppose us as we pass by, then we have no call to harm them or their houses.'

Evan ap Collwyn grinned. 'Indeed, but no doubt some of these fat clerics can be persuaded to "voluntarily" offer us sustenance. Is it not their Christian duty to aid any travellers who knock on their doors to ask for food and lodging?'

There was a guffaw from around the table and even Owain raised a smile as he replied. 'I doubt if any man of God would relish six thousand travellers knocking on his door ... so we will proceed with moderation.'

The leader was in a subdued mood, keenly feeling not only the loss of his brother and son, but the absence of his strange astrologer and prophet, Crach Ffinant. A superstitious man, Glyndwr took predictions and prophesies very seriously and missed the advice of Crach, with his reading of the stars and the clouds, and the behaviour of the birds and natural elements.

With a deep sigh, he sat wishing for some sign from heaven

that he was doing the right thing by marching deeper into the heart of England than anyone else since the Norman Conquest.

After vespers, the last service of the day, Prior Paul called his secretary into his parlour, bidding him to close the door firmly.

'Mark, you are my confidant and my friend. We must talk seriously about the tragedy that has befallen this house. Between us, we must try to come to some conclusion.'

It was true that the prior was extremely fond of the younger monk and an almost father-son relationship had grown between them. Mark was a nephew of the Bishop of Lichfield, who had been ordained from the same seminary as Paul, a fact that was likely to advance the younger man's career prospects, starting with this secretarial post in St Oswald's.

Mark sat on the stool opposite the table and looked expectantly at his mentor.

'How do we begin, Prior?' he asked.

'By posing a series of questions, I think. The first is whether we have to accept that it must be a member of our brotherhood that is the culprit.'

The secretary pondered this before he answered.

'I suppose we have to accept that John's death was murder, not some bizarre accident. Our infirmarian was adamant about that and I cannot see any hope of denying it.'

Paul nodded, his famous smile having deserted him. 'A lack of drowning and two blows to the head would seem to make his conclusion incontrovertible. Now what about anyone other than a brother being the perpetrator?'

Mark shook his head sadly. 'Little chance of that, I'm

afraid. The death occurred within the inner precinct and there was a guard on the only gate all that night. I cannot see anyone from outside scaling a ten-foot wall, especially when a stranger would surely have no motive to silence poor John's fantasies.'

Paul looked at his assistant. 'You feel sure that that must have been the motive?'

'I see no alternative. Why else would anyone wish to dispose of an obscure old monk who, apart from this recent aberration, never uttered a controversial word in his life?'

The prior rose from his seat and went to a window to stare out, though for once he was not searching the horizon for the approaching Welsh horde. He turned back to face Mark. 'So we are left with seventeen brothers as the only suspects?'

Mark turned up his palms in an almost French gesture, perhaps learned from Pierre or Louis.

'There was one lay brother in the precinct, of course: the night porter, Alfred, who rings the service bell. But he is almost as old and feeble as John, and has spent almost all his life here. Surely we can discard him as a suspect?'

The prior nodded his agreement. 'And there are two others we can discard as well.' The secretary raised his eyebrows in query as Paul continued, 'Ourselves, I trust! I certainly know that I am innocent and I am sure that you feel the same.'

Mark flushed a little at the implied compliment. 'Thank you for your confidence in me, Prior. But, of course, an episcopal or even papal enquiry, to say nothing of the secular authorities, could not eliminate us from suspicion any more than the rest of our brothers.'

Paul shook his head. 'There will be no enquiry outside the ecclesiastical fraternity. In these fraught times, with an enemy advancing on Hereford and Worcester, no coroner or sheriff will concern himself with an internal matter in a religious house. I doubt any bishop will be interested, either, for like us they will be too concerned with defending their brethren and their treasures.'

He sat down again and rested his chin on his clasped hands. 'So we now have fifteen suspects to consider.'

'I think we have one more to eliminate,' Mark said, 'and that is our brother Louis. He was the one who detected the murderous nature of the death and rejected any notion of an accidental – or miraculous – collapse of Beorwyn's statue upon old John.'

The prior saw the logic of this at once. 'Ah, you mean that if he was the killer, he would have gone along with the obvious conclusion that John had drowned under the statue? He certainly would not have demonstrated the two blows to the skull to us.'

There was a silence as each man digested this.

'That still leaves us with a considerable number of names to consider,' said Paul ruminatively. 'And no clear idea of how to proceed. I can hardly take each brother aside and demand to know if he killed old John!'

Mark pulled the top of his black robe away from his neck, as it was very hot in the chamber, even with the two glazed casements open.

'Can you not give them a stern warning at chapter about the peril to their souls and the prospect of hellfire if they do not confess – or even fail to offer you any information they have about this evil tragedy?'

Prior Paul sighed as he rejected this suggestion. 'I can do it, certainly, but I know it will be useless, unless we have a potential martyr amongst us, who is willing to sacrifice himself for having saved the reputation of our saintly Beornwyn.'

'What would happen to a brother who was found to be a murderer?' asked the secretary.

'I have never heard of such case, thank God,' Paul replied, crossing himself. 'As you well know, thanks to St Thomas the Martyr, who refused to submit the Church to the will of the second King Henry, we still have "benefit of clergy", so that we can avoid the lethal punishments of the secular law. But no doubt some very severe penance would be levied by archbishops or even the Pope, such as banishment for life to some remote cell.'

Mark was still not satisfied that the miscreant could not be persuaded to admit his crime.

'I find it hard to believe that a man devoted to God, as we all are here, could live with himself knowing that he had taken the life of another. Surely he would be bound to unburden himself to his confessor? Each one of us, even you, has one of the priests amongst us as his confessor.'

As was usual in any abbey or priory, most monks were not priests, but St Oswald's had four brothers who had been ordained, so could administer the sacraments and take confessions.

Paul's smile returned briefly at his secretary's youthful naïvety and unworldliness. 'Mark, you will learn that monks, like any other mortal men, will not tell their confessor everything. In fact they are more likely to keep major sins to themselves and be content to offer the smaller ones. In any event, you know as well as I do that all confessions are inviolate and even an admission of murder could not be divulged.'

He stood up to indicate that their discussion was over.

'I did not hope that we could solve the mystery today, but wanted to clear our minds about what we know and do not know. Let us both sleep on it and especially pray for guidance, then speak of it again after chapter tomorrow. Meanwhile, we have to see John laid reverently in the ground, in spite of Brother Matthew's doubts about his being possessed by the devil! And the other urgent matter is preparing this house against the advance of Glendower's horde.'

Next day, the monks assembled in their places in the quire for the solemn Requiem Mass that prepared Brother John's body for eternal rest in the small cemetery outside the church. The nave held all the lay brothers and many of the villagers who depended on the priory for their livelihood. For all his eccentricity, old John had been popular with the rest of the community until his fits became worse and his mind began to fail. The plain wooden coffin stood before the altar as Prior Paul officiated, ignoring the disapproving scowls of Brother Matthew, who still muttered that perhaps the devil had entered his soul. As the litany and chanting saw the old monk off to Heaven, some of the brethren suspected that when he arrived there, John would seek out St Oswald and berate him for cutting short his life.

The coffin was buried with all due reverence in the red Herefordshire soil and a simple wooden cross planted at the end of the grave. A final dirge was sung around it before the monks and lay brothers filed away to their normal duties.

The formalities were over, but an hour later a message from a shepherd tending priory flocks at the furthest limit of their land sent the prior into a flurry of agitation. The man had spoken to a party of refugees coming up from the west, who reported that Glendower's host, now strengthened by hundreds more French knights and foot soldiers, appeared to be making ready to move out of their camp near Monmouth.

Paul gathered the monks together in the warming room and urgently gave them instructions to hide the priory's valuables.

'The treasure chest in my parlour, the sacramental cups and plates from the aumbry in the chancel and, of course, the relic of Beornwyn, must be hidden securely. We cannot tell how long it will be before this ravaging host arrives from the edge of Wales, but we must be ready for them.'

As always, the sub-prior raised an objection.

'All that will not fit into a stone coffin in the crypt. The treasure chest alone would be too large.'

This provoked an immediate discussion, but it was a suggestion from the ever-practical cellarer that was soon accepted.

'Where the spring comes out of the earth beneath the chancel, there is a small chamber where the top end of the conduit that feeds Beornwyn's fountain is placed,' Brother Jude said. 'One of the stone slabs in the chancel floor is removable and there is sufficient space beneath to hide all we wish.'

The precentor, Brother Patrice, had a different question. 'With our relic hidden away, we will be unable to administer any sacred water to pilgrims,' he pointed out.

Arnulf, the hospitaller, answered this scornfully. 'There'll be no pilgrims for as long as the Welsh are advancing on us. I have had no lodgers in the guest-house since yesterday.'

Soon the inner ward was bustling with activity. All the lay brothers were kept out and the centre gate firmly closed, with one brother set to guard it against intrusion. Although all the rest of the community knew what was going on, the prior wanted to keep the actual hiding place of the valuables as secret as possible.

Although it was unmarked, Jude, who seemed to be best informed about such matters, identified the slab in front of the altar that covered the spring – virtually where old John's coffin had rested shortly before. With no strong labourers to help them, the brothers had to struggle with the heavy stone themselves, but when it was prised out and slid aside, they saw that the cellarer was right about the masonry-lined cavity beneath. It surrounded the small pool from which clear water bubbled out and then vanished down a conduit to the basin of St Beornwyn. There was sufficient room around the margins of the pool for the wooden chest that contained the mass of silver coins collected from pilgrims, as well as for the calvarium of their beloved saint. The silver chalices, patens and other precious items used in their religious observances, were fetched from the aumbry, a locked cupboard built into the wall of the chancel. All these were carefully wrapped in blankets and laid on the raised stones around the spring.

When the slab was replaced, dirt was rubbed into the cracks, then dust carefully brushed over all the slabs before the altar, to obliterate any signs of disturbance. When it was finished, Prior Paul stood in front of his brothers to contemplate the result.

'That is all we can do now,' he said sombrely, his famous smile having almost vanished in the turmoil of recent days. 'We can only commend the safety of our holy objects to God.'

As he led prayers on the spot, his secretary could not help

wondering how that chestful of silver pennies could be considered as 'holy objects'.

Later that day, a lay brother and a pair of men from the village were sent out westwards to give early warning of the approach of the advancing army. As disciples of the priory, they would get lodging with any cottager or forest-dweller who had not yet run away. When either the Welsh host or their scouts were spotted, they would ride back to Broomhill with the news. The prior, who had thought up this plan, was not really sure it achieved anything, but he felt that any warning was better than none.

In the meanwhile, Paul kept up the pressure on his brethren to reveal the killer of Brother John. At every chapter meeting and at prayers before each dinner and supper, he exhorted them to study their consciences and to safeguard their immortal souls. His normally mild manner had hardened in past days, and even Matthew could not carp about his laxity of discipline.

'For how long can you live a lie like this!' barked the prior at chapter one day. 'One of you has the mark of Cain upon himself, invisible though it be to all except the culprit.'

His voice gathered strength as he looked over the bowed heads of the abashed community. 'I will never understand why you, whoever you are, could not recognise that John had a disordered mind and that he could never be able to carry out his threat of informing the world of his morbid fantasy! You may have done this wicked deed in the honest, but mistaken belief that you were safeguarding the reputation of this house. That could be taken into consideration when you face the consequences of your action,' he cried, swinging a pointed finger around the assembled brothers.

'God and the bishops he has appointed as his agents on earth, are full of mercy and compassion. The secular law has no control over your punishment and anything that the Church can mete out to you is as nothing compared to the abyss you face without confession, contrition and absolution!'

He worked himself up to the finale. 'Repent and confess, or you will burn in hell and your miserable soul will suffer torments until the end of time! Confess to me and lift what must be an intolerable burden lying across your shoulders every minute of the day and night. Repent and confess!'

Paul continued in this vein for the next week, without any visible effect upon his reluctant listeners. He even began to wonder if his infirmarian's diagnosis of murder could have been wrong, though the facts seemed to speak for themselves.

The scouts he had sent out to spy on the Welsh had not returned, but on the fourth day, they sent a message with a shepherd to say that so far, there were no signs of even the advance guard of the Welsh.

'No doubt they are taking their time in destroying and plundering everything in their path,' muttered Arnulf glumly, as he sat sharing a cup of wine in the cellarer's room.

Brother Jude shrugged. 'Certainly this Glendower has wrecked almost every castle in Wales and the Marches. I have not heard that he has been slaughtering or pillaging religious houses, thank God.'

'We shall soon find out, Brother!' grunted Arnulf, gloomily.

But it was almost a week before the scouts returned, trotting up to the main gate of St Oswald's and breathlessly delivering their news to Prior Paul, who came to the steps of his house to meet them.

'They are but five miles away by now,' reported the lay brother, who normally was one of the millers. 'They delayed for several days to sack Ledbury, but the day before yesterday, moved on to Eastnor where they camped again.'

Ledbury was a small market town and Eastnor was a village with nothing between it and the priory, other than woods and open country. Pale with anxiety, Paul ordered his monks to call in the villagers from outside the walls and within the hour, about fifty men, women and children were camping in the outer courtyard.

'The women and children can stay in the guest-house,' ordered Brother Matthew, now striding around officiously, organising the influx. 'The men can remain out here, until we see what the situation is by nightfall.'

Several of the younger men had volunteered to stay outside to drive some of their best cattle, hogs and sheep up into the dense woods on the hills behind, hoping to keep them out of the clutches of the invaders.

'The rest of them, and all the fowls, will have to stay where they are,' said Jude sorrowfully. 'I doubt we'll see any of them again after this horde has passed.'

'If they *do* pass!' added Arnulf, looking askance at the ragged children running in and out of his tidy guest-house. 'This place will never be the same again.'

There followed an uneasy couple of hours when the priory seemed to be holding its breath. The birds still sang and the remaining sheep still bleated outside the walls, but there was still no sign of the dreaded Welsh.

'They move very slowly,' said the lay brother who had gone scouting. 'There are a few hundred mounted men in the lead, mostly French knights, but the main host is on foot, many of the men without shoes. And the slowest of all are the stolen carts, laden with food and weapons. Their oxen can only keep up half a man's walking pace.'

But eventually, they came.

The two porters were keeping a lookout from the top of the arch over the main gates, which were firmly closed and barred. The first signs they saw were a couple of men armed with spears, appearing on ponies on the track out of the woods. Alongside them walked a pair of archers, each with the famous Gwent longbows slung across their back, the bowstrings coiled inside their leather hats to keep them dry.

The lookouts cried a warning down to the crowd assembled anxiously in the courtyards below, then watched until they saw the advance guard reach the cottages a few hundred paces away. The men began searching them and brought out a few objects from the humble shacks, then turned their attention to the mill placed over the small river, which meandered across the pastures until it vanished into the woods beyond. There had been no time to bring the mill's stock of grain and flour into the priory, but Jude had been storing as much as he could in his cellarium over the past week.

When the soldiers emerged, they moved over to a point opposite the priory gates and began eating whatever food they had found in the cottages, sitting relaxed on the grass, obviously under orders not to approach the priory until the army arrived.

'Our hopes for the horde to pass us by seem dashed already,' said Brother Mark, who had been looking out through a small spy-hole in the main gate. 'These scouts are waiting for their leaders to catch them up.'

He made way for the prior to peer through the flap. After

a moment, Paul turned away and spoke gravely to his brothers.

'I must go out and confront this Glendower when he comes, to plead with him that he leaves this religious house in peace, for I have heard that he is a devout man.'

An hour later, the prior had his chance of confrontation. The porters above the gate gave a cry of warning, as they saw the vanguard of the Welsh host appearing through the trees, half a mile away.

The first to break out on the narrow forest track were horsemen, a score of whom rode in pairs. There was little by way of extravagant heraldry, as this was a fighting force wary of opposition, but the leading pair held pennants aloft, attached to spears. One displayed a gold French fleur-de-lis, the other the red dragon of Cadwalader. As they advanced at walking pace, the next sight the anxious watchers had was of a dozen men on larger steeds, some wearing armoured breastplates. As they came nearer, it was obvious which was the leader, as a very erect man on a horse with more elaborate harness pulled slightly ahead of the others as they emerged from the narrow track on to the more spacious fields. Behind them came a stream of mounted knights, many in the more colourful uniforms of the French, then a long cavalcade of foot soldiers with a motley mixture of clothing and weapons. Some carried swords or maces, others had spears or pikes, but many were archers. The stream of men seemed endless and they were still emerging from the trees when the leaders had reached the cottages in front of the priory.

'There's thousands of them, Prior!' shouted down one of the porters. 'Looks as if they are going make camp in the fields outside.'

With the monks crowding around him, Brother Paul peered through the squint in the main gate and saw that the leading men had dismounted and were conferring amongst themselves.

'I must go out and speak with their leader, this Glendower,' he said stoically. 'Throw ourselves on his mercy, if needs be.'

There was a babble of concern from his brothers.

'It is too dangerous, Prior!"' said his secretary, urgently. 'Let me go in your place to see if they are amenable to reason.'

'It will be equally dangerous for you, Mark,' said Paul gently. 'But you will come with me – and you both, Louis and Pierre, for you might be able to charm your fellow Frenchmen!'

Amidst a chorus of concern from the other monks, the bar was raised from the gates and the four men stepped out on to the track leading from the priory to the village. As they walked slowly towards the leaders of the army, more men were pouring across the fields, now followed by ponderous supply carts, pulled by both oxen and draught-horses.

When the quartet of monks got within fifty paces of Owain Glyndwr and his lieutenants, the front row of half a dozen riders dismounted, men running from behind them to hold the horses. In the warm summer weather, with their scouts reporting no immediate threat of opposition, most of the knights had discarded their armour, though some still wore a breastplate or a hood of chain mail which covered their necks and shoulders. Owain himself was bare-headed and wore a jupon, a short quilted jacket of green silk. His breeches were thrust into spurred riding boots and a heavy sword hung from a low-slung belt.

As he walked to meet the Benedictines, two of his companions coming close behind for protection, the prior saw a powerful man with abundant grey-brown hair and a forked beard and moustache of the same colour.

They stopped a few paces apart and regarded each other.

'I am Paul, the prior of St Oswald's,' began the monk hesitantly. 'Do you speak English, sir?'

The impassive face of the Prince of Wales suddenly cracked into a smile. 'I do indeed – and French, Latin and Welsh! Take your pick, Father.'

Paul felt a sudden wave of relief. Uncertain whether this war-like host had intended to slay him on the spot, he now felt that whatever pillaging of their goods might happen, this civilised man would not unleash an orgy of rapine and murder upon them.

'What are your intentions here, Sir Owen? We are a small house, with few people and no great riches.'

'How often have I had that said to me, Prior? But I have no quarrel with the Church – several of my most ardent supporters are of your cloth.'

He swept a hand behind him, where Paul noticed that several of the mounted men wore crosses around their neck

'What then do you want of us?' asked Paul.

Glyndwr regarded him coolly. 'We must be given – or we'll take – whatever sustenance we can gain here. Your grain, fodder and meat. And a place to rest up for a day, as I have many tired and hungry men here.'

One of the men in French uniform spoke up from behind the leader. His English was heavily accented. 'Are there no estates or great houses nearby? They are the places where we are more likely to find worthwhile stores to plunder.'

Before Paul could reply, Louis spoke up in his native language, addressing the speaker. 'None before Malvern or Upton. You need to move on a few more miles.'

Not to be outdone before a fellow-countryman, Pierre also made his nationality known, by using the same tongue. 'It is a pleasure to hear God's own language spoken in this outlandish country, Monsieur.'

Glyndwr's bushy eyebrows rose a little as he turned his head to speak to his Gallic comrade.

'We seem to have come across a nest of Frenchmen, Comte de Salers!' He swung back to Pierre and Louis. 'And what are you doing here, sitting on the Welsh border?'

'I am the sacristan, recently from the abbey of Fontrevault – and anxious to return there! This is Brother Louis, our infirmarian.'

'A Doctor of Physic from Montpellier.' Even in such a fraught situation, Louis could not resist flaunting his badge of fame, and the Welsh leader seemed interested.

'One reason for our need to halt here for a day or so is that we have sick and wounded men. Will you look at them or have you scruples about helping the enemy?'

This was a challenge to Louis's Hippocratic oath.

'They are not my enemies,' he snapped. 'All men in distress deserve Christian aid. You seem to have many of my countrymen in your retinue, so I will ask them how we might best aid the sufferers.'

Owain called the Comte de Salers forward and the two French monks went to confer with him, leaving the prior and his secretary facing the prince.

'If you have many sick men, perhaps they would be better housed in our infirmary and in the guest-house, rather than lie in carts or on the cold grass out there,' he suggested, pointing to the mass of men who were now covering the field, many sitting or lying down.

Already some were forming into groups and lighting

fires with sticks picked up on their journey through the woods.

'Where are your own villagers now?' demanded Glyndwr.

'Inside our walls. The women and children are in the guest-house, but we can move them to the lay brothers' dormitory if you wish to shelter your sick and wounded.'

Glyndwr regarded the plump prior critically. 'You are a compassionate man, unlike some clerics we confront! They often abuse us, resist and even try to offer us violence.'

Mark thought it was time he said something to support his prior. 'We are a house of healing, sir. The priory was founded centuries ago because of the miracle of the spring, above which the church was built. Much of our work is treating the sick, either by the magic of Beornwyn's fountain or by the expertise of physicians like Brother Louis.'

Glyndwr seized upon the idea of a magical spring. His fascination with divination and mystic signs made anything occult a welcome diversion from the years of warfare to which he had committed himself.

'We have a strong tradition of healing wells in Wales. Tell me of this spring you have here.'

Between them, Mark and the prior outlined the history of Beornwyn and St Oswald.

'Some two hundred years ago, we were given some of the bodily relics of that saintly virgin to keep in the church,' added Paul. 'Since then, the power of healing has increased, as has the reputation of the priory to attract pilgrims.'

The Welsh prince was no fool and knew that this meant that donations must have filled the coffers many times over since the spring and the relics attracted a stream of supplicants. But he was interested in the more mystical aspects of the story.

'I must see this famous fountain for myself – and touch your virgin's relics,' he announced. 'They may confer good fortune upon our crusade!'

Paul realised that the gold-banded skull was now hidden away, and they had carefully avoided mentioning it in treating the sick. Thankfully, he thought, they still had several other mouldering bones in the reliquary, which could be shown to Glyndwr to satisfy his curiosity. The more affable they could make their relationship, the better chance the priory had of getting away with a minimum of looting.

'Come in now, and bring your senior officers with you,' he invited. He led them back to the priory gates and called to the porters to throw them wide. 'And leave them open, there will be sick and wounded coming in shortly,' he commanded.

His two French brothers had gone off with some of Owain's captains into the now dense crowd of soldiers, to find men in most need of medical care, but Mark kept close to the prior as they led Glyndwr into the outer courtyard. Many of the villagers and lay brothers shrank back as the armed men strode through, but Paul called to the rest of his monks to follow them to the church.

He led the invaders up the steps and across the empty nave until they reached the marble fountain and the effigy of St Beornwyn. As Paul genuflected in deference to the high altar, he was surprised to see that Owain Glyndwr dropped to both knees on the flagstones, crossed himself and held his hands before his bowed head, as he murmured some prayers. Then he climbed to his feet and looked with interest at the unusual fountain that sat before the chancel arch.

'This is where your pilgrims come for a taste of your miraculous water, Prior?' he asked.

Paul nodded. 'They are also shown part of our blessed

patron's relics kept in that reliquary up at the altar,' he said, trusting that God would forgive his economy with the truth – though he assuaged his conscience with the fact that the other bones they possessed in the casket were relics and that omitting to mention the skull-cap was not an outright lie. 'And, of course, our infirmarian, a skilled physician, offers them medical treatment where necessary,' he added, to cover up any hint of evasion in his voice.

'I wish to avail myself of this same benediction from your saint,' said Owain, bluntly. 'She is an English saint, but no matter. Many of our Welsh saints were Breton or Irish – and the apostles were Palestinian Jews. The Kingdom of God knows no nationality.'

Paul was pleasantly surprised to find the Welsh prince such a devout man. It might be a good sign for hoping that the priory might come off relatively lightly from the attentions of the horde of invaders outside.

He beckoned to his sub-prior and the precentor and whispered in their ears, sending Matthew up to the altar to open the reliquary and reverently bring down a leg bone of Beornwyn, resting on a linen cloth. Patrice was dispatched to the aumbry in the chancel wall, from where he retrieved a communion chalice made of pewter, chased with silver ornamentation. As they had hidden their valuable vessels under the floor, this goblet was one used to take around the villages with Beornwyn's relics, when holding Mass during pilgrimages to raise funds for the priory. Paul hoped that it would look good enough for Glyndwr not to wonder if they had more valuable ones hidden away somewhere.

The monks filed into their places in the quire and began their familiar routine of chants as the prior extemporised on the ritual for administering the 'cure'.

Accompanied by prayers in Latin, he filled the chalice from under the angel's jet of clear water and set it on the rim of the large basin below. Then Matthew solemnly offered him the cloth carrying the ancient bone, which with more ceremony was presented to Glyndwr, who had again kneeled before him. Several of the other lieutenants, including a couple of the French officers, kneeled beside him and Paul gravely bent to present the crumbling thigh-bone to each man, who all touched it somewhat tentatively before making the sign of the cross.

Then he went along the row of kneeling warriors and offered each a sip of blessed water from the cup. After more prayers, and amid the soporific chanting from the quire-stalls, Matthew and Patrice returned the relics and the goblet to their resting places. The ceremony over, the soldiers rose to their feet and the prior rejoined them below the chancel steps.

'I see that your beautiful basin has recently suffered some damage,' said the observant Owain, pointing at the rim of the bowl. 'Is that not fresh cement in that repair?'

Hoping perhaps to increase the prince's sympathy for their house and further strengthen the good relations that seemed to be building between them, Paul began to recount the events of the past week.

'We have recently had a tragic episode, sir. One of our oldest brothers, weak in the mind from age and illness, caused us much anguish by his strange behaviour – and was murdered for his demented fantasy!'

His secretary, Mark, seeking to consolidate the prior's tactics, began to give Owain the details of Brother John's weird claims that he had been transported up to the ancient site on the hill above, to meet St Oswald and be told the shocking news of their patron's infidelity. Before he could continue with the description of John's violent death, the Welsh leader interrupted him, seemingly in a state of excited interest.

'What? And you all ridiculed the man? It may well have been true! Such visitations have occurred throughout history.' He glared around at the circle of monks, who began to look sheepish, then apprehensive as the Welsh leader's anger became obvious.

'We had no reason to believe the old man's claims,' said Paul, falteringly. 'He had been having fits for years and recently had been acting strangely.'

'That may be a manifestation of his contact with forces beyond our comprehension,' snapped Glyndwr. 'Many visionaries in the past have suffered from such seizures as they were used as a channel by mystical powers. You should have listened more diligently to what he had to say through your patron saint!'

The prior rallied his defence against these accusations.

'His claims that our beloved Beornwyn, revered for many hundreds of years, was a libidinous fornicator who desecrated a house of God, were repugnant to us,' he cried. 'It also damaged our reputation and threatened to ruin our healing of the sick!'

'And, no doubt reduced the contributions to your treasure chest,' observed Owain, scathingly. 'So who killed this poor man?'

'We do not know, sir,' said Mark, seeing that the prior had become too emotional to speak wisely. 'All we know is that to our great regret and anguish, it must have been one of us, as the circumstances permit of no other explanation.'

'And you have not exposed this villain?' roared Glyndwr. 'Is he one of these?' He flung a brawny arm around to indicate the group of monks now cowering on the steps.

Prior Paul stepped forward again, red-faced with a mixture of anger and apprehension.

'This is *our* business, Prince! It is not a secular matter, but one to be settled by the Church – even by the Pope, if need be!'

'Pope! Which one, eh? The true father in Avignon or the imposter in Rome?'

He had recently transferred the allegiance of his new parliament and Church in Wales to the pontiff in the south of France.

'We have done all we can to make the culprit confess,' cut in Mark, hoping to calm the developing dispute. 'But all the prior's efforts have been in vain.'

Glyndwr glared around at them all, his forked beard jutting forward aggressively. 'I'll soon alter that, priest! No one slays a man of vision chosen by God and gets away with it in my presence!'

He swung around and barked orders at Rhys Gethin, one of his principal compatriots, to call in a score of soldiers from outside.

'I want these monks hanged, for one of them is a murderer!'

'How do we know which one?' queried Rhys.

The reply he received was the one that the papal legate Arnaud Amalric had uttered during the Cathar heresy several hundred years earlier, when he ordered the killing of twenty thousand people in Beziers. 'Kill them all, for God will know which are the innocent!'

There was instant confusion, with the prior making vociferous protests, some of the brothers falling to their knees, hands clasped in supplication and others try to escape back into the chancel. But well-disciplined men-at-arms surrounded

317

the monks, though the two French brothers who had gone to see the sick troops had been forgotten. The monks were dragged into a line before Glyndwr, though he spared the loudly protesting prior the indignity of being a suspect.

'This is your last chance to save yourselves!' he said in an ominously level voice, full of menace. 'Don't think I will spare you, for King Henry's armies have slain scores of monks in Wales, burned their abbeys and massacred men, women and children by the hundred.'

He glared along the line as the ashen faces and trembling knees. 'Whichever amongst you is guilty, step forward!' he roared. 'This is your last chance to join the martyrs! Otherwise the weight of your consciences in letting your innocent fellows join you in death will load you down as you all take the last few steps to the hanging trees outside!'

His own followers had increased in numbers as curious soldiers had pushed into the nave to see what was going on. Their leader turned to them and waved an imperious hand towards the group of terrified monks.

'Help Rhys Gethin to take these murderous men to the nearest wood and hang them!' he commanded.

There was a sudden commotion as one of the brothers abruptly dropped to his knees in front of Owain Glyndwr and grasped his ankles in desperate supplication.

'Sire, have mercy! If I confess, I can tell you where the treasures of this house are hidden. But spare my life, I beseech you!'

The Welsh leader kicked him aside contemptuously, so that the monk fell onto his side on the cold stones.

'Don't try to bargain with me, you dog!' he bellowed. 'If you wish to confess, it can only mean that you are the guilty one. You should be hanged twice over for betraying your brothers, you treacherous coward!'

Arnulf, for it was the hospitaller who had caused this dramatic turn of events, clasped his hands before his face, tears running from his eyes, as he looked up at the grim figure of Glyndwr.

'It was not me who delivered the blows,' he gabbled desperately. 'Jude was the killer. I was drawn into helping him against my will!'

At this the cellarer, Jude, lunged from amongst the crowd of quaking brothers and tried to leap on his fellow monk, who was cowering on the floor. He was grabbed by a couple of soldiers, but still managed to screech denials of his guilt.

Arnulf continued to blabber his confession. 'Jude killed the old man after we agreed to get rid of him, as he was responsible for maliciously ruining the reputation of this house.'

'You liar, may you rot in hell!' yelled Jude, struggling in the grip of the two brawny soldiers. 'It was you that was afraid that your fleecing of visitors to the guesthouse would be damaged if their numbers were reduced!'

From his position on the flagstones, where he was now being held down by the riding boot of one of the French officers, Arnulf screamed his counterclaims.

'Be damned yourself, Jude! You feared that old John's slander would reduce the profits you make from selling priory stores to outsiders!'

At this, Prior Paul became so incensed that he even forgot the presence of the invading troops around him.

'You evil, foul men! How dare you shelter in this house of God merely to embezzle our substance! I have long had my suspicions about you, but had no means of proving it.'

At a sign from Glyndwr, the men holding Jude threw him to the ground to join his partner in crime.

'You miserable wretches, how dare you masquerade as holy men while all the time you were lining your own purses? I suppose when you had stolen enough ill-gotten gains, you would vanish to spend your loot in comfort.'

He turned to the prior, who was so devastated that his familiar smile had vanished, probably for ever.

'At least our invasion has solved your crime, Prior! I think, in return for our help, we deserve to see this treasure of yours.'

He aimed a kick at the prostrate form of Arnulf, still lying on the floor. 'Show us where it's hidden, swine! Though it won't save your neck from being stretched.'

Looking as if he had aged ten years during the past few minutes, the prior intervened, shaking his head in resignation.

'Let him be, Prince. I will show you where our hard-earned savings and our treasured relics are hidden.'

Wearily, he led a strange procession of armed men and monks towards the altar and indicated the slab beneath which the spring was concealed. It took hardly a moment for soldiers to use their pikes to lever up the loosened flagstone, revealing the wrappings that held the priory's wealth.

Glyndwr looked with great interest at the contents of the woollen blankets. The weight of the treasure chest brought a smile to his face, but his fascination was with the skull of Beornwyn, of now-dubious fame, as the prior's secretary explained how the calvarium was used in their healing ritual.

Owain held it up reverently and examined the wide gold band with its butterfly decoration. Then he kneeled on the edge of the well and reached down to fill the skull-cap with the clear water that was bubbling from the earth. He stood up again and offered it to Paul, who was by now totally bemused by the actions of this superstitious Welsh leader.

'Prior, though you gave me water in a goblet just now, I wish to take it again in its proper holy vessel. It may have a greater power in blessing my campaign with success.'

He handed the skull to Paul and, with his lieutenants grouped around him, Glyndwr kneeled again before the prior. Gathering his wits together with an effort, the monk held the libation aloft and murmured a stream of Latin as a form of blessing. This time, there was no background chanting from the monks, who were saving their prayers for their own souls in imminent anticipation of being hanged. Then, with more muttered incantations, Paul held Beornwyn's relic to Owain's lips and waited until he had taken a mouthful.

Then the prince rose to his feet. 'I think that we can now leave you in peace, Prior. I will spare the innocent brothers – though you will need to recruit two new ones after we have gone!'

This threat revived Paul's agitation and he thrust the relic at Owain, the remaining holy water slopping onto the floor.

'I beseech you, do not vent your anger upon these two men! Evil though they be, this is a matter for the Church's retribution, not for earthly princes.'

He attempted to push the calvarium into the Welsh leader's hands. 'Take this relic of our beloved patron. It may bring you good fortune, and there is much valuable gold around its rim.'

Glyndwr refused to accept the offering and gently pushed it back towards the prior.

'I will not take your treasured relic, priest. Keep it and

continue to do good in the name of that woman, whether she was virgin or whore. The gold is tempting, as I am sorely in need of the wherewithal to feed my troops, but I will not desecrate something that has been in God's service for centuries. Neither will I risk my immortal soul by committing the sacrilege of taking your communion vessels.' He gave a rare smile as he qualified this. 'However, I have no religious qualms about taking your treasure chest.'

Giving a sign to one of his captains, two soldiers lifted the heavy chest and made off with it towards the church door.

'We shall starve this coming winter without our money!' wailed Prior Paul, but the Welsh leader was unmoved.

'I doubt that, monk!' he growled. 'I'll wager you have cattle hidden in the forest and grain and silver stored elsewhere. If you insist on saving the necks of these two treacherous villains, then I will leave them with you and be damned to them! I will take your treasure chest instead, which seems a fair exchange.' With that he swung on his heel and marched to the main door of St Oswald's church, his retinue and soldiers following behind.

As he walked across the inner precinct, the blue butterfly that had been sunning its wings on the cross of old John's grave took to flight and fluttered twice around the head of the Welsh prince. Then it rose above him and flew off as straight as an arrow, up towards the peak of the Herefordshire Beacon, far above.

Historical note

The year of this story, 1405, was the zenith of Glyndwr's twelve-year campaign for Welsh freedom sparked by more than a century of indignity and cruelty heaped on the population since the crushing of independence by Edward I. Within five years he had regained most of the country, was recognised as Prince of Wales by King Henry IV, established a parliament at Machynlleth, had plans for an independent Welsh Church and two universities, and had formed alliances with the Scots and the French, the latter sending a large force to assist him. He invaded England itself, the first such foray since the Norman Conquest, and penetrated almost to Worcester, but his lines of supply were now too fragile and, faced by a large English army, there was a stand-off, then both forces retreated, His wife and two of his daughters were captured and died in the Tower of London and by 1412 he was reduced to fighting a guerrilla war. He soon vanished and there was never any record of his death or burial place, though it is possible that he took refuge with another daughter, Alys, who had married Sir John Scudamore, the Sheriff of Herefordshire and sheltered him in their home in Kentchurch in that county – where the Scudamores still reside. As with King Arthur, a legend arose that he was not dead, but would appear again when Wales was in peril.

Shakespeare makes a number of allusions to Glyndwr's mystical nature in his play *Henry the Fourth, Part I* and it is known that he relied considerably on portents and prophesies delivered by his soothsayer, Crach Ffinant.

ACT FIVE

Blidworth, Nottinghamshire, December 1541

'I call it theft!' Richard Whitney's heavy jowls quivered in outrage.

The butcher reminded Father James of an indignant cockerel and the sight would have struck the priest as comical had he not been so insulted by Richard's accusation.

'You should not have left the candle here in the first place,' Father James retorted. 'You know full well that Thomas Cromwell has forbidden the lighting of candles to any saints, and especially the placing of them before their relics. I know some of the old and ignorant in the parish have trouble understanding why they can no longer bring offerings to the saints as they have done all their lives, but as Master of the Butchers' Guild you should set an example for them.'

Richard Whitney took a step closer, thrusting his florid face close to the priest's. 'Do I look like a man who'd waste his hard-earned money on church candles? It was my frog-witted apprentice who left it here. That boy's so pious he'd make St Peter look like a non-believer. The lad's a fool, and I gave him a good thrashing when I heard what he'd done. But the point is, he spent good money for that candle and it wasn't his to spend. Alan bought that great candle with the purse his father gave him to pay his apprentice fees to me. Now it's been stolen.'

'I hope you're not suggesting I took it,' Father James said, with as much dignity as he could muster.

But the priest was a head shorter than his parishioner, and though not easily intimidated he found himself distinctly uncomfortable at the man's close proximity. Besides, Master Richard consumed far too much of his own meat and his breath always stank. Father James took a few paces up the steps of the chantry chapel so that he had the advantage of height, but that only seemed to antagonise the butcher.

'Don't you dare walk away from me, Vicar! I haven't finished with you. Alan says there was more than two pounds of wax in that candle, not to mention the worth of making it. That candlemaker makes an even fatter profit from the gullible than the Church does. So if that candle's going to be lighting anyone's table this winter, it'll be mine.'

Father James's chin jerked up. 'The candle belongs to this church. It's been offered to God in faith. Even if we should find it, you certainly can't use it to entertain your friends.'

Richard snorted. 'According to Cromwell, God doesn't want it, and it's my money that was squandered on buying it, so I'll be getting the worth of it, not you or your church-warden. Mark my words, he's the thieving bastard who's taken it. So you can tell Yarrow I want it back by nightfall, or I'll be round his house to fetch it myself, and you can be sure I'll make him regret putting me to that trouble.'

Master Whitney turned on his heel and marched from the church, slamming the heavy door behind him with such force it set the wooden cradle in the corner of the church rocking. The cradle was only used at Candlemas, when a baby boy, born closest to Christmas Day, would be rocked in it in honour of the Feast of the Purification of the Virgin. It was an honour the families often came to blows over, for it was said to bestow great good fortune on the child, but Father James found himself wondering if this too would soon be forbidden by one of Thomas Cromwell's numerous injunctions.

The priest had been trying to hold himself so tall, it was only now that he realised his back was aching from the effort. He shuffled a few paces to the carved stone rail that separated the faithful from the chantry altar and leaned heavily upon it, sighing.

If it was the churchwarden who'd removed the candle, it certainly hadn't been placed with the ones in the chest destined for the main altar, as it should have been. And this wasn't the first time offerings to St Beornwyn had gone missing over the past months. Many candles and tawdries laid at her feet had vanished without trace, even a costly ring given by a woman grateful for the life of her sick child.

Thankfully, the villagers of Blidworth had asked no questions. Assuming that their forbidden offerings had been hidden safely away in the church chest, they had not dreamed of asking for their return. But a man like Richard was never going to accept such a loss quietly. Not that the butcher could report the theft, for if he did so it would come to light that young Alan had left the illicit offering in the church, and a master could be held responsible for the actions of his apprentice. But that made it more likely Richard would mete out his own brand of rough justice. For by now whoever had stolen it would have surely sold it or melted it down to make a dozen household candles. Father James fleetingly wondered if it hadn't been taken by the candlemaker himself, who could then resell it to some other fool. He, above all in the village, would know the worth of it.

The priest glanced over at the source of all the trouble, the gilded reliquary in the form of the statue of the saint, which stood on the altar of the chantry chapel. St Beornwyn had been carved holding out her left hand on which rested a sumptuously jewelled and enamelled butterfly, the size of a raven in proportion to the height of the woman. Her painted robe was torn away on the top half of her body to reveal naked breasts, only partly covered by her right hand. Embedded in the back of this hand was a polished fragment of rock crystal beneath which lay a strip of the saint's own skin, flayed from her body when she was martyred. Two more pieces of crystal set into her bare feet encased two more fragments of skin. Not for the first time, Father James found himself entertaining the less than spiritual thought that if the saint had been half as voluptuous in life as her carving, then it was a miracle she had remained a virgin at all.

But why had that wretched boy taken it into his head to spend his apprentice fees on a candle? Was he praying St Beornwyn would rescue him from his apprenticeship? Father James could hardly blame Alan if he had. Richard had a notoriously short temper and the whole village knew he bullied his lads. It was even rumoured that a few years back, one of his apprentices was so miserable he had gone into Sherwood Forest and hanged himself, though the Butchers' Guild blamed it on lovesickness for a girl who spurned him.

But the priest was certain that Alan would never commit such a sin, however badly Richard used him. In fact, the boy almost seemed to revel in his ill-treatment as if it was a test of his faith and devotion to St Beornwyn. On numerous occasions both Father James and the churchwarden had each been forced to drag the boy away from the chantry, reminding him sternly that praying before relics was now forbidden.

The boy made no secret of the fact that he had wanted to become a monk, but with the monasteries being closed and the monks forced out into the world, there was no chance of that. Even entering the priesthood was no longer a safe choice. Little wonder then that Alan's parents had decided that in this fast-changing world only one thing was certain – people would always need butchers.

Father James glanced over his shoulder to ensure he was alone, then, crossing himself, he kneeled and muttered a hasty prayer that the blessed St Beornwyn would keep Richard's hand from the churchwarden's throat and Cromwell's enforcers far away from Blidworth.

Master Richard Whitney's temper had not improved one jot since hé stormed from the church and was, if anything, made worse when he flung open the door of his house and heard his wife's laughter ringing from the small chamber beyond the oak-panelled hall. He didn't usually return home in the afternoon, so could not reasonably expect his wife, Mary, to be waiting for him with the table laid ready with his supper. But Richard had never been an entirely reasonable man and was becoming less so with every passing year, especially since he had become Guild Master, an honour that was usually granted to the butchers who lived in the large towns, such as Nottingham.

He strode through the hall and flung open the door at the far end, which led to the small winter parlour where he and his wife ate when they were not entertaining guests. Mary was often to be found in there occupied with her sewing. He didn't know what he imagined might be the cause of Mary's laughter – some morsel of market-street gossip brought back by her maid, Jennet, or the lapdog rolling over to have its belly scratched. Who knew? It seemed to him that any ridiculous and trivial thing was enough to entertain the simple mind of a woman. But whatever he thought was amusing his wife, it was certainly not what he found.

Edward Thornton, one of his fellow guild brothers, and furthermore the one who had fought against Richard for the honour of becoming Guild Master, was sitting – or rather insolently lounging – in one of Richard's fine carved wooden chairs. His fingers were cupped around one of Richard's pewter goblets, half-filled with Richard's best wine. The floor around Edward's boots was strewn with honeyed spiced almonds, and as Richard flung the door wide, he saw that Edward's mouth was open and Mary was just about to toss another almond into it.

Mary's laughter froze the instant she caught sight of her husband standing in the doorway. Her plump cheeks flushed crimson as she sprang to her feet. But Master Edward did nothing except close his mouth, and continue, quite unabashed, to sprawl in the chair as if he was by his own fireside.

Edward Thornton was only a few years younger than Richard, but his curly chestnut hair and beard still showed not a smattering of grey, and he had a ready smile, which women apparently found quite charming, although Richard had long held that any man who smiled so easily was never to be trusted in matters of business or anything else.

'Richard . . .' Mary's breathing was rapid, like a trapped animal. 'I didn't except you back so soon.'

'Evidently,' Richard replied coldly. 'Do you often entertain my fellow guild members when I am about my business?'

'No, Richard, no, of course, not ... Master Edward came
with a message. He's ridden hard from Nottingham. I
thought it only courtesy to offer him some refreshment. I
thought you would wish it.'

'Is it customary to offer guests refreshment by throwing
nuts at them? You're not a child and he's not a pet bird. The
hall is the place to receive guests of Master Edward's rank.'

Although both men knew that the hall was reserved for
men of high social status, somehow Richard managed to
make it sound like an insult.

His wife looked close to tears. 'But Master Edward is ...
is an old friend. You often entertain him in here, Richard.'

'When there are confidential matters to be discussed,'
Richard said. 'But I trust there is nothing of a *confidential*
nature you have cause to discuss with my wife, Edward.'

Richard lowered himself heavily into the chair his wife
had vacated. She stood, hovering uncertainly by his side,
until Edward gallantly rose and offered her his seat.

Richard's jaw clenched. 'My wife does not require a chair.
She's just leaving to see to her duties.'

Mary flushed and lowered her head to hide the tears glit-
tering in her eyes. She hurried from the chamber. Richard
heard her feet running across the tiled hall.

'Come now, don't blame poor Mary,' Edward said lightly.
'It was my suggestion we came in here. I was frozen to the
marrow after the ride and this room is much warmer than
that great draughty hall of yours. I reckon we'll have snow
before Christmas. What do you say? Still, good for business,
what? Men always eat more meat in cold weather.'

Richard ignored Edward's attempt to divert him. He
stared down at the dish of spiced almonds on the table. 'I will
deal with my wife, Master Edward, any way I please, and I

will decide where the blame lies and what is to be done about it.'

It was the second time today that a man had tried to take what belonged to Richard. His hands were itching to seize Edward by the throat and hurl him into the nearest stinking ditch, but that would spread gossip round the guild quicker than lice round a swarm of beggars, and Richard had no intention of letting it be known that he was being made a fool of by Edward or Mary.

'My *wife* said you'd brought a message. It must be important to have brought you all this way and in business hours too.'

Edward leaned forward, his expression suddenly grave. 'One of Cromwell's enforcers has arrived in Nottingham, a man by the name of Roger Grey. He's here to search for relics and take them back to Cromwell to be tested to see if they are genuine or not. But we all know they're never returned to their owners. If the Virgin herself were to appear to Cromwell and hand him Christ's own foreskin and swear on the Holy Gospel she'd seen it cut from her son, Cromwell would still claim it was a fake and burn it. Unless, of course, it was encased in gold and jewels, in which case he'd throw away the relic and keep the valuables for himself.'

Richard felt a spasm of alarm. 'You think this man Grey will come here.'

'I don't *think* – I *know* he will,' Edward said. 'I heard Grey preach while I was in Nottingham. He told people to search their homes, byres and workshops and bring any charms, amulets or relics they could find to him. He made a big bonfire in the square, urging people to cast their relics into the flames. Course, the bits of relics people have at home are not housed in costly reliquaries, mostly just saints' teeth to hang in their byres or hair wrapped in a bit of cloth and tucked into the babies' cradles.'

'But did the people surrender them to Grey?' Richard asked, all thoughts of his wife forgotten in this far more important concern.

Edward chuckled. 'They surrendered something, certainly, anything to show their loyalty. But I reckon they were mostly just rags or bits of old bones they'd fished out of their midden heaps that morning. They'll have squirrelled the real ones safely away.'

'But Grey believed they were giving up their relics?'

Edward chuckled again. 'I doubt it. I reckon it was just a spectacle to get the people worked up and encourage them to inform on others. But we all know it's the church relics that Cromwell and his minions are really after. And he mentioned St Beornwyn by name in his sermon. He said praying before relics like hers was the worst kind of idolatry. Claimed she'd never been made a saint at all. So I know Blidworth'll be one of the first places he'll start with. He'll be determined to take her.'

Richard gripped the arms of his chair, his face flushing and not just from the heat of the fire. 'That reliquary belongs to the guild! It's been our property for nigh on two hundred years. It's Butchers' Guild money that paid for the jewels on that butterfly of hers, not to mention the gold crown on her head. He can't take that.'

'All very well to say he can't – he *will*, and he's got Cromwell's backing to do it.'

Richard shook his head impatiently. 'Every man has his price. When I was at the Mansfield fair, I heard about an enforcer who came to one town where the Guild of Cordwainers had a relic of St Crispin. They simply collected some money from the members and slipped it to the enforcer. Told him the relic had been destroyed two years since. He gave them the wink and went off to make his report, while they hid the reliquary in their church crypt. So what we must do is call an urgent meeting of the guild and—'

Edward did not let him finish. 'We could offer to pay twice what the reliquary is worth and we'd still lose it. I know some of the enforcers just take on the role to ingratiate themselves with Cromwell, hoping for advancement by clinging to his backside, and most do it to cream off what profits they may for themselves in jewels or bribes. But Roger Grey's an enforcer of the worst kind, a fanatic, one of those radical clerics who really believes he's doing God's work by destroying idols. If you'd heard him preach you'd know that any man who tries to buy him off is likely to end his days burning on a pyre along with the relics, with Grey warming his hands over the blaze.'

'Then we must hide it,' Richard said firmly.

Edward scraped the chair back and stood up. 'It's too late, Richard. You can't hide St Beornwyn in the church. Grey'll tear the whole village apart till he finds her. As Guild Master you should have seen this coming and whipped our little saint out of sight long before this. But no, you wanted to keep her on view just a bit longer to puff up the importance of your new rank. Was that why you moved here to this piss-poor church as soon as you became Master? You always wanted to be Guild Master for the glory of it, never for the good of the guild.'

Richard sprang to his feet. 'How dare you? We all know that's why you were so keen to be Master, because you were the one who wanted to possess the reliquary for yourself. I

moved her to St Mary's so that she could be given every reverence. If you'd been Master you would have had her hidden
away and deprived the people of her blessing.'

'Blessing!' Edward gave a mirthless laugh. 'Since when
have you sought any saint's blessing except to beg them to
make you Guild Master? I would have kept her safe until
this madness is over. How does it feel to be the Guild Master
who's lost the guild its most valuable possession? You can
be sure they'll remember you for the next two hundred years
for this.'

He strode to the door and flung it open. 'I came to give
you a friendly warning, Richard, to try to make sure you
didn't do anything stupid, like try to bribe Grey and get
yourself arrested. But now I'm going to give you another
warning. You carry on roaring at all those around you, like
a bull with a bee up its arse, and you'll end up losing more
than just St Beornwyn.'

Father James shifted his feet, trying to seep up the last little
warmth left from the warming pan that his housekeeper had
used to take the chill from the bed. It was a bitter night. The
old rectory had been built a century before and the incum-
bents of St Mary of the Purification had struggled to wrest
enough tithes from the parishioners to maintain the church,
let alone make improvements to the house. Most of the
ground floor was still taken up by a long open hall, which in
winter was as cold as a crypt, and what little heat was produced by the fire vanished instantly up into the open rafters
far above his head.

The priest was finally beginning to doze off when he was
dragged awake by the sound of the bell clanging in the hall
below, followed by the hum of voices. He turned over and

tried to bury his head beneath the blankets, hoping that his housekeeper would send the caller packing. But it was not to be. Moments later he heard her footsteps on the stairs and the door to the solar being opened.

'Father James, are you awake? It's Master Richard Whitney to see you. I've told him it's too late to disturb you, but he says it's urgent and won't wait until morning. He insists on seeing you, Father.'

Father Jones let out a curse that was far from godly, wrapped himself in a balding rabbit-fur robe to cover his nakedness and pushed aside the hangings round his bed. He forced his cold feet into his colder shoes, still cursing, and padded down the steps.

Richard was pacing impatiently up and down the hall.

'If this is about that wretched candle . . .' Father James said crossly.

Richard flapped his hand impatiently. 'It is not. This is a far more pressing matter. But don't imagine I've forgotten about the candle. If it isn't returned I shall insist on being paid the worth of it. But that matter will have to wait now. I've heard some disturbing news.'

He suddenly glanced up the staircase and Father James, turning, glimpsed the movement of a shadow on the bend of the stair. He guessed his housekeeper was standing just out of sight, doubtless listening to every word. Richard must have realised it too, for he beckoned urgently to the priest.

'Come with me and bring the church key. I shall tell you on the way.'

Father James felt his fury mounting. The boorish oaf actually thought he could turn up at this late hour, drag his priest out of bed and demand he go wandering through the village on a freezing night. What was it this time – a missing coin? Or did Richard want himself painted on the church wall sitting next to Christ in heaven? It wouldn't have been so bad if the butcher had even half the faith of his own apprentice, but Father James was certain the only reason Richard ever set foot in any church was to lord it over others, for it certainly wasn't to pray.

He folded his robe more tightly around his shivering body. 'Unless someone is dying and in need of the last rites, nothing can be so urgent that it cannot wait till morning. In case you haven't noticed, Master Richard, I have already retired. Now go home to your wife. God knows, the poor woman could do with some company.'

'What do you mean by that?' Richard demanded. 'What has my wife been saying?' His face had flushed red with fury. 'If she's confessed to you ... if she's admitted ... it's your duty to tell me.'

'Tell you what?' Father James blinked bemusedly at him. 'I only meant that you're so often away on business and guild matters that your wife must be glad of your company when you are at home.' He shivered again as the icy draughts in the hall crept up his bare legs. 'If I had a wife to warm my bed on a night like this, I'd be only too anxious to get into it and stay there.'

But Richard was not a man to be denied anything he had set his mind to, and against his will the priest found himself dressed and out in the street, hurrying up to the church with Richard striding along beside him. It was as dark as the Devil's armpit and bitterly cold outside. The street was deserted and in many houses the oil lamps and candles had already been extinguished.

Richard held the lantern at his side, half-muffled by his

cloak, and several times Father James stumbled on the path already slippery with frost. Finally he snapped at Richard that if he wasn't going to light their path, there was little point in having brought a lantern at all.

'I don't want to be seen entering the church at this hour.'

'Believe me, I don't want to *be* entering the church at this hour,' Father James retorted. 'And I think we can be certain no one is going to be standing at a freezing casement watching you or anyone else at this time of night.'

But Richard continued to hoard the light as if it was gold. Not until they were actually inside the church did he uncover the lantern, and then he was careful to set it where it wouldn't be seen shining out through the windows.

It felt even colder in the church than it had been on the street. Having spent a year in a monastery as a young man, before deciding that the life of a priest offered more prospects and considerably more comforts, Father James thanked God he was not required to attend those midnight services that the monks had once had to endure. He sometimes thought King Henry had done the monks a favour by closing the monasteries. He clamped his hands beneath his armpits to warm them.

'Now that you've dragged me here what do you want?' Father James asked irritably.

Richard could use words sparingly when he chose and he swiftly recounted the news Edward had brought.

'. . . so we must hide St Beornwyn without delay. She's the patron saint of the Butchers' Guild and we cannot lose her.'

For once Father James was in agreement, though he couldn't help thinking her value to the guild, and to Richard in particular, had less to do with the precious strips of skin flayed from the holy saint's dismembered corpse than with

338

the gold and jewels that even now glittered in the softly flickering lantern light.

The priest nodded. 'I've been considering what we should do if they came for her.' He nodded towards the church tower. 'I thought about moving her up there, hiding her in a box beneath the coils of rope stored there, but the Royal Forest Wardens sometimes climb up the tower to search for fires or signs that men are poaching. If they're left on watch for several hours, they might easily stumble upon her, especially if they start moving things to make themselves comfortable.'

Father James rasped his stubbly chin. 'No, the only safe place I can think of is to lay her in one of the tombs beneath the flagstones, though I am loath to disturb the resting place of the dead. Yet her presence would surely hallow the grave of any man and I cannot think the dead would object to protecting her, as she does them.'

'Out of the question,' Richard said. 'Have you forgotten that beneath the gilding her statue is made of wood? It would rot. Besides, tombs are the first places a man like Grey would look. He must be well used to all the hiding places in churches by now and he's bound to notice if a slab has been loosened.'

Richard unfastened his cloak and dragged down a large empty sack that was draped across one shoulder. Then he unwound a length of soft woollen cloth from around his waist. No wonder he didn't seem cold when we were walking, the priest thought.

'The only safe thing to do,' Richard announced, 'is to remove the reliquary from the church. I will take it.'

'What!' Father James said. He couldn't believe that he'd heard correctly. 'You can't take her. Where would you keep her? Your house is wooden – suppose there was a fire? Besides, as soon as the enforcer finds the statue missing he's bound to come questioning the members of the guild and he is sure to start with its Master, especially once he discovers you live in the village and had every opportunity to remove the reliquary.'

But Richard was already striding towards the saint. 'If he should question me, I assure you I'm more than capable of handling some snivelling little cleric.'

He laid the woollen cloth out on the ground, ready to wrap it around the reliquary. 'Don't worry, Father. I'll not burden you with the knowledge of where I shall conceal it. Then you may say in all conscience that you don't know where it is. I'd have thought you'd be relieved that you will not be forced to lie to a brother in holy orders.'

The morning sun shone brightly from a cloudless sky, but it may as well have been the moon for all the warmth it had in it. In the small slaughter yard Richard prised open the mouth of the freshly killed pig, searching beneath the purple tongue for any signs of the white ulcers that would give a man leprosy if he ate the flesh. Thomas, his journeyman, glowered at him behind his back. Thomas had inspected the pig thoroughly before buying him from the farmer and resented Master Richard checking up on him as if he couldn't be trusted to know his job.

Oblivious to Thomas's malevolent stare, Richard studied the line of the eviscerated carcass of a bullock hanging from the beam above to ensure the troughs placed beneath it would catch the dripping blood. He didn't intend to see a single drop go to waste. All the goodwives in the village were making blood puddings to keep out the cold. The carcass steamed in the cold air, as if it was already roasting.

Richard glared at young Alan, who was struggling to heave the wooden pail of guts and lights to the shed. He was a tall lad, but weedy as a sapling starved of light. Once again the boy had bungled the throat-cutting of the pig, forcing Thomas to step in and finish the job swiftly and cleanly.

'Swift and deep, lad, put some muscle into it. Then the beast will drop like a stone.'

Even then the brat had closed his eyes against the sight, rather than watching carefully and learning.

'You'll have to learn to kill, boy, if you're ever to make a butcher,' Richard said. 'What do you intend to do, lead the cow out to the shop and tell the customers to hack a leg off themselves if they want a joint of beef?'

Both men laughed and Alan flinched.

Thomas gave him a shove. 'You'll get the hang of it soon. After you've killed the first one, rest is as easy as shelling peas. Anyway, what's up with you? You've been right mardy this past week. Pining after some lass, are you?'

Alan turned and gave Richard a reproachful look, before lowering his gaze to the bloody pail again.

Richard knew at once what ailed the boy. He'd been sulking ever since he'd discovered the reliquary had been removed from the church three days ago.

'Beornwyn has gone, Alan. And it's as well that she has, for your sake. At least you'll not be tempted to break the law again and risk dire punishment.'

The boy flashed him a look of resentment and pain. 'I'm not afeared of the King's men. St Beornwyn risked her life for her faith. I'd risk my life for her too.'

The journeyman snorted. 'You'll be risking your life all right if you don't get a move on and shift those pails. Saints won't put food in your belly or a roof over your head, but a good sharp butcher's knife will. That's the only thing you want to be kissing, that and a buxom lass.'

'The boy doesn't need his head filling with thoughts of women of any kind, saints or tavern girls,' Richard said sharply. 'He doesn't even have room enough in his head to remember what he's been taught. Now, finish up here and don't be late opening the shop.'

Without even waiting for an acknowledgement of his orders, Richard strode out of the yard and made his way towards his house. Most tradesmen lived in the upper storeys above their shop, but Richard was wealthy enough to afford a separate house, well away from the stench of the slaughter yard, which had made the money to buy that house, at least what money he'd earned himself. Much of his wealth had come from his marriage to Mary, but Richard had long forgotten that inconvenient fact, as most men in his position did.

Ever since he found Edward sitting alone with his wife, Richard had taken to arriving home at unexpected times to see if Edward was paying any more visits. But each time he'd returned he'd found her alone or out walking or shopping with her maid. And on this occasion the house was once again deserted, with not even William, his manservant, answering his calls. This was not, he supposed, unexpected. The manservant had told him he was taking the wagon to fetch wood. With the nights as cold as they were, the stack of fuel for the fire had shrunk alarmingly these past few days.

But Richard was both annoyed and alarmed. He realised he should have left instruction that his wife and Jennet were to remain in the house whenever William was absent, and William should guard the house when they went shopping. Suppose someone broke in? It would be terrible to be robbed at any time, but with the reliquary in the house ... Not that his wife or the servants knew he had the reliquary. Nevertheless, he must impress upon them that the house was never to be left unattended. He would invent some story about a gang of robbers being reported as heading to these parts. That would frighten them into staying close to the house.

After calling out once more to ensure the house was indeed empty, Richard hastened to the solar and checked the lock still remained in place on the stout iron-banded chest. It was rather too obvious a hiding place, but it was the first place he'd found, when he returned that night from the church, where he could place the reliquary unobserved by anyone in the house. But a locked chest was the first place any thief or prying cleric would examine.

Richard had been pondering the matter ever since and finally resolved that if he could remove some of the oak panelling, he might be able to create a niche behind it where the statue could be hidden. The question was, who could he trust to carry out the work without talking? He would have to employ a craftsman, for though Richard could slice a pig into neat parcels in less time than it took a goodwife to pluck a chicken, he had no skills with wood, and any false panelling must appear indistinguishable from the solid walls when it was finished, else the hiding place would be discovered at once.

He was pacing the rooms, tapping on walls and trying to find exactly the best place for such a concealed compartment, when he heard someone else tapping on the door that led into the passage from the courtyard at the back of the house. Assuming it must be one of the servants, somewhat irritably he went to unfasten it.

But it was not one of the servants who stood there. Instead he was confronted by two men, both dressed in patched and ill-assorted clothes, their heads and half their faces muffled against the cold. Richard's first instinct was to slam the door, but one had already wedged his stave inside, preventing that.

Richard tried to muster as much authority as he could. 'What ... what do you want? If you want alms, go to the dole window in the church. I tolerate no beggars here.'

'We are not seeking alms, Master Richard. We have a matter of the utmost importance we would like to discuss with you.'

Richard was taken aback by the gentle, cultured tones of the man, in contrast to his appearance, but that only made him more wary. An educated man had no business to go around dressed as a beggar. He was obviously a knave or a thief.

'Come and see me at my place of business. I don't barter for beasts in my own home.'

'We are not here to sell you a cow, Master Richard. It concerns something altogether more valuable and it is we who wish to purchase it from you.'

Richard hesitated. He had no intention of admitting these men into the house. Two of them together could easily overpower him and he had no way of knowing if they were concealing any weapons beyond the staves in their hands. But the man seemed to understand Richard's wariness, for beyond holding the door open he made no move to force his way in.

The stranger glanced behind him. The courtyard was

deserted save for Richard's own horse in the stable, but even so, he lowered his voice, still keeping the cloth across his mouth and nose so that Richard had to lean towards him to make out the words.

'We seek the reliquary of St Beornwyn.'

Richard drew in his breath as if the man had just slapped him.

'Why ... why come to me?' he blustered. 'I know nothing about it. I've no idea where it is. It's probably been destroyed.'

'It is to prevent the destruction we are here. If you were to stumble across its whereabouts – by accident, of course – we would be pleased to take it to a place of safety, where no enforcer would ever find it. We'd keep it safe until this troubled time has passed. I assure you we would treat it with all reverence.'

Richard almost laughed. 'Smash it up to get to the gold and jewels, more like. Do you take me for a fool?'

The second man moved closer and Richard hastily took a step back, thinking he was about to push his way through the door, but he carefully laid his stave against the wall and held up both hands to show he was unarmed.

'We would never destroy a holy relic,' he said. His startlingly blue eyes darted nervously from side to side, as if he too feared to be overheard. 'We are Austin canons. The priory of St Mary at Newstead was our home until it was seized and we were evicted, ordered to leave the religious life God had called us to. We were thrown out like beggars with nothing, and our lands sold to Sir John Byron, who is even now tearing the priory apart so that he may live in it. He's even pulling our church down stone by stone to build his stables and pigsties. May God curse John Byron and all his descendants. But . . .' He hesitated, glancing at his companion, evidently seeking permission to say more.

The other man gave the briefest of nods.

'Some of us continue to maintain the order in secret, hidden from the eyes of Henry and that Devil's spawn Cromwell. We need no gold or silver. Ours was never a wealthy order. And any stone can be fashioned into a table, but it does not become a *consecrated* altar until a holy relic is placed on it, and without a consecrated altar we cannot say Mass and transform the bread and wine into the body and blood of our Lord. We need the reliquary of St Beornwyn. She's our only hope. Without that reliquary our order will die as Cromwell intends that it should, and we will not permit his evil to triumph. I assure you the reliquary will find no safer hiding place than with us. And we will pray to her for the health and protection of the man who entrusts her to us, and after his death we would offer Masses daily for his soul.'

To ensure that Masses were said to shorten the soul's suffering in purgatory was a costly affair, and most men would have agreed to such a bargain at once. But money for such Masses was usually left in a will, and to Richard's mind there was all the difference in the world between giving away his valuables when he was dead and no longer had any use for them and parting with them now while he was still alive.

'I can't help you,' he said firmly. 'And I cannot imagine why you should have come to me at all. The reliquary is the Church's affair.'

The man with the bright blue eyes reached inside his ill-fitting jerkin; again Richard jumped back fearing he might be reaching for a knife, but he withdrew nothing more threatening than a worn leather pouch. The man loosened the drawstrings of the pouch and tipped the contents into his grubby hand – a few gold coins, a garnet ring and other scraps of precious metal and semi-precious stones that had evidently been levered from some box or chalice. He thrust his palm up towards Richard's face.

'We've gathered together what valuables we could find to offer for the reliquary.'

Richard plucked at one of the broken fragments. 'And I don't doubt this is all that would remain of the reliquary of St Beornwyn if you laid hands on it.'

He let the scrap of silver fall back into the man's hand. 'As I told you, I know nothing of the reliquary. Now take this rubbish and buy yourselves another relic for your altar. There are bound to be dozens that have dropped off the back of the enforcers' wagons. And don't come knocking on my door again.'

He kicked the man's stave away from the lintel and slammed the door shut, bolting it as swiftly as his trembling fingers would allow. He leaned against the door, breathing hard. It was no coincidence the men had come to the door. They knew St Beornwyn was here or at the very least they must suspect that, as Guild Master, he knew where the statue was.

Only the priest knew he'd brought it to the house. Father James had opposed it being taken from the church. Was he behind this, trying to trick him into returning it? Did he really think Richard could be persuaded to part with the guild's most treasured possession for the offer of a few prayers or a bag of scrap that wasn't even worth the value of the gold in the saint's crown? Those men probably weren't monks at all, just rogues Father James had hired to intimidate him. But one thing was now clear to Richard:

he'd have to find a much more secure hiding place, and swiftly too.

There were few men more fitted to the names that birth had seen fit to bestow upon them than Roger Grey. He was a short, spare man whose hair and eyes were the hue of gathering rain clouds, and his dark, sober clothes only served to accentuate the lack of any colour in the cleric, as if he was a rag that had been washed rather too often. But his appearance belied a nature that was as hard as steel. And though his fond parents had simply thought Roger a pleasing forename for their infant, it was as if from birth their son had determined to become that very spear from which his Christian name derived, pressing the sharpened point of his zeal into the tender side of every priest and abbot in the land.

As Grey walked into the church of St Mary of the Purification in Blidworth in the company of Father James, his skin prickled in the presence of unseen idolatry, just as a hunter senses when a dangerous boar lies hidden in a thicket.

Grey cleared his throat with a dry cough. 'Since the observance of Candlemas is doubtless more important to this parish than to many others, as this church is dedicated to that feast, I trust, Father James, that you remind your parishioners that the candles are to be lit on that feast day only in memory of Christ himself, and not for his mother, nor are the candles to be used in divination to tell men's fortunes for the coming year.'

Grey addressed the empty air, before suddenly turning his gaze upon Father James at the end of his speech. It was a trick he found usually caught men unawares, leading them to betray their guilt in their glances. And Father James did indeed betray himself. His gaze had darted at once to the

Candlemas cradle. But Grey was not concerned with such petty customs, not on this occasion at least, and he made no comment, preferring to leave Father James to sweat a little.

Grey left the priest's side and prowled about the church. His practised eye could always spot where candles had recently been lit before the statues of saints, or fragments of leaves showed where images had been decorated with garlands or offerings had been left. But he was not on the hunt for such things now. His objective in this careful search had only one purpose and that was to make the priest nervous. They both knew why Grey was here, but the longer he delayed coming to the point the more likely it was that Father James would give himself away. Grey's father had been a tanner, and he'd learned as a boy that the longer a hide is left to soak, the easier it is to scrape clean.

Finally, when he judged Father James had sweated enough, he turned without warning to confront him.

'And where is the reliquary of the false saint?'

Father James moistened his lips. 'Many believe St Beornwyn to be a true saint. She's performed many miracles and her story is well attested. There is a book which details—'

'The story of Judas is well attested. That does not make him a saint. As to her miracles, it is God who grants miracles, not saints, and it is to him your parishioners should be lighting their candles and offering their prayers. But that aside, I am here to take the reliquary away to be examined. If my superiors find the relic inside to be genuine and the saint to be worthy of presenting an example of a holy life to sinners, then rest assured the reliquary will be returned to you.'

'Have many been returned?' Father James asked.

Grey allowed himself a faint smile. 'You would be

shocked, Father, to discover just how many of these relics have proved false. Bull's blood purporting to be our Lord's, chicken bones to be the finger of a saint, filthy scraps of cloth from martyrs, which were doubtless cut from some old beggar's clothes, and skin of holy men that is nothing more than pig hide . . . Your reliquary is supposed to contain fragments of Beornwyn's skin, is it not?'

'But the saint was flayed,' Father James protested. 'Her skin would have been reverently preserved.'

'As no doubt is her reliquary, but I do not see it. I understood it was kept on the altar in the chantry chapel. It was the property of the Butchers' Guild, was it not?'

'It was removed,' the priest said carefully. 'Cromwell said the people shouldn't place offerings before relics or light candles to the saints.'

For such a cold day, Grey noticed Father James was beginning to look rather warm.

'Removed to where exactly?'

Father James spread his hands. 'I honestly don't know. It has most likely been destroyed, broken up. As you say, it belonged to the Butchers' Guild.'

'And do you *honestly* believe they would destroy their own property?' Grey asked. 'Smash a relic that you have just told me everyone revered? No, Father, I can't believe it has been destroyed, though it has been concealed. Perhaps I should bring in men to search the church and help you find it. My men are known for their enthusiasm and thoroughness, though I regret they are inclined to be clumsy.'

He saw to his satisfaction a spasm pass across the priest's face and beads of sweat break out on his brow. Grey, however, was convinced the reliquary was no longer in the church. He could usually tell, catching the nervous glance towards the hiding place to check that nothing had been disturbed, the clumsy attempts to lead him away from the spot.

He had fought these kinds of priests all his life. Men granted an easy living as a vicar by reason of their privileged birth. Men who had little faith and less learning, who were more interested in hunting than in their devotions and yet were only too willing to fleece gullible parishioners, like his own parents, of what little they possessed. Grey, from his humble origins, had had to fight his way into the Church with all the zeal and persistence of the crusader storming the gates of Jerusalem, and he was not going to yield the battlefield to such a man now.

And indeed he did not, though Father James didn't confess easily. But fear of having his own church demolished about his ears and, as Grey hinted, losing his living entirely if he was seen to be obstructing Cromwell's injunctions was eventually enough to loosen his tongue. Grey left the church quite satisfied with the information he had received.

It was to Grey's lasting regret that he did not make his way straight to the house of the Master of the Butchers' Guild on leaving the church. But on learning from Father James that Richard's wife and servants were unlikely to be aware that the reliquary was even in the house, never mind where it was hidden, he decided to save himself a wasted journey by calling upon Richard Whitney when the butcher returned home after his shop was closed. According to Father James, Richard had little respect for the authority of the Church and was likely to resist if ordered to surrender his treasure, so Grey resolved to collect the two sergeants-at-arms who were currently warming themselves at the inn and take them with him when he went to search the butcher's house.

Father James had been sternly warned not to try to get word to Richard, and having put the fear of Cromwell, if not of God, into the priest, Grey permitted himself the luxury of lingering over the first good meal he had enjoyed in many days. To his surprise, the inn's meat pie was every bit as succulent as the serving maid had promised, as was the pork seethed in a honey and onion sauce, so it was a contented man who chivvied his reluctant sergeants-at-arms away from their ale and out into the cold night.

The moon and stars glittered like shards of ice in the black sky, and the men shuffled impatiently as Grey tugged the bell rope outside the door of the Master of the Guild of Butchers. They were ushered into a great hall by an anxious-looking girl and, before the servant had time even to summon her master or mistress, a woman came hurrying down the stairs, stopping in evident surprise when she saw the three men in the hall, for it was clear she was expecting someone else.

Alarm flashed in the woman's eyes when Grey introduced himself. She made a hasty curtsy.

'My ... husband is not here.'

'Where is he?'

'I don't know, sir. I was out most of the afternoon, paying a call on a friend. She's not long been brought to bed with child and I went to take gifts. Jennet, my maid, accompanied me. We stayed until it was near dusk. I hadn't intended to stay so long, but another friend came and we were all talking, and the baby was—'

'And your husband?' Grey interrupted, trying to get her back to the point.

'It was as we were returning home, that's when we saw him. We'd just rounded the bend in the path when we saw

Richard galloping away from the house at such a furious pace I was afraid he'd fall from the horse and break his neck.'

'And you've no idea why he left in such a hurry? Did a message come for him?'

Mary shook her head. 'Maybe it was guild business. He didn't often tell ...' She suddenly pressed her hand to her mouth, as if she was trying to stop herself crying, reaching for the back of a chair for support.

Grey eyed her suspiciously. A wife would hardly be so distressed if she thought her husband had simply gone out on business. There was something more to this, which she was not telling him. Did she perhaps think her husband was visiting another woman?

'In the absence of Master Richard, I must trouble you with the matter that brings us here. Your husband brought the reliquary of Beornwyn into this house. I am here on Cromwell's orders to take it to be inspected and authenticated.'

The colour drained from Mary's face and she took a pace forward, sinking into the chair.

'I don't ... know anything about a reliquary,' she muttered, without looking at him.

Grey paced slowly, very slowly, towards her. Not until he was standing over her with his knees almost touching hers did he speak again. He kept his voice low and even.

'Mistress Mary, understand I have the power to arrest anyone, man or woman, who tries to conceal a relic. I will take them for questioning and those who are suspected of deliberately defying Cromwell's orders or thwarting the purposes of the King's enforcers will be punished, that I can assure you.'

Mary gave a wrenching sob, shrinking back in her chair. 'I don't—'

But Grey cut her off, pressing his fingers to her mouth. He could feel her trembling beneath his hand, her breath coming in short, hot snorts.

'Think, Mary, think very carefully before you lie to me. I know the reliquary is in this house, just as I know that the hiding of it here was none of your doing. A wife cannot gainsay her husband. It's her duty to obey him. No one will consider you other than a virtuous woman for your loyalty to him, but now is the time to help him.'

Grey took a pace back from Mary and raised his voice so that the maidservant and any others who might be listening should hear him.

'Just tell me where the reliquary is, or where you suspect it to be, and I shall take no further action against either you or your husband. You'll be saving him by surrendering it to me. But if you don't tell me the truth, then both you and he and all your servants will be arrested, for you will all be deemed as guilty as Master Richard.'

He was gratified to hear a terrified squawk from the maid, behind him in the hall. It was exactly the reaction Grey had hoped for.

Jennet rushed to her mistress's side. 'Tell him, Mistress. Please tell him! You heard what he said, they're going to arrest us all. You have to tell him.'

Mary shook her head, struggling in vain to control her sobs.

Jennet stared at her, then turned to Grey. 'It was in the chest in the solar. Leastways, I think it was . . .'

Grey nodded. 'You're a sensible girl to tell me the truth. Your master and mistress will have much cause to be grateful to you.' He motioned to the sergeants-at-arms. 'Bring the reliquary here. The maid will show you where it is.'

But the girl shook her head, twisting the cloth of her apron in her hands. 'I can't . . . that's what I was telling you. It *was* there, but it's not now, sir. You go and look. You can see the lock's been forced; wrenched off, it has. I found it so when we returned. St Beornwyn's gone!'

Grey spent a restless night in the inn, lying awake in a guttering candlelight, for ever since he was a boy he'd never been able to bring himself to extinguish the light and fall asleep in the dark. The feather pallet on the narrow bed was hard and thin from being compressed by countless sweating bodies. The straw mattress beneath had evidently not been replaced for years, judging by the stink of it. But Grey had slept on much worse and it was not entirely the fault of the bed that he tossed and turned now. It was the missing reliquary that kept him from sleep.

William, the manservant, had been questioned thoroughly and finally admitted that contrary to his master's instructions he had left the house unattended to take meat to his mother and bedridden father, as he did most days. But, he was swift to add, only what meat the master allowed him as part of his wages. William hadn't troubled to wait for the mistress to return. He'd never done so in the past, and couldn't see any need to do so now. Though his master had told him about the gang of robbers, no houses had been broken into in Blidworth, and nor were they likely to be, for what cause would any robbers have to come to a little village when there were much better pickings in Nottingham or Mansfield?

William had had no reason to go upstairs to the solar on his return, so had seen nothing amiss. He'd occupied himself with chopping wood for the fire and drawing the water that the women would need for cooking on their return. He was adamant that while he knew the reliquary had vanished from the church, as indeed did the whole village, he did not know it was in the house.

Of course, William would have had every opportunity to steal the reliquary himself or to carry it off on his master's instructions to hide it elsewhere. But Grey suspected Richard would never have entrusted such a task to a servant, and as for William having stolen it, even broken up, the gold and jewels would be impossible for a servant to sell locally without arousing instant suspicion.

But if William was telling the truth, then either the reliquary had been stolen that afternoon and Richard, discovering the theft, had charged out in pursuit of the culprit, or more likely, Richard had removed it himself, breaking the lock on the chest to make it appear stolen, and had carried it off to a safer hiding place. It would explain why Master Richard had unexpectedly returned home in the afternoon without apparent cause.

Grey had waited in the butcher's hall until well past ten of the clock, but Richard had not returned to the house, and, utterly weary, Grey had finally made his way back to the inn, leaving the sergeants-in-arms in Richard's house, ready to seize him the moment he returned.

The following morning, Grey was half-way through his breakfast of mutton chops and ale, when one of the sergeants-in-arms appeared in the doorway of the inn. He scanned the dark little ale room rapidly and when he spotted Grey he came hurrying over.

Grey wiped his greasy mouth on a napkin. 'Did he return? Have you taken him?'

The man gazed longingly at the remains of the juicy chops and flagon of ale, almost drooling like a hound. 'Master Richard's been seized all right, but it wasn't at his house. It was at the Royal Hutt in the forest.'

Grey flapped the napkin at him. 'I don't care where he was captured, so long as he is safely held. But what of the reliquary, was that found with him?'

The sergeant shook his head. 'No sign of it whole or in pieces. But that's not the worst of it. There's been murder done.'

Grey leaped to his feet, almost overturning the table. 'Richard Whitney's been murdered!'

'Not him, sir. Master Richard's not the victim, he's the murderer.'

It was nearly noon before Grey and his two sergeants-at-arms arrived at the Royal Hutt in Sherwood Forest. It had taken some time to find a man who was prepared to guide them there. Most villagers denied even knowing of its existence, though Grey suspected that they knew very well where it was, but were not going to help an enforcer whom they all knew had come to take their saint from them.

Eventually, but only after he'd been offered a good purse, a wagoner who lived in another village offered to show them the track that wound through the trees. Grey and his men travelled behind the wagon on horseback at the wagon's infuriatingly slow pace until it eventually ground to a halt, and the wagoner pointed down a narrow path that led to a small stone lodge among the trees. It had, so he told Grey, been built to shelter the Royal Wardens of Sherwood Forest as they made their rounds searching for poachers and for any man cutting wood without leave or illegally carrying a bow in the forest. For centuries it had been a welcome refuge for the King's men, especially in the bitter winters.

Grey dismounted and tethered his horse close to the track. 'Stay here,' he said. 'We may have need of your wagon to move the body. Where is the nearest village?' He gestured ahead down the track. 'Is it that way?'

The wagoner shook his head. 'That way leads to Newstead Priory. Leastways, it was the priory till the bastards thieved it from the Black Canons and gave it to one of the King's fat lapdogs.'

Both of Grey's men took a menacing step towards the wagoner, their hands reaching for the hilts of their swords, but Grey motioned them back. Much as he was in favour of cleansing England of the foul corruption of the monasteries, he did not like the way in which such lands were falling into the hands of the wealthy supporters of the King, men no less corrupt than the abbots and priors they were displacing. He could understand only too well the wagoner's bitterness. Besides, it would not do to annoy the only man who had shown any inclination to assist him, even though Grey knew he would have helped the Devil himself if he were paid enough.

Leaving the wagoner, Grey and his men followed the path round until they came to the Hutt. Two men in forest wardens' livery were sitting on a bench warming their hands over a small fire burning in a shallow pit. A third man was sitting on the ground, his back to a tree to which he was tightly lashed. He was a stout man, and a wealthy one too, judging by his fine clothes, but his face was drawn and pale, the flesh sagging as if he'd scarcely slept at all, although a night spent out in the cold had evidently not been sufficient to cool his temper.

'I demand you release me at once,' he barked the instant he caught sight of the three men.

'Master Richard Whitney?' Grey stared down at him.

'If you know I'm Richard Whitney you must also know I'm Master of the Butchers' Guild, and I am not accustomed to being trussed up like one of my own pigs and left to freeze to death in a forest. It's a miracle I'm still alive after the way I've been treated.'

The forest wardens exchanged weary glances as if they'd been forced to listen to his protestations all night.

'Coroner's already inside if it's him you're looking for. It's Sir Layton,' one said, jerking his head towards the Hutt.

Grey nodded and pushed open the stout wooden door and peered into the gloomy interior. The Hutt was large enough to provide rough shelter for half a dozen men. Pallets and blankets were heaped in one corner, while in the opposite corner were several boxes and barrels of pickled pork and flour. A bundle of dried salt fish swung from a low beam. Deer antlers and goat horns were stacked up in a heap near the door. The thick stone walls were hung with spades, bows, bundles of arrows, coils of rope and mantraps, together with grappling hooks and long brooms for beating out fire. Between them, hanging in what little space was left, were the bleached skulls of foxes and wild boar.

Two men were bending over what looked at first sight like a heap of cloth, but as they straightened up Grey could clearly see it was a man who lay crumpled up on the stone floor in a puddle of his own dark congealed blood. His head was twisted to one side, revealing a gaping wound in his throat, wide enough for a man to put all the fingers of one hand through.

Growing up in a tanner's yard strengthens a man's stomach,

and Grey didn't flinch or avert his eyes, but found himself, as always, wondering what must go through a man's mind as he takes the life of another.

He stepped forward and briefly introduced himself, and the coroner frowned.

'Cromwell's enforcer? What business brings you out here then?'

'I believe Master Richard Whitney – the man you have tied up outside – to be in possession of a reliquary that he was trying to conceal. It's that reliquary I've come for. I've no wish to interfere in your investigation into this death.'

'Reliquary?' Sir Layton shrugged. 'You'll have to ask the wardens about that. It was they who caught Whitney, red-handed too, in every sense. Gave a good account of what happened. Observant men, the wardens. Makes a change from most of the witnesses I have to question. Most of the halfwits wouldn't notice if their own backsides were on fire.'

'The wardens saw the murder then?' Grey said.

'As good as,' the coroner replied. 'They were heading to the Hutt through the trees last night when they saw a rider come galloping up the other way. He sprang off his horse and ran inside. Naturally, they ran towards the Hutt too, thinking it might be a poacher. Burst in to find Whitney kneeling over the body, his hands covered in blood. Soon as he saw he'd been discovered, he barged the wardens aside and ran out, but one gave chase and threatened to put an arrow between his shoulder blades if he didn't stop. He had the sense to give himself up.'

'So he's admitted killing this man?'

Sir Layton gave Grey the kind of withering look school-masters reserve for particularly stupid pupils. 'Have you ever known a man confess to murder except to a priest, and then only when he's standing on the gallows? Naturally Whitney said what they all say when they're caught with a corpse: that he stumbled over the body in the dark and was just feeling to see if the man was actually dead. But the forest wardens have slaughtered enough beasts to be able to tell how long a man's been dead. They're certain this man had only just been killed when they burst in.

'According to them it was a clear night. Said they could see the walls of the Hutt glistening in the moonlight as they were coming through the trees. They're certain no one went in, save for Whitney, and there's only one door in or out.' Sir Layton jerked his chin towards the small opening on the back wall of the Hutt, which served as a window. 'A scrawny child might crawl through that, but not a grown man.'

The man who stood beside Sir Layton was evidently his clerk. He grinned broadly, showing a mouth full of blackened teeth. 'Master Whitney doesn't have to admit to murder. He's been shouting his mouth off ever since we arrived about how he's Master of the Butchers' Guild. And you've only got to look at this poor sod's throat to see it's been slit the same way as a butcher would cut the throat of one of his beasts. Be second nature to a man like him to whip out a knife and draw it across a neck quicker than you can say "I fancy a nice piece of mutton".'

Grey crouched down and peered at the gaping wound in the man's throat. The jagged and torn edges of the flesh were beginning to peel back as the cut skin dried. There was no arguing that this man's throat had been slashed. He straightened up.

'Have you got the knife he used?'

Sir Layton shrugged. 'Found one knife on Whitney, but that was clean. But a butcher would carry more than one –

a knife for the table and another for slaughter at least. He doubtless hurled it into the undergrowth as he ran from the cottage.' He nudged the body with the toe of his shoe. 'But if you know the murderer, Master Grey, do you recognise his victim?'

Grey shook his head. 'I hadn't even met Master Richard until just now, though I knew he'd taken the reliquary, and I've not seen this man before.'

Sir Layton grimaced. 'Pity. We need to identify the corpse and Whitney keeps saying he doesn't know him, though I don't believe him.' He sighed. 'But since we don't know where the victim comes from, the only thing we can do is take the body back to the village where his murderer lives and see if anyone there can put a name to him. If the two men did know each other, it's likely others will also recognise him.'

The body, wrapped in a blanket borrowed from the Hutt, was carried out to the wagon and the reluctant wagoner was persuaded, with the inducement of an even larger sum and promise of a bed in the inn, to drive the corpse back to Blidworth. Two horses had been found, one belonging to Richard, the other was assumed to belong to the victim. Both were tethered behind the wagon. Richard was hauled to his feet and had to be dragged to the wagon, for his legs were so numb from cold he could barely stand. He was forced to sit in the bottom of the wagon along with the corpse and the two forest wardens, despite demanding to be allowed to ride home on his own horse and insisting he would not be carried into the village like a common felon. But he was told firmly by one of the wardens that if he didn't hold his tongue, there'd be a second corpse in the wagon before the journey's end.

After Sir Layton and his clerk had departed, following the wagon, Grey and his men searched for the reliquary. They painstakingly took apart the stack of pallets and blankets, rooted through the boxes and poked sticks down to the bottom of the flour barrels, a common hiding place for valuables in many households, but there was no sign of it. Grey even sent the men to search through the dry brown undergrowth around the Hutt in case Richard had hidden it there, but they found neither reliquary nor knife.

Grey gazed into the mass of trees and heathland that lay all about him. Suppose Richard had hidden the reliquary somewhere in Sherwood Forest before he ever reached the Hutt? They could search for a year and not find it. But why would Richard have cause to murder a man if he had already safely hidden the reliquary? Unless, of course, the man had seen where he'd hidden it and Richard needed to ensure he couldn't talk.

Grey caught his men glancing anxiously up at the sky. The pale winter sun was already tangled in the tops of the bare branches of the oak tree. They were right to be concerned; if they didn't set out for the village now they might still be on the forest track when darkness fell and no one but a knave or a fool wanted to be on such a road then, for even strangers knew it was a notorious hunting ground for robbers and kidnappers.

Grey and his men reached the inn without mishap, and when he entered the ale room in search of supper, he found the coroner already seated at one of the tables, devouring a large wedge of rabbit pie. Sir Layton, wiping the pastry crumbs from his lips with a stained napkin, beckoned Grey to join him and, when the serving maid appeared, ordered brawn and sharp sauce for Grey and some of the roast tongue, which Sir Layton had evidently consumed as the first course. Grey, who didn't care much for either dish, found his objections swept aside.

'You'll be glad to know we've identified the victim,' Layton said breezily. 'Man by the name of Edward Thornton, fellow guild member of Whitney's, by all accounts. It seems the two men fought a hard contest to become Master.' He beamed contentedly. 'It would seem the two men were rivals. Quarrelled, no doubt, and Whitney killed him. From these past few hours I've spent in Whitney's company it's plain to me the man's of a choleric disposition, loses his temper at the slightest thing, I'd say. That's why Whitney refused to identify Thornton, do you see? Knew as soon as we learned who his victim was, it would put a rope round his neck without question.'

Grey frowned. 'I'd have thought Edward Thornton had more cause to kill Richard Whitney, not the other way round. After all, it was Richard who won the title of Master of the Guild. Edward would surely have the greater cause for jealousy and may even have thought that, with Richard dead, he'd become the next Master. I've known monks commit murder over who will become cellarer, so I supposed we can expect no better from laity.'

Sir Layton chewed thoughtfully on a mouthful of rabbit meat, before swallowing it. 'Perhaps Thornton attacked Whitney first out of jealousy, as you say, but Whitney got the better of him. He's much the weightier man. Could easily have knocked him to the ground and then in temper killed him, though if he's going to claim it was self-defence, he'll be hard put to prove it. We found no weapon on the corpse except for his knife, and that was still in its sheath.'

Grey poked listlessly at the unappetising slab of tongue. 'But that's the other thing. How did the two men come to be miles out in the forest? If they'd quarrelled in the village, I could understand it, but what business would butchers have in such a remote spot?'

'If, as you claim, Thornton was jealous, he could have lured Whitney out there to kill him. Ambushed him as he came through the door.'

'On what pretext, though?' Grey asked.

Sir Layton was beginning to look impatient. 'Buying deer or boar for his butcher's shop. I imagine the forest wardens often do a little poaching of their own, but they'd have to sell their kills quietly, well away from the towns. Half the butchers' shops in these forest villages are probably trading in poached venison. With the Christmas feasts almost upon us, both butchers might have been after the same carcass and quarrelled as to who should have it.'

He pushed his trencher aside irritably. 'Besides, it doesn't matter to me why they went out there. My job is simply to determine how the man died, see the body is identified and make sure Richard Whitney is arraigned at the next assizes. Who attacked who first is up to the judge and jury to decide.' He glanced sharply at Grey. 'And I'd have thought quarrels among butchers were of no concern of Cromwell's enforcers either.'

Layton was right, Grey thought, neither quarrels nor murders among butchers were any of his concern, except that one of those butchers had been trying to conceal a reliquary and now it was missing. Whatever Richard had been doing out at the Royal Hutt, Grey was convinced he hadn't been in pursuit of poached venison, and he wasn't about to let Richard take the knowledge of the hiding place of that reliquary to the gallows.

'Stinks a mite in there, Master Grey,' the constable said cheerfully. 'Bailiff sometimes uses it to hold stray beasts. There's certain men in these parts would think nothing of hauling their animals over the pinfold wall to get out of paying the fine for letting them wander.'

They were standing in front of the village lockup, a small round building shaped like a dovecote, built to hold felons until the sheriff's men could collect them, or to sober up drunks who had got into a brawl. It was still too early in the morning for many to be abroad, but the few who were stared at them with undisguised curiosity. The constable was taking an age unlocking the stout door. Although there were only three keys on the iron ring, the choice seemed to baffle him. Finally, the door creaked open and the constable stood aside.

'I'll have to lock you in with him, Master Grey, in case anyone tries to rush the door and help him escape, though I doubt even his own wife would do that. Terrible thing to do to a man, and one of his own guild brothers. I thought they were meant to look out for each other. Master Richard near enough cut his head off, he did. You should have seen the mess.'

'I did,' Grey said shortly, and marched in.

In the few moments it took for the constable to slam the door shut behind him, he saw Richard blinking up at him. He was looking even worse today than he had been after his night in the forest. His hair was matted with straw and his face was filthy, with dark rings under his eyes. There seemed to be a purple bruise on his cheek too, under the grime.

Once the door was closed, it took a few minutes for Grey's eyes to adjust to the twilight. The only openings in the walls were two slit windows, and the pale winter sun barely penetrated the chamber. The chamber felt so cold and damp that even though Grey was clad in a heavy winter cloak, his chest began to ache from sucking in the icy air. He shivered, wondering what it must be like to be alone here at night. The thought of being locked up alone in the dark had terrified him since he was a boy.

'Are you one of the sheriff's men? Have you come for me?' Richard sounded much more subdued than he had done yesterday.

Clearly the humiliation of being taken as a prisoner into his own village and then spending the night in this stinking filth had finally brought home to him just how much trouble he was in. Grey was pleased by the change in his tone. It would make it easier to get him to talk.

'I wasn't sent by the sheriff.'

Richard drew back against the wall, his body rigid, staring up at Grey as if trying to recall why he seemed familiar. Clearly the shock of the arrest had fuddled his wits.

In such a small space it was awkward trying to talk when Grey was towering over the prisoner. He realised that even in his present mood, making Richard feel as if he was being intimidated would only make him more stubborn. Grey crouched down in the straw so that he was level with him. The stench of dung and stale animal piss did not repel him as it would his fellow clerics. He'd grown up with it.

'Master Richard, I called at your house on the night of the murder. I came looking for the reliquary. I've orders to take it to be examined to see if it is genuine.'

Grey phrased his next words carefully. He didn't want to

make Richard think his wife or servants had betrayed him –
not unless it became necessary.

'I discovered the reliquary had been moved from the chest
where you had placed it for safekeeping. Did you—'

'He stole it!' Richard said vehemently. 'I came home in the
afternoon and recognised that little weasel's horse tethered
a short distance from the house. I hurried in, expecting to
find him in the winter parlour, but it was empty. I went
upstairs to the solar and I saw the chest had been broken
into. I heard a door bang, looked out of the window and
saw him running away across the courtyard.'

'You recognised the thief?'

'Of course I did, I'm not a fool. It was Edward Thornton.
But I didn't kill him, though I would have had every reason.
I gave chase simply to recover the reliquary. Once we
reached the forest I was gaining on him, even though he'd
had a good start on me; my horse is the younger and
stronger, and his beast was beginning to tire. It was dark by
that time and he rounded the bend of the track ahead of
me. But when I came round the curve there was no sight of
him on the road. I realised he must have turned from the
track to try to shake me off. It was only when I came back
down the track that I saw the path leading off through the
trees and that's when I noticed the Hutt beyond. The moon
was glinting off the stones.'

'You saw him go in and followed him,' Grey said.

Richard rubbed his neck, trying to ease his stiff shoulders.
'I glimpsed Edward by the door, but before I'd even dismounted he'd slipped inside. I knew how the little rat's mind
was working. He imagined I'd carry on down the track for
miles, leaving him free to ride back to Blidworth, brazen as a
cock on a dung heap. Then he could return at his leisure to

retrieve what he had stolen from me. But I'm not a fool. I hid my horse well away from the Hutt and I crept up to the door, planning to catch him hiding the reliquary. It was pitch-dark in the Hutt, and I'd taken only a pace or two inside when I tripped over something lying on the floor ...' He paused, rubbing his eyes as if trying to wipe the memory from his mind.

'What happened then?' Grey prompted softly.

'I ... I was shaken up by the fall. Must have lain there a minute or two trying to get my breath. I clambered up and I started groping round to find out what I'd fallen over. I thought it was a dead animal. I'd only just discovered it was a man when those fools of wardens came bursting in and accused me of murder!'

'And it would be perfectly understandable if you had murdered Edward,' Grey said soothingly. 'After all, a brother guild member breaks in and steals a valuable object, and when you demand its return, he threatens you, attacks you, and in the heat of the moment ... I'm sure a jury would be sympathetic.'

Grey thought it politic not to remind Richard that he was as much a thief as Edward.

Richard slammed his fist against his leg. 'Are you deaf? I told you he was already dead when I found him. If I'd got my hands on the louse I would have cleaved him in two and hung him up like the pig he is. But I didn't get a chance. Someone else got there first.'

Grey tried to maintain an understanding tone. 'You say you saw Edward enter the Hutt. Did you see anyone leave?'

'Yes, yes, I did!' Richard pounced on the idea, a little too eagerly. 'That's exactly what I saw, someone running from the Hutt after Edward went in. Whoever it was took off along the path in the opposite direction to me.'

Grey knew he was lying. The wardens had been walking towards the Hutt. Anyone running away would have charged straight past them and they were adamant they'd only seen Richard enter, no one leaving. They'd no reason to speak anything but the truth.

'It was dark,' Grey reminded him. 'Didn't you think it was Edward you were seeing leaving the Hutt and chase after him?'

Richard hesitated. 'It didn't look like Edward ... the man was ... was taller, broader. Besides, I was only interested in recovering the reliquary. So I saw no point in charging after him and I went straight into the Hutt to search for it.'

Grey heard the bluster in his voice and was convinced Richard had only just thought of this.

'And did you find it?'

'Haven't you even got the wits you were born with?' Richard snapped. 'I didn't get a chance to search the Hutt. I told you, I fell over Edward's body in the dark and then those numbskulls lumbered in, dragged me out and tied me to a tree. They refused to let me go back inside.' He leaned forward, staring into Grey's face. 'Have you found it? Was it in there?'

'We searched thoroughly, Master Richard. The reliquary isn't there. Wherever Master Edward hid it, it was not in the Hutt.' A thought struck Grey and he plucked at his lip. 'How would Edward have known you had the reliquary in the house? Did you tell him?'

'Him! I'd have told Cromwell himself before telling Edward. I didn't even tell my wife. It could only have been Father James who betrayed me. He didn't want the reliquary removed from the church. He probably put Edward up to this. I wouldn't be surprised if they were in on this together.

That priest's already tried once to trick me into giving it to him, so when that didn't work, he arranged to have it stolen. It's Father James behind all of this. He probably killed Edward himself, once he'd brought him the reliquary. You know, the more I think of it, the more certain I am it *was* that priest I saw running away from the Hutt. I'd swear to it.'

Grey didn't believe for one moment that Richard had seen anyone running from the Hutt, much less Father James, but he was convinced that Richard had pursued Edward because he genuinely believed he had stolen the reliquary, and had killed him. Certainly the theft would have given a man like Richard reason enough, and that made a great deal more sense than Sir Layton's belief that Edward had lured Richard to the Hutt with the intention of murdering him.

But if Richard had followed Edward in close pursuit, how had the man managed to stop off along the route and hide Beornwyn's statue? If he had it with him, he'd surely try to hide it in the Hutt. But he hadn't had much time to conceal it there, so why hadn't they found it?

Grey left the lockup and made his way slowly towards the church. He had no idea if Father James would be inside, but was pleased to find the door of the church standing open. But when he stepped inside it was not the priest he saw.

A spindly young lad was standing up near the altar. He seemed to be handing something to a man standing in the shadow of one of the pillars. The boy spun round as he heard the sound of footsteps on the flagstones. As he turned, a meaty hand shot out from behind the pillar and cuffed the boy's head.

'I've told you before, brat. You can't leave offerings before the statue of the Virgin Mary. 'Gainst the law, it is. Don't let me catch you again.'

The lad turned and ran back down the church. Grey tried to block his way, but the boy was too nimble. He evaded his grasp and was out of the door before Grey could stop him.

The man, whom Grey took to be the churchwarden, emerged from behind the pillar and ambled down the church, shaking his head.

'Can't get the new laws into their heads, some of them. Old women, it is mostly, won't give up the old ways, but you get a few of the young ones at it, too. That lad's one of the worst, devoted to the Church he is. Should have been a priest or a monk, by rights, not a butcher's boy. I do my best to keep 'em out, but I've my own business to attend to. Can't be here every minute to watch 'em and they sneak in behind my back.'

From the stench of wet fish that clung to his skin and clothes, Grey could make a good guess as to what the man's business might be. He glanced at the warden's hands, scarred with a hundred old nicks and scratches, but they were empty. Whatever he taken from the lad had disappeared quicker than a starving dog gobbles a scrap.

'What did the boy give you?'

The man gave a puzzled smile. 'Me? Nowt. He was trying to leave some tawdry at the feet of the Virgin Mary, but, as you saw, I sent him packing.'

Grey was certain he had seen the boy hand something over. But he didn't press the matter. Better the warden confiscate the offering than leave it with the lad to try again.

'What's the boy's name?'

'Alan. Master Richard's apprentice.' Yarrow shook his head sorrowfully. 'Bad business, bad business. But can't say

I'm surprised. Only a matter of time, if you ask me. Master
Richard always did have a violent temper. I reckon young
Alan there would testify to that. Lashed out at the lad regu-
larly, he did, and at his wife, too, so the market crones say.
Not that you can set much store by women's gossip.'

That was motive enough for any hot-headed apprentice to
commit murder, Grey thought, especially if he attacked the
wrong man in the dark.

'Did you happen to see Alan the night Edward was murdered?'

Yarrow gave a wry smile. ' 'Course I saw him. Had to
drive him out of here, so I could lock up at dusk.'

If the boy had borrowed a horse and ridden to the Hutt,
he would have had time to get there before Richard, and he
was certainly slim enough to squeeze out through that
window at the back, or even to have hidden inside until the
wardens were occupied chasing Richard and then slipped
out of the door. But even so, it didn't seem likely that he
could have killed Edward. The lad was so skinny, he'd have
had trouble overpowering a cat, never mind a grown man
with the brawn and muscles of a butcher. All the same, Grey
resolved to speak to Alan as soon as he could. In his experience, inquisitive boys often noticed more than adults realised,
especially the quiet ones.

'Where is Beornwyn's reliquary now?' Grey asked suddenly, hoping the abrupt change of subject might catch the
man off guard.

But Yarrow was not thrown. 'Father James took it. You'll
have to ask him what he did with it. For all I know he's
chopped it into firewood. Up at this church at least twice a
day, I am. It's as well I never took a wife, for she'd still be a
virgin waiting on me to come home. The church would fall

down round the vicar's ears if it wasn't for me tending to it night and day. But for all that, I'm the last person he'd consult about such things as reliquaries. I'm only the churchwarden, after all!'

There was a bitter note in his voice. Clearly there was no love wasted between the churchwarden and his parish priest.

'Richard Whitney tells me it was he, not Father James, who removed the reliquary from the church,' Grey said. 'He hid it in his house and Richard believes Edward Thornton stole the statue from him, which is why Richard pursued him to the Hutt. But if he did, the reliquary was not found with his body. Have you any idea where Edward might have hidden it?'

The churchwarden laughed. 'There's a bloody great forest out there, or hadn't you noticed? If Edward hid it, I reckon that's where you want to be looking, but even if you had every soldier in King Henry's army hunting for it, they could search till their beards turn white and they'd still not discover every hollow tree or thicket or yard of leaf mould where a man might bury such a thing. Can't see why you're even bothering to question folk. If St Beornwyn's vanished, then you've got what you wanted, for no man will be able to worship her relics now.'

'I've known other reliquaries *vanish* until the enforcers have left a parish, then miraculously they reappear,' Grey said.

Yarrow shook his head. 'That might be true for other parishes, but unless dead men can talk, there's no likelihood of St Beornwyn appearing in this church again. Edward's taken that secret to his grave.'

He moved past Grey and stood at the door of the church, pointedly holding it open and swinging the ring of iron keys around the great knuckle of his finger. Grey took the hint.

The small row of shops in the village was bustling, for it was Christmas Eve and every woman in the village wanted to prepare a fine feast. Neighbours would be calling on each other daily, for it was said to bring good luck for the following year to eat a minced pie on each of the twelve days of Christmas in a different house and no goodwife wanted to be shamed by others whispering that her pies were not as good as the next woman's.

Such superstition annoyed Grey, although it was as much because he remembered the shame of his own childhood as for any religious objection. Unlike the other boys, his mother never cooked such delicacies, for who would brave the stink of the tanner's yard to eat with them?

He threaded his way through the women struggling with baskets and bundles. They jostled around the wares laid out on the open benches in front of the little houses. The exotic smell of aniseed, mace, nutmeg and cloves from the grocer's stall mingled with stench of eels, herring and dried cod from the fishmonger, while the fragrant steam of newly baked bread and spiced meat pies made the stomach grumble to be fed.

The crowd seemed thickest round the butcher's stall. Hunks of bloody meat and offal were ranged along a stone bench. A harassed-looking woman was slicing a fat purple cow's tongue, while a strapping young man was tying a rope around the back legs of a skinned goat and heaving it onto one of the vicious-looking iron hooks that stuck out from under the overhanging upper storey of the building behind. The carcass of the goat swayed gently as spots of blood splashed onto the cobbles below.

Grey pushed his way to the front of the gaggle of women. They protested indignantly until they saw who he was, then they stepped aside, hauling their children behind their skirts as if he were a leper. But they didn't move far, their chatter ceasing instantly as they craned their necks to listen.

'Is this Richard Whitney's stall?' Grey asked.

'Do you want to buy anything or not?' The woman continued to cut thick even slices from the cow's tongue, without looking up.

'I'm Roger Grey and I want to know if this is Richard's stall.'

Her head shot up and she pointed the sharp blade straight at Grey's chest; the furious expression on her face told him that if he annoyed her any further she might well use the knife on him instead of the tongue.

'Look,' she said. 'I don't know nothing about any murder, so it's no use your asking.' She gestured behind her with the point of the knife. 'Thomas here's the journeyman, so I reckon he's the man in charge now. You go ask him. I shouldn't even be working here today. Wouldn't be if that brat of an apprentice of his hadn't gone missing, yet again.'

'Now don't you go spreading rumours that Alan's gone missing. Folk'll reckon he's been murdered 'n' all,' Thomas said.

He stared at Grey over his shoulder, while running his blade down the spine of the kid, peeling the flesh back to the bone. Grey winced for him, sure he would cut his own hand off, but it seemed the journeyman was so skilled at his craft, he could slice a carcass open with his eyes closed, or even, Grey suddenly realised, in the dark.

'Alan's run off again, but I know where he is all right,' the journeyman added. 'He'll be hanging around the church again. Haven't had a decent day's work out of the little runt since the statue of St Beornwyn went missing, not that we ever did before. I reckon he was in love with that statue; spent all his time gazing at her breasts, he did. Can't get a real lass to look at him, so he has to drool over a wooden one.'

'The boy was devoted to the statue then?' Grey was more willing to put the lad's interest down to religious fervour rather than lust, but both states could produce a blind and unreasoning passion in the young. He might not have been strong enough to murder a man, but he could certainly have stolen the reliquary from Richard's house before Edward got there, in which case, it might never have been taken to the Hutt at all.

'Can you remember where Alan was on the afternoon Edward was murdered?'

The journeyman took off his filthy cap, and ran his fingers through hair already matted with grease, dung and blood. 'Here, I should think, but I couldn't rightly say. I was away m'self buying a couple of pigs.'

The woman snorted. 'He wasn't here, not one of you buggers was. Left me on my own again, same as always.'

'You get paid, don't you, you old besom?' Thomas said.

'The runny-nosed squabs who pick up dog shit for the tanner get paid more than me.'

'So why don't you ...'

Grey left them bickering, gesturing recklessly with their knives to the amusement of the customers, who were evidently well used to this. He picked his way up the street towards the church, his thoughts whirling as he walked.

So, the journeyman had also been absent. Either he or Alan could have stolen the statue from the house or from Edward. The journeyman certainly had the butchering skills to kill Edward, just as easily as Richard. But Grey still couldn't see how he had got out of the Hutt without being seen by either Richard or the forest wardens, and Richard would surely have recognised Thomas if he'd seen him running away. There was something else nagging at the back of Grey's mind. Something that didn't fit, but he couldn't seem to grasp hold of it.

But neither Alan nor Thomas knew the statue was in Richard's house. According to Richard, only one man did and that was Father James. Was Richard right to suspect him after all? The priest also knew Grey was going to Richard's house to seize it later that day. Could he have got there first? But no, Richard said he arrived home in the afternoon to find the lock of the chest broken. His wife and maid saw him riding off shortly afterwards. The reliquary must already have been missing when Grey was talking to the priest in the church.

Richard had said his wife hadn't known the reliquary was in the house. Yet she and her maid had both told Grey it had been in the chest. And for a woman who claimed her husband had gone off on business she had seemed unusually distressed by his absence that night. Grey turned and hurried back up the road towards Richard's house.

When he arrived, he found a group of women standing across the street, talking earnestly, repeatedly glancing up at the casements as if they expected to see blood running from them or the Devil to come flying out of the chimney.

After Grey had tolled the bell several times, the maid, Jennet, finally opened the door a crack. She shook her head when Grey asked to speak to her mistress.

'She doesn't want to see anyone. She's in a terrible state. Been sobbing all night, she has, and she's not eaten a bite.'

Grey tried to sound sympathetic but firm. 'Her husband

has been accused of murder. It's only to be expected she is distressed; nevertheless, whether she wants to see me or not, I must speak with her. This is the King's business.'

Reluctantly, Jennet opened the door just wide enough for Grey to squeeze through before slamming it shut again, as if she feared the entire village might force their way in behind him.

'She's in the winter parlour, sir,' Jennet said, leading the way to a door at the back of the hall.

Grey nodded. 'I may wish to speak with you and William later. Do not leave the house.'

Jennet gave him a frightened look before ushering him in with the briefest of announcements. Mary was sitting by the fire staring into the flames, twisting a kerchief in her lap. She did not look round as Grey crossed the room.

'I told Jennet I can't see anyone,' she said. 'Please have the goodness to leave me alone.' Her voice was hoarse, as if her throat was dry and sore.

'I understand your distress, Mistress Mary,' Grey said, taking the seat opposite her without waiting for it to be offered. 'You're naturally worried about your husband.'

'Husband?' Mary lifted her head.

Her eyes were swollen from crying, but they were dry now as if she was drained of tears. She gazed at him uncomprehendingly.

'Your husband being accused of murder,' Grey reminded her, wondering if shock and exhaustion had dulled her wits.

She made a little gesture with her hand, which was almost one of dismissal. 'I cannot think about that now.'

He could understand that. She was probably more worried for her own future. If Richard was hanged she could well see herself evicted from the house and Grey had no idea if Mary had relatives who would take her in or who would even be prepared to acknowledge her after this disgrace. The guild, which was supposed to provide for the widows and orphans of its members, would hardly be prepared to provide for a murderer's wife, especially when the victim was one of their own. Nevertheless, Grey could not afford to be too understanding. The longer that reliquary remained missing, the greater the chances of someone else finding it and spiriting it away.

'Mistress Mary, I spoke this morning with your husband. He tells me that he returned to the house earlier than usual and found the chest broken into and saw Edward Thornton hurrying away. He gave chase, assuming that Edward had taken the reliquary. But he says he did not tell Edward the reliquary was in the house. Did you tell him?'

She hastily turned her face back towards the fire, but not before Grey had glimpsed the expression of alarm that flashed across it.

'I knew nothing of the reliquary.'

'But you and Jennet both knew that the chest had been broken into and the reliquary was missing, so you must have known it was there. Think, mistress, it's important, could you have let slip anything by accident, perhaps to a friend or neighbour?'

She shook her head vehemently, but still did not look at him. Grey gazed about the small chamber, thinking back over the exact words Richard had used. He suddenly leaned forward.

'Your husband says when he returned to the house, he saw Edward's horse tethered a little way from here and he rushed to this room expecting to find him here. Why this room in particular? Surely it is more usual for servants to leave guests waiting in the hall for their master's return.'

A slight flush crept over Mary's pale cheeks. 'My husband often entertained fellow guild brothers in here. It was more private if they had guild matters to discuss.'

'But Master Edward knew that your husband would be about his business at that time in the afternoon. Why would Edward call on him here at a time when he knew Richard would not be at home?'

'One of the men must have told Edward he'd returned here.'

'And why did he return here?' Grey persisted.

'I don't know! All I know is my husband is arrested and Edward is . . . dead.' Mary sprang from her seat and paced over to the window, staring out at the bleak sky through the tiny diamonds of glass. Grey could see her shoulders shaking as she fought to stifle her sobs.

He felt a twinge of guilt. He disliked harrying women, but she was lying to him. He knew that.

'Edward came here to see you, didn't he?' he said sharply. 'Was that why your husband returned unexpectedly, because he had his suspicions that you and Edward were playing him for a cuckold?'

Mary's legs buckled and she sank down onto her knees. For a moment, Grey thought she had fainted, but she remained kneeling at the casement, sobbing uncontrollably into her kerchief.

He hurried over and lifted her up, settling her into the window seat.

He waited, until she quietened a little.

'Mistress Mary, you have my word I will not utter a word to any about your dalliance. That's no concern of mine. But if your husband's lawyer learns of it he might raise the matter at your husband's trial. Juries tend to be sympathetic to husbands who've been wronged. They are, after all, husbands themselves. Although from what little I know of Richard, the fact that he didn't mention it to me probably means he would sooner be hanged than have the world know he'd been cuckolded. But there is one thing that is my concern. Did Edward take that reliquary?'

He saw the muscle in the side of Mary's face twitch as she clenched her jaw.

'Edward is dead, Mary. It cannot harm him now if you tell me the truth. And that reliquary has already brought enough misery to this household. Don't force me to add more by having my men tear this place apart looking for it.'

She swallowed hard, then took a deep breath. 'I'm not as stupid as my husband thinks. I heard him lumbering up the stairs that night long after the servants were abed and I heard the chest in the solar being opened. It's right next door to the bedchamber. Next morning, the rumour was all round the village that St Beornwyn had vanished from the church in the night. I know how much my husband likes to show off the reliquary for its gold and jewels. He wasn't interested in her holy relics, just the statue that housed them. I guessed at once he had taken it and where he'd put it.'

'And you told Edward.'

Her head jerked up. 'We were not lovers,' she said fiercely, 'at least not in the way you mean. Edward was kind and intelligent. He should have been Guild Master, not Richard, but half the men were afraid of Richard and dared not vote against him. I enjoyed talking to Edward. He didn't treat me as if I was one of his apprentices. He took to calling on me and we enjoyed spending time in each other's company.

Richard came home unexpectedly one day and found us in here laughing together. He was convinced I was betraying him, but I wasn't ... not then. After that Richard began coming home at odd hours, trying to catch us, and his moods got worse. Edward could see how miserable I was, how Richard treated me, and asked me to run away with him.

'But taking St Beornwyn was my idea. Edward would be giving up everything for me and we needed money to begin a new life far from here. Besides, Richard had taken all the money and property I brought with me as a bride, so why should he have the statue as well? He deserved to lose it!' she added vehemently.

Clearly, Grey thought, Mary cared as little for the relics as her husband. Her only thought was to use the reliquary to finance her new life with her lover, and to spite Richard too, of course.

'William always slips out to his mother's in the afternoon, so I arranged that Jennet and I should sit with a friend, so that if Richard checked, we could prove we were not in the house when it was robbed. My husband had warned us there was a gang of robbers come to this village, so I knew if the house were left empty Richard would be bound to think it was them. Edward was to take the reliquary and hide it. In a few days, after the fuss of the reliquary had died down, I would join Edward and we'd disappear. But Richard returned early in the hope of finding us together. He must have seen Edward and followed him, and then ... then he killed him. He ... he cut his throat as if Edward were nothing more than a pig in his slaughter yard!' She broke down into sobs again.

Grey thought that it was as well for Richard that a wife could not be called as a witness against her husband, for she'd surely put a rope around his neck herself, and probably offer to kick the ladder away, too.

'You said that Edward intended to hide the reliquary. Where?'

Mary scrubbed at her tear-stained face. 'He didn't tell me in case I was questioned. He thought it would be easier to deny everything if I didn't know.'

Grey could understand that, and he was inclined to believe her, but once again he felt a growing frustration.

'Then where were you to meet?'

'The village of Linby; it lies beyond Newstead Priory. Edward has a distant cousin who owned a watermill there, but it's not been running these past few years, since one of the landowners diverted the stream and put him out of work.'

So, in all likelihood, Edward was planning to hide the reliquary in the disused mill – a good hiding place – but plainly he never got that far. Realising that Richard was about to overtake him, he turned aside to the Hutt. But where was Beornwyn's statue now?

As Grey walked back down the street towards the inn, the last of the goodwives were clustered around the stalls, bargaining for bread, fish and meat, and anything else they thought the shopkeepers might be persuaded to sell cheaply on the grounds that it would not keep over Christmas Day. Apart from at the baker's they were having a hard time convincing the shopkeepers to bargain, for in this cold weather even meat and fish would stay fresh for several days.

Dusk was settling down over the village and icy mist, heavy with wood smoke, curled itself around the houses. Grey was anxious to get back to the inn's fireside. He was so hunched up against the cold that he found himself walking past the butcher's yard without even realising it, and would have carried on but for the bellow of anger that caught his attention. He paused and glanced through the open gateway.

The journeyman was nowhere to be seen, but the slovenly woman he'd spoken to earlier had trapped someone in the corner and was giving him a good drubbing with her tongue, punctuated by several smart raps to the head. Grey couldn't see much of the figure cowering under her blows, but he guessed it was probably the errant apprentice. He strode in and pulling the woman away from Alan, seized the lad firmly by his jerkin and marched him out of the yard.

Momentarily stunned by having her victim snatched from her, the woman recovered herself and ran after them down the road.

'Here, where do you think you're taking him? The little bugger's been gone half the day. I need him here to clear the meat and fetch water from the well to sluice down the slabs.'

Grey ignored her and hurried the boy on.

They heard her voice rising to a shriek behind them. 'Bring him back here! You're not leaving me to do it all myself again!'

As soon as they had turned the corner safely out of sight, the boy tried to wriggle free, but Grey pushed him up against the wall of a cottage.

'Alan, isn't it? You're not in trouble. I just want to talk to you.'

The boy looked plainly terrified.

Grey tried again, softening his voice. 'I don't think you want to face that woman tonight, do you? Why don't you come along with me and I'll buy you a good hot supper?

We can sit by the fire and I'll ask you a few questions. That's all, just a few questions, then you can leave or stay as you please.'

He saw the look of temptation on the boy's face and guessed it had been some while since he'd eaten and probably only scraps when he had.

'What if I don't know the answers to your questions?' Alan said warily.

'As long as you speak the truth I'll be content with that, and you'll still have your supper . . . I believe there is meat pie tonight and green codling pudding. I saw a man delivering woodcock too.'

The boy hesitated, but Grey could see from the excitement in his eyes that he needed no more persuasion.

As soon as he ushered the boy into the inn, Grey asked for food to be sent up to the small chamber where he slept. There was a good fire burning in the hearth in there and he thought Alan might be more inclined to talk if they were well away from the curious eyes of the villagers who'd come to sup their ale. He saw the innkeeper and serving maid exchange knowing glances, and guessed he was not the first guest to take a village lad up to his bedchamber, but he was too weary to bother explaining. Besides, he'd learned long ago that men and women always preferred their own imaginings over the truth.

He let the boy eat his fill in silence, though that took quite some time. The boy was still stuffing himself long after Grey was replete, having devoured a woodcock basking in a rich wine sauce, a wedge of meat pie and several slices of cold pork and bread. Alan was eating at such an alarming speed he was certain to give himself a belly ache, but Grey had known hunger himself at that age and knew that no word of caution would stop the boy taking another slice. When have warnings of future pain ever prevented the young from succumbing to temptation?

When Alan finally pushed his wooden platter from him and refilled his beaker from the jug of cider, Grey finally permitted himself to speak. He didn't look at the boy, but leaned forward, spreading his hands over the blaze in the hearth as if addressing himself to the flames.

'The churchwarden tells me that you often visited the statue of Beornwyn. You must have been upset when it was removed.' He heard only a noncommittal grunt. 'Do you know who took it from the church?'

Silence.

'It was your master and your priest who removed it. Did you know that, Alan?' He risked a sideways glance at the boy and caught a brief nod.

'Did you know Master Richard had the statue of Beornwyn in his house?'

'He shouldn't have taken her,' the boy said savagely. 'She didn't belong to him.'

'No, he shouldn't,' Grey agreed, 'but later someone else stole the statue from Master Richard's house.'

'I didn't do it! I swear it.' The boy was half-way out of his seat.

'I know you didn't,' Grey said soothingly. 'Master Richard believes it was another butcher who took the statue, Master Edward Thornton, and that night he was murdered at the Royal Hutt in the forest. You've probably heard people say it was Master Richard who killed him, but that is not yet proved. Someone else might well have slain Master Edward.'

'It wasn't me,' Alan said sullenly. 'I was in the church all night.'

'All night? Are you sure?'

The lad grunted. 'Thomas said he'd tell the master I'd refused to cut a sheep's throat and I'd run off again. He said the master'd kill me this time for sure. I was too afeared to go back to the master's house, so I ran to the church and hid behind the altar. Yarrow never checks there. I knew old Yarrow'd come and lock the door soon as it were growing dark. Then even if Master came to the church looking for me, he'd not be able to get in.'

Grey frowned, puzzled. 'Are you sure it was the night Master Edward died? You're not confusing it with the evening before? Because on the night Master Edward was murdered, Master Yarrow said he drove you out before he locked up.'

The boy took a swig of cider and burped loudly, rubbing his belly. 'Nah, he didn't lock up at all. I lay awake half the night, ready to creep out in the dark if the master came looking for me, but he didn't come neither. Church was still open next morning when I left, and that afternoon Master Richard was brought into the village in the wagon. I saw them pushing him into the gaol.' He bit his lip. 'St Beornwyn prayed for those who slew her, I suppose I should pray for him.' He didn't sound as if he was eager to do it, whatever the example the saint had set.

To console himself the lad reached for the remains of the leg of pork, but realising that not even he could manage any more meat, he sliced off the sweet honey crackling, which was evidently his favourite part, and chewed happily on the crispy wedge.

Grey idly watched the blade of Alan's knife as he sliced off yet another piece of golden-red crackling. Then as if the wisp of mist at the back of his head had frozen into a solid and tangible form, he suddenly realised what had been troubling him all this time. The meat that lay on the platter was sliced with a straight, smooth edge.

He pictured in his head the woman slicing through the lump of tongue and Thomas running his great blade down the spine of the young goat. They were all clean straight cuts. Butchers' knives, or the kind of knife any man would carry in his belt to cut his food or defend himself, all had smooth blades. That's what you needed to slice flesh and meat swiftly. But the wound on Edward's neck was not a clean cut. The edges of the flesh were jagged and torn as if his throat had been slashed with a serrated blade, and there was only one profession he could think of where serrated knives were used.

Grey pushed back the chair and rose swiftly. 'I have to go out. It may be very late before I return.'

He saw a look of alarm flash across the boy's face. 'You're welcome to stay here, lad, if you wish. No one will bother you.'

He crossed to his bed and kneeling, pulled out a low, narrow truckle bed from beneath his own and dragged it to the far corner. The truckle bed was intended for servants travelling with their masters, but he guessed it might be warmer and more comfortable than any sleeping place Richard had assigned the boy.

'You can sleep on this.'

He'd no wish to find the lad curled up in his own bed when he returned and he knew the boy would be tempted.

Grey did not trouble to rouse his two sergeants-at-arms from their warm seats in the ale room. He was not intending to make an arrest – not yet, anyway. Once the murderer was under lock and key there would be little hope of getting him to divulge the whereabouts of the missing reliquary. He would know that even surrendering such a valuable object would not save him from the gallows.

Grey had the stable boy saddle his horse. The lad was sulky at being dragged out into the cold from his supper, for he plainly hoped all of the guests would be settling down for the night in the inn and would not be venturing out again until morning.

The streets were quiet. The horse's iron shoes rang on the stones. A couple of men lumbered wearily past, returning from their workshops, their breath hanging about them like a cloud of white smoke in the cold night air. They scarcely bothered to lift their heads to stare at the rider.

Grey slowed his horse to an amble along the street, which just a couple of hours ago had been bustling with housewives and shopkeepers. Now the stone benches in front of the houses were empty of goods, and candles flickered through the holes in the shutters of upper storeys, where the shopkeepers and their families were eating their suppers. Grey looked up at the crudely painted signs above the shops, which indicated what each traded in. A pig's head for the butcher, thread and scissors for the cloth merchant, and a camel that looked more like a cow with a hump for the spiceseller. He found the sign he sought, and counted the houses down to the end of the row, then he turned his horse, and made for the street behind. He counted the houses back along the row.

Dismounting, he tethered the horse a little further down the road in the shelter of the trees and crept back again, until he had the courtyard at the back of the house within his sights. He could hear a horse stirring in the ramshackle stable in the yard, though it was too dark to make out much beyond dark smudges which might have been a cart and stacks of kegs.

Slivers of flickering yellow light crept out around the edges of the shutters on the upper storey, but they were too feeble even to reach the ground, never mind illuminate the spot where Grey stood. At least, Grey thought, it proved the man he sought must be at home. No one would go out and leave candles burning. The question was – would he leave? If the murderer realised the reliquary was still being sought, he might be panicked into moving it. In the meantime, there was nothing Grey could do but wait, watch and hope.

But by the time the lights were finally extinguished in the upper storey, Grey was so numb with cold and fatigue that he didn't even notice. In fact, it wasn't until he saw the light of the lantern coming across the yard and heard the whinnying of the horse in the stable that he realised the man was on the move. Grey's legs were so cold that it took quite a time for him to move himself and it took several attempts before he could heave his stiff body onto his own mount. He had only just settled himself in the saddle when he saw the horse and its rider trot out of the yard.

He dug his heels into his horse's flanks, urging her to follow, while trying to keep as much distance as he could between himself and the rider ahead without losing sight of him. He quickly realised they were leaving the village and heading straight down the road that led to the Hutt. Grey felt his stomach tighten in excitement. The thief was doing exactly what Grey had hoped he would do: leading him to the reliquary.

On such a still night, the hoofbeats of the horse he was following rang out as clear as a church bell and as the iron struck the stones on the track it sent up a shower of blue sparks in the darkness. It occurred to Grey that if he could so clearly hear the other horse, its rider would also hear him following. He turned off the path and forced his beast to walk on the grass, but Grey was anxious to keep as close behind as he dared. If the murderer had hidden the reliquary in the forest then he could turn off the track without warning and Grey might lose him, just as Richard had done.

Low wisps of white mist wrapped themselves around the roots of the trees, snaking over the track. Grey prayed it would not rise any higher. As the road wound deeper into the forest, the bushes crept closer to the track and the grass verge disappeared, so that several times Grey was forced to leave the line of the road and weave his way through the trees. But that was no bad thing, he told himself. If the rider ahead did happen to glance round, the forest would hide him.

Then, as Grey emerged from the trees, he saw to his consternation the track ahead was empty. Only a swirl of mist hung between the trees, glowing like a spectre under the starlight. Grey reined in his horse and listened. Then he heard the sound of breaking twigs away to his right and a little ahead. He coaxed the horse forward and suddenly saw that they had reached the narrow path that wound away to the Hutt. Even as he stared along it he glimpsed a figure on foot moving towards the door and, moments later, slip inside.

Grey quickly dismounted and, tethering his horse in the cover of some trees close to the track, he edged along the path, keeping his eyes fixed on the door, ready to dart into the undergrowth should the man re-emerge. Several times, he heard the sharp retort of a twig snapping beneath his feet and cursed himself for his own clumsiness. But the door didn't open and he guessed that the Hutt's stone walls were thick enough to prevent such sounds being heard inside.

Briefly, the yellow glow from a lantern shone beneath the door, vanishing almost at once. Grey crept up to the door and put his ear cautiously to the wood. Inside he heard a scraping, as if something were being dragged across the stone floor. Someone was searching for the reliquary. It must have been in there all along, but so cunningly concealed that neither he nor his men had found it.

He waited until there were no more sounds of movement within, then, assuming that the thief must by now have it in his hand, Grey drew his sword with his right hand, while slowly and noiselessly lifting the latch with his left.

He edged into the room, every nerve and muscle taut, his sword arm braced for immediate action. But the man he expected to confront was not there. The room was empty. A lantern stood on the floor. The flames guttered, sending shadows stalking round the walls. But the only other thing moving in the Hutt was Grey himself.

His heart thumping, he cautiously began a systematic search, edging round the walls and using his sword blade to probe between barrels, stabbing it into piles of blankets and straw pallets. The man had to be in here somewhere. He couldn't just vanish. Grey hadn't taken his eyes from the door, and the walls were solid stone. There was no other way out. Unless . . . A sudden thought struck him and he stared up into the beams above. The candle flame in the lantern on the floor illuminated the boxes and piles of bedding on the floor, but by contrast the rafters above were in deep darkness. Anyone might have climbed up there and be looking down on him, ready to drop as soon as he stepped beneath.

Keeping the blade of his sword pointing upwards, Grey backed across the floor, feeling for the lantern behind him with his heels. He banged into it and heard it rolling across the floor, though mercifully the candle did not topple out of the socket. He crouched, grabbing the handle with his free hand, then raised both lantern and sword as high as he could, searching through the shadows between the dusty, cobwebbed beams.

So intent was he on searching the rafters that even when he felt a sudden draught on his legs, it did not at first register on his brain as significant. And when he sensed the movement behind him it was already too late, far too late. Even as he tried to turn, a sack was dragged down over his head and shoulders, pinning his arms to his sides. He heard the clang as the lantern and sword fell from his hands. His wrists were grabbed and bound tightly behind him. He struggled to breathe through the coarse cloth.

'You can shout if you want to, but you'd be wasting your breath. No one'll hear you. I'm going to take the sack off now. We don't want you breaking your neck on the steps, not just yet anyway.'

As the sack was pulled free, Grey, gasping for air, smelled at once the odour he had recognised in the church – the pungent stench of fish. He knew without even having to turn his head that the man standing behind him was Yarrow, the churchwarden.

'Down there!' Yarrow gave him a shove towards a dark hole, which had suddenly appeared in the corner of the floor. The slab of stone that had covered it stood tipped up against the wall directly behind it.

'I warn you,' Grey said, 'I'm not alone. My men are keeping watch.'

Yarrow laughed. 'I dare say they are keeping watch – over a flagon of mulled ale back in Blidworth. Do you imagine I didn't see you following me long before we even left the village? I know you rode here alone. Now walk.'

Grey felt the prick of the knife in his back. He shivered, thinking of Edward's torn and gashed throat, and he felt sick with fear, expecting any moment to feel the blade ripping at his own throat, but the point did not move from his back.

As he shuffled the three steps to the hole, he thought that he was about to be pushed down a deep pit or well. But when Yarrow retrieved the lantern and held it up over his head, Grey could see a set of stone steps leading downwards from the trapdoor in the floor.

He descended awkwardly, trying to step sideways, so that he could brace his shoulder against the rough stone wall. With his hands bound he was terrified he was going to slip and by the time he reached the bottom his legs were trembling.

At last he found himself standing in a long low tunnel carved out of the rock. It smelled damp and musty at first, but as Yarrow prodded him along it he began to catch the scent of beeswax and something stronger, which he could have sworn was incense.

He rounded a bend in the tunnel and blinked furiously as his eyes were blinded by a sudden burst of light. They had emerged into a cave that glittered like a crown of jewels. Slender candles blazed all around them from rocky crevices and outcrops, while two fat church candles burned on a broad rocky ledge that had been hewn out at the back of the cave, their light sparkling and glinting from a great silver crucifix, and from the golden crown and jewelled butterfly of the reliquary of St Beornwyn.

Grey was so dazzled by the scene that it took a moment or two for him to realise that they were not alone. Several figures, dressed in the dark robes of the Black Canons, were seated motionless, like a flock of monstrous black birds, on ledges around the edges of the cave, the deep hoods of their black cloaks pulled down low, concealing their faces.

Grey tried to moisten his dry lips. 'What . . . what is this place?'

One of the canons rose and slowly glided towards Grey, his hands folded beneath his cloak, his eyes and nose concealed beneath the shadow of his hood. Only his full lips were visible.

'This . . . this is now the church of the priory of St Mary. Since we were driven from our home in Newstead, which our order has occupied for nearly four centuries . . . since we were forced to watch our holy church demolished to build byres and pigsties . . . we have had to find another place to worship. God will not permit that heretic King Henry and his satanic servants to destroy us or our faith.'

Grey gaped at him. 'You've been hiding down here all these months? But how have you managed to conceal yourselves and survive?'

'There are many caves beneath Sherwood Forest and many tunnels connecting them. That one leads straight into the crypt in Newstead Priory.' The canon pointed to a dark hole on the opposite side of the cave from where they had emerged. 'At night, after John Byron's builders have left for the day, we've been able to return to our home and remove what is ours. It isn't much. Most of the valuables were stripped out before we could rescue them, and the workmen rarely leave food behind, but such tools and trappings that are small enough to carry through the tunnels we bring away when we can. As long as we take only odd things here and there, the builders think they have simply forgotten where they left them or grumble that one of their fellows has stolen them.'

'What they can't use themselves, I sell for them,' Yarrow said.

Grey jumped at the sound of the voice behind him. In the shock of discovering the cave, he'd forgotten the church-warden was there, until he remembered the knife still pointed at his back.

'Master Yarrow has always been a faithful friend to the Austin Canons,' the hooded man said quietly. 'And the vil-lagers have helped us too. They bring candles and offerings to St Beornwyn and the Virgin Mary, which by order of Cromwell's own decree, Yarrow, as churchwarden, is obliged to remove and so they find their way to us, where they are used for the glory of the saints and in the service of the true Church, as the villagers intended.'

Grey remembered seeing Alan hand something to Yarrow. Had the boy too been in on the secret of where the offerings were really going?

'Father James – does he know about this?'

'Him!' Yarrow said contemptuously. 'He doesn't know half of what goes on in the village.'

'He would have betrayed us had he known,' the prior added. 'The regular priests have always been jealous of the Austin Canons. We minister far more faithfully to their parishioners than ever they do, sitting through the night with the dying, absolving them of sins their own priests don't even recognize, for they're too busy committing their own.'

Grey, his wrists still bound, gestured with his chin up at the altar. 'And did you absolve Yarrow of the sin of stealing that reliquary for you?'

'I didn't steal it!' Yarrow said indignantly. 'I'm no thief.'

'But you are a murderer,' Grey said coldly. 'Edward was slain with the kind of serrated knife that fishmongers use to scrape scales off fish and to gut them, not with a straight butcher's blade. In fact, I suspect he was murdered with the very knife you are pointing at me right now.'

Before Yarrow could admit or deny it, the prior spoke again. 'When someone is forced to kill in order to defend the servants of God and the True Faith, it is neither a sin nor is it murder. A soldier who kills the enemy in battle is guilty of nothing save bravery and courage. And make no mistake, this is war between the servants of light and Cromwell's forces of darkness.'

He gestured back to the reliquary. 'We needed a relic to consecrate the altar. We asked Master Richard to sell the reliquary of St Beornwyn to us, but he refused. So we prayed and God answered our prayers. Edward stole the reliquary from Richard, though it had no more meaning for him than it did for Richard. Both were only interested in the value of the gold and jewels, not in the precious relics of the virgin saint. We didn't know Edward intended to take it or why he brought it here. But finding himself pursued, he must have tried to hide in the Hutt, hoping Richard would ride on by.'

'I didn't know it was Edward in the Hutt,' Yarrow broke in. 'I was half-way out of the trapdoor, and the first thing I knew was when someone burst in through the door. Whoever it was gave a yelp and I knew the man'd seen me for there was a candle burning on the stairs below me. But I couldn't see the man's face. It could have been anyone – one of the forest wardens, even you.'

Yarrow fingered the wicked-looking knife as if regretting it hadn't been Grey. 'Had to stop whoever it was yelling out or running off. If the passage were discovered they'd have found the canons. So I silenced him. Only thing I could do. I heard the thud of something hitting the ground, just before the man crumpled up. Muffled it was, something heavy wrapped in cloth. I was going to drag the body down into the passageway, but I heard someone else outside the door. So I just grabbed what the man'd dropped, thinking it might be food, and slid back into the hole. I pulled the trapdoor shut, just as the door opened.'

The prior took up the story again. 'It was only when we examined the contents of the sack that Yarrow brought us, that we saw that God had answered our prayers with a miracle and delivered St Beornwyn into our safekeeping.'

All the canons crossed themselves as one, bowing their heads reverentially.

'But now that you have found us,' the prior continued, 'we must move St Beornwyn to a place of greater safety. We've been fortunate so far and no one has noticed us coming and going through the Hutt, but now that there has been a killing here and the reliquary is missing, there will undoubtedly be others, like you, who will be keeping a closer eye on the place in the future. Sooner or later one of us will be seen as we go to minister in secret to those who need us and we cannot risk that. We had already been preparing to leave even before you stumbled upon us, Master Grey, but your presence is a sign that we must depart at once. Although I regret that you, Master Grey, will not be leaving, at least not unless your sergeants are disposed to search far more diligently for you than they did for the reliquary, and with tomorrow being Christmas Day, I doubt they will trouble to make a start soon.'

Grey sensed a movement behind him, and threw himself to the ground, as Yarrow lunged at him with the knife. The churchwarden missed, but recovered himself, grabbing a handful of Grey's hair and dragging his head backwards to expose his throat. Grey, with his hands bound, was helpless to defend himself. He screamed as the murderous blade flashed in the candlelight, but before it could bite into his flesh, the canon caught the churchwarden's wrist, dragging the knife upwards.

'No! I will not permit this sacred chapel to be desecrated by bloodshed. Besides, there is no need.'

Yarrow backed away, his head bowed. The canon crouched down and pulled Grey into a sitting position, though he did not help him to rise.

'I neglected to mention, Master Grey, that before we consecrated this place, it once had another use when Newstead Priory flourished. It was used as a carcer, a place of correction for those among us who broke the rule.'

He gestured towards the cave wall nearest the tunnel to the Hutt, from which dangled a set of heavy iron chains.

Then he beckoned to two of the other canons. Before Grey could grasp what they intended, the men rose, lifted Grey on to his feet and dragged him over the rough floor to the chains.

Grey twisted and fought with every ounce of strength he had, but it was useless. They threw him once more to the ground and hauled him into a sitting position against the sharp jagged wall of the cave. The two men pinned him there while a third forced his neck into an iron collar and manacled his hands above his head to the chains on either side.

The prior stared down at him. 'Do you wish to make your confession? If you do so in all humility I will absolve you.'

Grey stared up into the face, seeing only the lips move. The eyes were still masked deep in shadow.

'You ... you can't mean to leave me here like this. It could take days for my men to find me.'

'*If* they ever find you,' the prior corrected.

Grey was still pleading desperately to be released as the canons busied themselves packing the crucifix, chalice and other items of value into their packs, which they distributed among themselves before each one kneeled and kissed the reliquary of St Beornwyn. Finally they wrapped her in woollen cloth and stowed her away in a plain wooden box. The canons quickly changed into clothes of beggars, merchants and pedlars, hiding their own robes in their packs. Each kneeled for a blessing before their prior, who dispatched them two at a time along the tunnel towards the Hutt, carefully leaving a few minutes' gap between each departing pair.

The prior was the very last to leave. Even then, even as the Black Canon stood over him, Grey was sure he did not mean to leave him there. Now that the other canons were all safely dispersed, the prior would surely release him from the chains.

The prior bowed his head gravely. 'I shall leave the candles burning. They will be a comfort to you until they go out.'

Grey tried in vain to wrest his arms from the chains. 'No, no, please, I beg you. You can't leave me here. This cave is so far beneath the ground, no one will hear me shouting for help ... You can take my horse. By the time I manage to walk back to the village you'll be long gone. Please ... I give you my word, as God is my witness, I will not hunt for Beornwyn's relic. I'll report that it has been destroyed. I'll be no more threat to you. I swear it on my mother's grave!'

'You and all of Cromwell's men are a threat to every true servant of God. If you cannot destroy St Beornwyn, then you will hunt down other relics, destroying the holy things that God has sanctified and through which he works his miracles in this dark world.'

Grey could not believe the man could sound so calm, yet was preparing to leave him helpless, trapped in the cave.

'But you said you did not want this consecrated chapel desecrated by death and I will die if I am not found!'

'Desecrated by *bloodshed*,' the prior corrected. 'And there will be no bloodshed. If God chooses to save you then you will live. If he decrees you will be punished by death then you will die and your spirit will guard this holy place until another comes to take your place. That will be your atonement. Your fate lies in God's hands now, not mine. I suggest that if you hope for a miracle, you should pray to St Beornwyn to save you.'

The prior bowed his head, and to his horror, Grey heard him softly chanting '*miserere nobis*' – 'Have mercy on us' – and realised he was reciting the prayer for the dying. Then the Black Canon turned and walked away down the tunnel, still singing softly, until it seemed as if the rocks themselves were whispering the prayer as they closed around the chained man.

Grey's screams and pleas echoed through the cave, but the prior did not return. In the distance, he heard the hollow grating of a stone being pushed back into place. And knew he was utterly alone.

The candles flickered in the draught that rushed down the tunnel as the stone fell into place. Then they steadied themselves, burning steadily again. The soft yellow light filled the great empty cave. But even as the full horror of what the next few hours and days would bring filled Grey's terrified mind, the first of the candles guttered and died, leaving only a wisp of black smoke that rose momentarily into the shadows above and dissolved. Darkness snuggled a little closer to poor Roger Grey.

Outside, though Grey couldn't hear them, the midnight bells in the distant churches rang in the Christmas morn. And as Edward had predicted, the first flakes of snow began to fall, covering tree and stone, footprints and tracks. It would be a white Christmas.

Historical Note

Newstead Abbey was built between 1164 and 1174 by King Henry II to atone for the murder of Thomas Becket. It became a priory of Austin Canons, known as the Black Canons from their robes, who were not monks, but ordained priests living under monastic rule. King Henry VIII drove the canons from the abbey and on 28 May 1540 sold the lands to one of his loyal supporters Sir John Byron who promptly converted the abbey into his family home, demolishing most of the priory church to reuse the stone for farm buildings.

The romantic poet Lord George Gordon Byron inherited the title and estates in 1798. The house was in such a ruinous state, thanks to his great-uncle stripping it of its valuables, that the poet could only afford to refurnish a few of the rooms, where he lived amid the ruins. He excavated the North Cloister in the hope of finding the fabled treasure of the Black Canons to restore the house, but found only skeletons.

The Royal Hutt was built around 1400 just outside the present entrance to Newstead Abbey as a shelter for the Forest Wardens who patrolled Sherwood Forest. Legend has it that there is a tunnel stretching for about a mile from the Hutt to Newstead Abbey, which was still in use up until the seventeenth century. This is quite plausible as the whole area is riddled with underground caves. The tunnel from the Hutt is said to be haunted by the ghost of a man who died of starvation, having been chained up in it. The tunnel has since been blocked off and 'The Hutt' is now a popular pub and restaurant of that name, where you can still see some of the ancient features of the buildings.

The Church of St Mary of the Purification in Blidworth is one of the few remaining churches in the country to hold the ancient rocking ceremony at Candlemas, in which a baby boy of the parish born closest to Christmas Day is rocked in an ancient cradle during the service. This is thought to bring great blessings to the child and family. The churchyard is the legendary burial place of Will Scarlet, one of Robin Hood's men, and Maid Marian is said to have lived for a time in the village. Only the west tower of the original medieval church survives; the rest was later rebuilt.

EPILOGUE

Boris Malenkov gazed from his top-floor window at the high summer clouds. He glanced again at his Rolex, then stared out of the window once more. Young Deverill was late by all of eleven minutes. When he arrived, Boris would give Mikhail ... he would give him ... He struggled to remember the right English expression. A piece of his head, was it? Or maybe it was a piece of mind? Anesha could have told him which one was right. He always relied on her to correct him when he made mistakes in his English. But Anesha was no longer here to put him right.

Boris Malenkov's thoughts turned from his wife and back to his visitor. His irritation at Mikhail was tempered by a reminder of what the young man was bringing. If he really was carrying it – the text message had been no more than the single word 'BUTTERFLY' – then there would be no reproaches for his lateness, none at all.

There was a tap at the door. Boris trundled round expectantly but it was only Eric Butler.

'Excuse me, Mr Malenkov, but is your guest staying for lunch?'

'How did you know I had guest?'

'Sonia mentioned someone was coming to see you and I thought that you might be requiring me to cook for two.'

'No guest for lunch,' said Boris, and then corrected himself. 'I mean, no lunch for guest.'

'Very well, Mr Malenkov.'

As Eric Butler made to close the door Boris raised his hand. 'I do not want lunch myself. And please find something to do yourself downstairs. In fact, take afternoon off.'

'Thank you, Mr Malenkov.'

After the door closed, Boris waited for the clank of the lift taking Butler to the ground floor. While he waited, he looked at the icons arrayed on the walls of this top-floor room, part of his private quarters. He looked at the icons without really seeing them. The autumnal glow of their background was as natural to him as the sun, while the elongated, clear-cut features of the saints were familiar, like the faces of his long-dead parents. The exterior wall with its windows giving a view across the treetops of Eaton Square was the only one not covered with icons.

He heard the soft thump of the lift as it reached the ground floor. Boris had not even been aware that Eric Butler was up here on this level, in his little kitchen at the back. Generally Boris liked his unobtrusiveness. He liked the people who worked for him to be quiet and discreet. Sonia should not have mentioned to Eric Butler that a visitor, a guest, was coming to call. He would have a word with her, he would give her a . . . suddenly he remembered the expression he'd been searching for. It was 'a piece of his mind'.

If Boris Malenkov had eavesdropped on the scene now taking place on the ground floor, he would most likely have given both Sonia Davies and Eric Butler a piece of his mind. Eric strolled over behind the desk where Sonia sat working her way through a book of sudoku puzzles. He waited to catch her attention and when she did not look round, he reached down, pushed his hand inside her blouse and gave her right breast a friendly tweak.

'Eric, no,' said Sonia, dropping the book and wriggling away from him, but not doing so especially quickly. 'What if he's watching? You know he doesn't like that kind of thing. Thinks I'm still a virgin, probably.'

She nodded towards the CCTV camera tucked below the elaborate cornice over the door and angled directly at her desk. Another camera covered the entrance porch and a third surveyed the small walled garden at the rear of the house. All of them fed into a composite picture on a monitor on Sonia's desk as well as to another screen on Boris Malenkov's floor.

'It's never switched on these days upstairs,' said Eric, taking his hand out of her blouse but not moving from his position behind Sonia. 'Or if it is on, Boris never looks at it. Why should he? When was the last time he had a visitor?'

'He's expecting one now,' said Sonia. 'The gentleman is a few minutes late. Mr Malenkov will not like that.'

'That's the *mysterious* gentleman visitor, the one you won't tell me about.'

'Because I don't know much about him, except he's young and good-looking. Get away, Eric. I don't like you behind me.'

'You don't?'

Eric Butler moved around and stood in front of Sonia. He was a small man, with deep brown eyes. Sonia was a round blonde. She and Eric had started sleeping together about three months ago. Coincidentally or otherwise, that was about the time it became obvious that the Anesha Foundation was on the skids. The purpose of the Foundation, named for Boris Malenkov's late wife Anesha (which means chaste in Russian), was to restore purity to the motherland. It was an almost missionary enterprise, one set up when Boris decided on London as his home after making his money – and making enemies – in the newly liberalised Russia. Now in his early seventies, Malenkov had once been no more than a Soviet Party bureaucrat working in the gas industry. Luck and a little arm-twisting enabled him to earn a fortune after the old system fell apart.

But Boris Malenkov was no oligarch in exile. Once in England, his latent spirituality emerged, spurred by the death of Anesha. He set up the organisation in her name, using the Eaton Square house as office and residence. Yet the fortune he brought from Russia eventually dwindled until only a small deposit remained. Where once a dozen or more dedicated young men and women – some English, but most of them expatriates – had prepared pamphlets and flyers, organised appeals and meetings, and liaised with similar organisations, all for the sake of holy Russia, now there was no one left at the house. No one apart from Eric Butler and Sonia Davies. Not that these two engaged in any missionary-style work, they simply held the fort. Eric Butler did a spot of cooking, as well some tidying up and sorting out of papers. Sonia Davies was the receptionist, although there was rarely anyone to be received these days. In between the ground floor and the top one where Boris himself worked and ate and slept, there were rooms full of slightly out-of-date office equipment, printers and filing cabinets, whole floors where the lift never stopped.

'Where're you off to then?' said Sonia.

'Going for a walk,' said Eric. 'He doesn't want me up there, he doesn't want me to do lunch for him and his mysterious visitor. Just as well, since there's nothing in the kitchen. The cupboard is bare. I'd have to break into the petty cash if he wanted food.'

'You'd be lucky,' said Sonia.

'Why doesn't he sell some of those religious pictures?' said Eric, reluctant to leave Sonia's company. 'He'd get more than petty cash.'

'Mr Malenkov will not sacrifice the icons,' said Sonia. 'Not unless he's up against it, and probably not even then.'

'It's real, is it, this religious thing?'

Eric Butler had been working for Malenkov only since the beginning of the year. Sonia had been with the Anesha Foundation almost since its inception. She knew that the Russian, of whom she was fond, had been motivated to found it partly by his distaste, even outrage, at the way in which his homeland was sinking into a mire of materialism and corruption. Also, there had been the unexpected death of his wife, who happened to be half-English. Malenkov had sunk all of his fortune into the Foundation. Now the money was running out. Of course, he could sell some of those strange golden pictures on the top floor but somehow Sonia didn't think that he would. It wasn't worth explaining why to Eric.

Instead she said to her lover: 'Stop staring at my chest.'

'Who's to see?' said Eric Butler.

'I am. Besides, you never know if he's ...' She nodded again in the direction of the CCTV camera. 'Later, you can look as long as you like.'

'Good. Let's have a takeaway. Pre-shag? Or post-shag?'

'I don't understand you when you use vulgar terms, Eric. Or foreign ones either. Pre-this, post-that.'

'Indian, Chinese?'

'Decisions, decisions.'

'Your place or mine?'

'There's a new Thai restaurant round the corner.'

'That must be round your corner, Sonia. So it'll be your place, then.'

'Get out now,' said Sonia, her eyes flicking towards the monitor on her desktop. 'I can see Mr Malenkov's visitor has arrived. Oh, and we'll be having that Thai takeaway pre-shag, if you don't mind.'

Meanwhile, on the top floor, Boris Malenkov was again staring at the high white clouds in the summer sky. He looked down just in time to observe Michael Deverill emerging from a taxi and automatically casting an eye up at the very window where Boris stood. Was the young man carrying anything? From this angle, he was unable to see properly.

Deverill disappeared under the portico entrance. Moments later Sonia buzzed to indicate that the visitor was on his way up. Boris sat down at a writing table in the corner nearest the windows. His back was to the door. He picked up a pen and examined it. When the tap at the door came, he waited a moment before answering and also before turning round. Then he pretended to be surprised.

'Ah, it is you, Mikhail. *Kak vashi dela?*'

His visitor paused for a moment as if trying to recall the right response to 'How are you?' Then he answered simply: 'Yes, I'm fine, Mr Malenkov. You got my message?'

Boris said nothing. He rose from the chair. His heart beat a little faster as he noticed that Deverill was carrying something before he realised that it was only a plastic bag from a supermarket. Some surprise or query must have appeared on his usually impassive face for Deverill said: 'Don't worry, Mr Malenkov, I haven't brought my shopping with me. Instead

I have the item that I mentioned, the one we discussed. The one I texted you about.'

'That is good.'

'I often carry around valuable things like this. No one is likely to mug a person with a Sainsbury's bag.'

Boris Malenkov thought there was something a bit cheap about such deviousness, something almost sacrilegious, if his visitor really had the genuine 'item'.

'My father sends his regards,' said Michael Deverill.

'You make good side, Mikhail, you and your father Patrick. No, that is not right, not good side. I mean you, you . . .'

'Make a good team, Mr Malenkov?'

'Yes, good team.'

For a moment, Michael Deverill looked uncomfortable at the idea of making a good team with his father. Malenkov seemed not to notice. He went on: 'Come now, Mikhail. Show.'

They were standing on opposite sides of the Chippendale dining table in the middle of the room. Michael Deverill reached into the plastic bag and brought out something wrapped in what looked like a strip torn off a sheet, none too clean either. He laid it gently on the shiny surface of the table and peeled back the folds of cloth. Inside was an unmarked wooden box with a sliding lid, the kind of box – it occurred to Boris – in which you might keep chess pieces. Michael Deverill removed the lid and handed the box to Boris Malenkov.

Malenkov took the box and carried it to one of the windows. He tilted it so that he might see the object inside more clearly. Then he eased a hand under the object and lifted it right out. In his palm he was holding another hand, a hand that had been severed violently from its arm, to judge by the jagged, splintered stump. The hand rested comfortably in Malenkov's own wide palm. If you'd been asked to estimate the height of the owner of the hand, you might have said that he – or she – would have been about three feet tall.

The hand was made of wood painted a realistic pinky-white, although the paint was thin and flaking in places. But the most striking thing about it was that in the cupped wooden palm there rested a butterfly, also carved out of wood but enamelled and perhaps studded once with jewels, for there were regular little pits on the butterfly's wings. The carver had done a fine job, for the hand and the insect seemed to be composed of quite different materials, one thick and fleshy, the other thin and airy.

Boris Malenkov looked at Michael Deverill, still standing on the other side of the table. The young man was gazing at him, waiting for his reaction. His long fair hair flopped over his ears and the collar of his jacket. Boris thought he looked worried.

'You have done well, Mikhail.'

Again, for a moment, Michael looked not reassured but more uncomfortable, but he quickly said: 'Thank you, Mr Malenkov. There's something else.'

Deverill drew another item from the bag and walked round to pass it to the Russian, who took it while continuing to clasp the butterfly. This second item was much smaller, no more than a fragment of wood. In it was embedded a piece of what looked like rock crystal, which, in turn, contained an unidentifiable scrap of greyish material. Boris Malenkov peered and puzzled over this. He turned to Deverill.

'What you are seeing is a piece of human skin. It belongs to our saint, Beornwyn.' He paused, gratified at the Russian's response, a start of surprise amounting almost to fear. It was as if Malenkov were to suddenly glimpse a familiar face in the street, an old friend – or enemy – he had long thought dead. Boris moved away from the window and placed the items – the severed hand cradling the butterfly and the fragment of rock crystal – on the table. He stood back and gazed at them with his hands folded respectfully in front of him. Michael Deverill picked up the thread of what he had been saying. 'We *believe* it belongs to St Beornwyn, my father and I. The quartz, the crystal, was most likely embedded in one of her feet, I mean the feet of the statue depicting her, and which served as her reliquary.'

'Reliquary?' repeated Malenkov after a time. He had difficulty saying the word.

'A container for a saint's relics, objects such as a bone or a phial of dried blood, a shred of clothing or piece of skin. It's normal for reliquaries to take the form of a box or chest, but sometimes a statue may be used. The image of Beornwyn herself has been lost, apart from these two pieces.'

'Where did you find them, Mikhail?'

'Of course, you do understand it was not we who found them, Mr Malenkov. All I can say is that they were unearthed somewhere in Nottinghamshire, from a place where the cult of St Beornwyn was very strong in the days before the dissolution of the monasteries. That was during the reign of—'

Boris Malenkov waved an impatient hand. He did not want a history lesson. But there was something he needed to be sure of.

'St Beornwyn, she does not come from Notting-ham-shire?' Boris broke up the name of the county into its component parts. 'She comes from north?'

'From Northumbria, yes,' said Deverill, who had done

some research into Beornwyn so he could talk with authority on the subject. 'She was the daughter of a local king.'

'My wife, she came from that part of the country too. Not
the daughter of king, no, but daughter of Russian, yes.'

Boris smiled to show that he was making a bit of a joke but
there was pride in his voice too. Deverill knew that one of his
reasons for collecting Beornwyn relics was because of the
association with his wife, Anesha, whose Russian father had
married a woman from Newcastle. Anesha Malenkov and St
Beornwyn came from the same remote, northerly area of
England, though many centuries apart, of course.

Michael Deverill continued: 'The strongest evidence that
these Nottinghamshire relics are connected to your saint,
Mr Malenkov, is not so much that they were found together
near this site which was once holy ground, but that the hand
cradling the butterfly – rather a finely wrought carving,
wouldn't you agree? – confirms the link with Beornwyn.
Consider how, after her martyrdom, her modesty was preserved by a cloud of those beautiful flying creatures. And of
course the crystal containing her skin, her pale flayed
skin . . .'

Michael Deverill put the slightest emphasis on 'flayed'.
Then he paused. He was a good salesman. He knew that
the most rewarding results came when the clients did the
work, persuading themselves of the value of what they were
looking at rather than having to be persuaded of it by others.
In any case, he did not want to go into too much detail on
this fine early afternoon in the house in Eaton Square.
Michael Deverill was in a hurry, a desperate hurry.

He needed to wrap up a deal quickly and return to the
flat in Wimbledon that he shared with his father, Patrick.
Together they had to catch the 18.50 flight from Gatwick

to Malaga and thence to their bolt-hole outside Cordoba, a villa that had been bought long ago in anticipation for just such a day as arrived last week. On the previous Tuesday, to be precise. It was then that the Deverills, father and son, heard that one of the clients to whom they supplied objects of interest – pictures, manuscripts, small pieces of furniture, relics even – had grown suspicious of the provenance of a certain item. This caused the client to query a couple of other items he had purchased through the Deverills.

Unfortunately for Patrick and Michael, this client was like Boris Malenkov in only one respect. He was Russian. But, unlike Boris, Vladimir Zarubin was genuinely rich and genuinely ruthless. He travelled with a palisade of bodyguards and stick-thin blondes. He had a dirty reputation, even in Russia. Vlad the Impaler was one of his nicknames. The nickname was not altogether a joke. Michael had warned his father against dealing with Zarubin but Patrick asked what harm there could be in something as insignificant as a Sheraton commode, followed by a little-known Rossetti painting and then a second picture, this time by the pre-Soviet artist Larionov. To a billionaire like Vladimir Zarubin, the sums involved were piddling. Besides, he was so pig-ignorant he couldn't have told the difference between a Constable and a Kandinsky, let alone between a carefully wrought fake and the real McCoy.

Unfortunately for the Deverills, father and son, Zarubin employed people who could tell the difference. And when they finally got round to checking up on the commode and the Rossetti and Larionov and some other items, they smelled a rat. Word got back to the Deverills that Vladimir was intending to pay them a visit himself as soon as he

returned from a business trip to the Ukraine. He was returning to England that very night. By then, Michael and Patrick
planned to be on Spanish soil and inside their Cordoba villa,
where they could live happily on the back of several Swiss
accounts.

Therefore Michael Deverill needed to conclude his business with Boris Malenkov as fast as possible. Needed this
amiable old man to buy the bits and pieces relating to St
Beornwyn, so that he, Michael, could scoot off and collect
his father.

Boris was still looking at the butterfly-in-hand carving and
the fragment of crystal. There were two key features in the
legend of St Beornwyn. One was that she had been flayed,
a detail that gave a *frisson* to even the most minute scrap of
her skin. The other and more attractive feature was that her
poor, despoiled body was discovered shrouded in butterflies.
Did Boris Malenkov believe these items to be relics of the
cult of Beornwyn? Michael himself did not know if they
were genuine, whatever 'genuine' meant when it came to a
saint's relics.

The main thing was to get the business over with, fast.
Patrick Deverill hadn't told Michael to make a rapid trans-
action, to take what he could and then get out. He hadn't
needed to. Nor had he told his son where he obtained the
hand and the crystal. Michael preferred not to know. In the
past his father had proved himself an adept faker, though
on canvas rather than with wood or stone. Patrick Deverill
possessed real talent. That talent and the training at the
Slade meant that he could have earned his living as a painter.
But something in the Deverill blood pushed him down a
more winding path.

Michael coughed slightly, a signal that Boris Malenkov

should say something. Do something. Preferably buy the Beornwyn relics right now.

As if reading his thoughts, Boris indicated that Deverill should follow him into a smaller room that led off the dining room and that was next to the kitchen where Eric Butler produced the meals. With another gesture Boris directed Deverill to bring the wooden hand cradling the butterfly and the crystal containing the scrap of skin. The inner room, unlike the larger one overlooking Eaton Square, contained only a handful of small icons. It was a place where business was done or might once have been done, with a small table, a couple of upright chairs and a filing cabinet. On the table was a computer and near to it a monitor screen, which Boris used to keep an eye on the ground floor of the house. Both were switched off. There were sets of worry beads coiled on the table. Or perhaps, thought Deverill, they might be rosaries.

Once both men were inside, Boris shut the door and went towards a picture on the wall. This picture stood out, not because of its subject matter – like the icons, it was religious in nature – but because it was a small gilt-framed oil depict-ing the Madonna and Child. Malenkov carefully detached the picture from the wall and placed it on the surface of the table. He noticed his visitor's appreciative stare.

'The work of Lorenzo Gelli, the Florentine,' said Boris Malenkov. 'Is good, no?'

Better than good, thought Michael Deverill, and wonder-ing who this Gelli was before realising that the Russian had mispronounced the name by using a hard 'g' rather than a soft one. Lorenzo *Gelli*, of course. The name of that minor Italian master of the Renaissance was familiar to him. So, too, was the picture itself now he looked at it. The face of the

Madonna, especially. He must have seen it reproduced in some catalogue. He stooped to look more closely. Through an arch behind the round-faced Madonna and the plump Child on her lap was a delicate landscape composed of hills and rivers, hamlets and little scattered figures. The sky was a delicate azure deepening in colour towards the top of the arch. Altogether, it was a very attractive picture.

But the function of this Western Madonna was not so much decoration as concealment. Set into the wall behind where it hung was a safe. Without troubling to conceal his actions from Deverill, Boris Malenkov twisted the dial and opened the safe. He reached inside and took out several items. These, too, he placed on the table top.

They were: a fragment of manuscript encased in protective plastic together with three boxes, one about six inches long and the other two small and square, all covered with velvet. Malenkov opened the boxes, flicking at hasps and catches with his thick fingers. Michael Deverill had seen the contents before – indeed, he had been responsible for supplying one of them to the Russian. The smaller boxes held a single bone or piece of bone, from a finger or foot perhaps. The long one held what looked like most of a rib. The fragments nestled in velvet, their yellowish pallor contrasting with the purple material.

The common factor to these relics was their connection to the sainted Beornwyn. The piece of manuscript was part of a poem by the medieval writer, Geoffrey Chaucer, who composed a poem about St Beornwyn, to be recited at the court of John of Gaunt. Nothing of the poem survived except this fragment, whose very subject might have remained unknown had the writer not mentioned Beornwyn by name in the first dozen lines. The story went that the scrap of manuscript had been unearthed during excavations at Aldgate, one of the old entrances to London.

Michael Deverill deposited the reliquary objects, the butterfly in the hand and the skin in the crystal, beside the bones. Absently he picked up from the desk a string of worry beads or rosary and poured the chain from hand to hand. Boris walked over to the single window in the room. He stared out across more trees and rooftops. Deverill wondered what was going through his head. Surely Malenkov would agree to purchase these sacred treasures? He still had the means, hadn't he? Although Deverill had heard stories that the Anesha Foundation was running low on resources. Certainly, the Eaton Square house felt very empty now compared to when he'd made earlier visits. Apart from large Sonia down in the reception area and a man who passed Deverill as he was on the way in, he'd seen no one. For sure Boris was not one of those ultra-rich oligarchs, he was not even a proper multimillionaire. He had no yacht or private Boeing, he owned no football club in London or estate at Cap Ferrat. What he possessed was a driving desire to take Russia back to her spiritual roots. Somehow, Michael assumed, the amassing of these relics and objects connected with a virgin saint was going to help in that task.

Michael Deverill liked Boris Malenkov, certainly by contrast to Vladimir Zarubin, for example. Malenkov was not intimidating. Indeed, there was something almost benevolent about the podgy man.

'I can't offer you any money,' said Boris. 'I have cash-flow crisis. Next month maybe . . .'

Next month was too late. The next day would be too late. Somehow Deverill wasn't surprised by any of this. He said: 'But you do want those things of Beornwyn, don't you?'

If Boris noticed such an off-hand way of referring to the relics, he didn't mention it. Instead he said: 'I am ready to do exchange, though.'

'Exchange, Mr Malenkov?'

'The Madonna on desk, the one you are admiring. By Lorenzo Gelli.'

'The Lorenzo Gelli,' said Deverill, taking care to pronounce the name correctly (*Jelly*). 'Well, it *is* a fine piece of work.'

'A far exchange, as you say.'

'Yes,' said Deverill. He didn't bother to correct Boris's mistake over a 'far' exchange. He glanced at his watch. He had to finish the business with Boris and return to his father. They had to catch that Gatwick flight in the early evening. More worrying, much more worrying than any to-do over relics and pictures, was the return of Vladimir Zarubin from the Ukraine. Through Michael Deverill's mind there flashed the image of burly brutes picking their way through the flat in Wimbledon, looking for evidence of fakery and fraud. No, not picking their way through, but smashing things up. Not just things either. Yes, yes, take the painting. Get out of here. Get out of town. Get out of the country.

So it was concluded. Michael Deverill left the Eaton Square house with the Lorenzo Gelli unceremoniously wrapped in the same cloth in which he had carried the Beornwyn relics, inside the same plastic bag.

When Michael returned to the flat in Wimbledon, his father was cramming things into a last-minute case.

'Well,' he said. 'Did our Boris go for them?'

'Yes. But he had no money – no ready money, at any rate. I had to take this in lieu.'

'Let's see.'

When he saw the Gelli, Patrick Deverill let out a sound between a groan and a laugh.

'One of mine,' he said. 'From the old days. This isn't a genuine Gelli. No more than the woman in the picture was a real virgin.'

'You're sure?'

'Of course I'm bloody sure, Michael. The model for the Madonna was your mother. Oh, but it's nice to see her again.'

Michael wasn't sure whether his father was referring to the Madonna or to his mother, who had been dead these many years. He said: 'I thought her face looked familiar.'

'And the baby is you. You were the model when I did it.'

'Jesus,' said Michael.

'You could say,' said his father. 'Too late to return it to Boris now.'

'Perhaps Vlad the Impaler will take it instead.'

'That's a joke, right? We are not staying to find out.'

Patrick Deverill dithered for an instant before stuffing the Lorenzo Gelli into the case. He did seem pleased to be reunited with the old fake. Minutes later, the taxi arrived to take father and son to Gatwick airport.

Meanwhile, back in Eaton Square, Boris Malenkov was casting his eyes over the collection of Beornwyn relics, picking up one, now another. He considered that he had got the better part of the bargain. That painting by Gelli he never really liked it. He had bought it in his early days in London through a dealer who later introduced him to the Deverills, father and son. But he had never believed in the Mother or Child in the picture, to him they looked false. There was something bourgeois about their features compared to his beloved icons, there was no real suffering or spirituality to them. So, obtaining the butterfly and the crystal was far exchange. Boris paused for a moment. A far exchange ... was that the right expression? Anesha could have told him.

And downstairs in reception Sonia Davies was preparing to leave the house in Eaton Square. It hadn't been much of a day. Half the sudoku book finished. One visitor. That bloke, Michael Deverill was his name, he'd left in a hurry still carrying the Sainsbury's bag he arrived with. Hardly paused to say goodbye to Sonia. Otherwise no callers. Not even Eric coming back. But he had sent her a text. Rather a naughty message, as it happened, combining food and sex. So now what she was looking forward to was a takeaway from that new Thai place round the corner, followed by a good session with Eric Butler. For a moment she wondered what the old man upstairs would make of that. A tiny part of her was concerned by Boris's opinion. Then she shrugged. No virgin she.